THE UNMARKED WITCH

Unmarked
© 2022, Miranda Lyn
All rights reserved.

Cover Designer – Tairelei – www.facebook.com/Tairelei/

Copy/Proof Editor – Second Pass Editing

CONTENT WARNING Violence, Language, Sexual Content, Death

ALSO BY MIRANDA LYN

FAE RISING:

BLOOD AND PROMISE

CHAOS AND DESTINY

FATE AND FLAME

TIDES AND RUIN

www.authormirandalyn.com

To those that need a little magic ... and those that need a heaping pile ...

1

I wondered if he'd watched her die. Or had he hanged her from that old oak tree and turned his back on her as he had the rest of his scarred kingdom? I couldn't bring myself to look up at my coven leader's withered face, now as still as her worn black boots, hanging before me, framed by her tattered skirts.

"A coven leader?" Kirsi nudged me with a shoulder as we stood, mouths slackened in shock. "That's bold, even for him, isn't it, Raven?"

A single black feather lay on the ground like a signature at the end of a long letter. He'd been here.

"Not for the Dark King."

I stared at the wrinkled hands that had held me as a small child the night my grandmother died. The ones that brushed the tears from my face when she promised to teach me the proper way to use magic. My blue eyes trailed up her elderly, lifeless body. A fist gripped my heart, banging it against my rib cage. Splotchy, purple, and nearly unrecognizable due to the swelling, the woman who had shown me kindness when she didn't have to was dead. We hadn't been close in recent years, but the ringing in my ears, the taxing on my heart, didn't care.

"Do we know for sure it was him?" Kirsi stepped away, seemingly unbothered.

"Isn't it always?" I asked, pointing to the damning feather that could have only come from the monster.

Something within my stomach lurched as my mouth turned dry. She was dead. Gone. Now a decaying body left as a message from a dangerous king. He was still here. Still watching, still merciless. But Tasa, her soul, she was worth so much more than that. Every wrinkle on her thin, pale skin, each magical marking upon her body, proof of the long life she'd lived, of the deep-rooted power she'd once had. But in the end, none of that mattered. She hadn't been able to save herself, anyway. As no one could, when caught in the Dark King's grasp.

A pounding of heavy footfalls yanked my attention away as I spun, backing into Kirsi, ready to fight, to flee, to panic. But it was only Nikos, perfect blond hair falling into his eyes as he ran toward us, cheeks flushed and shoulders heaving. He hadn't seen the body yet, instead his focus remained on catching his breath.

"There's been another Thrashing. The Daniels' sons. Ricker's alley is covered in blood, I'm told."

"That makes two this week alone," Kirsi said. "Not including this."

She pointed to the witch hanging from the tree and the color drained from Nikos' face.

"Look away, my darling. I know how much she meant to you." He put a hand on my shoulder, turning my back to her. "I'm so sorry. Shall we bring her down?"

There was something disingenuous in his tone, but we'd all gotten so used to death, to funerals, to murder. If it wasn't a Thrashing, it was the Harrowing—a sickness that attacked the witches. No one was safe. Not before the war, and certainly not now, during this time of *peace*.

I slipped away from Nikos, nodding as I pulled power forward, letting it crackle beneath my skin. Moving into a circle around Tasa, we lifted our hands. A single thin marking glowed, a blue band, on Kirsi's forearm as she sliced through the frayed rope with a spell she'd received seven years ago.

It was uncommon to know every spell another witch had, but Kirsi was like my sister. I knew every time she acquired one, and she, I. Flicking a hand in front of me, I slowed the descent, the gentle thud of Tasa Moonbreak's fallen body whispering through the crisp, mid-autumn air. Nikos stepped forward, flourishing a hand over her until her eyes were closed and the rope had vanished entirely.

An eerie breeze whipped by, rustling the vibrant leaves on the tree-lined path. Looking around, it seemed no other witches had been down the cobblestone road that connected a few small homes to the main road toward the village. The significance of this moment struck me from nowhere. The death of a coven leader was no small thing. In fact, it was the very event that would spur the Moon Coven into the hands of the Dark King.

I cleared my throat, pushing away the unexpected emotion. "We have to tell the others."

"You know what this means," Kirsi said, raising an eyebrow.

I did know what it meant. And for my whole life, I'd thought this moment would come with so much more excitement. I'd always glossed over the part where Tasa had to die in order for someone to take her place.

"The Trials are dangerous." Nikos stared at me as if the rest of the world had vanished and it was only me standing there with his warning lingering between us. He'd never agree to me entering. But he didn't know about the promise.

Kirsi coughed, stepping in to get a closer look, if only to save me the awkward conversation. Her familiar, Scoop, a calm tempered panther followed hot on her heels, his dark coat showing each of the lithe muscles displaying his strength.

Leaning down until she was all but nose to nose with the old coven leader, she said, "Remind me to beg the goddess for the same number of markings, but far fewer wrinkles."

"Kir!" Nikos barked. "She's not even consecrated. Show some respect." Removing his cloak, he promptly covered Tasa's face, his usually well-kept hair falling onto his brow.

My best friend's eyes lit with mischief. "Did you know they swelled up like that . . . before they . . ." She slid a thumb across the base of her throat.

"Kirsi!" I gasped, yanking her back. "She'll come back as a wraith just to haunt your ass."

"She'd never stoop so low." Looping arms with me, she started back on the path. "We'll let you handle this, lover boy. Someone's got to alert the other coven leaders, and we have a shop to run."

"I have a job too, you know," he said.

I turned over my shoulder, mouthing my apology. Nikos' soft blue eyes met mine as he flashed a charming smile my way. He'd deal with it. With complete poise and chivalry, as he always did. He hadn't been my first choice for a partner. To be honest, I wasn't sure he had been my choice at all in the beginning. But we'd somehow found a familiar bond by each other's side. A friendship was slowly blooming into something more, highly encouraged by my parents. Though he was an outcast, he worked hard and cared for me. That was enough.

"Someday he's going to wonder if you actually like him."

Kirsi halted, looking over her shoulder. "You know I like you, right?"

"Yeah, yeah," he called back, hoisting Tasa from the ground.

"Okay. Just checking." She yanked me forward. "See? We're fine."

Using my free arm, I lifted the long, curly locks of my onyx hair, pulling them to the front to help block the chilly breeze, wishing for the sun to warm my unmarked skin.

"Oh no." Kir skidded to a halt, the small pebbles scattering along the road beneath her. "It's Tuesday."

I thought for a moment before it dawned on me. "You're more worried about Shayva Stormridge than you are about the literal dead body we found, or the Thrashing in the square?"

"Don't act like you're surprised. Shayva's an asshole."

"Come on. If we're late, she'll be ten times worse."

We hustled into the market village without stopping to speak to anyone—to tell them of Tasa. The remaining coven leaders would want to handle this their own way and would only chastise us for making the announcement. It wouldn't take long though, gossip spread like wildfire throughout the witch covens.

Gaunt faces met ours the closer we got to Ricker's Alley. We didn't pass the massacre but could feel the remnants of it in the streets. The Dark King liked to send his men into the village—in and out before they could be seen—killing witches for unexplained reasons and leaving us to deal with the wreckage. Thrashings, the witches called it.

The Dark King's wrath, ever present, ever threatening. The Moon Coven saw fewer massacres than most, but even one death was one too many.

Navigating the pebbled streets, small puddles dampening the hems of our skirts and aprons, we rushed forward. Approaching the familiar arched door of Crescent Cottage, I reached into my pocket and pulled out a twisted iron key. Sometimes coming to the shop which used to belong to my grandmother felt like stepping into a memory. As if my childhood waited for me to return. Other times, it felt like leaping into a world of wonders. Not a place I owned, but something specifically curated for the incredulity of others, feeding their curiosities like a loaf of bread to a starving man.

It was worse, before. When my grandmother ran the shop and busted her ass every day to conjure and brew the rarest and most highly coveted spells. Now, most witches came to browse the wares, hardly ever purchasing them, or to get a better look at me, the only witch ever born with power and no markings.

But when I was a child, they would come from across the seven territories for my grandmother's Fountain of Youth elixir or her Devil's Breath healing potion. They would wait in the streets for the doors to open. She'd worked every night to create them. When she was murdered, though I knew the ingredients and recipes for all, I let the world believe my grandmother had taken them to her grave. I still kept a small collection of the best ones hidden in the shop, but hardly anyone knew they existed. I would not become a slave to this store, would not take my final breaths on the floor, as she had.

The doorknob stuck most days. I needed to replace it, but Kir said it gave the shop character, which truthfully meant we couldn't afford it. When we pushed inside, the bell pealed above the door. I paused for a moment, taking in the familiar smell of the room: red currant and shaved cedar, chamomile and honey, even the old pages from the small bookshelves we kept in the far corner. A crackle of power moved below my skin, and I waved my hand through the air, lighting the scattered candles throughout Crescent Cottage.

"Here she comes," Kirsi warned, stepping around the stacks of empty terracotta pots, whipping her silvery blonde hair over her shoulder as she moved. She hid behind the wall of devil's ivy concealing our back room, Scoop directly behind her. "I'll be back here ... counting the blades of grass through the window."

"You're the worst," I hissed.

She poked her head out, lifting an eyebrow, the once smooth marking on her forehead distorted. "If I come out there, I'm going to punch her in the throat. This is me picking my battles. You're welcome."

I took a long breath, steadying my nerves as the door banged open, rattling the wall. A plump woman, dragging her red-haired son by his ear, came storming up to the long wooden counter, cheeks flushed, and huffing as if she'd run the entire way.

"Cast a single spell and I'll ship you off to the human lands where there is no magic at all," she swore at the boy.

"Good morning, Mrs. Stormridge. The usual?"

Turning, she crossed her chubby arms over her chest as she glared at me. "Why do I bother coming back here?" She smashed a glass vial on the counter. "Clearly, the charm isn't working."

I could hear the snort from the back as I smiled, squeezing my hands into fists behind me. "Sometimes fertility spells can be fickle. You have to get the timing right and both parties have to be willing, as you know."

"Well," she heaved. "I'm not sure what you're insinuating, Raven Moonstone, but I can assure you both parties are very willing."

"Of course," I said, turning my back to hide the eye roll. "Give me a moment and I'll have it ready for you. I think I'll add rose quartz this time."

"Be quick ab—"

Her son gasped, and I whipped around. The woman's eyes glowed with a pure golden light as she froze, suspended in time.

"It's a receiving," he breathed.

"Yes, it is. Give her a few minutes."

"I wonder which power she'll get," he said, eyes locked on his mother.

I turned away again, pulling a vial from the shelf behind me. "That's the mystery, isn't it?"

A dash of coriander for fertility and passion, dried yarrow to stimulate her moon cycle, a pinch of lavender to calm her anxious nerves, and a tiny rose quartz to inspire compassion. Glancing up to see the witch still frozen in place, I crossed the room, laying each of the items inside a circle made from salt and nine white candles, ready to spell them. I lifted my hands, infusing amplification magic into the elements before placing them in the jar and sealing it with the dripping wax of the seventh candle.

Though some witch's spells were the same as others, none were guaranteed, which is what kept my store running. One witch might have had the power to induce sleep, but also no need for the spell. Yet another could have had trouble closing their eyes at night. A simple elixir would be the solution.

We didn't only serve the witches. I welcomed the other creatures from this world, though I remained wary of shifters. Most witches refused to work with them, the remnants of our past, and the cause of the current state of the world, weighing heavily on us beneath the rule of the Dark King. The wraiths were usually no problem, except if they chose to haunt the store. But that was nothing a little sage couldn't fix.

Kirsi came storming out from behind the wall of plants, ignoring Shayva's catatonic state as she approached her son. "Hand it over, boy." She jammed one hand on her hip, holding the other out to the child.

"I—I don't know what you mean," he stammered.

Kneeling in front of the boy, Kirsi lowered her voice to a dangerous level. "Do you know what I am?"

He pressed his lips tight, shaking his head.

The intricate marking on her forehead glistened blue. She waited until Scoop padded around the corner, his feline ears twitching as he came to a stop before Kirsi with a disgruntled huff. Scoop had two sizes, a kitten and a full-grown beast. Though usually in kit form, Kirsi loved intimidating people with him. She trailed her hands down his furry spine as she glared at the boy. "I am spirit blessed, boy. My familiar tells me there is something of mine in your pocket. Hand it over."

7

Without warning, the boy bolted around the corner, tangling himself in his mother's skirts as Kirsi cursed and chased after him.

I intercepted, circling the workbench to cut her off before she tackled the boy and his mother to the floor. "Kirsi, don't you dare."

She lifted her arms, ready to cast a spell on the naughty child. "He's a liar and a thief. I think a pig's snout would be appropriate."

The boy screeched and ran off again. I clapped my hands and the stacked pots on the ground toppled around him, causing him to stumble and fall. It was enough of a distraction for me to catch him by the collar. He fought against me, trying to wiggle free, but my grip was firm.

"You can deal with me, or you can deal with her." I jutted my chin toward the spirit blessed witch, panther pacing before her. "Your choice."

He stopped fighting and glanced at Kir, who'd picked up the knife we used for cutting stems, never taking her gray eyes from the boy as she cleaned the dirt from below her fingernails.

"You. You." He gripped my wrists, eyes wide. "I pick you."

"If you give me back whatever you've taken, I won't tell your mother. If you don't, I'll decline her sale and blame it all on you. Again, your choice." I couldn't afford to refuse her business and I was confident that was the only reason Kirsi hadn't threatened her life yet, but the boy didn't need to know that.

He gulped, pulling a small jar of worms from his pocket. "I'm sorry."

"You always have a choice in this world. You can be the hero or the villain. Never both. Think hard about which path you want to walk."

"Erix?" his mother shrieked, grabbing his collar and yanking him toward her, eyes still slightly glossed over from her receiving. A fresh spell glowed golden on her arm, tangled in the mixture of her other markings.

"I wasn't going to keep it. Honest. I only wanted to look."

Kirsi leaned over the counter, pinning the boy with a glare. "Be careful which lies you let slip from those lips." She flourished her hand for dramatics and the boy screeched again, dashing below his mother's skirts.

8

Shayva turned on the boy, grabbing him by the ear. "What did you do, child?"

"I gave it back. I swear. I was only looking."

Kir snorted, and the woman's head snapped toward her. "Stay out of this."

"Gladly," she answered, throwing her long silver hair over her shoulder as she turned away, pretending to fidget with the mortar bowls shelved on the wall.

I cleared my throat, plastering a smile on my face. "He apologized and returned the item. No harm done."

"No harm done? I'll not raise a thief." She slammed three sliver glints on the counter and swiped the fertility charm from my hand. "You keep it up and the Dark King will steal you away as easily as the Grimoires."

Kirsi and I shared a stunned glance as the woman dragged her weeping son from the store.

"Did she just ..."

I nodded. "She absolutely did."

The most traumatic incident of my life had been the night the king's soldiers broke into this shop and stole the Moon Coven's Grimoire, killing my grandmother for using magic against them. And Shayva Stormridge had just flippantly referenced it like that night hadn't changed every living witch's life forever.

2

Twelve years ago ...

Thunder so loud I thought it severed the world shook my grandmother's apothecary shop. The bottles full of elixirs, salts, and herbs rattled on the wooden shelves. Gnarled shadows cast from hanging leaves crept toward me like spindly fingers in a nightmare. Bolting upright on the tiny cot I'd claimed as my own when I came to visit, I shrank back, watching the lighting from the storm illuminate the aged walls of Crescent Cottage. I lifted the small protection charm tied around my neck as I closed my eyes, ten-year-old heart racing faster than a herd of wild horses.

Calm, child, it's only a storm.

My young soul wrapped around that comforting voice, only slightly jealous of the telepathy spell Grandmother had. Someday, I'd be just like her. Strong willed and equally influential, even though we'd only just discovered I had any magic at all. I stared at the creamy skin along my arms, wondering why I was the only witch that remained unmarked.

Rubbing the soft blanket between my fingers, I let the calm wash over me as I settled back into the little nest I'd made on the cot and closed my eyes again. A tendril of shame crept over my skin as I remembered the way the other children had balked and pointed at me. One had gone so far as throwing a stone, claiming I was not truly a witch at all, but an abomination.

Rain fell in sheets outside, crashing against the little round window along the back wall. Another strike of lightning flashed so bright, for the span of a breath, the entire room illuminated. I jumped and threw the covers over my head. There was power in potent storms, but Grandmother had seen the red ring around the moon. Trouble was coming.

The thunder that followed less than a second after the lightning shook the whole cottage. Glasses fell from the shelves, shattering onto the wooden floor. Varying shades of salt poured from the cluttered counters. Pots toppled over, likely breaking and scattering fresh soil all over the ground. Grandmother would probably make me clean it tomorrow.

She screamed. A horrifying, ear-piercing scream that seemed to halt time, to pause the storm, to make every hair on my body stand.

No matter what you hear, Raven, don't you come out of that room. Hide. Now.

Fear, unlike anything I'd experienced in my life, struck me hard. Shaking, I sank to the floor and tried to crawl beneath the cot, but it toppled over. I froze, holding my breath as my grandmother screamed again. She needed help. I could hear men's deep voices now. So many of them. Crawling toward the door, I peeked out. Soldiers filled my grandmother's shop. She stood before the pedestal that held the Moon Coven's Grimoire in nothing but a thin nightgown. Her long silver hair fell in waves around her as she lifted her hands in the air like a deadly promise.

"Don't come any closer," she warned, blocking the ancient book with her old body. "You have no rights here."

A soldier stepped forward. Hatred filled his eyes as he spoke behind clenched teeth. "The king has every right. Stand down, witch."

I could feel the power my grandmother was prepared to use, as if it were a tangible thing, hanging like static in the air. The world hummed. Several of the king's men stepped back, away from one of the most powerful witches born to this world, nearly every inch of her body, aside from her face, smothered in magical markings.

The soldier in front leaped forward, arms outstretched as he shifted forms. Halfway between man and bear, my grandmother whipped her hand through the air; a marking on her wrist glimmered, and the man fell to the ground, bleeding out from a million tiny cuts covering his entire body.

That was all it took. One moment, she was standing there stronger than I'd ever seen her, and the next, they were on top of her. I wanted to cry out, to scream for her to protect herself. But I couldn't move. Couldn't save her as I heard her final words in my mind.

Close your eyes, baby. Close your eyes.

Hot tears left fiery trails down my cheeks. Her head rocked to the side and lifeless eyes met mine. I stared into my grandmother's empty soul, unable to blink or swallow the sharp lump that grew in my throat, as those men stepped over her fallen body to steal our Grimoire and escape into the stormy night.

I waited, watching the arched door as if the monsters would return. Or the rain would flood the world as thoroughly as my silent tears. Nothing happened. I inched forward, crawling across the broken bits of glass and pottery. A crack of thunder sent me surging ahead, throwing myself over my grandmother's body as if I, a ten-year-old child, could have protected her, though she was already gone.

Another flash of lightning lit the silhouette of a hooded figure standing in the open doorway.

Allowing steel to creep through my veins, I raised my hands, attempting to shield my grandmother just as she had tried to save the Grimoire. "Stay back. I'm warning you."

The hooded figure moved forward, seeming to float across the floor toward us.

I'd received one spell. And though it didn't show on my skin like the other witches, it was there. I raised my hands, ready to light all the candles in the room, when the stranger swept her hood back, taking in the scene of the shop with absolute horror on her aged face. Tasa Moonbreak, the Moon Coven leader, stood before me, stricken.

She reached a shaking hand toward the empty pedestal before falling to the ground in a wail. She crawled toward my grandmother, pulling her into her lap, then held a hand above my grandmother's body. Several of Tasa's markings glowed as she closed her eyes. I waited, swiping my tears, until she gasped. "The king's soldiers did this?"

I nodded, scooting backward through the layer of fresh dirt covering the damp floor.

Dropping her head, she pushed the hair from my grandmother's face and tucked it behind her ears. "I should have been here, Viana. I'm so sorry."

We sat, steeped in the sound of the thunderstorm, until Tasa began to hum, rocking my grandmother in her arms as she combed through her hair and remembered her closest friend. They'd been in the Trials together. My grandmother would tell their stories over dinner, or as we pruned the overgrown leaves of the various plants in the shop or the gardens. Tasa had barely beaten my grandmother, who'd always been the more powerful witch. But the Trials were never about being the most powerful. A statement my grandmother had told me time and time again as she made me promise that when the time came, I too would enter and do everything I could to win.

Eventually, Tasa reached a hand for me. We stood together for a moment, looking down upon the matriarch of my family one final time. "I'll take you home, Raven. We'll tell your mother. But never forget what happened this night. The loss of your grandmother may haunt you, but the loss of the Grimoire is a far greater tragedy."

With that, we left, shutting the door with a sticky knob behind us as we traveled through the pouring rain, watching for the king's soldiers to come back and kill us both.

THE FUNERAL FOR TASA MOONBREAK WAS NOTHING LIKE MY grandmother's. Though Viana Moonstone was known for her creative elixirs and potions, it was nothing compared to the reverence deserved by a coven leader. Kirsi and Nikos stood on each side of me, holding my hands as we took in the crowded clearing nestled within the darkest reaches of the haunted Whorlwood Forest. Before, there had been only the Moon Coven present. But now, at the funeral for a coven leader, it seemed the entire world felt the need to pay its respects as we consecrated the body of a fallen matriarch.

Dressed in a long black gown, lace covering the faces of the women, we waited as Endora Mossbrook clapped her hands to silence those that had come. Holding her title as Moss Coven leader the longest, Endora wore her age in her posture, stooped over a knobby staff, a twisted silver braid falling over a shoulder with markings along her neck and on her hands, showing off her abundant power. I pulled away from her, intimidated by her reverence.

With a sidelong glance, I nudged Kirsi because she wasn't paying attention. Instead, she studied the wraith representatives floating high above the forest, their gauze-like forms and haunted faces coating the setting in somberness. They drifted back and forth, back and forth, watching.

"I caught you staring at the shifters earlier. Don't judge me," she hissed.

I pressed my lips together, shaking my head. Kirsi was never comfortable in emotional situations and she kept her familiar close and the crowd at bay. She understood me in a way few did. Being spirit blessed was incredibly rare. There were only a few others that we knew of and all had the same marking on their brow. She and her familiar Scoop practically shared a soul. They could communicate on a level I would never understand. He curled his soft tail around my ankle, a show of companionship, and I reached for his wide head, stroking behind his black ear as he leaned toward me.

Since we had been the ones to discover Tasa hanging from the oak tree, we were ushered to the front of the crowd to be the first to light our candles and then the coven leaders. There were only five of them now, and a representative for the king's coven. He'd never been seen amongst the witches of any coven but his own, and we'd preferred it that way.

Endora pressed her palms over one another on her walking stick, dipping her chin to her chest before raising one arm into the air. Flourishing a hand, she used her magic to cover Tasa's body with a pure white sheet the moment the nearly full moon cast a sliver of light into the clearing. She then walked to the edge of the salt circle surrounding Tasa and lit the first black candle.

"As ancient as the moss that coats this world, sister, I consecrate thee."

The next coven leader, again an old woman draped in black lace, stepped forward, lighting the second candle. "As powerful as the storm that rages in the night, sister, I consecrate thee."

And so, they continued, each leader speaking for their coven.

"As rooted as the forest that anchors our magic, sister, I consecrate thee."

"As fluid as the river that binds us together, sister, I consecrate thee."

"As limitless as the whisper that sweeps through the land, sister, I consecrate thee."

The king's representative stood, dark blond hair unkempt as he followed the lead of the others, lighting the sixth candle. He spoke in a deep voice that filled the clearing almost as much as the hesitant silence at his presence. "As searing as the fire that ignites our souls, sister, I consecrate thee."

Then it was our turn. Hand in hand, the three of us walked to the salt circle standing before the candle that represented the seventh and final coven. "As steady as the moon that reigns over the dark, sister, we consecrate thee."

I knew it would draw attention I didn't like as I swept a hand forward, casting a spell to light the candle. Small gasps and subtle shifting sounded within the curious crowd, as most of them had never seen me perform magic. Even those from the Moon Coven had doubts unless they'd visited Crescent Cottage.

Try as I might to blend in, I was a novelty. The only witch among thousands that remained unmarked, though not silenced. There were days when I wondered whether it would be better if I was silenced; a witch with no magic at all. But then, if I really wanted that, I could just go live in the human lands across the ocean. Magic didn't exist outside of our pocket of the world.

There was a chance it wasn't me they longed to get a peek at. Maybe it was Kirsi, the spirit blessed with Scoop, who hadn't left her side. They could have been staring at Nikos. Perhaps he was the most likely target because his family had renounced their position within the Moss Coven. They'd willingly performed a bloodletting to transfer their power from their old coven into the Moon Coven's Grimoire. Fortunately for them, this was before the king swept through five of the seven covens and stole the remaining books. He already had his, of course. And one had been missing for over twenty years.

No one knew why Nikos' family had left the Moss coven, but staring at the leader now, her old face and hard eyes, one could imagine.

As we sank back into the crowd, Endora took over once more, inviting the other races to come forward to pay their respect before they were asked to depart from the clearing, leaving only the earthen races, the witches and shifters, though the shifters were hardly welcomed.

The wraiths came first; their translucent, floating bodies swooping close to the ground as they hummed a haunting melody, circling Tasa before vanishing. Water sprites were next, the tiny beings swarming forward as one to leave a gentle mist above the body before they flew away. A phoenix, perched on a treetop at the edge of the forest, spread his bright red and orange wings as he threw his head back and screeched until he burst into flames. He would be reborn, but his beautiful sacrifice for an old woman that had probably never considered the phoenix race at all was telling of the witch's stance within the lower portion of this world. Alongside the shifters, we reigned over all. Below a tyrant king that was half shifter, half witch.

Endora's voice filled the clearing again. "Of blood and bones, of earth and sky, Tasa Moonbreak, let your soul rest with the goddess as your power returns once more to this sacred ground."

She turned to the king's messenger. Eerie silence fell over the crowd, purer than the first breath of a fresh babe as the blond-haired man stepped forward. Dressed in black from head to toe, with a chest as broad as any I'd ever seen, he lifted his chin, pulling the Moon coven's Grimoire from the deep folds of his cloak.

Kirsi squeezed my hand so hard the blood stopped circulating to my chilled fingers. It was there. Right there. And had it not been for the undisputed fear the Dark King had instilled into each of us, the memory of every funeral after the Thrashings, the massacres, that messenger would have likely died on this day. Instead, he pricked the finger of the fallen coven leader and took her final drop of blood. We watched in stunned silence as he placed the drop onto the book and vanished.

3

As with any gathering of the seven covens, though the Fire Coven had been notably absent, gossip followed. The main topic? The sighting of a Grimoire outside of the black castle. They had hardly been seen since the Dark King stole them twelve years ago. We needed those Grimoires. Every witch born to the coven since the birth of witches had placed a drop of their first and last blood into their coven's Grimoire. That stored power bound the families in a coven together. Without them, we grew more and more distant. But more so, should a Grimoire be destroyed, so would an entire coven fall. And how could we trust something so ancient and fragile to a treacherous king who left dead bodies in his wake, left his people to starve, abandoned all but the shifters of his father's lineage and the coven of his mother's?

We were weakened by the loss of our books. But also by the wars between witches and shifters that had dragged on for a millennium before this fragile state of peace, a truce bonded in blood, and by the marriage of the shifter king and his chosen witch bride. The Dark King's fallen parents. But as the population of the witches dwindled, the shifters living amongst us grew. It was clear the tyrant preferred his father's stock.

We moved from the sacred clearing, through the thick forest and onto the hillside lit only by the silver moon, scattered stars and a thousand floating candles. That uncanny scent of crisp October air settled among the gentle rolling hills surrounding us. My eyes flashed to Endora. She'd removed the black lace from her aged face, watching the crowd intently. Studying the witches, likely hoping her daughter, who'd been missing for over thirty years, would magically appear. There was power here. Tremendous power in a gathering of so many witches, but even so, Eden Mossbrook was never coming back.

An offering, they'd called her. Thrust toward the Dark King's father before his marriage as a peace offering, a prospect. Eden had gone missing the same night she traveled to the castle. After all these years, her mother still believed her alive, even though the previous and current king were known for their brutality. If the rumors and whispers, spreading even now, were to be believed, Eden had stolen the Moss Coven Grimoire. It'd been missing as long as she had. Some said Endora's obsession was one of a grieving mother, while others said she hunted the Grimoire, intent on destroying her daughter for what she had stolen. But none of that mattered because the witches with the power to scry couldn't find Eden. Although, one swore she'd heard her heart beating within her seeking spell.

As I watched the mingling covens on the hillside, I noted the animosity growing like poison ivy between them. Those that couldn't farm or garden stood out amongst the others. Thinner, more haggard. I'd always made a priority of sharing when we could, but the gesture was rarely returned. More and more witches grew hungry and angry, and it was far easier to be jealous of what others had, to be cruel to each other, than to thrust ourselves back into a war we could never win. Though they'd come today, custom and tradition always strong amongst them, the witches hated the shifters with so much passion, if they could have eradicated them, many would have tried.

"Raven?" Kirsi waved a hand in front of my face. "Are you in there?"

I swatted her away. "Just observing."

"Be careful, or they'll think you've caught the sickness, staring off into space like that. I'd hate to have to fight a bitch today."

I laughed. "Even if it was the sickness, why would you have to fight anyone?"

She looked me dead in the face, eyebrows slamming down over her eyes. "For fun? Casual Tuesday? You pick."

Rolling my eyes, I pointed. "Look at Endora. Tell me what you see."

She turned, following my line of sight to the witch. "I see an old hag with too much power."

"You hate all the coven leaders. But imagine being one of them. Getting to lead all the rituals. Having a voice. No one staring at you, wondering if you even belong."

"First of all, shut the fuck up about belonging. You're possibly a better witch than I am. Second, leading the rituals is definitely the best part and third, wrong. I actually liked Tasa. She was kind."

"They're all probably kind." Nikos wrapped his arm casually around my shoulder, his blue eyes sparkling in the candlelight. "I imagine being at the top comes with its own sort of battles."

"Just because they won their trials and took on difficult jobs doesn't mean they are pleasant, Nikos. I'm confident old Endora would love to get her hands on you."

"Kirsi!" I snapped. "Not okay."

"What? You both know it's true. She hates your parents for leaving her coven. And why was that again?"

"Can we not talk about this here?" I asked, noticing the surrounding crowd had fallen silent to eavesdrop. "He doesn't know anything about it."

"Sorry," she whispered, winking at Nikos. "We can talk about how evil you are later."

She said it to rile up the eavesdroppers, but as Onyx Moonshade pivoted on a heel behind us and inserted himself into our conversation, everything changed.

"Hey, Leech." He jutted his chin forward, his jet-black hair seeming to soak up the surrounding shadows. "Talking about how weak Moss was, so you had to come suck the Moon coven's tit?"

Nikos said nothing, taking the higher road as he always did, his lips setting into a hard line.

Onyx shot me a disgusted look as he noticed the arm hung over my shoulder. "I'm entering the trials. And I'm winning. When I do, the first order of business will be to send you and your disloyal family back to where they came from."

Each word only escalated the fury within me. Nikos wouldn't speak up for himself, but I sure as hell would. I stepped out of Nikos' embrace and came chest to chest with Onyx, though I had to look up to stare into his golden eyes. "It's a lot easier to build your own narrative when it's based on lies and hatred. And that's exactly why you won't win the trials. Power and asshole tendencies will only get you so far."

"You need a woman to fight your battles for you, Leech?" Onyx jeered before he scowled down at me. "Overcompensating for your lack of markings?"

Kirsi launched herself at him, shoving me out of the way as she hauled back and punched him right in the throat. "Say what you want about Nikos, he can fight his own battles, but come after my best friend, and I'll end you. Coven rules or not."

Choking, Onyx turned and stalked away. Kirsi meant what she'd said, and I loved her deeply for it.

Nikos grabbed my arm and spun me toward him. "Why did you do that? I could have spoken for myself if I'd wanted to."

I drew back, blinking slowly. "Because you didn't. And someone has to stick up for you. You can't just let them say stuff like that all the time. It gets old."

"Exactly." He dropped my arm. "It's old news, Raven. That guy isn't a threat to me. Why would I bother bantering with him? It'd get me nowhere. I'm used to it by now. It's been over a decade of this."

"You're mad at me for sticking up for you?" I shook my head.

"I'm upset that you let him get to you. It wasn't about you. It was about me. You needn't stoop so low."

Steel inched its way through my veins. "I didn't stoop. I stood."

"If I'd wanted your help, I would have asked for it." He stormed away and left me standing there, shocked.

"Why would he be mad about that?" I asked Kirsi as we watched him disappear into the crowd.

"Because you just added fuel to a fire he didn't want. Like he said, it's been like twelve years of him defending himself. He's not a child anymore. Let him take the higher road."

I rolled my eyes. "What would you know about the higher road?"

"Oh, nothing. But I've heard great things."

"Should I—"

"Have you guys seen Talon?" Nym, the other spirit blessed witch in our coven, asked, cutting me off. "I hate to call him away if he's hunting."

I'd always thought Nym was the most beautiful witch. Even as a child, her dark brown skin glowed with a golden hue. I was convinced she draped herself in gold fabrics and bangles to increase the regal aura she seemed to carry with her. She looked around, her emerald eyes searching for her white tiger familiar.

"I'm sure he's run off with Scoop." Kirsi tucked her light blonde hair behind her ear as a flirty smile rested on her lips. "I could help you look for him."

"Would you?" Nym grabbed Kirsi's hand.

They would be so perfect together. Such a pure balance of each other. But Nym, as smart as she was, was completely oblivious to Kirsi's advances.

They left me alone in a crowd of gossiping witches. I thought I'd search for my parents, but as I shuffled through, a shiver ran down my back, and an awkward feeling that someone was watching me settled on my flesh. I whipped around, wondering if it was Endora, the only witch I'd seen really studying the crowd. But she had her back to me now, talking with the other coven leaders.

Surrounded by so many powerful beings, it could have been the magic that filled the space. The thousands of witches marked with spells all over their bodies. The lingering emotions from consecrating a witch who had been such a strong presence in our lives for so long. But it was probably just the palpable hatred of each other that hung in the midnight air. Though I truly believed the coven leaders were doing their best to show peace among themselves, sidelong glances and fisted hands were blatant proof that if something didn't change, everything would.

As if someone had pulled on an invisible string attached to me, I jerked my head to the side. The feeling that someone was watching me turned into something far more sinister, like a thousand invisible spiders creeping over my body. My heart sat in my throat as I eyed the thick line of forest we'd come from. Hoping it was Nikos with some kind of spell he'd kept to himself, I set off.

I couldn't let him stay mad. He didn't have to understand why I'd snapped, but I needed him to know it wasn't malicious. He'd fought that battle a thousand times. I knew he was tired. I knew it wasn't worth it to fight back, to try to explain that he'd had no say over his parents' decisions when he was only a child.

One step after another, I walked into the tree line, pushing heavy branches full of colorful leaves to the side. "Nikos?"

A rush of heat stung my back. I whipped around, facing the clearing, taking in the dancing flames as I realized they'd lit a bonfire. A witch's magic, no doubt, as each floating candle vanished. I thought they'd all leave, that the fading crowd was only a marker of our growing disdain toward each other. It was hard to leave a gathering though, to walk away from the collected power you could feel in your veins. Plus, a meal would be served and for some, that was worth enduring whatever discomfort we had.

I turned my back to the fire, the eerie feeling pulling me deeper into the mesh of trees, snarled branches reaching for me from the growing darkness. As the witches chanted a haunting melody behind me, I moved, carefully stepping on the mossy forest bed as I searched the shadows for movement.

"Honestly, Nikos, I'm sorry. Can we talk?"

I was certain it was him pulling me deeper into the trees and further from the gathering, power tingling against my skin. No one else would take such interest in me. My breaths were short as I progressed, anticipation settling into my stomach with each movement.

"I'm coming." I huffed, pushing aside another branch. "You could have just asked me to follow you."

Silence was my only answer as I played his game. Looking over my shoulder, I was deep enough now I could only make out the silhouette of the branches with the flickering fire in the distance barely visible. A twig snapped close by. I froze, turning back toward the fire, toward the sound.

"Hello?"

A surge of magic gripped my throat, freezing me in place. My heart beat so fast, within seconds my chest ached. I tried to open my fist, to counteract whatever spell I'd been hit with, but I couldn't. Seconds turned into minutes as my muscles protested the strain. The tension in my neck throbbed, moving around to my jawline. A single tear trekked down my cheek. In my peripheral vision, I could see it was red. Blood. Now dripping from my nose, as well. A thick, warm tingling moved down the side of my face. More blood. From my ears.

My heart stopped.

The Harrowing.

No one survived the witch's sickness. I wanted to burst from my own body and flee. Mere feet from a powerful gathering of witches, I was slated to die, frozen in a forest. I couldn't scream for help, couldn't draw power to save myself. Couldn't move. My tongue swelled, scraping against my teeth and along the back of my throat. The world was getting darker, my heartbeat slower. They'd find my body here, smothered in the blood dripping from every cavity.

The world went completely silent. The sound of birds' wings high above me vanished, the inaudible murmur of voices faded away and branches no longer rustled against each other. In a moment of pure peace, terror filled me. I was locked in my own body, trying to leap, to surge forward, to scream.

The gentle faces of my parents flashed through my mind, and I wondered who would tell them. Who would tell Kirsi? At least she would have Scoop to help her through the hard days. Maybe she and Nym would become closer. And Nikos? Ugh. Nikos. He'd tried so hard to be patient with me and I'd hurt him. Now, I wouldn't be able to apologize.

As the edges of the world faded into shadow, I watched the glowing embers from the fire dance. Something darted in front of me. A tendril of blond hair dashed out of the corner of my eye. Kirsi, searching for Talon with Nym. Another drop of blood fell from my eyes, weighing down my bottom lashes.

I couldn't signal her, but somehow, she turned, stepping right into my view. The color drained from her face as she took me in. Rushing forward, she gripped my arm, but I couldn't even acknowledge her. I couldn't hear the screech that likely pierced the world.

Kirsi screamed over and over again, falling to her knees before me as she took my hand, holding it to her forehead. Her markings glowed as she tried and failed to save me. But then more witches entered the clearing. I could only see those directly in front of me, and even they began to blur. There was no mistaking Endora, though. Or the other coven leaders that joined hands around me, one spreading a pocket full of black salt into a circle as the forest filled with witches, their markings glowing sporadically.

Another jolt of magic as the gathered witches' compounded power struck me. Not all would have had a spell to help, but those that could, did. Having no control, my head fell backward, my arms limp at my side. Gravity no longer held me to the forest floor as I lifted from the ground, power shooting through me in waves of battle. Something within me snapped. A murky rolling magic seemed to command my entire body in a seductive caress as a final faint scream erupted from my lips and the world faded away into absolute darkness.

4

The grainy texture of dry eyes behind heavy lids didn't touch the pain throbbing through my bones, over my muscles and through my skin, though I was half asleep. I tried to swallow, but my tongue refused to cooperate, and I gagged instead, gasping for breath as I shot up from the bed I'd been laying in, trying to catch my breath.

"Easy, Rave," a familiar, gentle voice said.

"Kirsi?" Pushing through the pain, I willed my aching eyes open, only to shy away from the harsh sunlight pouring into my childhood bedroom. "I'm so sorry."

She stood from my side and crossed the room, closing the curtains so the room was dark enough for me to handle. Everything was the same. From the quilt draped over the chair in the corner of the room to an old, dusty bookcase holding trinkets and keepsakes I'd made as a child. My eyes flashed to the tiny protection charm my grandmother had made me. The Harrowing would have cracked that little vial had I been wearing it.

I dropped my arm from my eyes as she strode back to the bed and fell to her knees, bringing my hand to her forehead as she had in the forest. "Don't you dare apologize to me for living. Don't you dare."

My mother cleared her throat in the doorway. "Perhaps our Raven would like a cup of that fresh tea I've brewed. Would you mind, Kir?"

She dropped my hand and rose, slipping out of the room.

"She hasn't left your side, you know."

"I figured. Have you seen Nikos? I thought he'd be here."

Her face smoothed, the shadows of new wrinkles disappearing as she relaxed, a warm smile hiding the dark circles. "He's been by a few times. I'm sure this will be his first stop after work."

My mother always gave me space until she couldn't handle the distance, and then she smothered me. I opened my mouth to speak, but she threw her hand in the air to stop me.

"Save it, Raven. You've been resting for three days."

"Three days?" I screeched, bolting upright again.

She sat on the edge of the tiny bed, fluffing the pillows behind me, a smile I didn't trust on her face as she refused to look me in the eye.

"What is it?"

Pushing a black curl behind my ear, she sighed. "You're the first to survive the Harrowing. You're very lucky. We are very lucky."

I shook my head. "It wasn't a sickness, Mother. I could feel the power before it struck. Someone cursed me."

I studied her face for an ounce of understanding, getting nothing but a tear-filled stare. "I'm sure you were very confused. Had you been feeling well that day? Was Tasa's funeral too much for you?"

"I was fi—" I began coughing. Trying and failing to catch my breath as my lungs rattled in my chest.

"That's enough for now, dear. Lay back down. We have all the time in the world to discuss this."

I shook my head. "No. It could happen to someone else. You have to tell the coven leaders. Endora has to know. Someone is cursing the witches."

"Later," she snapped, pinning me with a stare as cold as steel. I wouldn't win. Not when she'd made up her stubborn mind.

I nodded slowly, resting against the pillows as Kirsi came in carrying an old tray with my mother's finest mismatched teacups and a few small cookies. Setting it on my empty dresser, she poured a single cup and handed it to me.

"Equal parts lemongrass and lavender mixed with a pinch of poppyseed and peppermint," my mother said as I lifted the steaming cup to my lips. "You'll feel better in no time. But just in case," she cast over the drink and lifted a charm from her neck. "Take this, too."

"I don't need a protection spell," I insisted, tasting the bite of peppermint on my tongue. That was far more than a pinch, and she knew it.

"If not for yourself, then wear it for me. You gave your father and I enough of a scare."

"Where is he?" I asked, setting the cup on the bedside table.

"He's gone out to chop wood."

I exchanged worried glances with Kirsi, but she lifted her palms. "I tried to help him. He wanted to be alone."

"That sounds like him." I forced a smile, the warmth of the tea coating my throat as I settled back into the cozy bed, pulling the blankets up to my chin. "I think I'll rest now."

My mother kissed my forehead and walked out without another word.

The bed sank as Kirsi took her place.

"You just might be the luckiest witch on the planet." She grabbed my hand and squeezed. "You don't get to die on me, Rave. We've got shit to do together."

I tried to roll my eyes, but instead they fell shut and sleep stole me away once more. My mother's potion, no doubt.

"What if she does?" my father barked.

"Then we support her as we've always done," my mother answered, though there was no conviction in her statement.

I should have announced that I was awake, but morbid curiosity got the best of me.

"No, Yara. I won't have it. She's too fragile. We love her too much."

A snort from my mother. "What is a parent's value if they don't love their children too much? We cannot control her any more than we can control the harvest, Dein."

"I could strap her to that damn bed for two more weeks. Keep her asleep with herbs."

His voice faded as I realized I was falling back to sleep. He meant well, but if he kept me here longer than necessary, I'd never speak to him again. A fact he knew well.

"RAVEN, IT'S TIME TO WAKE UP. YOU NEED TO EAT."

My stomach growled in response and I peeled my eyes open, subtle moonlight pouring into the room, falling softly onto the foot of my bed. Feeling a bit more like myself, I sat up, taking my time as the room spun.

"Nikos went home to bathe, but he'll be back soon. I thought you might like to freshen up while he was away."

"Where's Kirsi?" I asked, rubbing my eyes.

"She and Scoop went for a walk, but she isn't far," my mother said, handing me a hot cup of broth with a few floating vegetables.

I sipped the concoction, letting the soup take me all the way back to my childhood. To winter colds and scraped knees, to chilly nights and dry logs heating the house. I considered bringing up the witch's sickness again but, once Mother made up her mind about something, that was it.

She held her hands out for me to take, and I did, letting her help me because I needed it, but so did she. I undressed and she dipped a cloth into a warm pot, wiping down my skin. There was no dried blood, no sign of what had happened on the outside. Inside, I was weaker than I'd ever known, though still thrumming from the power of the gathered witches. That final strike of magic had been so dominant I'd been released from the curse but locked into a deep sleep for days.

Brushing through my tangled curls, my mother hummed a lullaby as she had when I was a child and refused to sleep. I didn't come home enough, especially when life and the world was overwhelming, but there were reasons, days when my parents forgot that I was grown. I was the center of their universe ... to a sickly degree. I needed space. I needed to be my own person.

Refreshed, I sank back into the bed, reaching for the soup. "Where's Father?"

"Dein?" she shouted. "She's awake."

He appeared in the frame of the door, looking so much older than I remembered him to be. They both did. My mother's black hair had streaks of silver and my father's broad shoulders turned inward.

"You nearly died," he said by way of greeting, his voice cracking on that final word.

I could only nod in response.

He waved his hand through the air and the tear I hadn't noticed vanished from my cheek. Stepping into the room, he commanded the space until he loomed over me, blocking the small bit of light I'd had.

"Sometime in the next moon cycle there will be a Trials announcement."

"Dein!" my mother chirped. "You cannot interfere. You know this."

"She's our daughter, Yara."

My mother conceded, sitting on the edge of the bed, content to pull the layers of blankets higher around me. Though some were threadbare, she clung to them simply because I'd worn them down myself over the years.

"You're a grown woman now. I cannot tell you what to do, but I pray you'll heed this warning and stay away from the Trials. There's nothing you need to prove to this world, Raven. People will believe whatever they want about you, no matter what you do. You'll only be putting yourself at risk."

I needed to make a choice. To confide the deepest desires of my heart, telling my father how much I longed to join the Trials just as my grandmother had, or lie through my teeth and come up with an excuse later, should I ever be chosen.

He didn't know what it was like. To be at the very bottom of the totem pole. To live life, even as an adult, beneath a spectacle of catty whispers and pointed fingers. I could show them all the truth of the secret power that lay within me. I could command the weather, could move the earth if I wanted. I'd never known another witch with such power. It could be enough to gain their respect. Especially now, when the stares were going to be longer, the voices louder. I was not only the unmarked witch, but I was also the only witch to ever survive the Harrowing.

I sighed. He'd never understand. "I hadn't intended on joining. I've no desire to become a coven leader."

Crossing his arms over his chest as he lifted his chin, his posture growing into the man I'd always remembered him to be, he narrowed his eyes. "Would you be willing to bind those words to me?"

"Dein!" my mother shrieked, leaping from the bed. "She cannot. It's forbidden."

Holding my father's stare, I lowered the cup of soup. "I will not make a binding promise. I've told you I have no intention, so let that be enough for now."

"Raven, listen to your father."

My head whipped to the door to find Nikos standing there, hands casually placed into his front pockets as he pinned me with a look I didn't care for. Setting the soup back on the bedside table, I shifted my feet, poised to stand. Nikos rushed over from the door, grabbing my arm to help me up. I pulled away.

"I'm not fragile. I'm not going to break. I don't need you."

The hurt in his eyes stunned me.

"I'm sorry, Nikos. I didn't mean that. Of course I need you. I'm just feeling ..."

"Smothered?" my mother answered, repeating words I'd said to her the day I moved out.

"Yes." My shoulders lowered as I sank back onto the bed. "I love that you all care about me so deeply. I love that you want to make sure I'm taking care of myself." I stared directly into my father's blue eyes that mirrored my own. "I love you. But you have to trust me. Even if you don't agree with everything I do."

He grunted and walked out of the room. My mother patted my back, but as anticipated, followed my father, content to bring him solace for my harsh words.

Nikos kneeled on the floor before me, taking my hands in his as he kissed the palms. His blond hair fell over dark lashes as he looked at me with eyes that spoke a thousand words with only a glance, the marking on the back of his palm glowing amber as he rubbed his thumb over my knuckles.

"Please don't use your magic to try to soothe me. I know you mean well, but I need to feel what I'm feeling right now. I need to know I'm just as alive as I was before I—" I paused, unsure if he would believe me. But also, unsure if I could forgive him if he didn't. "You know. I'm sorry for what I said at the funeral. I didn't mean to involve myself. Onyx just knows how to get under my skin."

"I stormed off instead of staying with you. I'm the sorry one, Raven." The glowing mark faded to black, but he didn't pull away. "Does it make me such a bad person that I agree with your parents? That I look at you and think about my whole world. Our future. I'm allowed to be a little selfish when it comes to you. I've earned that, haven't I?"

I tugged on his arms, pulling him onto the bed. He wrapped his strong arms around me and, for the first time in what felt like forever, I could breathe again.

"I'm sorry," I whispered.

"It's been a rough week. I think we're all on edge."

I nodded.

"Just think about what they said, Rave." His voice rumbled in his chest and my eyelids grew heavy as I sighed. He didn't know I'd already promised my grandmother I'd enter the Trials. That I'd promised myself I would. That the mere thought of being the last witch standing made something deep within me come alive.

A banging outside my parents' home rattled me awake hours later. Nikos shifted behind me as we took in the commotion of voices and hammering outside. I threw the layers of blankets off and swung my feet over the edge of the bed. Nikos reached out to stop me from standing, but I pushed away, content to do it on my own.

He circled the bed, grabbing my waist to help me stand. "Let me help you. I want to."

Nodding, I wrapped my arm around him as he helped me to the

front door. Stepping out and past my parents, who stood motionless on the front lawn, I watched as one of the Dark King's soldiers drove a giant nail into the trunk of the tree. I glanced back at my parents, but their faces were expressionless. Neighbors poured from their humble homes, huddling together as they tried to see around the man's broad shoulders to the message he hung.

"What is it?" I asked Nikos.

"I'm not sure."

"It's the announcement for the Trials," my mother whispered from beside me. I hadn't heard her approach. "They aren't going to wait for the new moon."

I could feel my father's gaze pinning me to the spot before I had a chance to process her words.

5

"You moved out for a reason, Rave." Kir kicked a pebble down the dark cobblestone road as she held tightly to my arm, our billowing sleeves intertwined.

The silvery moon led the way from our small home to Gravana lake. I'd walked this path so many times. Often feeling like it might be a second home, or possibly third if Crescent Cottage counted. Midnight gatherings were not unheard of in the Moon Coven and, though we could have walked there navigating from memory alone, tonight's sky was a blessing from the goddess. The night appeared dangerous, though. Ominous. And while the path was tree-lined, it seemed to be the shadows within the wood that threatened to swallow us whole as we traveled together, several witches ahead of us and even more behind. Solidarity in numbers would hopefully guarantee our safe journey.

"I know. And they mean well." I shuffled my feet to keep her pace.

"I think we should do it. Have you ever seen a coven leader skip a meal or patch a skirt? Work overtime in a shop just to keep her home?"

"No. Listen, I thought I would join. I made a promise. But my parents, and even Nikos, asked me not to."

She snorted, the wisps of her long blonde hair catching the blue moonlight. "Nikos asked you not to? That's your first sign to do it. It's best for him to learn now that you don't answer to him."

We turned down the next path as I shook my head. "I care about him. His feelings and opinions matter to me."

Bumping me with her hip, she smirked. "He doesn't know you like I do. You hide your fire. You hide that crazy power, but I know it's in there."

"I don't hide my fire." I stopped walking and she jerked backward. "Seriously, Kir. I don't. I just know when to pick my battles."

She held her pinkie in the air between us, brushing her hair from her face. "I know you. This means everything to you. But if you swear it doesn't in a promise, I won't mention it again."

Stepping toward her, I stared down at that calloused finger. Could I swear it? Biting my lip, I moved back.

"I knew it." She smirked, taking my arm again. "Don't worry. Your secret is safe with me, you cute little liar."

"I want to think it through, that's all. But imagine if one of us became a coven leader, Kir. We could make changes. Encourage the covens to work together to help people struggling. The witches are determined to rise above the wraiths, the shifters, even the Fire Coven. Imagine if there wasn't such a divide."

"Does the Fire Coven even count anymore? We never see them. They've taken sides with the Dark King because he's their coven leader. They probably walk around their territory without an inch of fear in them. Why would he kill his coven of witches when he has us to pick off? The real reason to win the Trials is to band together and find a way to protect the rest of the witches from the Thrashings."

"True. I heard Moss and River won't speak to each other."

She flipped her hair over her shoulder. "So, we're doing it?"

"It's dangerous. This king has never hosted the Trials before. He's a different kind of evil. No. I changed my mind. I'll make the promise."

"Too late. We're entering together."

We merged into a crowd of Moon Coven witches, all headed to the gathering on Gravana Lake. Our covenstead, the place we held our casual gatherings, resided where the moon could pour over us from the sky and in its glass-like reflection on the water below. Fog, lit by the stars, settled atop the lazy water, holding a spider web of docks that joined in the middle of the lake. Thirteen families would meet with no excuses made.

I searched across the water for Nikos but couldn't see him mixed amongst the hundreds of witches gathered. On nights like these, even the silent witches were to attend. Though they were born with no power at all, this was a familial obligation. I shuddered, remembering I was once considered a silent witch. Unlike the others, I had no power until I was nine years old. We still had no explanation as to why it unexpectedly came, nor why the markings remained invisible.

The central platform was empty, a reminder that Tasa was no longer among us. This would be the first Trials announcement in my lifetime and, while I knew we wouldn't have a coven leader present, I was surprised to see seven cloaked figures, their faces hidden in the shadows of their hoods as they crossed over the swaying dock and took center stage. Kirsi gripped my hand as one of the broader shoul-dered figures stepped forward and removed his hood.

The king's messenger from Tasa's funeral studied the coven surrounding him as he drew a curved blade from the folds of his robe and dipped it into the moon-soaked water. A wave of his fingers and a basin the size of a bar of soap drifted from the bank, across the foggy water, and right into his hand.

Setting the basin on a pedestal carved from bone, more ancient than my grandmother's grandmother, he lifted the blade to the palm of his hand and sliced, just deep enough that the royal coven's blood could open the ceremony. He was not a fool, though. One drop was all he allowed before he healed the wound and lifted his hands into the sky. We were too far away to hear the words he murmured to the moon. But as his giant hands fell to his sides, a burgeoning wall of darkness formed around the perimeter of the lake, closing the entire gathering into a dome of shadows, apart from the window above, left for the full moon.

"Have you ever seen power like that?" Kirsi whispered. "And who's the figure standing in for Tasa?"

A subtle shake of my head was all I could answer, feeling claustrophobic from the shadows so deep they could have been crafted from the space between the stars, or the deepest parts of the earth. A cold hand wrapped around my forearm, yanking me backward. Only then did I realize I'd been moving toward the wall. Kirsi had saved me from walking straight off the dock and plunging into the lake.

"Still feeling weak?" she asked, holding tight to my hand as I nodded, my stare vacant.

The king was the only one allowed to have a representative by proxy, but this was still the king's magic. His infamous darkness pouring over the gathering. I wondered if housing the stolen Grimoires made the Fire Coven stronger. And more so, how close was the Dark King to have cast the spell at just the right time.

One by one, the other coven leaders, except for the mysterious stand-in for the Moon Coven, gave a drop of blood to the basin, speaking a spell to the moon before they moved back into line. Again, the Fire Coven witch stepped forward, his silver-blond hair glinting in the moonlight as he gestured and a cauldron, sizable enough to fit a full grown shifter inside, slid across the top of the Gravana Lake and settled onto the platform.

His smoky voice echoed off the shadowed walls, spreading his words for all to hear now. "Each of the four lunar phases last approximately seven days. For this reason, the witches have seven covens. And perhaps the most sacred of all is the one gathered here tonight. Beneath your namesake, bathed in the magic of rebirth and cleansed power."

"As if we haven't heard this a thousand times," Kirsi mumbled under her breath. "He probably thinks he's winning us all over right now."

A woman in front of us whipped around, shushing Kir for her comment and giving me a weary look, before turning back to the platform. Kirsi lifted a middle finger to the back of the woman's head, and I bit my bottom lip to hide my smile.

"You have thirteen days to enter yourselves into the Trials held by the Fire Coven leader, our king. To enter, you are to place a single drop of your blood into this cauldron."

Kirsi snorted. "So archaic. I wonder if we'll fly to the castle on broomsticks as well."

I bumped her with my shoulder as I faced forward again.

"The shadow wall around this lake will serve as a barrier. Once the other coven members on this platform have crossed the threshold, it will be magically sealed for the next thirteen days. You'll be able to come and go as you please, but only the Moon Coven will be allowed to cross through.

"Once the shadows fall, the cauldron will select her thirteen Chosen. There will be no question who is selected. If it's you, you'll know." The king's proxy turned to face the other direction. Though his back was now to us, his voice was just as clear as before. "If you are Chosen, there is no turning back. Make your decision wisely. The witch Trials are not for the weak of heart, soul, or power. Your coven leaders will eliminate the first five, and eight of you will join your king in his castle. The number eight represents authority, inner-self and inner-wisdom as well as ambition. The number eight is fed with the energy of both sorrowful endings and strong beginnings."

He lifted his vibrant green hood over his head and, just as before, vanished.

Six figures remained cloaked on the platform. Five coven leaders and one special Moon Coven witch, chosen for symbolism to open the Trials. My grandmother had the honor of that role in her time. Before Tasa won their Trials. A deep sense of envy seeped over me as I watched, jaw slackened.

All the cloaked coven leaders, aside from the mysterious stand-in, kept their heads bowed as they stepped down from the platform, pushing through the magical barrier as they left. All that remained were the members of the Moon Coven. The last cloaked figure walked forward, moving to the edge of the obsidian cauldron. Thin, tan fingers poked out of the long robe sleeves as they caressed the edge of the magical vessel. The gathering was completely still and silent as we watched Willow Moonhollow remove her cloak, prick her finger and let a single drop fall silently into the basin. She swiped her dark curly hair from her eyes and turned, following the coven leader's example as she walked out.

She'd just officially submitted her entry.

"Come on," Kirsi said, dragging me forward as soon as the spell that had mesmerized us all broke. "I want to be among the first."

My heart raced in my chest. I wanted to join her. To be the very second in line. But my parents were here somewhere, watching. And so was Nikos.

"I can't." I pulled out of her grip. "I have to wait."

"Fine. We'll wait until no one's here to watch and then do it."

We shuffled down the docks, dodging the witches going in both directions until we were face to face with the black barrier. Being this close to something so powerful made every hair on my body stand on end. A part of me wanted to bathe in those shadows, be seduced by them, but the other part, the sensible part, recognized the true, uninhibited danger they really were. A product of the Dark King.

Still, I lifted my hand and skimmed the shadowed wall with my fingers. Nothing happened.

"Stop being so dramatic, Raven. If you still want to stop by the shop tonight, we'd better go. We aren't going to be home before four am as it is."

She was right.

"I'm exhausted, and I'm not ready to go back to the store yet. People will only come to stare and be nosy about what happened."

"You won't hear me argue." Kirsi stepped through the barrier like it didn't bother her at all.

I held my breath and followed, growing warmer by the second. For a moment, everything inside me came alive. I could feel it all. Every nerve ending in my body thrummed with an overwhelming desire to be touched by a man, to be filled and aching for release. To be lost in passion like I'd never known. What were these shadows that caressed me? My body wound tighter and tighter as I stopped moving. The friction of my thighs alone, the heat, threatened to be my undoing. I gasped, wanting nothing more than to run my hands over my heavy, sensitive breasts, to reach under my skirt and bring myself to climax. No one would see me here, hidden in the shadows.

I pushed away the wicked feeling that accompanied the barrier.

Gritting my teeth until my feet moved. It was as if the king's magic had set my soul on fire. And then I was out. Walking right behind Kir.

"What *was* that?" I asked, running my hands up and down my arms as I fought the urge to go back.

"That was the king's magic."

"But why did it feel like that?" I could hardly catch my breath.

"Feel like what?" Kirsi stopped walking and grabbed me by both arms. "You look like shit, Rave."

"Yeah. It's, uhm. I'm just tired." I moved my hands into my curls and decided not to mention the sweat beading on my forehead.

"Let's go home before Lover boy shows up. You need to rest."

I DIDN'T TELL KIRSI I WAS FRIGHTENED TO JOIN THE TRIALS. SINCE childhood, I had been determined to win, to find my place among the witches and prove myself worthy. For the next twelve days, I lived in a constant state of contemplation, self-doubt, and fear. Every piece of me knew I wanted to join—knew I'd never forgive myself if I didn't fulfill that promise to my grandmother—to not only enter, but win. That was all before we'd known the true threat of the Dark King, who I imagined sat on a massive throne of fallen witch bones, plotting ways to steal our power and kill us all. I also needed to consider Nikos and my parents' wishes for my safety. Their warnings were not without merit.

Kirsi, though? She was all fire and persistence. She had no doubt we'd enter, and it would come down to her and me, just like it had for my grandmother and Tasa. When we were younger, we'd acted out our Trials, having no idea what really happened during them. Even my grandmother, though she loved to talk about the times she'd beat Tasa, never painted a full picture. The Trials were secret and sacred and full of the perfect amount of mystery to stir a child's vivid imagination. She and Tasa had always said, 'The Trials are what you make of them'. From that day forward, we'd promised to be just like them.

Kirsi insisted we take time off from Crescent Cottage. I didn't have the energy to go back to working from sunup to sundown after flirting with death, but the more I thought about the garden over-flowing with leaves from the past two weeks, the more I knew we needed to get back to work. We were blessed with green thumbs, and we'd never go hungry as long as we could garden, but some were not so fortunate. And our patrons might fall ill and need our tonics.

The morning air was crisp and welcoming on the walk to Crescent Cottage. I found myself looking up at the tree we'd found Tasa hanging from and wondering how she'd truly gotten there. Had the Dark King shown his face before he'd hanged her? Had he attacked from his powerful shadows? The single feather left behind was long gone.

Chills crept down my spine, and I wrapped the shawl tighter around myself as we walked.

"Raven?" Nikos' soft voice called from behind us, and I stopped to let him catch up.

Sharing a smile, he leaned down for a kiss, rubbing his hands up and down my arms to help warm me. "You'll catch a chill in your condition."

Kirsi rolled her eyes hard enough I thought I'd heard it. "She's not *in a condition*. She's completely fine, I promise you that."

"I'm glad to hear it." He took my hand in his and kissed my fingers as we walked on. "I've missed you."

The sincerity in his voice warmed me. He'd been working hard at his apprenticeship. Someday Nikos would be a scholar, keeping all accounts of our history. He worked long hours within the record halls every day. But he had a brilliant mind. It was the perfect job for him.

"Raven and I have a meeting with Greer Moonbreak tonight to discuss putting some of our items in their shop on the other side of town. We won't be free this evening, unfortunately."

Nikos drew back. "You never told me you were considering that."

"Nothing's decided. We're just looking at our options," Kirsi answered.

"If it makes us a little extra money, it's worth the additional work." I glanced away from Nikos, knowing he wasn't a fan of the idea. He didn't think we should keep Crescent Cottage at all, saying it took far too much of my time for the small return it warranted us. But it kept food on the table and wood for our fire. "It's just a consideration."

"Of course." He tucked his hands behind his back. "It's not something I would do if I had a business. I'd insist my clients came directly to me. But to each their own."

"Excellent. So we'll see you tomorrow." Cutting off the conversation now was the easy route when it came to Nikos. He would inevitably go out of his way to make sure we were doing what he felt was best and, while it was endearing that he cared so much, I preferred to be my own woman. To make my own choices.

He smiled warmly, pulling me into a hug as we stood outside the shop. "Don't overdo it on your first day back. I'm worried you're pushing yourself too hard."

I moved to my tiptoes to kiss him as Kirsi unlocked the door. "I promise I'm not. Kirsi does all the work around here anyway."

He chuckled and kissed me soundly. I let the world fade away, lost in the feel of his arms around me. He slid his hands up my back as his tongue caressed mine. We took a moment to get lost in each other. Something I hadn't known I'd needed until he stood here before me.

Pulling away from his eager grasp, I smiled up at him through long, dark lashes. "You can stop by early tomorrow and we can have tea before we come to work?"

He moved in, pressing his head to mine until I thought I'd drown in his eyes. "I wouldn't miss it for the world."

I stepped into Crescent Cottage beaming as I pressed my back against the door with a sigh.

"Still want to be just friends?" Kirsi laughed, already watering the plants inside.

She'd teased me endlessly when I'd skirted around Nikos' advances when we were younger. Over and over, I'd insisted we should stay friends. Thankfully, things changed, but Kirsi liked to remind me of my stubbornness from time to time.

"You can't judge my past when you won't tell Nym how you feel."

Several of the bundles of dried flowers had hung too long and shed their crisp petals along the dusty floor. I stepped away to grab a broom, just as the bell above the door rang behind me.

"Oh, thank the heavens you're back, Raven," a rumble of a voice said from behind me.

"Yetu?" I turned to face the troll. "What's wrong?"

He pulled the worn hat from his wrinkled head and took a knee before me, unable to stand fully erect in our shop.

"It's my hand. I keep getting those cramps in my fingers and I can't work. Everything just locks up. But if I can't work, I can't feed the children."

"Let's take a look, shall we?"

He nodded and followed me over to the counter, plopping his calloused fingers down for me to look at. I waved my hand over his, calling forth a healing spell I'd acquired when I was seventeen. The relief in the troll's shoulders was indication enough that it had worked, though I never doubted it.

"I'm afraid that's not going to keep it well forever. But surely the Forest Coven has a healer you could see that would be closer? Instead of coming all the way down to me?"

He fished three coins from his pocket and put them in my hand before cupping it tightly. "Hardly any witches will see anyone outside of their race. I went to every market practically begging, but got turned away. Polly said she went to Gretha's last week looking for a new basket for her yarns and had the same trouble. Seems the witches don't want nothing to do with the likes of us anymore. We might as well be shifters."

He turned to walk away.

"Yetu, wait." I crossed the cottage and plucked a stone from a display. I closed my eyes and called power forth, enhancing the energy of the stone.

"Keep this in your pocket. It will help with the arthritis. And I promise I'll never turn you or Polly away. If you need something, please don't be afraid to ask. Even if I have to go down to crabby Old Gretha's myself to buy her basket."

"You're too good for this world, Raven Moonstone. Too good."

The rest of the day carried on the same. Agatha Rivercast, who usually came the third day of each month to purchase our leftover dried flowers, made an unexpected stop. But most of the day's patrons were not witches but the wraiths, trolls, and sprites seeking remedies and spells, earthen crystals and unique flowers. The wraiths, though they lacked the need for sustenance, loved to collect our crystals to calm their wary souls. We'd hardly had time to tend to the garden. But a busy day meant for a good supper.

Turning the key in the lock, I slipped it into my pocket as Kirsi took my arm.

"How tired are you?" she asked.

"Honestly, I feel rejuvenated. There's something so empowering about being needed."

She smirked. "Fantastic, because we're not meeting with Greer tonight. I mean, we are, but it has nothing to do with the shop."

I tried to protest, but she held a hand out to me. "This is the final night to submit our names for the Trials."

My mouth turned dry as I envisioned that tiny drop of blood sinking into the darkest part of that cauldron. "We're really doing it," I said, filled with awe.

She winked. "We really are, but first, we're going moondancing."

My eyes lit up. "Who's in charge of the wine?"

"Me, of course." She laughed. "Who else?"

6

It was said, if a moon witch danced below the moon when it was weakest, it would draw upon your power and the next full moon, you would be blessed. I was sure the moon enhanced our power, but not about the blessing. Either way, dancing with twelve other witches, half naked, drunk on wine and singing at the top of our lungs seemed like a brilliant idea. It was just the escape I needed. The perfect level of fun. Kirsi had invited Nym and they swung around in lazy circles, holding their empty glasses, the wine long since sloshed over the sides. There was joy here in the clearing. And a little bit of mischief.

"Dance with me." Greer held out her open arms and I took her hands, laughing as we circled each other, barefoot on the cool autumn grass, her copper hair covering her face, her dimpled smile and dusting of freckles.

The shoulder of my snowy white dress had fallen and after several times adjusting it, I just didn't care anymore. Moondancing was a time to be carefree and happy. To send the moon your reserved magic, to draw power and ground yourself to the Earth. To let go. And so I did. Spinning and spinning until the world beyond Greer was nothing more than a blurred reality of overgrown trees and drunken girls in a forest.

"Stop, stop." Greer giggled. "I've spilled my wine. I can't breathe."

"Me either," I panted behind my smile.

Crashing into the swells of grass below me, I stared at the stars and waited for my breaths to slow. Kirsi lay beside me, taking my hand as she shuffled until her head was touching mine, her blonde hair practically glowing next to my black.

She pointed to the sparkling expanse of energy above us. "Each one you get wrong, you have to drink."

Biting my bottom lip, I nodded, half the world tilting with the gesture. "Deal."

She shifted her pointer finger to the east.

"Tigress. And there's her cub," I said, directing her arm. "The mother fell into a ravine and her cub followed. When the goddess asked her whose life should be spared, the mother refused to answer, stating they would never part and so they were placed into the sky for eternity. Your turn." I pointed to a cluster of stars to the north. Kirsi was far better at astrology than I was. I rarely stumped her when we played this game, so instead, I preferred to make it annoyingly easy for her.

"You always pick her." She groaned. "At least try. That's Sirain. Winged warrior of the dark kingdom of ancient times. Cast to the sky because it was the only way to separate her from her lover and defeat her. Even now she draws her bow." She took a long draw out of her goblet. "I got that one right, but I'm still drinking. What's that one?"

Kirsi filled my cup as I stared into the sky, trying to connect dots that had begun to wave, leaving traces behind them.

"That's Atulle. The rabbit."

"Wrong. Drink. I get to go again. That one?" Again, she pointed.

"Celcian. The king of kings."

She burst into laughter. "His name is Tlecan and he's way over there. That one is Arturus. Drink."

"The clock is ticking," I said, lifting the cup to my lips while I approached the subject that had occupied my mind for twelve days.

"It is." She sat up on an elbow staring down at me, bathed in starlight, the moon illuminating her curious face. "You know how I feel, Rave. I won't do it without you. It's all or none. I think you should be the change you want to see in the world. We've waited for this since we were kids. Fuck Nikos, fuck your parents, be a big girl and show these assholes what you're made of. For once in your life, make a decision for yourself without concern of what others think. You've earned the right."

"It's not just that. It's him. What if we all die at the hands of the Dark King?"

"Everyone dies. It's just a matter of when, my girl." She clinked her glass to mine and we both drank again.

BEFORE THE SUN COULD CREEP THROUGH MY BEDROOM WINDOW, BEFORE the rooster crowed, murmurs as constant as the river sounded outside of our small house. Though the wine was long gone, the hangover was in full force.

"Go away," I mumbled into my feathered pillow.

The cold air smelled like stale fire and ash, proof that summer was only a memory, and the autumn solstice would soon be here. It did nothing to coat my churning stomach or ease the pounding in my head as the noise outside continued. I moaned again, expecting Kirsi to be up to something as I folded my head into the pillow and cursed the morning.

But each footstep outside the door grew louder to my sensitive ears until I threw my pillow across the room and shot out of bed, steadying myself as the world tipped to one side. I loved the wine, but it did not love me back.

Cinching my robe at the waist, I stumbled through the house and flung the door open, all for the world to fall silent. I stared at the gathered crowd in disbelief as they stared back at me. Witches of all shapes and sizes had gathered outside my home.

"Well, what is it?" I asked, folding my arms over my chest.

A small child in the front row, held back by only a knee-high iron fence, pointed to me, but said no words. I lifted an eyebrow until the woman beside him spoke.

"Your door."

My ears rang as the memories of last night came flooding back. Flashes of Kir and I dancing and drinking all the way to the shadowed barrier. I remembered standing in the wall of shadows, hypnotized by drunken lust, then Kirsi yanking me out as we stumbled across the docks, giggling as we tried not to fall into the water. And then a single prick of my finger as I entered myself into the Witch Trials.

And now staring back at me were two letters, 'R' and 'K' smeared in blood upon our door.

I backed slowly into the house, my heart racing though no words came to me. The floor cold beneath my bare feet. The world tipping once more as I rushed to a bucket and lost any remaining contents of my stomach. I'd done it. To myself. Unaware if I was excited, or scared, or both, the walls crept toward me. I swiftly became a small child, staring into the dead eyes of my fallen grandmother. As soldiers clad in black rushed over her body to steal the Grimoire. Our king was younger then. And only freshly crowned. What types of evil had he learned since?

A hand swiped the hair back from my face as I crouched over the bucket. Kirsi rubbed my back in small circles as she tried to soothe me. "I thought you actually wanted to join the Trials, Rave. I'm so sorry."

I shook my head, wiping away the tears. "I did want this. My whole life, I did. But we could die."

"I won't let anything happen to you, Rave. I promise. We're in this together."

"You *what?*" My father stormed across my childhood home; strides longer than his body was tall. "You promised you wouldn't."

My mother hadn't spoken a word. Wide-eyed and unmoving, she

relied on my father for the outburst as she sat at the small table, gripping the sides of her teacup so hard her knuckles had turned white.

I studied the careful embroidery on the tea towels as my father carried on, raging about his disappointment and concern. I had to keep reminding myself that he loved me. That he wouldn't bat an eyelash if he didn't care and that would have felt so much worse. When I was a child and everyone thought I was a silenced witch, my father had taken extra precautions to make sure I'd have a place in this world. He was the one that thrust me into my grandmother's arms to make sure I understood how to grow plants. How to study them and learn their uses without magic. How to guarantee I could grow my own food so I would never starve, even when my mother had her own reservations.

I stood, placing my hands flat on the table, and stared down my father until he stopped wearing the path into the kitchen floor. "I'm sorry you're disappointed. I'm sorry I went back on my word. But unless you know of a way out, I'm in this now. And I can either go in half-heartedly, or I can go in with nerves of steel and no self-doubt. Which would you prefer, Father?"

"Just tell me why." His voice broke on the last word, but that would be the extent of his weakness.

"There's a small part of me that wonders if I can do this. If I can do something good with the coven leader's position. I might not be the most powerful, nor the strongest. But I have something to offer this world and, at the very least, I hope you can see that."

His mouth formed a flat line as he jerked his head to the side, staring out the window. His heaving breaths turned slow, calm. "There's no way out now, Raven. I wish I knew one, but I don't."

"I don't need a way out. I need you to look at me and understand this is my decision. No matter how much of a mistake you think it was. I'm not a child."

Rubbing his knuckles against his palm, he let his shoulders drop and walked out. His version of a concession. It wasn't ideal, but I'd take it. I turned to my mother, waiting for her outburst of tears.

Instead, a single drop fell down her cheek as she peered at me with a solemn face. "You have no idea what you've done."

She stood and walked out in the same manner my father had.

"I THOUGHT WE'D TALKED ABOUT THIS?" NIKOS SAID, LOOKING AT ME over the top of the book he'd been reading.

I didn't want to come to this place. The dimly lit record hall was quiet in all the wrong ways. Eerie even. The ancient history of the witches, dating back to a time when magic was frowned upon, sat nestled on the old wooden shelves caked in dust. Solid wood tables with mismatched chairs filled the center of the silent room, as if the witches would really come to spend time here. But only the scholars did. Only those dedicated to the history of our kind found solace in a past as treacherous and scarred as our present and likely future.

I drew a steady breath. "I promised my grandmother if the time ever came, I would put my name in. I couldn't break that promise, Nik."

"What's a promise to a dead woman when you're risking your life?" He huffed, a billowing of dust falling from the worn edges of his book.

Biting the inside of my cheek, I held myself back. "I came here to talk to you about this, not argue. My promise mattered then, and it matters now. Can you really sit there and tell me you didn't even consider putting a drop of blood into that cauldron?"

"I'll spend the night here in the record hall. I'll get you out of this. The Thrashings are happening more frequently. The Dark King is deranged." He finally set his book down, moving around the table to place his heavy hands on my shoulders. "Only a fool would be tempted by fire."

His words sank into my gut like the weight of the book he'd been reading. I tried. Really tried to remember all the good things that had been between us but couldn't. I pushed away from him, shaking my head. "I am not a fool. And you cannot control me, Nikos. I can go where I please, when I please."

"Agreed. Unless your safety is concerned and then I think we need to discuss it. One day—"

I threw my hand up to stop him. "No. That's not how this works. I am not a child, and I will not ask for permission. I don't understand why you insist on treating me like this."

"If you act like a child, you get treated like one. And I know that burns to hear, but how else am I going to get through to you? You're overreacting. We've known each other for a long time. I know you better than you know yourself. This isn't you, Rave, and I'm afraid I'm going to have to forbid you—" The words were out of his mouth before he could stop them. He pulled back, the look of shock on his face at saying them, mirroring my own.

I backed away from him. "We have known each other for a long time. We were friends. Good friends. But ever since this," I gestured between us, "became more than that, you've been overstepping. I'm not sure when I made it okay for you to treat me the way you have been, but I'm done. I can't even listen to you speak. I don't want this anymore, Nik."

His eyes doubled in size. "I think we both know you don't mean that. You need me, Rave, and I need you. I didn't mean it like that."

I shook my head, inching toward the door. "I thought I might love you. I thought we'd marry one day." I scoffed. "My parents definitely thought so. But I have to go be my own person. I have to do this. And if you can't stand beside me, then get out of my way."

I spun on a heel and stormed toward the door.

"Raven, wait."

Heart hammering in my chest, adrenaline pumping as if I'd just moved a mountain, I paused. A beat. A single second. Time for him to change his mind. Me to change my own. I wasn't sure. But a second, suspended in time as I dropped my head and turned toward him. But then I saw it there. In his eyes. The look my father had given me. The disappointment, the chastising lecture on the tip of his tongue. And that was it for me. Everything between us snapped as clean as a dry bone. I whirled once more and walked out.

Only Kirsi saw me cry.

7

I 'd stood in the square a million times. Where the four corners of the market met, two streets away from Crescent Cottage, the cobblestones were still wet from last night's rain. The sun had barely risen, but through the heavily overcast skies and the dark storefronts nearby, most of the light came from oil lamps and a floating orb of blue light one of the thirteen Chosen had cast above us.

Half the coven had come to see the king's carriages. And each of them had been equally disappointed when none appeared. Instead, a lone glass door, taller than the lamp post close by, appeared right in the middle of the street, wide open. The world beyond the threshold of the door was nothing like the Moon Coven territory, with its common bouts of dreary rain and fog and damp ground. Instead, the sun had risen; the sky was vibrant, and a river rushed by, cascading over rocks, rushing away from a waterfall in the distance. I couldn't hear that world beyond, but I imagined the water was refreshing and cacophonous.

The blond man that had acted as proxy during Tasa's funeral and as the Dark King's messenger during the Trial's opening ceremony stood, broad chested, a black leather vest straining over his muscles, with his arms tucked casually over his chest. A questionable smirk on his face showcased a single dimple as he stared down the line of thirteen witches, shoulder to shoulder, before him.

The crowd fell silent as he stepped forward, his polished boots thudding on the ground while he moved down the line, assessing each of the Chosen. He stopped before Ender, Greer's little sister, and she smiled nervously up at him. I gulped. This was danger incarnate, sizing up his prey before delivering us on a silver platter to a king that would sooner see us dead than allow us to sleep in his castle. I caught Greer out of the corner of my eye, clutching her hands below her chin as she likely held her breath. They could have been twins, if not for Ender's fuller, younger face.

The king's messenger reached forward, twisting Ender's copper hair in his massive fingers as he smirked at her. She dropped her head, a blush feathering across her face as he winked and kept walking. He stood before Nym next. She carried herself like a goddess, her brown skin shimmering like golden sunlight no matter the weather. Staring straight ahead, she set her jaw and ignored the man. He chuckled and walked on, keeping a wide berth from Scoop, who sat at Kirsi's heel, gray eyes locked on the man. He might have stopped, might have gawked as all men did before her, but instead, he moved on. As if he'd known she wouldn't give him the time of day.

I was next, but he passed by without a glance. Onyx, the egotistical asshole, snorted from beside me. The messenger halted, spinning toward him, potentially only an inch taller, but he looked every bit double Onyx's size as he stuck out his chest, speaking for the first time.

"Something funny?"

Onyx leaned back on his heels; his golden eyes dull in the lackluster morning light. "The odds are heavily in my favor, it seems. We could just skip this process and finally put a man in charge."

"*Another* man? Feeling pretty confident?" the messenger asked, leaning over Onyx until he took the smallest step away. He clicked his tongue against his teeth, shaking his head before moving on.

Breya, a petite witch known for her clumsy nature and genuine lack of awareness, hid beneath the tattered edges of her blue cloak, staring up at the man as he stopped before her. She smiled timidly in his direction, bowing before him, her long red locks nearly grazing the ground.

Sorin, the male witch to the side of her, reached down and grabbed her elbow, yanking her upright. "He's not the king, you ninny. Get up."

Breya gasped. "Then who is he?"

The king's man wrapped his arm around his waist and bowed to Breya. "Those that love me call me Grey, those that tolerate me call me Sir, and those that dislike me rarely find their tongues to call me anything at all."

The line of thirteen witches stilled with his threatening admission. The man's eyes, green as fresh, springtime grass, flashed over the assembly one final time until he was satisfied in his assessment and spun, stepping toward the open glass door, placed by someone's magic.

"The Witch Trials are a ritual as old as any of our lineages. The rules and the stages are just as ancient. If you're lucky enough to make it to the castle, any weakness will mean your failure. The Trials have been curated by our ancestors to test you all. They are not for the tenderhearted, the weak, or the submissive. The coven leaders will test you first, eliminating five before you have a chance to step foot in the black castle." He took a deep breath, careful to look each of us in the eye before moving to the side. "The River Coven awaits."

Stepping through the door was as easy as walking through any threshold. One moment we were in the Moon Coven square, and then the next, we were standing beside that rushing river, watching a looming waterfall pour over the slick gray rocks from above. The smell was just as I'd imagined it would be, standing at the beginning of a web of rivers, spreading from this single point into a hundred.

"Welcome."

Nearly in unison, the Chosen twisted to see Circe Rivervale standing behind us, the door we'd stepped through gone. Circe was perhaps the youngest of the coven leaders, only a decade older than my parents. With a warm smile and beautiful golden hair, she was likely also the least intimidating. What seemed to be the whole of the River Coven stood behind their leader, waiting for the ceremony.

Many loitered with eyes pinned on Grey, aware of the danger he presented from his presence alone.

"As this is the beginning of your tour, let me be the first to congratulate you on being Chosen. It seems like only yesterday, I stood where you stand now, staring at Tasa Moonbreak as she welcomed thirteen overconfident witches to our Trials." Her face turned solemn as if her eyes held a warning. "Do not be fooled, Moon Witches. You are not walking into a bout of children's games. While we can say the Trials are what you make of them, they do not come without excessive risk. Chins up. Eyes open. Even now. By the end of this visit, one of you will be returning home and only twelve will move on."

I couldn't help but feel the way her eyes lingered on me, scanning my naked arms, thoroughly searching for something that she'd never find. I remembered seeing her enter the woods to help save me from that deadly curse. She'd given me the same look she did now, full of pity and doubt.

"Follow me," Circe said, her coven splitting down the middle, allowing us to follow her into the heart of the crowd, until they closed around us, and we were directed to sit on the ground in a circle. The king's man, Grey, hadn't followed. Kirsi sat next to me, giving me a look that said she was not impressed, and once I was seated, I quickly learned why. The ground was not only chilly, but wet, of course.

Ophelia sat on my other side. Being the oldest witch to join the trials, she seemed the least phased by the discomfort, though it did take her the longest to get down to the ground, having to rely heavily on my arm and her cane for support. As the gathered crowd around us shared smirks and glances at one another, I did my best to sit perfectly still, noting the fidgeting in the circle across from us. Onyx might have been thoroughly annoyed, but it seemed Drea was the most uncomfortable, standing to move around the circle to a spot that was likely just as soaked as the other. Zennik was not far off from her though, rubbing his arms for warmth and looking at the rest of us as if he expected someone to protest.

Circe sat as still as the mountain; her eyes closed as she grounded herself. I nudged Kir with my knee and pointed with my chin. Understanding, she bowed her head as well and we followed the coven leader's example, letting ourselves become one with the earth and the water that was so prominent here, in respect to this territory.

When I was a child, my father had explained the geographics of the witch territories like the spaces between the spokes of a wheel. While the northern continent did harbor magical beings, there was no magic there. Our magical lands stemmed from the center of the wheel, the Fire Coven territory. He'd loved starting his lesson with the River Coven because he and my mother had traveled here so often for ingredients for my grandmother. He'd said the entire land was separated by a thousand rivers, though until today, I wasn't sure I'd believed him. I should have. My father wasn't known for his wild imagination.

Once the Chosen had settled and the crowd quieted, Circe took a deep breath and clapped her hands once. Opening my eyes, I found her staring directly at me, smiling, though it didn't quite meet her eyes. It was in that precise moment the reality of the Trials settled within me. I'd spent so much of my life waiting to be a part of this secret society of witches, and now I was here. But this single witch had the power to toss me out, and based on the way she watched me, I couldn't help but feel the giant target that seemed to be growing on my forehead. Still, I sat quietly, cold water seeping up my thighs as I waited, knee to knee between Kir and old Ophelia.

Circe flared a slender hand in front of her, a marking on her middle finger glowing green as a deck of midnight black cards appeared, the edges shimmering gold in the sunlight. I'd heard she had an affinity for cards laced into her magic, but I'd never witnessed her use them before.

"Thirteen witches, thirty-seven cards. You will each take one. You may look at your card and decide if you choose it, or if you'd like to redraw. Your blessing will be divined within your choice, so take the card that speaks to you the loudest and trust the goddess to bless you with the message you're meant to receive."

She stood from the ground, dry as bone and walked the circle, starting with Drea, who had always kept her distance from me, believing I was cursed from infancy, which was why my spells didn't show. It'd gone so far that when we were children, her mother had come to my door, offering to cleanse me free of charge. When my mother slammed the door in her face, Drea was never allowed to speak to me again.

She didn't hesitate to draw from the middle of the deck Circe held. She peeked at the card, locking eyes with Circe as she shoved it back in and drew another. The coven leader lifted an eyebrow, waiting for a response. When Drea shook her head again, several members of the crowd began to murmur. Back and forth they went until the witch was satisfied, holding her card to her chest as she smiled and nodded.

With a subtle dip of her chin, she moved to the next witch, Zennik. His rich brown skin was a shade darker than Nym's, and he was so attractive, with one blue eye and one green, that several of the River coven witches giggled as they watched him draw a single card. He nodded to Circe without looking at it. The second Circe shifted away, Zennik winked at two of the witches in the front row.

Kirsi's snort was quiet, but even if I hadn't heard it, I would have known she'd done it. Zennik had chased her for years until she finally enlightened him, she preferred women. He hadn't taken the news well, insisting she was lying until he caught her kissing his ex. It had been strategic on Kirsi's part, but it worked. He hadn't spoken to her since. And his ex had been more than happy to play the part.

When Circe got to Kir, you could see the anticipation in her eyes as they shifted between Scoop, in kitten form, and Kirsi's blue marking on her temple. Pulling the very end card from the coven leader's hand, Kirsi peeked, but kept her face neutral as she indicated she was satisfied with her card. I couldn't let the curiosity settle for too long because I was next.

Circe kept her perfect smile. Looking down at me, she held the fanned oracle cards forward. One of them was caught at just the right angle in the sunlight, the shimmering edges calling to me. I reached, plucking out the card. Her eyes narrowed as I peeked, and my heart sank into my throat. I didn't want to trade my card and seem scrupulous or weak, but everyone was watching and would know I'd chosen to keep the card with a cloaked figure, face hidden in shadows as he held his scythe, the word *death* scrawled across the bottom in beautiful golden script. Had this card really called to me?

I swallowed. The pressure built with each second I sat there, debating what to do. Growing frantic, I handed the card back to Circe, my ears turning red as she placed it into the deck and shuffled the cards, expressionless. Again, she held the cards out for me. This time I didn't overthink it, just reached in and grabbed a random card. I clutched it to my chest and dipped my chin without looking this time, content with whatever blessing I might receive, as long as it wasn't laced with my demise.

Ophelia, the old witch beside me, flourished a hand. One of the cards flew toward her and she snatched it from the air, peeked at the design and waved Circe on. And so, the coven leader went around the circle, most keeping the first card they selected, but others peeking and trying again until satisfied.

"It is time," Circe said, the smile she carried vanishing as she took on a far more serious expression. "Drea, since you drew the first card, you will receive the first blessing. Please, come stand before me."

As the witch, with eyes so dark they could have been black, stood, the coven leader cast a spell to dry her clothing, gesturing for her to stand before her. She held out her hand expectantly and Drea gave her the oracle card, face up. A marking on Circe's neck glowed green and the card grew in size as it lifted into the air and spun on a slow rotation for all to see.

"Opportunities," the coven leader said, reading the scrawled word at the bottom of the card. "Heed my warning, girl. Do not spend so much time curating your own opportunities that you refuse to see those that are already there waiting for you. I bless you with patience from the goddess."

Drea's face turned from olive to red as she took her place in the circle once more. Circe called for the next witch. Zennik, stood, and shuffled forward.

"You didn't look at your card until after I walked away, Zennik. Why?" the coven leader asked.

"I trust the goddess to give me the blessing she wishes me to have, regardless of my own ambition." Zennik had been born exuding confidence, but as Circe shook her head and lifted the enlarged card for everyone to see the word, his powerful shoulders shrank inward.

"Arrogance. Tell me, had you viewed this card, would you have kept it?"

With his back to me, I couldn't see his expression, but the pause of thought said more than enough. "I would have considered it."

"That is not an answer, Zennik Moonfall. But no need to continue these games. Your blessing also comes as a warning. Your arrogance will only carry you so far in the competition. You must keep your wits about you. You may be able to fool others, but you cannot fool yourself."

She walked away from him without waiting for a response, beginning a slow path around the circle, her feet never sinking into the muddy water we sat in, no longer waiting for us to approach her. By the time she got to me and I stood, I wasn't breathing, just letting the edges of the card press firmly into the palm of my hand. She cleared her throat, and my ears rang, handing over the card I hadn't seen. She held my gaze as she enlarged it, an audible gasp coming from several of the river coven witches as well as a sharp inhale of breath from Kirsi beside me. I gulped and glanced at the card, the massive letters far more ominous this time. *Death.* I'd somehow managed to pull the card twice.

Circe stared at me, waiting for a reaction. I held myself still but, on the inside, panic and fear were thrumming through me, awakening every nerve ending, every muscle tightening until I was internally begging for absolution.

"Death." She said the word like it was a promise and I knew then she'd eliminate me first. "Fitting, considering you've cheated death, is it not?"

I had no doubt she waited for an answer. A semblance of guilt on my face as if I hadn't deserved the magic spent to save me. I raised my head, shaking it. Something lit in her eyes as her smile reappeared.

"There you are," she said, quietly. "May you never fear the death that surely haunts you. The Dark King may very well be death himself. Do not let yourself be coaxed by death. And if you are the weakest link, may your death be swift since you drew this card twice. A rarity indeed."

She dipped her chin, the smile vanishing as she moved to Ophelia. I didn't hear a single blessing after that, instead replaying the words she'd spoken to me over and over as I saw that word flash across my mind. If I'd cheated death, when would he come for vindication? Was I truly the weakest link?

I was sure more than half those gathered had wagered I'd be the one eliminated. I appeared to be the weakest; I'd drawn the death card ... twice. We stood, all dried by Circe's magic, as we were guided back to the tall glass door. I thought the king's man would be standing there, but he was nowhere to be seen. Couldn't say I blamed him, considering the many warnings laced into Circe's blessings of the Dark King and his danger. Just more carnage for a war that hadn't been officially declared.

Nerves had settled into the thirteen witches standing in the line with me. Some fidgeting, several cleared their throats, swaying from one foot to the other as we waited for Circe's final decision. I held an empty feeling in the pit of my stomach, remembering the way she'd looked at me. The way everyone did. I wanted nothing more than to prove to them all that I was more than worthy, but that couldn't happen if they wouldn't give me a chance.

"Raven Moonstone, please step forward."

My ears began to ring, my hand brushing Kirsi's as I moved forward out of the line of Chosen. That butterfly of nerves in my stomach grew into a boulder, tumbling around as I prepared my heart for the words she would say. I hadn't even made it to the second territory. I would not be following in my grandmother's footsteps. I'd broken my promise on the very first hurdle.

Shame filled me, but I would not let them see me break. I lifted my chin, hardened my stare and swallowed any sign of emotion. Though my knees had gone weak, though I wanted to sprint through that door so they couldn't watch my failure, I set my jaw.

"Onyx Moonshade, please step forward."

My head whipped to Circe, though she did not return my stare. If she hadn't called me forward to eliminate me, then why? Onyx stepped from the line. On she went, calling Nym, Willow, Sorin and Visha. Then Kirsi, Breya, Ophelia, Fawn and Ender, who could be heard sniffling, likely convinced she was out. All that remained were Zennik and Drea. The indecisive and the arrogant.

Kir slipped her hand into mine, and I could feel the relief as she squeezed my fingers. She must have thought the same as me. It could have been me going home, it could have been any of us, if the reason was based on a random card draw. Though Circe would never believe a draw was by luck alone.

"You may all return to the king's man and step through the door, which will now take you onward, to the floating isles of the Whisper Coven. I wish you all well in the tasks that lay before you."

We walked through that door in a line, leaving the water behind for erratic bouts of howling wind and crashing waves far, far below us. Holding my hair from blowing in my face, I only chanced a glance at the lush green grass below our feet and the looming edges of the floating isle. It smelled of ocean tides and a warm summer breeze, but the height of the isle stole the pleasure.

Grey leaned against the frame of the magical door, counting us and then recounting, annoyance clear on his smooth face as he realized Circe was taking her time. He pushed his blond hair out of his eyes and rocked back on his heels, whistling as he waited.

The rest of us shared a single thought as we stared at the door and wondered whether Drea or Zennik would walk through that door.

8

I stood smashed between Nym and Kirsi, both holding their familiars in kitten form as they eyed the edges of the isle. I'd never heard of one of the isles falling into the ocean, but standing here now, it felt like a real possibility. Either that, or the wind would become strong enough to shove us over the edge, sending us plummeting to our deaths.

Grey crossed the distance we'd kept from him and stopped before me. "Heard you pulled the death card twice. That doesn't always mean death, you know. Sometimes it's just the end of one thing and the beginning of another."

I shared a look with Kir before turning back to the king's man. With a small voice, I answered, "How could you have possibly heard about that from so far away?"

He smirked, wiggling his fingers in the air as if he were speaking to a child. "Magic."

I pressed my lips together and turned away as my cheeks burned. *Idiot.*

Only minutes passed before Zennik came walking through the magical threshold, his face solemn as he tucked his hands into his pockets, lifting his shoulders to cover his ears from the gale as he joined our line. I wasn't his biggest fan, but I was happier to see him than Drea. She had too many prejudices against me and the silenced witches.

A clap of magic sounded behind us, seeming to rattle the isle, as five people appeared before us out of thin air. Dasha Whispercove and four witches with their arms crossed, their eyes hard as stone.

"Messenger, if you would please wait for the Chosen by the next door. He's left it across the way." She pointed to a different isle directly across from us and Grey vanished without a single word.

One man with skin as golden-brown as Nym stepped forward, assessing us. "Three witches were found dead this morning on the outlying isles. They'd been discarded by the Dark King, one alive only long enough to deliver a warning. They'd foolishly gone to the king for food for their families, and not only were they turned away at the gate, they also got no more than four paces away before they were attacked. It wasn't a Thrashing. This happened in broad daylight right outside the castle."

I glanced over at the isle Grey had gone to. How could anyone work for someone so monstrous? My heart ached for the families of the fallen. They were hungry and they'd died because of it. What a broken world we lived in.

"Thank you for your report, Callum," Dasha yelled over the wind, walking slowly forward, hunched over a cane.

Her legs moved smoothly, though. I'd begun to wonder if the show of age and frailty from the coven leaders was merely that, a show. A clever move to allow the Dark King to underestimate them.

"I've asked Callum to share this grave news with you today, so that you're all aware of what you're walking into. Though it would be much easier, and likely safer to call off the Trials, it cannot be done, lest the magic of your coven weaken. Who can tell me why the king is overseer?"

Ophelia raised one frail, wrinkled hand into the air. Willow followed right behind, full of eagerness as she waved hers.

"Ophelia, darling," Dasha shouted, "It's so nice to see you among the Chosen. How is your husband?"

"Dead," Ophelia answered, not a hint of emotion.

"Oh dear," Dasha said, pulling down her hood. "May the goddess keep him. Please." She gestured for Ophelia to answer the question.

"The leader of the coven with the greatest power hosts the Trials. That line of power has been with the Fire Coven for oh ..." she paused, tapping her lip with her finger as she glanced up to the sky, "Well over five hundred years."

"Five hundred and seventy-three, to be exact," Dasha yelled, nodding as she held her long silver hair gripped in her hand to keep it from whipping across her face in the powerful wind. "The Fire Coven is the only coven that is not beholden to the ritual of Trials. Who can tell me why?"

Again, Willow's hand shot up, as did Fawn and Ender's. Kirsi and I raised ours at the same time, seconds behind the others. Dasha surveyed us, eyes lingering on me for only a fraction of the time Circe's had.

"Miss Moontide?"

Nym hadn't raised her hand. Kirsi held her breath as her friend cleared her throat. I knew Kir would be heartbroken if Nym went home.

"Because the Fire Coven is the royal coven and, as such, the power is passed by birth and not acquired by Trial. That is also why the Fire Coven oversees the Trials. In previous selections, they've been a non-biased party."

"Correct," Dasha said, a bit of surprise in her tone. "The king is half witch, half shifter and therefore, still beholden to the ancient magic of the witches. Which means, whether any of us like it or not, the Trials will continue. It also means you must all watch your backs. Don't pin targets on yourselves." Her eyes shifted to someone down to the far end of the line, but I wasn't quick enough to see who she seemed to be talking to.

"You're a relatively young batch of Chosen. Who can tell me the significance of the Grimoires to our magic?"

No hands raised. Not one.

She glanced up and down the line before her eyes landed on me. "Ms. Moonstone, your grandmother was the keeper of the Moon Coven Grimoire. Surely, she told you many things."

I nodded, kicking myself for not raising my hand. "The Grimoires of each coven date back to the Breaking. When the society of witches grew too populous, the root of our power spread too thin. Our ancestors performed the Breaking, splitting all the witches into territories, appointing seven coven leaders through a set of Trials. We've been that way ever since. The first and last drop of blood, placed into the book, along our family trees, to recycle our power back into our coven. Our bones are consecrated to the earth and our blood to family." I dipped my chin. "At least that's how it was."

"Keep going dear," she said, stopping before me to place her hand on mine. "What is happening with them now?"

I forced the words out. "After the Moss Coven Grimoire was lost, those witches haven't been able to recycle their power and currently grow weaker. And since the Dark King has stolen the rest of the Grimoires, we may only have access to them if granted."

"Correct," she said, moving away from me. "The king is doing everything in his power to weaken the witches. Do not forget it." She took a deep breath, the weight of the witches' problems settling upon her frail body before she turned, pointing to the south. "Your test this day will be a simple one. You're to cross the plank bridge from this isle to that one."

Fawn, with hair the color of her namesake, raised her hand.

Without turning, Dasha acknowledged her. "Yes, Fawn?"

"I only wondered if we're permitted to use our magic for the task."

She turned, a slight smile on her old face. "Ah, thank you for asking, dear. You may use any form of magic at your disposal."

Relief washed over the three of us sandwiched together. Kirsi and Nym could use their familiars' traits, which gave them incredible feline balance. I'd have to be more creative if I didn't want to die. So fun.

As the twelve of us approached the plank bridge, my hands began to tremble. It was exactly what I'd feared it would be. A long, bowed plank ran from one island to the other, no wider than my foot, a single rope on each side running the length of the swaying board. There was no way in hell that rope was going to save anyone from falling, especially in these winds.

"Wonder what would happen with a little push," Onyx said, breathing against my neck.

I rolled my shoulders, a failed attempt at shaking him off as he pressed close behind me. Onyx was a dangerous foe. The moment I'd heard he was Chosen, I knew the stakes had been raised. Where Willow would navigate the Trials with cunning, Onyx would be ruthless, feeding his opponents' fear.

"You're welcome to go first," I hissed. "I'll keep the shove to a minimum."

"You just want to get those hands on me. Can't say I blame you," he rumbled from behind.

Scoop, now a full-size male panther with a maw bigger than Onyx's fist, stepped away from Kirsi, squeezing himself between us, staring down the man that would see me dead for his own gain. I didn't turn to look at Onyx's face, but guessing by the sudden space and silence, Kirsi's familiar had won the battle.

Our single line shifted into an arc around the bridge as Dasha stepped forward, sweeping her cloak to the side so she could properly lean against her cane as she called us in turn. Sorin was to go first. He shared a conspiratorial grin with Onyx as he marched forward, not an ounce of fear on his hard face. You'd think, being so stocky, he'd be afraid of the wind, shoving him to the side, but he used magic to create some sort of shield and shuffled across the plank with ease.

Boosting my confidence, as the bridge hadn't swayed as much as I thought it might, I prepared myself to go. Knowing I could be next or last.

"Don't die. Go slow. It's not a race," Kir whispered as she stepped forward.

The blue spirit blessed marking on her forehead glowed as she drew attributes from Scoop. They both walked across to the other island without a single issue. Nym was called after her and she and Talon were like graceful gods crossing the board. They'd made it look far too easy, and that was such a dangerous truth. Kir was so far away I could hardly make out her face from the island across the gap, but I could feel those gray eyes pinned to mine as sweat formed on my palms.

Breya was next. Her red hair whipping across her face made it difficult to see if she was scared or confident. Perhaps a little of both. She'd cast a spell, but I couldn't see what it did as the wind did not falter, and her steps were not steadfast. Her feet shook the board, her hands trembled on the rope, and three times she slipped and nearly fell. Though far slower and more aligned with what I thought would happen, she somehow made it across unscathed.

Ender was next. She tied her coppery hair back, staring across the way at her best friend Nym, who'd moved to the far end, ready to catch her when she stepped off the plank. A substantial gust of wind sent the bridge soaring to the east with Ender on it. She took off running, refusing to look back as she reached the end and leaped into Nym's arms.

I was next and nervous didn't begin to explain the way I felt. I cast a spell, controlling the bridge's movements below me. I could shift the board to the left or right with a single thought, but I wasn't sure if I could hold it steady and I couldn't battle this wind. Sending the same spell down the ropes to keep them taut, I inched my way onto the boards, getting a feel for the motion below my feet. I'd forgotten to tie my hair back, so it blew across my face, but I could still make out the blonde-haired witch and her black panther standing at the end of the bridge, refusing to blink as I moved. Step by careful step, I shuffled down the board, over the ocean that tumbled below me. Before I knew it, I'd made it to the other side and the task that had seemed impossible was no longer so.

I watched for spells used to cross the bridge as the last of the Chosen made their way carefully across. Onyx used some sort of magical tether to link himself to the rope, which was honestly clever. Ophelia was perhaps the slowest, her old age showing tremendously as she used a magical wind shield to block the weather, but still struggled across.

When it was Fawn's turn to cross the bridge, she made a colossal show of casting a spell that seemed to stop the movement of the swaying ropes. But the moment she stepped onto the bridge, the spell released, and the board nearly came out from under her. The surrounding crowd fell silent as we all held our breaths, watching her.

By halfway, she was shaking more than the plank and she overcorrected, the board shooting out from beneath her. In the blink of an eye, she was falling. And screaming.

There was no thought given as I cast my magic toward her, taking control of her descent and lifting her to our side of the isles, though she thrashed and screamed the whole way. When she landed softly in the grass beside us, she remained on her knees, weeping. Ender and Breya both came to her aid, wrapping their arms around her as they helped her to her feet, whispering their quiet promises of her safety.

With a crackle of magic, Dasha landed beside us, gaze locked on Fawn. "Who cast the spell to save her?"

"I did," I said with pure conviction in my voice.

The coven leader's eyebrows raised as she examined me carefully. "Why?"

I drew back. "She would have died."

The old woman pushed her hood back, exposing her thin, wrinkled skin as she hobbled toward me with her cane nearly dragging on the ground. "She would have died, but wouldn't that have made your Trials easier? To have one less witch to worry about in the fold?"

I shook my head. "I'll sleep better knowing she lived to be my adversary rather than died while I stood idly by."

Kir nudged me with an elbow, recognizing the fire she knew sat within my soul, but I didn't care. Not when it came to this.

"Inspiring," Dasha said, though the tone of sarcasm was great enough that Onyx snorted and Sorin chuckled.

I flashed them both a glare as I stepped back into my place in line. Dasha moved to stand before Fawn, who studied the ground through her tears. She knew. We all knew.

"Your journey in the Trials is over. You are fortunate to leave with your life when death was seconds away. Had you been in my Trials, you would not have been so lucky." She nodded to her guards, and they flanked Fawn, grabbing her arm as they disappeared with that same snap of magic I'd heard several times.

Dasha ushered us to another door. This time it was black, save for a lightning bolt etched in silver down the middle.

"You each have my blessing to continue in your trials. I wish you all luck, but more so, I hope you remember the careful balance this world teeters on. As you've witnessed, death awaits in the blink of an eye, keep your wits about you and remain steadfast in your journey. Remember that the Trials are as ancient as our bloodlines. Trust the tasks you're given, not the overseer." With that, she snapped her fingers and vanished.

"I think we've found our weakest link," Onyx said, shoving his shoulder into me as he passed.

"I'll kick his ass, if you want," Kir offered, taking my side.

A small gesture and the grass in front of Onyx grew into a vine, with enough subtlety that he could have tripped on his own. He hit the ground with a thud, looking around as if someone had shoved him before leaping to his feet and yanking down on the ends of his jacket, his golden eyes furious.

Kirsi raised an eyebrow. "Have you been walking long or just trying to quit?"

"You don't want to make an enemy out of me," he threatened. "I'm not afraid of your beast."

"No?" Nym asked, tilting her head to the side as she approached. "Let's say hypothetically there were two beasts. Would you be afraid then?"

"Why should he be?" Sorin asked, stepping forward. "You lot wouldn't harm a witch now, would you?"

Kirsi's gentle face turned severe. The deep rumbling growl of an enormous black panther at her fingertips was enough to scare anyone as she leaned over the top of Sorin, grabbed his earlobe and pulled him to her until they were inches apart. "Never mistake someone's humanity for weakness. Did you see Raven lift that body with her magic and save her? Did you stop to think she could have done the opposite? Dropping your scrawny ass over the edge with merely a thought? Every second you breathe, remember she decided you were worthy of it."

I loved her. Her fire, her spirit, her unwavering faith in me as a person.

"I never thought to throw him over the edge, but now that you mention it ..."

She laughed, looping her arm with mine. "There's a reason witches like me aren't given that level of power."

"The tasks are only going to get harder and more dangerous, aren't they?" Ender asked, the worry in her voice prominent.

"They aren't warning us of death for no reason, E," Nym said. "Don't worry. I've got you. We'll figure it out together."

They were as close as Kir and I, and something in that gave me hope. Beyond the probability of peril, there was still good here, nestled within the witches I'd known my whole life. But as we stepped past Grey and through the magical door into Storm Coven territory, the ominous sky lit with a scattering of lightning that stretched as far as we could see, I wondered if any of us really had the ability to make promises we could keep.

9

Thirteen witches had turned to eleven within the span of a few hours and now we stood in the middle of a gathering hall in the Storm Coven, surrounded by a thousand witches who watched our every movement. The pods, as they called them, were unlike anything I'd seen. Where we lived in cottages and even small huts, the Storm Coven lived in buildings similar, but connected by tunnels that ran above and below ground.

Visha, the Chosen who had been the most observant and disconnected, pushed herself to the front of the line as we were led through the tunnels. When Ender asked about them, Visha had scolded her for her curiosity. The women leading us hadn't been so stern though, explaining that the tunnels kept them mostly safe through the bouts of severe weather.

Isolde Stormburn, their mighty coven leader, stood from her seat as we entered. Though she was also similar in age to Endora and Dasha, her hair remained as black as night, her eyes even darker. Towering over everyone around her, she spread her hands wide, smiling down at us from the platform that only made her bigger.

"Today is a rare day as we gather together to share a small feast of autumn soup in celebration of your arrival." She cleared her throat.

"The meal is humble, but the best we can provide. Please introduce yourselves to my coven while we wait for the meal to be brought in."

Years ago, the witches would mingle through the covens. While they lived in their respective territories, most traveled through all of them for visiting, shopping or foraging materials they couldn't find in their own. But now, it was different. The animosity and hatred had grown and this simple request to introduce ourselves felt a little like exposing our open backs to enemies. And that was the problem that seemed to be growing as the Dark King became more untouchable. Though not these witches' fault, trusting anyone was complicated.

Still, spinning in a circle to look into the witches' eyes made me feel like a traitor just for thinking that way. They were not my enemies. I moved first, stepping into the crowd of cautious people with a smile on my face as I reached my hand forward to one woman with hair that reminded me of my own and eyes as gray as Kir's. "I'm Raven Moonstone. Thank you for having us."

The shock melted into warmth as the woman grasped my hand and gave a curt nod. "Bedalia Stormblossom. Welcome."

As if a veil had fallen, the room erupted into chatter. The rest of the Chosen sank into the crowd to introduce themselves. Grey remained propped against a wall in the back corner of the room. A cat in a barn chock full of mice. Kirsi didn't stray too far from me, and she kept Scoop in full beast form, but she smiled and let a few people pet her familiar. There was even a man toward the back with a bird on his shoulder and the same spirit blessed marking on his forehead as her and Nym, only his glowed red. His bird was a variation of a phoenix, it seemed, vibrant in color, but smaller, at least for the moment.

A tug on my dress from a small child with massive brown eyes grabbed my attention as I knelt before her.

"My mam says you're different than the others."

I nodded. "I suppose we're all different in our own ways."

Slowly shaking her head from side to side, she looked me over, searching for markings. "You're not supposed to have magic. You were supposed to die."

My heart stopped. Parents spoke through the mouths of their children, and it wasn't the first time I'd heard such heavy words, but none had said I was meant to die. The death card flashed in my mind, as did the warning of death from Dasha. The theme of the tours was growing heavy as I stared into the eyes of that little girl. "I'm not sure what you mean, but of course I wasn't meant to die. You cannot cheat death."

"You had the Harrowing like my aunt. Only she died and you didn't. You cheated."

"I was only lucky," I said, standing to walk away from the child as the room began to fill with savory scents of salty broth and nutty wild mushrooms. "I'm sorry to hear about your aunt."

The child said nothing more. I shifted toward the back of the room, shaking more hands and making more introductions, though the child had rattled my thoughts.

"If you could all make your way to your seats, we will begin the show. Moon Coven witches, the table in front is for you."

I glanced at the eleven chairs seated around a circular table, hoping there'd be a space away from Sorin and Onyx by the time I made it up there. Smushed in the shifting crowd trying to make their way back to their seats, I almost didn't see the little boy directly in front of me until he took my hand.

"I can't find my parents. Can you help me?"

I looked to our table, catching Isolde in the corner of my eye. She was watching me. Had the interaction with the other witches been our test? My head snapped away, looking down at the blond-haired boy.

"Tell me what your parents look like."

"My da's got brown hair and a long beard. Mam's real fat and she has red cheeks and red hair."

I bit the inside of my cheek to keep from smiling. From the mouth of babes, indeed. Moving to my tiptoes, I scanned the room, but everyone was moving so much it was hard to make sense of anyone for too long. I lifted the child up and let him scan the crowd also, but when he turned and shared a smile with Onyx, I set him back down.

"Did that man ask you to come over here and distract me?"

He nodded, grinning from ear to ear. "Gave me a candy, too. By the way," he lifted his leg and stomped directly on my foot before running off, screaming over his shoulder, "my mam's not fat."

Wincing, I stood straight, glaring at Onyx from across the room. He smirked, lifting a glass of water in my direction before he leaned over and whispered something to Sorin. Frowning, I weaved my way through the mostly settled crowd and to the table. Only there were no longer eleven chairs. There were only ten.

For a moment, I thought I'd been eliminated. That my lack of seat meant I'd failed the challenge. But when Sorin jutted his chin toward a different table, one chair didn't match the others.

"There's a seat over there for you, pigeon."

The silenced witches' table. They'd moved my seat on purpose, hoping to humiliate me in front of an entire coven. Embarrassment was the last thing I felt as I crossed the room, sitting at the table full of witches with no markings and no power. I was furious, my breaths carefully restrained as I considered how I would retaliate. But I was not ashamed. Of them, or of myself. Fuck him.

I stared the men down, seeing only red as I dared them to look at me, limbs trembling, wondering which spell would do the most indiscernible damage. It wasn't until Kir crossed my line of sight, purposefully dragging her chair over the floor, the screeching sound stealing my attention, that I remembered where I was. Who was watching. The silenced witches at the table shuffled around so she could slide in next to me, blocking my view from both of them.

Kir nudged me. "As far I can tell, you have two choices. One: make a show, right here and now in front of everyone and hope you don't get eliminated. Or two: you let this go. For now. Save that fire until we need it."

I nodded, melting into my chair as I lifted the glass closest to me and sipped the cool water, convinced I could feel it sizzle as it coated my angry throat. The silenced witches were no less than the rest of them, born without a choice, like me, and not. Kirsi was right, though. Isolde was watching.

"They say you're the lucky one," one of the witches at our table said, her voice quiet. "Blessed with magic."

I shared a calming smile with her, letting loose a deep sigh. "They say a lot of things."

She smiled, showcasing two dimples. "Isn't that the truth?"

"You're Margreet, aren't you?" Kirsi asked, reaching for the soup that had been delivered to our table. "I think I just met your father. He says you've got the most thriving garden in the coven."

"He's being generous, of course. I don't have the magic some of the other witches do to help keep the crops, but I do seem to have a green thumb. Yes."

"She's being modest," another from the table said, scooping soup into her bowl. "She supplied the vegetables for today's meal."

I served myself next, lifting the spoon and savoring the full, rich flavor of the soup with a moan. "It's glorious."

"Are these morels?" Kirsi asked of the mushrooms. "How did you find them?"

"They grow abundantly down by our place. You have to catch them in season, and they aren't easy to get to, but they are worth the work."

"That's it. We're moving in." Kir took another mouthful, reaching for a dinner roll to dip into the broth.

"I wish we could eat like this all the time," another from the table said. "Our lands are riddled with the aftermath of the storms. It keeps the powers of the witches strong, but the gardens have to grow in pods."

"We're blessed all the same," Margreet said as she shifted in her seat, staring up at the platform.

Isolde stepped to the edge of the stage, clapping her hands to get everyone's attention. "As you know, I am burdened with selecting only ten witches to move on to the next stage. One at a time, you will rise from your seat, come to the stage and demonstrate your power to my coven. You're allowed to be modest, keeping the best of your spells to yourselves. We ask for only one to see how well you wield your power."

I swallowed my next bite, confident it was audible as Kirsi and I shared a look. An open display of magic, just for the sake of magic, was infrequent. We shared small spells here and there with the public, but most witches did not broadcast their powers. Something in the request, knowing we were surrounded by a group of witches from another coven, felt incredibly invasive. Still, Isolde gestured to Ophelia at the end of the other table and the old witch shuffled forward, taking center stage.

She formed a ball of water the size of a head of lettuce in her hands with ease, moving it this way and that between her open palms. The crowd clapped at her simple magic, and she bowed with a smile, moving back to her seat.

Well, that was easy enough.

Next was Nym, who took Talon to the stage with her in kitten form. The marking on her forehead shimmered gold and he transformed into his full size, roaring into the crowd. It was a trick most of us had seen a thousand times, if we were close enough to her, but here, among these witches, it was a rare treat. She'd chosen wisely as the crowd's applause was nearly twice what Ophelia had received.

Ender was next, surprising the group of us with a spell that enlarged her chair. The marking on her hand that beamed orange was not new.

"Why didn't she use that spell on the board between the isles?" I asked Kirsi.

"I promise you the majority of the Chosen are keeping their spells a secret. She probably feels the pressure to impress Isolde, though."

I shook my head. "She could have died."

"Ender's a pleasant person, Rave, but I'm not sure she's the brightest watermelon in the patch."

"I guess," I whispered, watching Willow take the stage with extra sway to her hips as she moved, pressing her fingers into the mass of dark, chestnut curls that hung around her shoulders.

She winked directly at Ender before casting the same spell we'd just seen, enlarging Ender's chair, with her still on it. She didn't stop there, though. She should have, but didn't. Twirling to Kirsi, her sweet smile turned into something mischievous and all together wrong as she cast once more, striking Scoop with the same spell. Kirsi was out of her seat in a blink, arms raised. Scoop, still a kitten, but enlarged, didn't so much as wake from the nap he'd been taking on the floor.

I reached for Kirsi's hand and yanked her back down. "You have two choices," I hissed. Reminding her of the words she'd spoken to me.

Willow flourished her hand through the air and Scoop was back to his regular size. The crowd's applause was hesitant as they watched the pure, animalistic rage surging from Kirsi, who gripped the sides of her chair to keep herself planted. When Willow beamed over the crowd and waved with a giggle, I was sure I heard something in Kirsi snap.

It was clear from that point forward, whatever we'd thought the Trials were going to be, we were wrong. Because Kirsi would wake up and choose violence every single day if anyone so much as looked at her familiar. And now Willow had crossed a line she could never return from. Sure, Sorin and Onyx had been picking on me, but this was wholly different. This was an unforgivable punch to the gut.

The other witches moved through their spells as quickly as possible, likely as eager to get out of the room as I was. But when Kir rose from her chair, walking to the stage like a predator, I could only hold my breath. Only pray to the goddess that whatever she'd planned, it would not be murder. Or we'd have to take this entire room down, just to run.

A spark lit Kirsi's gray eyes as she studied her fingers, taking her sweet time with a dangerous smile on her face. Her eyes flicked up to Willow and did not move again as she thrust a hand toward her target. The entire room erupted into pure chaos. The banquet table vanished, transforming into a pile of serpents, hissing and slithering directly toward Willow.

A majority of the witches were leaping from their seats, some moving to the tabletops, some running for the back of the room. The silenced witches sitting at my table held in their laughter as Willow scrambled, lifting her feet onto her chair, praying for the goddess to show her mercy. Nym hadn't moved at all, smiling from ear to ear, stroking Talon.

"That's enough now," Isolde announced.

Kirsi snapped her fingers and the table returned to normal, the room flushed with surprises as my best friend walked down the steps, stopped in front of Willow and leaned over the table. "Next time, there will be no mercy, but thank you for your prayers."

I didn't miss the prideful smirk on Isolde's face as she watched Kirsi take her seat. Only I knew her well enough to know this would not be the end. That there would never be enough revenge for what Willow had done. But I had to let that go for now, because I was next, and I had no clue what I should do.

I hated the thought of being a spectacle, but truly, that's what the coven leaders were. Envied by witches for their power and control, they were nearly the top tier. All decisions, every move the witches made, came from that elite group of women. And I could be one of them if I could just get past the Trials.

"Raven?"

I jerked my head up to see Isolde staring down at me.

"Right. Sorry," I mumbled, trying to slide my chair back to stand.

But I couldn't. Couldn't move my feet from the ground, couldn't slide my chair at all. Couldn't shift the lower half of my body. I could feel the embarrassment seep in bright tones of reds down my cheeks as I looked up to the coven leader, jaw slackened, trying once more to move.

"Rave?" Kirsi asked, sliding back in her chair, eyes narrowed. "What's wrong?"

"I can't move," I said behind a forced smile. "Someone's cast a spell on me."

Isolde cleared her throat. "Is there a problem?"

I hated to admit it, hated to show weakness here, of all places, especially in front of her. But what choice did I have?

Taking a deep breath, I met her dark eyes. "Someone has cast a spell and I'm unable to move. I'm so sorry, but could I show my magic from here?"

Her face hardened as she glanced over the crowd, dipping her chin to someone before turning back to me. "You may."

Still firmly in my seat, I raised my hands, casting a wave of fire through the air, letting it dance around the room like a ribbon before vanishing into a puff of smoke. The crowd was awestruck. Likely not from the type of magic I'd shown, but from the fact that I was truly an unmarked witch, full of power. The doubt would always follow me.

A short man with a large midsection hobbled onto the stage. While everyone remained distracted, I glanced at the table full of Chosen witches and didn't miss the snickering from Sorin and Willow. Onyx had sat me at this table, and Sorin had made sure everyone saw. *Dicks.*

"Sorin Mooncave, please join me on stage."

The glee vanished from his face as quickly as the color. He slid his seat out with measured ease and walked to the platform, climbing the steps two at a time.

Isolde held her hand out. "Please, hold your hand like mine."

He did as he was told and the man that had also come forward cast a spell on his hand.

Isolde pointed to the faint beam of green light that appeared. "This is trace magic. Caliso here tells me you've cast a spell on Raven. Why?"

He shrugged with an easy smile. "It was a joke."

I wasn't sad. Refused to let myself feel that at his admission. He'd made a mockery of me in front of everyone for his own entertainment. What Willow had done was wrong, but so was casting on me. I'd built a wall so high, these things couldn't affect me anymore. Not like they had when I was a child. But as Margreet reached under the table and took my hand, I knew she understood. Knew that we were the same and I was proud to sit at this table.

"Release her," she demanded, then turned to the other Chosen. "Willow, come forward."

As Willow slid out of her chair and took the stage, Isolde addressed the rest of us. "Your Trials are what you make of them. If you choose to turn against each other, that is your right. If you choose to keep a peaceful manner, that is also your right. But I'll warn you, you are *not* in the Trials yet and you must not turn against your fellow witch. You must learn that our true enemy and our old enemy are one and the same. The Dark King." Her eyes flicked to Grey in the back of the room, but only briefly before she continued. "Do not let yourselves get distracted by each other and land in the hands of that man. He will kill you without a second thought.

"Willow and Sorin both turned on their fellow witches today.

Willow cast upon a familiar, but Sorin cast directly upon a witch with ill intent. This is not how we grow stronger than our enemy. The rest of you may see yourselves out."

We moved from our seats and rushed to the back of the room, to the tunnel, and following a guide, made it back to the glass door. Not a single one of us hesitated to step into the Forest Coven, turning to watch the door for the last person to step through.

10

When Willow walked through that door, I think Kirsi grew three inches, content to loom over her and threaten her very life. Whatever lesson we were supposed to have learned from Sorin's elimination, it hadn't sunk in for her. Enemy number one was always going to be the witch who'd cast upon her familiar. Willow kept her distance, though, chin still high enough she'd be the first to know if it rained, but the wide berth was notable.

"Welcome, Moon Coven," a soft voice said from behind us. Xena Foresthale was perhaps the kindest of the coven leaders, her cheeks always rosy, her smile always warm. "I won't keep you. I know it's been a long day and you're down to ten witches. Your task here will be simple. Follow me. You may come as well." She gestured to Grey to join us as she swiftly spun and ambled on.

The Forest Coven was picturesque. Full of vibrant colored leaves, snow-capped mountains not too far in the distance, and possibly the freshest air I'd ever taken into my lungs. I could hear a trickle of water somewhere beyond the birds singing and leaves rustling in the breeze, and could have happily napped in the aura of calm that came with the abundance of nature and peace.

We walked down a wood chip path into the forest, stopping at the bed of a tumbling river. Kirsi, Nym, Ender and I stayed close together, while Breya remained only a few paces back with Ophelia and Zennik. Visha, as independent as ever, kept away from everyone, and to my utter dismay, Onyx and Willow were shoulder to shoulder.

Xena twisted her wrist and a candle shot out of the river, landing in her hand. She scooped several more from her pocket.

"Winter is nearly upon us, and my coven must harvest what we can to prepare. I don't have a long time to host you, so rather than having a dramatic display of power and twisted magic, your task today is simple. You'll each draw a candle. As you can see, they all look and feel the same, but one has a wick that will not light. Whomever draws that candle will be eliminated. If you are meant to be coven leader, the goddess will bless you. If this is where your journey is to end, fate will tell us. I wish you all luck."

She gripped the candles upside down, walking down the line as we each plucked a white candle from her fists. I hated this challenge perhaps most of all. It had nothing to do with brains or cunning, nothing to do with power or kindness. Sheer luck would see us through. Holding the wax between my fingers, I tried to feel for any sign of water, but I knew Xena was smarter than that. As kind as she was known to be, she would keep things fair across the board.

"I will light all the candles on the count of three. If your candle doesn't light, please step forward."

My heart began to race, confident I'd pulled the wrong candle. Or Kirsi. But it couldn't be either of us. We had to do this together. We both needed to move forward. Holding my breath, I waited until Xena flicked her arm and one by one, all the candles before us ignited. All but one. The warm glow of my candle and that of Kir's beside me was all I cared about at that moment. My shoulders sank with relief as Visha stepped forward, face fallen, holding a candle with no flame.

"Come with me, my dear. I'll see you home. The rest of you are to go with the king's man. I bless you all and wish you well on your journey."

And with that, there were nine witches left. One more elimination to go. And they'd saved Endora for last. I glanced over my shoulder once to see Visha's stunned face as we walked away, following the broad shoulders of Grey. That could have easily been me.

A new door stood over the wood chips we'd previously walked on. This one was covered in moss, leaving no question as to where we were headed.

"All the witches hate you and yet you stick around as the glorified babysitter. Pretty sure we can walk through these doors on our own," Onyx said to Grey as he scowled at him.

"After you, then," Grey answered with a sweep of his arm as he stepped aside, letting him pass.

Lifting himself taller, as if he'd won something, Onyx stepped toward the door. From nowhere, a gust of wind shoved him from behind, planting him face first into the hard ground. If anyone but me saw the marking on Grey's neck glow, they didn't mention it as Onyx jumped from the ground, stomping through the threshold.

"Bit breezy, isn't it?" Grey commented, his single dimple showing as he winked at Breya.

Though I couldn't stand Onyx, I much preferred him over any of the king's men.

While each of the lands was connected through bridges leading to the Fire Coven territory in the middle, the ease of using the magical tour doors was far superior, keeping us from having to travel for days around the entire kingdom. I wondered whose magic created the intricate doors, lovely and covered in artistic detail but thought better than to ask. I doubted anyone would know anyway.

The Moss Coven was as beautiful as the Forest Coven, a bit greener, the mountains not quite as high, but impactful nonetheless with the same fresh air and cool breeze. Endora Mossbrook stood waiting for the nine of us to walk through, her long silver hair pouring from inside of her cloak, falling in waves down to her waist. Though her hood was up, she kept it back, so her wrinkled face was as easy to see as the markings covering her neck and circling her brow. She exuded power in the truest form. Her watery blue eyes even seemed to glow from within.

She took a moment to stare each of us in the face. When she got to me, my heart stopped beating as though she were reading my entire soul. Nikos had said he thought all the coven leaders were kind. And while I believed the others to be, while I felt awed by them and their position, Endora was a different kind of witch. The kind you'd never say no to, you'd never turn your back on, you'd never question. She was perhaps the sole reason the Dark King hadn't just sent his shifter army into each of our territories, annihilating all but the Fire Coven. Endora Mossbrook was a beast of her own kind—scorned by the loss of her missing daughter—and she wore every bit of hatred toward the Dark King on her face.

I swallowed, failing to hold her stare as my eyes dropped to the mossy ground. One by one, she broke each of us with that stare, but that was her right. Her earned privilege from winning her Trials long, long ago.

She stuck out her cane, jamming it directly into Zennik's chest. "You have two different eye colors. I knew a witch like that once." She dragged the cane up his chest until it rested under his chin as she stared at him. "Is your magic affected by such an affinity?"

Zennik shook his head, gulping.

"Interesting," she said, moving down the line until she stood in front of Breya, who didn't bother hiding her trembling hands. "I know your father well, Breya. I hope you will follow in his footsteps."

The red-haired witch nodded, saying nothing as Endora moved down the line again. Breya's father worked as a liaison between the covens for Tasa. Her family could typically be seen mingling through all the covens during gatherings because they knew so many of the other witches. It didn't seem Breya had gotten many traits from her vagabond father. She was shy, meek even, and far more reserved.

When Endora stopped before me, she used her cane once more to lift my chin, forcing my eyes to hers. Silence thrummed in my ears as she scrutinized me from head to toe. Those eyes, so light they nearly bled into the whites of her eyes, making her ghostly, held my entire soul.

"You lived," she said simply and walked back down the line. She stopped before Willow next, reaching for her cheek. "Such a pretty thing."

Kirsi's hands tightened into fists. Even Nym shifted closer to her as Endora fawned over Willow. Eventually, the evaluation of each witch as if we were soldiers in her army passed and she stepped a few paces away, the hard face she'd given us now a little softer.

"You'll each join me here, where we will speak in private." Her lips fell into a hard line. "Consider your words, consider your posture, consider each and every move you make from now until you leave the black castle, witches. You're entering a battle ground and each breath could be your last. Ophelia, you will be first, and we will make our way down the line."

She waved her arm in an arc over her, and something between us shimmered in the air. We all watched as Ophelia crossed the barrier and began speaking with Endora, though not a word could be heard. The face of both witches remained stern as they conversed, the coven leader asking a question and Ophelia answering.

"So much for winning her over with my good looks," Kirsi whispered.

"Guess I'll give my winning personality a shot," I answered.

She didn't turn to me, but bit her bottom lip to hide her smile.

"I mean, we're both fucked," she said. "But at least we've got Breya as a buffer."

"Kirsi!" I whispered.

She rolled her eyes. "Don't even try to convince me you weren't thinking it."

I pressed my lips together and faced forward as Ophelia stepped out of the domed barrier, passing Onyx as he walked in. His exchange with Endora was brief. It was hard to read their lips and know what either of them were saying, but I noted how he shifted slightly to the side, an attempt to put his back to us, though it didn't work.

One by one, the Chosen entered that space and answered questions. Breya looked as if she might throw up as she walked out, Ender was hardly better. Nym held no expression at all, leaving Talon behind as she entered. By the time she was done, the tiger had curled into a ball to sleep on the ground while Nym remained placid.

Kir was next. As expected, she took Scoop, full sized, with her into the circle. He sat immediately, his tail swishing back and forth as he stared up at old Endora, just as attentive as Kirsi, who answered each question without a single eye roll. Impressive for her, really.

She exited, sharing a quick nod with me as I passed her. Stepping through the barrier caused a brief pull on my skin, just enough to let me know it was there, before the sensation was gone and I was standing directly in front of Endora, very much alone, though eight other faces stared at us.

"What can you tell me about the Harrowing?" she asked with no hesitation.

What could I say? She likely wouldn't believe that it was a curse, something a single witch would have cast upon me, not a sickness. I had no proof, but if I lied, maybe she'd know.

"It's a curse-like illness that has been plaguing the witches since ... well, I'm not sure when it started, actually."

"No one knows, child. But I want to know what it feels like. I want to know about your rescue. Each detail."

"It was like being stricken. One moment I was walking, the next, I couldn't move, couldn't feel, couldn't react. Blood trickling down my face was the only sensation. I thought I'd die. And then I was found. You were there when the witches came running. I don't remember a lot after that. Just a surge of power and then waking up in my parents' house."

An omission was not a lie.

"Why do you think your spells do not show on your skin?"

She studied me as I considered her question, nearly content to lift my shoulders and remain silent. It wouldn't do, though. She expected an answer, and I could not fail this.

"I honestly do not know. My family and I thought I was a silent witch for years. But one day, I received a spell to light a candle. A late bloomer, my grandmother said."

"And do you receive spells *now*?"

The way she'd dipped that last word in a vat of skepticism made my skin crawl. She'd never select me to move on if I couldn't change her mind, and this was my final chance.

"I do. And it's like I feel the markings placed on my skin each time, yet they just don't show. My grandmother believed it was a gift from the goddess. She'd said I'd be able to hide my powers, which would work to my advantage."

Intrigued by this, she tilted her head, eyes narrowing. "How so?"

I lifted the corner of my mouth in defiance. "You will *all* always underestimate me."

Her eyes lit with delight as she smiled. Perhaps the first I'd ever seen from her. "Indeed. You may go."

As I passed through the barrier, it vanished. Endora waited for me to take my place before she beckoned us to follow her. We walked at a snail's pace for what felt like hours. Until the nourishment of the mushroom soup had long worn off, my feet ached, and the emotional roller coaster of the day had started to set in. The matriarch's hard demeanor kept us all silent as we blindly followed over rocks and mossy ground, passing a forest, walking up a hill and finally descending into a small valley with a gathering of cottages, smoke billowing from some chimneys.

We followed Endora into the center of the tiny village, where a handful of witches stood behind a long, worn table built from stone. As we approached, they lifted a cloth from the slab, revealing several items.

"Approach and select an item," Endora ordered.

As I studied each of the items, circling the table with the others, I wondered about their significance. This was the final stage before the Trials actually began. The final elimination. Was it similar to Xena's candles? Luck driven more than anything, or closer to Circe's oracle cards, where each piece had a specific meaning? The mask was intriguing, covered in feathers. But then there was a golden goblet, a crown, a tree branch, and a candle. A stick of dried sage, a sizable amethyst, a dagger and a spoon. Nine items, nine remaining witches.

Having no clue what to select and knowing I didn't want to be stuck with whatever remained, I reached for the spoon and walked back to my spot in line. Once the table was empty, Endora stepped forward, looking over each of our items.

"Kirsi chooses the sage, content to keep herself safe. The wise choice. You may join me here." She gestured to her side. "Breya, the tree branch represents a connection to all. Well done. Please join us."

She walked down the line, studying the items. "Zennik, the goblet. Nourishing our minds and our bodies is important." She tilted her head to the side, indicating he could step forward. "Willow. The candle you hold represents the core of magic itself, showcasing your dedication to coveted rituals. Very fitting. And Nym with the amethyst, content to keep your mind clear, well done."

She paused for a moment, studying the remainder of us as I held my stupid spoon clutched between my fingers. Why, of all things, had I picked something so damn simple? What meaning could possibly come from a utensil? She moved in front of Onyx next, taking the dagger from his hands. "The dagger is one that comes with multiple meanings. You must be cautious not to turn your hand to the witches that join you, Onyx. But you're also smart enough to know you will need protection. Please," she gestured to the side. "Join us."

Only Ender and I remained. Me with the damn spoon and her holding the crown. The *crown*. Why hadn't I grabbed that crown? Kirsi and Nym stood hand in hand, both unblinking. My heart stopped. One of us was going home. Sweet Ender, Nym's best friend, or me.

Endora held out her hand and I placed the spoon upon it. She then turned to Ender, reaching for the crown.

"The crown represents the ambition to win, the end goal in sight, but one must never covet power. The spoon is the shovel, representing the grave. Death. While it is wise not to fear death, it is far wiser not to chase it."

My mouth went dry at her words. Death. Again. As if it really did follow me, lurking in the shadows of my choices. I locked eyes with Kirsi and I waited for a name to be called, my journey to end before it ever started. I thought of my parents and how happy they'd be to see me return, though my heart would be shattered, my promise to my grandmother broken.

"Ender ..."

My mind went blank, my ears ringing as whatever Endora Mossbrook said was lost to me. I'd been eliminated before I even got a real chance to show them what I could do. Arms heavy at my side, I focused only on hiding the tears that threatened to show. My throat grew thick as I swallowed, focusing on a single breath in and then out over and over until I thought I could walk away. It was only when I moved my gaze to Nym, only as I saw her crumble into Kirsi's arms, did I realize the coven leader hadn't eliminated me. She'd eliminated Ender.

I turned in slow motion to the coppery haired witch beside me, opening my arms to crush her between them. I was there, in that moment with her. I knew what she was feeling, and I wished more than anything I could have saved her from it all.

"You'll go back to your homes for one final night," Endora said, her voice nearly lost in the emotion surrounding the Chosen. "Tomorrow you will begin the real battle. Remember who the enemy is. Remember the witches that starve. Remember the faces of the witches you've seen die. May you each move forward with my blessing as well as the protection of the goddess as you enter the lion's den." She pointed to a door, with a beaming moon carved into ash wood. "Go home, Moon Coven witches. Sleep well in your beds one final night."

11

A dense fog settled above the ground as the final eight Chosen witches lined up in the square the next day. When Kirsi and I had finally broken away from Nym and Ender, we'd decided to pack together, not taking a moment for granted. We'd plucked through our small wardrobes and done our best to celebrate the small win. We'd lasted one day when five hadn't.

I'd chosen a simple dress over my chemise, belted at the waist with loose sleeves and a long gray cloak. I'd caught Kirsi combing through her silvery-blonde hair more thoroughly than she'd ever done in the past, but that had far less to do with a tyrant and everything to do with a certain witch standing close by with stacked golden bracelets all the way up her arms that jingled when she walked.

"Our whole lives, Rave. We've thought about this day and it's finally here." She grabbed my hand. "One of us could win this."

"Could but won't," Onyx said, shoving by us to make his way toward Willow, who stood right at the edge of the street, no family nearby, no anxious waiting, just staring straight ahead as if the rest of the world were an inconvenience to her. She'd donned a beautiful cream lace gown cinched so tight at the waist, I wondered if she'd faint before the king.

A thunderous roar of hooves pounding cobblestone grew so loud a group of children covered their ears, darting to hide within the crowd. Eight royal black carriages, each led by two monstrous obsidian horses, filled the square. A single sliver of self-doubt settled in my mind, but I forced it away as quickly as it came. I was damn well going to do this. And I wasn't going to be afraid.

The king's messenger, Grey, stepped out of the cart in the center of the square. He moved his hand through his hair as every whisper fell silent, each witch staring down the handsome man who worked for the Dark King.

He cleared his throat, lifting his sharp chin. "The eight Chosen will step forward now. You're not to speak to one another. You're not to use magic at all. You're to hand your coachman your bag and step inside, where you will each find a letter from your king."

I made to step forward, ready to start this journey, when a heavy hand landed on my shoulder. Turning, I was immediately struck by familiar blue eyes. "Nikos? What are you doing here?"

"I couldn't let it end that way between us. I see now that you can't back out of this. But let's talk when you come home, okay? As friends?"

There was no time, the other witches were already getting into their carriages. I had a million things to say to him, and nothing at all as I opened my mouth, shut it quickly and let Kirsi yank me away.

"Don't let the king get to you," he called out. "Keep your head down until you can come home."

I looked back once, but Nikos had already been swallowed by the crowd.

"I'll see you there?" I asked Kirsi as our hands broke apart.

Kirsi pressed a finger to her lips, remembering the rule that we were not to speak to each other. She dipped her chin, chose a carriage, and crawled inside with Scoop right behind her. And then it was only me. Standing before the last open carriage door. With one final deep breath, I stepped forward, my boots clicking on the stones as I handed the coachman my small bag. He set the leather case beside him and jerked his head toward the open door.

"Get in. We're wasting time."

"Sorry. I . . ." There was nothing worth saying that would explain the rush of mixed feelings I had. Instead, I shook my head and crawled into the beautiful carriage. I moved to pull the door shut and a massive hand caught mine.

"How about some company?" Grey asked.

I jerked my hand away and shot across the seat of the cabin as he let himself in. His bulky, muscled body barely fit through the door as he shook the whole thing trying to settle in.

"I'll take that as a yes," he said, swinging the door shut.

I didn't respond. Just held my scowl and stared out the window, avoiding the fact the uniform he wore was the same as the soldiers that had murdered my grandmother. And I was willingly putting myself into the path of the man responsible for her death and so many more. Each of the coven leaders' warnings rang through my head as I steadied myself.

"First time at the castle?"

I pressed my lips together, refusing to acknowledge the beautiful man. He'd given the silent order regarding the other contestants. I'd happily pass that courtesy onto him as well.

"Not much of a talker? That's fine. I can carry the conversation for both of us."

I turned to face the small octagonal window opposite the door. *Great. Chatty Cathy.*

"I came into this world one balmy midsummer night. Mother said—"

"You have *got* to be kidding me. I'm not interested. There's not a single piece of me that wants to hear a word from you. I'm here for one reason only, and it's not to make friends."

He smiled as if he hadn't heard a word I said. "Ah. You can speak. Excellent." He reached into his coat pocket and pulled out an envelope. "This is from the king. You're to read it on the journey."

"You could have started with this and saved the small talk," I said, plucking it from his fingers.

He shrugged. "I like the small talk."

"Shouldn't you be out there riding a gallant stead, leading the caravan while you murder every innocent creature from here to the castle?"

"Thought I'd save that for the ride back."

I rolled my eyes, flipping over the envelope, noting the flame pressed into the black wax. At least he'd acknowledged the royal coven. There were those of us that had questioned if he only claimed his shifter side. Nearly denouncing the powerful witch blood that ran through his veins.

My name was carefully scrawled across the front of the envelope. I wondered if Kirsi's letter would say the same as mine. I placed it onto my lap, staring back out the window as I watched the world pass by, listening to the wheels crunch on the gravel below our carriage.

"Aren't you going to open it?"

A very real part of me wanted to break the king's rule and cast a silencing spell over the messenger. I needed this moment to collect myself. To prepare for whatever I was about to go through, each passing moment the fear within me grew. But clearly that was too much to ask for.

"Here." I held the envelope out to him. "If you want me to open it so badly, you read it. I don't really care what he has to say. The Trials are a sacred event for the members of my coven. It has nothing to do with the Dark King or his castle of nightmares. He's only there to spectate. But by all means, help yourself."

Flaring his fingers, a marking lit on his neck as the envelope opened without breaking the seal. The letter unfolded midair, and he cleared his throat. "Ms. Raven Moonstone."

"Stop. Stop." I snatched the paper, crumbling the corner as I turned the words to face me. I glanced down at the letter and back to the messenger, making eye contact for the first time. "It doesn't even say my name."

He wiggled his eyebrows. "I was going for dramatic."

"You're supposed to be dark and murdery."

"You've got a lot of opinions about what I'm supposed to be for someone who's never formally met me."

"You work for a tyrant king with a penchant for murder and thievery. My opinions are valid."

He clenched his jaw, finally taking a hint, and turned away. Satisfied, I opened the letter I'd crumpled, and read to myself.

The rules are simple. Don't wander through my castle. You go where you're told, when you're told. The guards are stationed for my benefit, not yours. Stay away from them. The scheduled events are not optional. You're in the Trials for a reason. You could win. You could die. You could vanish. Remember that.

This is not a game.

The Spectator

"What the—" I glared at the man filling over half of the cabin, but he hadn't bothered to look back, the anger on his face still present. *Fine.* "Your king is eavesdropping, Messenger."

"My name is Grey." Cold eyes met mine. "And like it or not, he's your king, too."

"Unfortunately." I lifted the hood of my cloak and brought it up to hide my face, hoping that he'd just leave me alone.

I felt his subtle glances as we traveled, but I was used to those. People that didn't know me stared at my bare skin as if they'd never seen anything like it. I'd been ten, standing in my grandmother's shop, when every single candle lit at one time. The only one more surprised than me was my mother. Clearly, no one could get over it.

Eventually, we arrived at the castle. I hadn't been able to see it from the small carriage window. But as I stepped outside, taking in the obsidian stone that seemed to grow from the ground, the spires grazing the afternoon sky, I hardly noticed the rest of the contestants.

"Your jaw's on the ground, Ms. Moonstone," Grey said, moving to my side, peeking at the castle. "Wouldn't want the king to think you were in awe of him."

I snapped my mouth closed, pushing my hood down as I walked toward Kirsi. I got no more than four paces before a woman began clapping her hands as if she'd command the world with the gesture, barking orders to a full line of staff that poured out of the castle.

Two women dressed in simple gray gowns, and a single guard surrounded me. I peeked around them to see that the other contes-

94

tants were also being assigned staff. My breaths became short as panic set in. We'd simply offered ourselves up to the worst king this world had seen. And now he was separating us.

"Good luck," Grey said as he walked freely around the ladies orchestrating the chaos.

"Follow me," the largest of the two women assigned to me said, spinning on her heel and walking away, her chestnut hair swaying behind her as she moved.

"But my things," I protested, pointing. I turned back to the carriage, but it was gone. They all were.

The other woman, with softer features and lighter brown hair cleared her throat, though she didn't look me in the eye as she said, "They'll be in your rooms. Hustle. Clariss doesn't like to be kept waiting."

Sparing a glance at the guard I'd been assigned, I grabbed the bottom of my skirts and jogged after the first woman, hardly getting a chance to take in the pitch-black castle. I'd barely caught up to the maid hustling through the corridors when she turned a sharp corner and came to an abrupt halt outside of a door. The first in a long hallway of rooms, it seemed, though it was hard to tell with the lack of light.

She reached into a pocket, pulling out an iron key. "These will be your assigned rooms for as long as you remain. You're not to wander the castle, or the grounds without our king's permission. And don't expect that to be granted to you." She turned to the guard. "Thank you, Armious. We can take it from here."

She shoved the key in the lock and swung the heavy wooden door open. It seemed every other surface of the castle was made from black stone. Even the plethora of candles that lit the echoing corridors we'd hastened down didn't give enough light. Each corner of the Dark King's castle was nearly invisible as it faded into heavy shadow.

The slighter maid followed right behind me as I crossed the threshold to my assigned room. A fire crackled in the corner, warming the antechamber. Shiny black walls boasted high ceilings and alcoves that held more candles, and some intricate statues of beasts and the goddess. Something was missing, though. Something so pivotal, the moment I realized why the room felt so foreign my heart ached. No windows. No natural sunlight, no moon peeking through the night. This was a prison. My small bag sat on a deep gold printed rug in the middle of the elegant sitting room, equipped with a chaise, trivial desk and another chair the same color as the rug.

"My name is Clariss and this is Tavia. We are here to serve you during your trials. Have you got a fire spell?"

Though I'd never had a witch blatantly ask me what my spells were outside of yesterday's tours, I reluctantly nodded. She snapped her fingers and the fire vanished.

"Show me."

My breath caught in my throat. They didn't believe I had magic. Couldn't trust me because I had no markings. My welcome here would be equally as warm as it was in my daily life.

"My spells are not for your personal entertainment."

The other witch, Tavia, stepped forward, her voice a bit softer. "It's our job to make sure you are comfortable, my lady. You'll have to show us this one thing so we know you can warm yourself in the night when the castle gets cold. Otherwise, one of us will be assigned to sleep here."

I flashed a hand through the air, igniting the fire. "Shall I make it blue for you as well?"

Clariss didn't bother responding as she stepped toward the bed chambers. Another snap of her fingers and a warm glow from freshly lit sconces came from within. I swallowed, moving forward to take in the opulent room. Everything was still a careful mixture of black and flecks of gold, but four thick bed pillars seemed to grow up from the floor and down from the ceiling, as if the space in the room was carved out of a solid rock. I'd never known anything could be so foreboding, yet so beautiful.

I moved to the bed, smothered in silky sheets and a thousand pillows, hardly able to hold back my smile. There wasn't a single hole in the blankets. Nothing threadbare. I expected it, but it was still notable.

Even now, that massive bed lured me. I wanted to crawl in, get lost in the sheets, and never leave. First, I needed the others to go. I needed a moment to breathe and be. To sit in the space that would be mine for as long as I remained in the Trials. But they didn't leave.

Tavia, whom I'd already declared the more tolerable of the two, crossed the room, hiding her smile as she pushed open a heavy door in the corner that I hadn't even noticed.

"Your bathing room, my lady."

She swept to the side as I entered, watching me marvel at the space.

"There's a chandelier in the bathing room?" I whispered, barely taking my eyes from the painting of two lovers embracing along the ceiling.

"Yes." Tavia giggled as I spun, studying every careful detail.

"I've never seen anything like it."

"You'll have plenty of time to stare later, my lady," Clariss said. "You're to be presented to the king and have your evening meal in only a couple hours. We need to get started."

"Get started with what?" I asked, stepping away as they moved toward me.

Tavia waved an arm through the air and the bath began to fill, steam rolling. "We're to make you presentable for the king, of course."

Clariss's eyes flashed up and down my body before she turned to Tavia. "Pull the blue and green. Let's save the black."

"I'm quite sure I can prepare myself, thank you."

"For all the tragedy that befalls this castle, there are also indulgences. Take heed to embrace them while you can, Raven Moonstone. They will not last."

12

Each inch of the steaming water helped to release the tension I'd been holding. Tavia conceded the lathering soap, letting me wash in privacy, but there were no such deals given in regard to the mass of dark curls currently floating around me. Clariss, all six feet of muscle and judgment, had dunked and scrubbed my hair over and over, brushing with her fingers, grunting and groaning as she poured in different oils and scented soaps.

Eventually, she turned away satisfied and agreed to five minutes of soaking and meditation before I was to be dressed. And in exchange for these five minutes, I'd agreed to let them dress me without a fight. We were stuck with each other, it seemed. With Onyx here to cause problems, the Dark King somewhere nearby, and guards all over the place, I didn't need another battle.

Closing my eyes, I rested my neck against the ledge of the bath, breathing in the lavender infused steam as I pushed every thought from my mind, simply focusing on the energy around me. The power that seemed to pulsate through the castle as if it were a conjuring of ancient magic settled into this world by its own right. Being here within these walls, twisted the power inside me, coaxing it, caressing it, moving it, as if it were muted below the water of this bath, but something had pierced the surface.

I knew this would be one step at a time, just as the tour was. No one anticipated the witch with no markings to win. Most probably doubted I had significant magic. Maybe I didn't in comparison to the others. But winning wasn't all about power. And I would do none of this half-heartedly.

Rejuvenating my sense of determination, I stood from the bath, water dripping, ready to take on whatever the night would bring with my chin high. I slipped into the chemise left on a hook and stepped into the bed chambers. The maids were debating the color of dress I would wear. In the end, they settled on an emerald green gown with gold embellishments.

I'd never worn something so fine in my life. Though, for all its beauty, sitting in a chair came with its own challenges. It took several tries to learn to sit with my back arched enough that when I settled, I could still breathe. Clariss raked through my curls with vigor as Tavia handed her pin after pin. A small diadem was the final piece as they stepped away, critiquing their work.

"A deep red lip should do it, and easy on the eyes. The last time you did this magic it was too heavy," Clariss said, gesturing for Tavia to move closer.

The younger maid flourished her fingers in front of me, a small tingling braised my skin and then they stood back, contentment on their faces.

I lifted from the chair, moving to the ornate, gold mirror. Tavia had painted my face with her magic. The makeup was subtle everywhere but the crimson lips.

"Well, then," Clariss said, clasping her hands in front of her. "You're a stunning little witch ... when all that hair has been tamed."

I glanced down to the full green skirts, moving my fingers up the golden embroidery on the bodice. "Will everyone be dressed this fine?" I asked, thinking of Kirsi and wondering what sort of maids she'd been assigned.

"We can't have a bunch of wild witches looking half-starved and in need of a bath running about."

I spun, pinning Clariss with a glare. "You should ask yourselves why we are half starved. Why *your* king allows his people to suffer, when clearly he could do so much more."

"Even so," she answered, her cold face matching mine. "You'll wear the dress, attend the meals, perform at your Trials and try not to get yourself killed. What *our* king does with his country is no business of mine."

"Isn't it? The witches suffer. He's killing them faster than they can be born. The Thrashings are a complete massacre of our kind. Over and over again. You're witches. We are all linked, our power equally divided amongst the seven. And you ... how are you not offended by his hatred for the rest of us?"

She waved her hand in the air and, though I tried to shout, my voice had gone. Anger boiled within me. She knew I was right.

"Not another word about this." She leaned in until her hot breath warmed my ear. "Witches have died for less, girl. I am not your enemy."

She snapped her fingers and my voice returned.

"Please," I gasped, gripping my throat. "Leave me."

They turned, leaving the bed chambers, but as they stepped into the adjacent sitting room, Clariss stopped. "Keep that fire, little witch. You're going to need it."

I'd wanted nothing more than the easy comfort that giant bed promised, but dressed in three hundred layers of maddening fabric, even if I managed to crawl into it, I'm not sure how I would have gotten down. Unless I rolled to the floor ... I considered it, biting my thumb as I stared. No. This wasn't the time. I'd be summoned soon.

Opening the carved wardrobe, enriched with tasteful carvings painted in careful gold detail, I was stunned to find more gowns hanging inside with as much elegance as the one I was wearing. Life within the castle was a deep contrast to the outside world. Perhaps those here were grossly unaware of the king's firm grip on the witches' throats.

Marching soldiers passed by my door and I found myself opening it to peek. The sound of synchronized boots faded away as the darkened hallway seemed to swallow them whole. And then there was no one. Only a flickering candle from the alcove across from my room.

I waited, peeking out through the crack in the door as I held my breath. Standing in the home of a murderer had been my choice, but finally being left alone with my own thoughts, I realized just what that meant. I was now prey to whatever game he could orchestrate. And I'd never seen his face. I knew he was young, though older than me. I knew he was half shifter. But the witches only spoke of the Dark King in passing whispers and sharpened threats.

Even now, the thought of opening the door fully and stepping into his hallway sent so much fear through me, I backed into my room instead. If fear was his goal, the price of those lives, he'd accomplished it.

Waving my hand through the air, I used unnecessary magic to close the door. There was comfort in unbridled power, even if it was only a sliver of magic. It was too bad I didn't have the key. But I was sure it was superfluous anyway. If I was to be murdered here, a simple lock wasn't going to save me. I stepped away from the door, walking the circumference of the room. The fire was still rolling, the candles all perfectly lit in their arched alcoves, but no matter how much I tried to imagine staying here, I couldn't do it. It was all meant to be warm and inviting. A carefully laid trap for the thoroughly warned mouse.

A firm knock sounded once on the door before the handle jiggled.

"Time for presentations," a small voice said.

I gestured once more, and it swung open.

A small child with charming amber eyes stared up at me with a weary smile. She didn't cross the threshold, instead grabbing the sides of her skirts and lifting, she curtsied. "You're to follow me, my lady."

My stomach turned over the words. This was it. The single moment of this whole competition I'd been dreading. The presentation to the king. Marking myself as a target for him, rather than him having to do any of the work. The coven leaders had warned us to be vigilant. Keep our guards up. But as I stepped toward the quiet child, I realized even the most innocent could be deadly in a castle built of deception.

"Isn't it beautiful?" Kirsi asked as we stood in a line formed outside two tall doors blocked by guards.

"The blue is stunning on you." I smiled, though I'm sure it didn't reach my eyes. "Just be careful, okay? It's dangerous here."

Her eyes widened as she moved in closer, Scoop sleeping in her hands as she leaned in to whisper. "Have you seen him?"

I shook my head. "No, only the two maids that forced me into this dress."

"It is exquisite, Raven. We've spent our whole lives waiting for this moment. Even though it feels wrong, we should embrace the good things." Her eyes flashed behind me. "Like her for example."

Nym. She made her way forward, joining us, and a twinkle lit her eye as she took in Kirsi's form-fitted blue gown with a deep neckline.

"You're stunning," Kirsi said, brushing the fingers of her free hand over the gold bands stacked on Nym's arm.

"So are you," she answered, reaching for Kirsi's face.

"I've always meant to ask you what the bands represent," Kirsi said.

Nym twisted some of the bangles up her dark arms, a smile lighting her face. "One for each generation of witches in my family. The thirteenth one is for me. It is to represent our generational power."

Kir brushed a hand over the highest band. "Incredible."

I turned away, respecting their private moment as my heart soared for Kirsi. It seemed Nym had finally seen her. Really seen her. And that alone made today's trip worth the worry. Especially when I knew Nym's heart was full of sadness from saying goodbye to Ender this morning.

The doors swung open and a short man carrying a rolled parchment stepped forward.

"You're to be presented to our king, Chosen. You don't speak to him. You don't look him in the eye. You simply walk forward when your name is called, bow, and wait for him to dismiss you. If you can count to ten in your head and he has not acknowledged you, take that as a dismissal. You'll follow the west wall of the hall and form a line at the back of the room. Once you have each been presented, the king will say a few words, and then you'll be released for dinner. Questions?" The eight Chosen shifted, each looking at the next, though no one spoke. Not even Onyx, surprisingly. "Right then. Follow me."

In single file, we stepped into the first room that had been properly lit in the entire castle. I peeked over the shoulder of Onyx in front of me, but I couldn't see much from this distance. Only domed ceilings smothered in detailed paintings of shifters depicted in various shades of black and gold.

"Zennik Moonfall, Your Grace," the man shouted.

Zennik adjusted his blue pressed jacket and shuffled forward. I listened and waited. Rather than hear the voice of the Dark King, or even sense his domineering presence, there was absolutely nothing but sharp footsteps that echoed in the hall as Zennik made his way forward, a pause and then footsteps again to the back wall, as we'd been instructed.

"Willow Moonhollow, Your Grace."

The only thing I could see was a flash of red as Willow's satin skirts flared when she stepped forward. Onyx let out a discreet chuckle as muffled voices came from within the room. He may have ignored Zennik, but it seemed he had acknowledged beautiful Willow. I couldn't say I was surprised.

The line shuffled forward. Breya and then Ophelia presented. As the line drew closer, I'd finally been able to see around the brute in front of me. In the spacious room, only guards and the Chosen were present. And the Dark King, who, from this distance, seemed to be lounging on his throne having a conversation with Grey beside him, paying absolutely no attention to the rest of the Chosen as they were introduced to him. Only Willow had gotten his attention.

"Onyx Moonshade, Your Grace."

Finally, my view opened entirely. Icy chills ran down my spine as I stared at the Dark King. His midnight, shoulder-length hair blocked most of his face as he carried on with his casual conversation with Grey. He couldn't be bothered with the likes of us witches and, though I should have preferred that, it infuriated me.

Onyx swept forward, chin high as ever while he tried and failed to impress the king. After a long-held bow, he moved his hands through his chestnut hair as he stood there, waiting for a response. When it became clear he also would not get one, he spun on a heel and stormed away, clenching his fists at his sides.

"Raven Moonstone, Your Grace."

I didn't raise my eyes. Jaw set, I stormed forward, the small flats of my shoes clicking against the black marbled floor as my skirts muffled the sound. Stopping at the base of the dais, I deigned a small curtsy and waited, wondering why I'd ever wanted this. Torn, I stayed frozen in place, by fear or frustration at this treatment, I wasn't sure. I didn't want the attention of the villain, but something within me demanded to be defiant. To let him know that the witches still had guile. To let him stare into the eyes of the granddaughter of Viana Moonstone. One minute passed. Two minutes. Dread began to over-take my nonsensical conviction.

Another moment passed. The voices silenced as two powerful footsteps made their way toward me. I didn't bother lifting my head. Perhaps the king would make an example of me for showing the slightest discontent. Maybe he could feel my fear, being half beast. But then he'd also have to feel my hatred.

"Rise, Raven Moonstone."

Adrenaline mixed with regret as the voice that ruled the world commanded me. Head down, I stood straight, willing my hands to steady as I readied for anything. Anything but the black leather glove that reached forward and lifted my chin, forcing me to stare into the gray eyes of the man that had commanded my grandmother's death. But blessings, he was gorgeous. His markings snaked down his neck, disappearing beneath his clothing. Wings so dark they must have commanded the shadows spread wide as he stood before me. A sharp jawline and sun kissed skin with eyes that could stop the world stared back at me.

"Are you lost?" His voice was smoky and deep. The kind you'd hear in a bedroom after hours of exhausting pleasure. Something warmed my belly at the tone, drifting down, pulsating, as the edges of the world darkened beneath his shadows. It was not the response I wanted to have to this beast, but as I clenched my thighs, I realized I had absolutely no control over myself. Clearly.

I gulped, allowing my head to sink again. I could die with only the wrong words. Shaking my head, I pressed my lips together.

Again, he gripped my face, pressing his fingers too hard into my cheeks. "You will look at me when I speak to you, unless I've ordered otherwise."

I nodded, forcing my chin high. "Forgive me, Your Grace."

He stepped away then, clasping his hands behind his strong back, just below those wings as he circled me like a predator, studying me carefully. The room was silent, though I could feel the eyes of the Chosen on me now.

"I've never seen a witch without markings." Pulling the glove from his hand, he pressed his warm finger to my exposed collarbone, dragging from one side to the other. "What spell do you use to conceal your nature, witch?"

"The—there is no spell, Your Grace. I do not know why I have no markings."

I noticed the tick in his jawline and instinctively moved away from the Dark King. I'd stuttered. For all the hatred and anger I felt, fear had been the dominant emotion. He circled once more, the shadow cast along the ground from his avian wings barely discernible as he moved like a carnivore. I needed out. I needed a full breath to fill my lungs. I needed clarity. He'd taken all sense of reason the moment he'd entered my space and now, as he stood before me staring at me, as everyone stared at me, the only thing I could think to do was run.

But I was frozen. My mind racing a thousand miles per hour as I waited for him to kill me. As he had Tasa and countless other witches for no reason. He hadn't moved in minutes. No one had. I doubted anyone had dared to breathe as they watched. The Dark King cleared his throat.

"You're holding up the line, Ms. Moonstone."

I jolted. Had he dismissed me? Without another word, I spun only to have my arm gripped tight as he pulled me close enough to whisper into my ear. My eyes doubled in size as his timbered voice trailed down my spine. "A pleasure."

I jerked my arm free and hustled to the back of the room, refusing to look at the stunned faces that stared into my own as the towering Dark King with wings that swept the polished floor marched back to his throne and continued his conversation as if he hadn't just made a spectacle of me. He'd talked to Willow also. I wondered if it had been of the same nature.

My heart didn't slow as the last two witches, Kirsi and Nym, were presented. They were ignored as thoroughly as the first half. Though Kirsi held her head high as she joined the rest of us against the back wall, flashing me a wink. Whatever target I'd placed on myself, at least I still had her.

The Dark King rose from his throne and the line of witches shuffled closer together. Our fear was a shared emotion, even though we were to compete against one another.

The man that had introduced each contestant walked forward, kneeling before the king for a moment before he rose and swept his hand to the side, gesturing to us. "Come forward, Chosen."

We moved until we were standing in a group down the center aisle. I'd tried to hide myself toward the back, but Kirsi shoved me forward until it was only Onyx, Willow, and I in the front row.

"You've been given the rules of my home. You're not to wander. You're not to mingle. You're not to do anything but prepare for and perform your Trials to the best of your ability. Do not forget who I am. The stories you've heard of me. The fear I've elicited. Break a rule, and you'll wish you could go home."

He hadn't looked at me until that final word. A word that burned into my soul as he spoke it. As if he knew I had spent the majority of my life dreaming of being here. He snapped his fingers and the doors behind us slammed open. Two guards dressed in the garb that haunted my nightmares dragged a man forward between them. His boots screeched along the ground, and he twisted and turned, screaming in protest. We parted, letting the spectacle through. The guards said nothing as they tossed the poor man with sandy blond hair to the floor before the king. He crawled forward, tears splashing onto the marble as he pleaded.

"Please, Your Grace. It was only a goblet. Only one, I swear. My daughter is sick. She needed the med—"

A snap of the king's fingers and the man said nothing more as he went deadly still, all signs of life falling from his face as he fell backward, stiff as stone. Dead. Just as quickly as his tears had fallen.

Anger ignited within me as I stared into the hateful eyes of the Dark King. The monster. The killer. He smirked, reading my face as easily as I'd hoped he could while stepping over the man he'd just murdered. "Let this stand as a lesson, Moon Coven witches. You live by my will alone."

Wrapping his wings around his body until he was cocooned within them, he vanished, leaving behind a single black feather that landed softly at my feet.

13

I was used to the side eyes and gawking. The doubt on strangers faces when they saw me amongst the witches; the pity some held, believing I was a silent witch. The markings upon a witch's skin were a blessing. A rite of passage. And oh, how I'd envied them when I was a child. I'd burn the dried flower petals in Crescent Cottage and press the ashes into my skin, dreaming of the markings that would make me normal. Now, I only pitied the people that stared. The witches that found me weak or lacking because they could not see the amount of power I wielded. After all this time, I'd taken on a new mantra: No matter how long or hard they stare, they will never really see me.

But this? The casual glances from some of the king's guards as their eyes flicked over my body, I couldn't handle those. The envious glances from Breya and even Nym as we sat for dinner made an already uncomfortable situation worse. The only time one would want the attention of the Dark King was during the Trials he presided over, but now having that attention, I already wished I could take back my stubborn will. At least I could concede that Willow was receiving the same treatment. Though Kirsi's glares toward her were full of threats and dangerous promises.

The black walls of the hallway continued into the dining hall, the room dark yet beautiful, although the tone had not changed. Fresh lilacs and hydrangeas filled a row of tall, slender vases placed down the center of the table, warmth radiating from the overabundance of candles with flames that reflected off the shining walls, onto the ceiling and upon the floors like flecks of stars. The high backs of the chairs made each contestant seem so small in comparison.

No one, besides the king at the head of the table, had spoken a word. Not even Grey, who stood guard by the door. We'd been given a feast worthy of any solstice, with plates loaded with meats and gravy, and breads of all kinds. There were more fruits than we could eat. At every other place setting stood a server, waiting with a jug to refill icy drinks.

The king watched me. Probably no more than he was studying the rest of the Chosen. I'd forced Kirsi without words to sit toward the end of the table, but that didn't seem to help. Willow had taken the seat closest to the king, with Onyx right beside her. He'd leaned in to whisper to her once, but she hadn't answered, holding eyes for only the Dark King.

Someone had died. A man. Right in front of us. And now we would eat as though we celebrated that death. The wrongness rolled my stomach enough times to turn my appetite as I pushed the roasted chicken through the gravy on my plate and wished I hadn't filled it at all. I couldn't let this go to waste. Not when I knew there were children starving, or near so, on the cobblestone streets at home.

The king stood, his chair scraping against the cold marble floor as his great black wings pushed it backward. Turning to dip his chin to Grey, he lifted those wings high into the air. If it was an attempt to get everyone's attention, it was unnecessary but highly effective. Most of these witches hadn't interacted with the shifters like Kirsi and I did occasionally in the shop. In fact, they hated them. The shifters were the reason the witches were impoverished.

"Eat," he commanded with that voice that could melt the world. "You're going to need your strength. Tomorrow will be your first Trial."

Kirsi kicked me from under the table. She'd finished two plates, likely concluding the same. As soon as the king was good and gone, a tumble of whispers rose from the Moon Coven witches sitting at the table.

"Assume everyone is an enemy. We need allies," Kirsi hissed. "They are all looking at you like you're their next meal, now that you and the king are hooking up."

I jumped back in my seat, nearly tipping it over. "We're not ... I'm not ..."

She smiled.

"I hate you." I smiled back.

"You love me. We all know he's probably got Willow in his sights as well. She's undoubtedly going to leave her door unlocked, just in case." She pressed her shoulder into me. "That's the first smile I've seen in days."

"Probably the last."

"I'm going to need you to be less dramatic." She glanced over my shoulder at Grey. "Before we get in trouble for talking, we need to plan. We've got Nym already. Tonight, we need to scope out the rest of these witches and figure out who might be good to make friends with."

"If we make friends, eventually we're going to have to betray them. This isn't a team sport. There's only one winner. Even you and I ..." my voice trailed off as I circled back to the truth that haunted me. Kirsi and I were going to have to go against each other.

"You have your talents and I have mine. We use them to help each other until it comes down to you versus me. And then the best witch wins. We take nothing personal. We're still in this together."

"Fine. Let's keep an eye on Breya, and Ophelia. I'll never be able to trust Onyx or Willow. I'm not sold on Zennik but let's watch him as well."

She lifted her fork and pointed at my plate. "Eat, Raven. If you have to run tomorrow, you'll want the calories."

After only a handful of bites, I pushed my plate away.

"Our glorious king has asked me to send you all back to your rooms the moment your forks stopped moving. I'm feeling a bit generous, though." Grey leaned against the door frame, hands in his pockets. "Carry on with your gossip."

No one trusted him. Not a soul said another word or moved.

"Fine," he drawled. "What if I turn my back?"

Making a show of rolling his eyes, he winked in my direction before he turned. Annoyed, which always seemed to be the case with that man, I pushed away from my seat. Kirsi followed, and then Nym, and soon everyone stood.

I walked over to Nym, petting the tiny white tiger that circled her feet. "Kir says you'll be allies with us. Are you sure?"

She scanned the room carefully and then leaned into me. "I think the entire room wants to beat you right now. Even Willow didn't get the attention you did. They're saying he only gave her a brief introduction and he was definitely watching you at dinner. You're going to need all the allies you can get, Raven."

"I think the king will be the first to kill me. I foolishly challenged him the second we met. He seems far more interested in Willow, though."

"It didn't look like he wanted to *kill* you. Sleep with you, probably, but not kill."

"Agreed." Grey's voice crept over my shoulder.

"Mind your business, Messenger."

"I like your business so much more than mine."

Kirsi pulled Nym away from the crossfire as I rounded on Grey, my skirts heavy as they spun in waves of fabric.

"What has intrigued him so much?"

He smirked, that dimple showing. "I think it's the guts. We don't seem to scare you or intimidate you."

"You would if you weren't so annoying. Or if the king hadn't taken all my fear for himself."

"He's really not that bad, Rave. May I call you Rave? I feel like that's such a good nickname for your fiery spirit."

I stepped toward him, my hands in fists at my side. "No, you may not call me Rave. Your king won't even allow me to speak to my friends. Your *generosity* gives us these few moments. The sheer thought of communication scares him. We," I gestured around the stricken room as they all stared us down, "have come here to compete. We aren't here to cause problems."

He moved backward with that infuriating smirk still on his face. "I'll be sure to relay your message to the king."

"You do that," I replied, casually lifting my skirts to see myself out, though guards flanked me in the halls.

Something in this castle was getting to me, and every move I made was followed with a deep sense of regret. I wasn't a fool. I knew if I kept mouthing off, kept letting myself fall over the edge of control, I was going to reap what I sowed. But I couldn't help the fury. This damned place coaxed my anger forward. But perhaps it wasn't the place. Merely the man.

I SAT ON THE FLOOR OF MY ROOM WITH MY BACK PRESSED AGAINST THE door. Clariss had told me she'd be back after dinner to help me out of the elaborate gown that threatened to drown me, but so far, I'd been left to my own thoughts. Which was such a terrible place to be.

"Do you always sulk?"

The deep voice sent my heart directly to my throat as I jumped to my feet, fell forward over the length of my skirts and landed in the arms of the most dangerous man in the world. The king held me firm, hoisting me up until my feet cooperated. I curtsied low as the damn dress flourished beautifully on the floor.

He pressed a single finger under my chin and lifted until I was face to face with him again. The gray in his eyes shimmered like silver, betraying the hard lines of his beautiful face as he looked at me. "I'm told you have something to say to me?"

Oh fuck.

I blanched as if he could hear those words cross my mind, and stepped back, dropping my head.

Again, he lifted my face with a thick finger under my chin. There was a moment, a single second, when the world stopped. My heart stopped as I stared at him. The well-groomed, dark stubble that lined his sharp jaw, the full lips, and the way he pulled his hair back, as if the goddess had built the perfect trap. The beautiful beast to lure you in before he unleashed hell with his endless darkness and venom.

"I've commanded you to look at my face when I speak to you. Will you need a reminder each time we speak?"

"No, Your Grace." Biting the inside of my cheek to remain calm, I gripped the sides of my dress, hoping it would steady my trembling hands.

Looking down, a smug smile stretched across his wicked face. "You're afraid of me."

"I'm not afraid," I answered, the lie hot on my tongue.

He raised his eyebrows. Something in the way he scoffed, the way he so clearly found pleasure in my discomfort, brought back all my annoyances from earlier. All the injustice as I thought of the food that would go to waste, the children that suffered, the witches he'd killed, Tasa hanging from that tree. And then I realized something.

"It's you," I said quietly. "You're the one that's afraid. Why else would you block us off from each other?"

"I don't fear that which I control." Anger roared behind his calm words, though he remained perfectly poised.

I grew warmer beneath his gaze as he ripped the air from the room.

He began to circle me like a vulture, his hands clasped behind his back, mirroring the assessment he'd carried out in the throne room. "Do you want to know something about fear, Ms. Moonstone?"

The cold tone in his voice shifted something within me. I shook my head, but he ignored it.

"Fear is power. Fear is seduction." He traced his finger down my cheek as he leaned in close, his warm breath a whisper on my ear. "Fear is the darkness that calls to you."

"I am not afraid of you," I managed.

A low and calculated chuckle left his throat as he gripped my face again, forcing my eyes to his, only a breath of space between us. "Say it like you mean it, little witch."

I swallowed, staring as his shadows began to rise around us. The pull to them had never been as strong, as urgent as I felt them then. "I am not afraid of you."

"Well done." He stepped away, though the shadows lingered on the floor like a low-lying fog as his wings appeared behind him. "I almost believed you. As it stands, this is my kingdom. This is my home. And you will follow the rules I've set in place." He turned his back to me, his wings dropping as he looked to the fireplace beside him. "Make no mistake. The rules are in place for your safety, not mine."

He vanished. The shadows lingered, gathering at my feet before they snaked up my body, caressing me with phantom hands that gripped my throat, stealing my breath before following their master into oblivion.

A black piece of paper drifted down from the carved ceiling, seemingly from nowhere. I snagged it from the air, running my fingers over the soft golden script.

A gift for the fearless.

I whipped around, searching for him. Anticipating him to appear from nowhere, as he had the first time, but he wasn't there. The edges of the note became fiery embers, turning it to ash before it had a chance to burn my fingers. I waited until I was sure he was gone for good before I let my shoulders down, taking in a full breath.

Wondering what gift he meant, I surveyed the room again, afraid I'd find a dead body or maybe a gift box with a severed head. But there was nothing. Stepping into the bedchamber, I nearly tripped over my own feet as I noticed a piece of the wall, no, a hidden door had been left slightly ajar. I moved across the room to investigate, noting the black iron sconce that would act as a handle.

As I reached to swing the door open, three solid knocks came from my sitting room. Afraid I'd be caught sneaking out, I did the only logical thing and pressed the new door shut, praying it didn't lock.

"I've got a whole night's worth of work to do, girl. Let's get this over with." Clariss pushed into the room gesturing for me to turn, her dark hair pulled back into a perfect bun. She wasted no time tugging at the ties on my sleeves and lifting the dress over my head. "I expect you can remove the pins from your hair on your own?" she asked as she tugged on the cords of the corset, releasing me from its death grip on my rib cage.

I nodded as I stood nearly bare, wearing only a chemise as she swept back out of the room, my dress over her forearm. I couldn't help but feel the eyes of the king on me now. Knowing he could simply appear in my rooms whenever he pleased. I quickly ran for the wardrobe, selecting a long nightgown to throw over my head.

Waiting only a few moments to make sure she wouldn't come back, I strode back to the secret door, lifted to my tip toes, gripping the cold sconce in my hand and pulled. The door swung open with no resistance.

I wasn't sure what I expected, but it wasn't baby Scoop launching himself at me from inside Kirsi's room.

"Raven?" she asked, setting down the book she'd been reading. "What are you doing here?"

"Apparently we're neighbors," I said, gesturing to the hidden door.

She squealed, hopping off the couch to hug me, squishing Scoop between us as I held the little black fur ball in my arms. "It'll be just like home."

Leaning around me, she peeked into my bedroom and let out a low whistle. "I'll show you mine if you show me yours?"

Setting the cat on the floor, I agreed. She swept into my room, wiggling her eyebrows as she took in the ornate carved posts surrounding the bed.

"It's incredible, isn't it?" she asked.

I traced the carvings with my fingers. "It is."

I wanted to hate that it was his. That someone so undeserving could live in a place like this. But maybe a castle surrounded in cold black stone was the punishment he deserved. We had trees and water and the open sky above us, whereas the king's covenstead was barren, nothing but ash surrounding a castle. I didn't even know where the Fire Coven witches lived or what their territory looked like. It'd been black from the moment we crossed the bridge from the Moon Coven.

Kirsi's rooms were similar to mine, only instead of gold details, she had deep rubies and bedding made of scarlet satin. She swiped the blankets from her bed and followed me back to mine. "There's room in here for two. Only for tonight."

Kirsi hated being alone. Since her mother had died in childbirth, taking her little sister as well, she'd never been the same. She had her father, but they hardly spoke anymore. She'd been raised by an aunt until we decided to reopen Crescent Cottage and live together. We'd never spent a night apart since. Not even after the Harrowing.

Scoop curled into a tiny ball between us, and within minutes, they'd both fallen asleep. I couldn't. The first trial was tomorrow, but it was more than that. It was knowing the king could be standing in a dark corner, hidden by his shadows as he watched me. But why had he given me access to Kirsi when it was a clear defiance to his own rule? I supposed the rules didn't apply to the executioner.

14

At some point in the early morning hours, Kirsi snuck back to her rooms, afraid to be caught away from them. Not long after that, probably before the sun had risen, though it was hard to tell without windows, Clariss and Tavia arrived, pushing me out of bed.

Feeling more tired than I had since being attacked in the forest, I worried something was going to happen to me again. I pushed that thought from my mind as I dressed.

"This is far more comfortable than last night," I said mostly to myself as the two witches hustled around me, using magic as needed to quicken their pace. Or maybe it was me that was sluggish. I used a healing spell on my queasy stomach. Nothing too powerful, but instead of feeling better, it seemed to make it worse.

"Pants, boots and tunic are all you'll need until dinner," Clariss said, pulling my hair as she braided it behind me. "A satchel and cloak are the only other permitted items today."

"Here," Tavia said, handing them to me. "Best of luck, my lady." She shared an empathetic smile that said I was not nearly as scared as I should have been.

"You're to go to the end of the hall and let yourself in the very last door on the left."

"Thank you." I swung the satchel over my head.

The dark hall was quiet and completely empty. Only when I reached the door I'd been directed to did I hear someone else moving behind me. Rather than waiting, I pushed the door open and stepped into the middle of another coven's territory. The bright blue sky in the small clearing was broken only by a smattering of billowy clouds. Dense trees surrounded us, swaying in a soft warm breeze, and the ground was covered in grass, the deepest green I'd ever seen. Studying the myriad of colors on the leaves in the woods, remembering the fresh, crisp air, I knew exactly where I was. The Forest Coven.

A throat cleared. I whipped my head around, taking in a group of six Chosen, and Grey, standing with his hands clasped behind him as he smirked at me. Eyeing Kirsi, I walked to her side, and she reached for my hand in silence as we waited for the final Chosen to join us.

Onyx. He approached, taking the space between Breya and Zennik in front of us. Breya swayed on her feet slightly and Onyx shoved her to the ground, her silky red hair covering her face as she moaned.

I rushed forward to help her up, staring at Grey, daring him with a look to do something to Onyx for being such an ass. Instead, he shrugged and walked down the line, counting us. Satisfied we were all there, he moved back to the front of the group.

"You'll notice we skipped breakfast this morning, though I doubt many of you felt up to it anyway. You've all been poisoned. Welcome to your first Trial."

"No shit," Nym said from the other side of Kir, Talon full-size at her heel.

Grey's dimple showed as he tried and failed to hide his obnoxious smile. "You're to find a remedy as quickly as possible here within the Forest Coven lands. Take heed, everything you need has been carefully placed at your disposal, though some items may be limited. Once you've taken the remedy and are confident it's the right one, you're to come back to this spot with a list of the ingredients you used. The first to arrive will earn eight points. The second seven and so on down the line. The winner will also receive a hefty advantage in the second

Trial. If you're last, you will start the next trial with a punishment. Begin."

There was no hesitation. The moment we were dismissed, the Chosen all started to run.

"How bad are your symptoms?" Kirsi asked as she, Nym, and I left the group behind.

"Not bad. A headache and sour stomach. Manageable," I answered.

"Mine are similar," Nym added, keeping pace as we moved, two great felines chasing closely behind us.

"What's the poison, Rave?" Kir gestured to the side, pointing out a slightly worn path in the grass leading toward a tree line and we shifted directions.

"I—I don't know. I need a minute to ..."

"We don't have a minute. It's getting worse. And I can't use my healing spell, that only speeds it up," Kirsi said.

"Right. Of course, it does." I pulled them to a stop, looking over my shoulder for any signs of the others as I shuffled through a list of poisons in my mind. Seconds felt like hours as I checked options off until it came to me. "It's snakeroot. They must have fed it to the chickens we had for dinner. We can't use magic to heal it."

I began to pace back and forth, remembering everything I could about the dangerous poison. My eyes doubled in size as I froze, staring at Kirsi.

"Don't look at me like that, just say it."

"It's deadly. If someone ingests too much and doesn't get the anti-dote in time, they could die."

She pulled her long hair back, revealing a sheen of sweat on her forehead. Tying it into a knot, she scowled at me. "Not helping."

"Agreed," Nym added, gripping her stomach.

"We're going to need river water, slug's grass." I pinched the bridge of my nose as I wished we could go to the shop. We'd have everything there. "Nine candles, all black but one, and a ram's horn."

"He picked a difficult remedy. Naturally." Kir turned toward the mountains. "Should we split up? Each take an ingredient to find?"

"Yes and no. You should stay together and use your familiars to hunt a ram while keeping an eye out for slug's grass and river water.

I'll stick to this path and try to find the candles and look for the grass also."

"Be careful," Kir warned. "You have no idea what's in these woods or if the Forest Coven will harm you. And if not them, surely the other Chosen."

I waved my hand over my body and a jolt of power crackled under my skin. "I'll be silent."

Satisfied, they turned and ran together toward the mountain, markings already glowing. I rushed off into the dense forest, sticking to the path as much as possible as I searched the ground for slug's grass. As Grey had said, all the items we needed were here, but how difficult the king made them to find was a wholly different story. If we all died, it would end the headache for him.

I pushed away a wave of nausea, gritting my teeth in response as I gripped the trunk of a tree. I couldn't get distracted. The reaction to the poison would only get worse. Candles. We needed candles. I doubted I'd have enough time to make nine candles out of beeswax before we all died. We were going to have to find the Forest Coven witches.

Following the trail, my footsteps silent as I moved, I ignored the needlepoint pain in my head. These witches lived scattered through their beloved territory. Aside from the tour, I'd been here one other time. A winter solstice. The place had been covered in snow and ice back then, and I mostly remembered sliding and falling over a lot. I couldn't have been older than four. Thankfully, this terrain was far less treacherous.

Listening to the birds' caws and the leaves rustling in a slight breeze, I hurried down the path. Keeping my ear open for a river, I nearly moved off the trail, but a plume of smoke caught my attention. Slowly approaching a small cottage, overgrown with moss and smelling of rotten straw bales, I swung the small iron gate open, flinching at the squeal of metal against metal.

A trail of planted stones led to the rounded front door of the adorable lodge. Removing the cloaking spell from below my feet, I turned back to the path. Surely Kirsi would be along soon with Nym, unless they ran into trouble. They'd know I stopped at the cottage.

Even still, I cast a spell near the gate that would make Kirsi think of me as she walked by. It was the best I could do without raising an alarm to the owner.

I knocked three times and waited, rubbing my hands together. With no answer, I knocked once more and on the third rap, the door inched open.

"Hello?" I leaned in to peek around the door.

The only light inside came from the dust-caked windows and the fireplace. The walls were covered in cobwebs and dried flowers. The smell, like swamp water, was hardly better.

"You're quick." A croaky voice came from behind me, and I spun so swiftly, traces filled my vision, a side effect of the poison, no doubt.

An old woman stood on the path I'd come from with long gray hair and several crooked yellow teeth stared up at me from the shadows of the patchwork cloak she wore.

"My name is Raven. I need assistance."

"Surname, girl. What is it?"

I smiled beyond the pain in my stomach. "Please. If you could hear —"

She pushed past me and up the steps to her home. "I know why you're here. This is the only cottage along the trail from where your Trial started. You're the first, but won't be the last. If you want help from me, you'll start by giving me your full name, or this conversation is over."

"Raven Moonstone."

She smiled a wicked grin, each of her crooked teeth showing in the dim light. "Ah, Moonstone. I knew your grandmother well. Talented old witch."

"She was. Until the Dark King—" I paused, realizing she was working with the king. She'd expected my arrival. "Until he changed everything."

"I cannot offer you the knowledge of your poison or the list of ingredients."

"I know what it is. And the ingredients. I need the candles for the antidote. I think I can forage everything else."

"You are your grandmother's kin …" The woman pressed the tips of her fingers together and only then did regret creep up on me. "Everything comes with a price, you know?"

She pushed the door all the way open and beckoned for me to follow.

The cottage was small, but sitting upon the small table beside an empty teapot and a few dusty glasses, was a collection of black and white candles. The old witch crossed her small house and sat on a chair at her little table, pulling a hand-woven blanket from behind her and spreading it across her lap for warmth.

"We weren't allowed to bring anything but a satchel. I'm afraid I don't have anything to trade."

She lifted a candle from the table and pressed her dirty fingernail into the soft wax below the wick. "Value can be found in more than physical things. Knowledge can be exceedingly powerful. I happen to believe you have something quite valuable indeed."

My ears began to ring, and I wasn't sure if it was the poison or the concern for what she might ask for.

"The recipe to your grandmother's Fountain of Youth elixir will do, Raven Moonstone."

I shook my head, stepping backward. I couldn't. Wouldn't. Kirsi and I had spent our first year running Crescent Cottage convincing all my grandmother's patrons we didn't know how to make her elixirs. I'd witnessed my grandmother a thousand times, slaving over her cauldron late at night, creating the complicated serum. She'd leave for weeks at a time to collect the ingredients needed from all seven territories. Neither of us wanted the responsibility, and there was also a blood sacrifice to be made with each batch. We'd secretly decided we wouldn't condone it. Blood magic was as dangerous as it was rare.

"Do you think you're the only one who will come knocking at my door for candles?" She leaned over my shoulder, looking out of the dusty window. "It is a race, but beware, your life is still at stake. Time's nearly up, girl."

"Okay, okay. But only if you'll make a binding promise with me. You can use the elixir for yourself, but you can never share my grandmother's recipe."

That same wicked smile from before slathered across her face as she rose, reaching out an arm and clasping mine. "I bind your will to my actions. I will not share the recipe you give."

I looked over my shoulder again in time to see Onyx's crown of dark hair. The sight made me worry for Kirsi and Nym. He was running down the same trail I'd taken through the forest. I had clearly underestimated him. Searching my mind for the recipe, I debated if I should have stolen the candles from the witch and run. It would have been faster, and far less costly.

"Blood of the lamb raised in the hills of Moss Coven. Thrice spoken the name, a powerful moon witch must twice pierce the heart under the peak of the moon's gaze on the sacrificial stone in the center of Gravana lake. Black of stone, freely given in the Fire coven, a vial of water from a moving stream traveling backward from the sea. Tail feather of the phoenix, freely given from the highest floating aisle of the Whisper coven's territory."

I bit my lip trying to remember the rest.

She flourished her hand through the air, slamming the door shut as she gestured me on. "Hurry girl, the boy waits."

"Come out, witch. I have need of you!" Onyx yelled, banging on the door.

"Troll's toe weeds from here, dipped in the waters of the Storm Coven when the moon bleeds red. Each item is to be boiled in a cauldron for seven nights, from dusk until dawn, stirred without stopping. It's to be poured in an obsidian vial and buried beneath the earth's surface for no shorter time than one moon's cycle."

"Hm," she said, weighing my words. "You wouldn't be giving me the wrong recipe now, would you?"

"I wish I had," I mumbled.

Onyx banged again on the door, this time hard enough to rattle the old walls while he continued his demands from the porch. The dust seeping from the cracks of the cottage caught in the faint light leaking from the window.

The witch held eight black and one white candle out for me. "Pleasure doing business with you, Raven Moonstone. I wish you well."

Stuffing the loot into my satchel, I turned in time for the door to fly off its rusted hinges, landing in a heap on the floor, dust spreading in the dappled sunlight. Onyx burst into the room, the dagger in his hand catching a glint of light as he made his way toward the old woman.

I cast a spell, sending the dagger flying. "What on Earth are you playing at Onyx? There's no need for weapons."

"Not all compasses are driven by morality, child," the old witch said as the markings on her body began to glow.

Before she could utter a word, he charged forward, shoving me to the side. With a swipe of her hand, she cast all the remaining candles into the fire, looking in my direction to mouth the word: run.

But I couldn't do it. I couldn't leave her to his mercy for a batch of candles. Something reckless in me sparked to life as I screamed, "Onyx! You're here for candles and I've got the only ones left."

His fist, mid-air as he made to hit the old witch, paused long enough for her to cast a spell, sending him flying across the cottage, his back crashing into the hutch.

I didn't wait to see what he would do next. I tore out of her little hut, hoping he would follow and leave the witch behind. She may not have deserved my grandmother's elixir, but she didn't deserve to die either. Though it was Onyx's clear intention.

At first, I didn't think he'd come, but within minutes of running through the trees, I could hear his pounding footsteps behind me. I had to think, and think fast, but the hammering in my head was getting louder and my fingers were starting to go numb. The poison's grip on my body was worsening.

I darted behind a tree, hoping he would run past. But the moment Onyx's black cloak whipped by, he turned. I didn't want to do this. I really didn't. But what choice had he given me? I swiped my hand through the air, lifting him from the ground. He struck back fast, sending me crashing into a tree. Breath whisking from my lungs, I lay stunned. Giving him enough time to stomp over, grabbing me from the ground and lifting me by the neck.

"I should kill you and be done with it," he seethed, black hair falling into his face.

My body stilled as I realized he meant those words. He would kill me.

The trees began to shake around us, the ground rumbling as I struggled in the witch's grip. His eyes held mine alone as his breaths quickened. Searching for the strength to take a life. To tighten his fingers on my throat and deprive me of air.

His hesitation was all I needed to kick him as hard as I could in the crotch, break away and cast a spell to send him high into the air, his life in my hands. His exposed arms were covered in markings. He had to have had a plethora of spells, yet he didn't move, didn't cast as his gaze slowly lifted beyond me. His golden eyes doubled in size.

"I need those candles," Onyx breathed behind clenched teeth. A single hand gesture and the satchel began to lift from my shoulder, though he didn't look away from whatever was behind me.

I tangled my arm in the leather, fighting against his magical pull as I turned, facing down a hoard of trolls towering over us. A single troll was one thing, but a hoard of ten was quite another.

"Someone causing you trouble, Ms. Raven?" a voice called from the back of their group.

I knew I was a fool to turn my back on Onyx. A laceration from a knife sliced up my arm. I hissed at the slight pain. Deep enough to sting and bleed as the bag continued to be pulled away. I'd forgotten he was marked with a spell binding his knife to him, and now blood poured down my arm.

"Yetu?" My lips, still numb from the poison, could barely manage the name.

The troll pushed forward as I held my arm to my chest, blood cascading down my body. Everything mixed with the headache and nausea threatened to take me down as the troll I'd treated in my shop from time to time took a knee before me.

"Tell me what you need, Raven Moonstone, and it shall be done."

"Don't kill him," I said as my grip on the satchel loosened. "Find … a way to make him stop, please."

Gesturing forward, my magical hold on Onyx released and he dropped to the ground in a heap.

"You heard her, brothers. Bind his arms or he will cast against us."

In his fall, Onyx lost his concentration, and his spell was broken. But now I held the only candles available for the antidote and there were six other witches who would need them. And they would come. I'd underestimated the dangers within the Trials. Why worry about the king killing us when we'd kill each other?

"What are you doing here?" Yetu asked as he helped me up.

"The Moon Coven's leader was murdered and I'm competing to take her place. There's a witch in a cottage nearby and I'm afraid of what he might have done to her."

"It's not our place to interfere with the witches," another of the trolls said, placing his giant hand on Yetu's shoulder. "We've done our part, let's be on our way."

Yetu shook his head, the messy hair flopping into his eyes. "It is my job. This here's Raven Moonstone. She's the only witch I know that'd save the likes of us. She deserves the same."

"I've no doubts, brother," he looked over his shoulder up the path, "but others are coming, and we can't fight a full coven. "Bring your friend if you wish, but we need to go."

"Come." Yetu held out his oversized hand.

Reaching for him, the world spun below me, my knees falling weak.

"Woah, witch," he said, grabbing firmly onto my injured arm. "Let me help you."

"Kirsi's here with me, Yetu. We've been poisoned. I need to find her." Darkness filled the edges of my vision as I looked down and the world spun.

He pushed me toward the other troll who had spoken. "Take her down to the cave by the river. I'll be right behind you."

"Thank you, Yetu," I tried to say, but it came out as a jumbled mess of tongue and teeth as the world around me faded to black.

15

Harsh whispers of words I couldn't connect filled my unconscious mind as I tried over and over to pull myself back to reality. Poison mixed with the blood loss had weakened me before darkness had called; caressed me as I'd fallen into oblivion and even now, though I fought against it, something here comforted me.

"Raven?"

The voice was smoky and deep. Slow and coarse. My unconscious mind shifted into the direction of the voice calling me. Lured me. But it felt as it had before. Wrong. Dangerous. The same as the woods before I was attacked.

My body began to shake. I gasped, lurching forward as if a bucket of water had been dumped over me, yanking me from the world of oblivion and right into Kirsi's arms.

She cried my name as she hugged me close. "I'm so sorry I left you. I should have stayed. I'm so sorry."

I shook my head, but the pounding was worse than before as if it echoed off the walls of the cave we were in. The sound of trickling water cascading nearby brought attention to my dry mouth.

"My ... mouth ... fingers ... numb ... water."

She nodded her understanding and turned to one of the trolls. "She needs something to drink."

"She needs more than that," Yetu said, stooped over, the ceiling far too low for him to stand comfortably. "Found these two hiding in trees." He tilted his head toward Nym. "That one tried to kill me."

"Still not sorry," she said, crossing her arms over her chest as she kept her eyes on the exit.

"She doesn't mean that," Kirsi assured him, hiding her smile before she turned to me. Gaunt eyes and sweaty skin drew my attention more than her words. She was more sick than before. "We were attacked by Willow. Had to hide to keep myself from killing her."

She handed me a makeshift cup of water, bringing it to my lips to help me drink, though her hands trembled.

"We have to go," I managed with a numb tongue. "Ram's horn?"

Kirsi turned to Yetu. "We've all been poisoned. Do you have anything made with ram's horn? I will give you shop credit for the value."

The troll stuck his hands in his pockets, shaking his head, but another stepped forward, pulling a horn from the necklace he wore.

"Makes for a good mug on the road," he said. "S'yers if ya want it. For helping with Yetu's hands n' such."

I thanked them generously and performed the healing spell on Yetu once more before we left, then the three of us leaned on each other for strength as we left the trolls behind.

"Slug's grass," I said, pointing to the riverbed.

"I've got it." Nym dropped to her knees ripping at the grass.

"The roots. We need the roots," Kirsi corrected her.

A flash of red from the line of trees in the distance had us lumped together, all back-to-back as we searched, waiting for another attack.

"There's a hoard of trolls who will hear us scream and come to our aid!" Nym shouted.

"Or me. I'll kick your ass, Willow. Don't think I won't." Kir followed, lowering her voice before saying, "You're going to have to do it here, Rave. The longer this shit continues, the worse it's going to get."

Dropping to my knees, I dug the candles into a circle on the ground as Nym and Kirsi stood watch. I needed them to stay upright long enough to make the remedy. "Roots," I mumbled the word getting caught on my swelling tongue.

Nym dropped the long brown grass into my hands as she raised hers into the air. The marking on her forehead began to glow and she called forth her magic.

"Wait. Wait. Please," someone called, stumbling forward from the trees. Breya.

"Please. I don't have a team and I don't know the poison. Please help me."

Nym dropped her hands, looking at Kirsi who turned to me. "We aren't assholes, right? Team decision here. Breya's not a threat?"

I nodded, wiping the sweat beading on my forehead away.

"Agreed." Nym said, lowering her arms. "There's no use for dead witches."

Breya approached slowly; the rip in her pants from Onyx's shove nothing compared to the cut on her forehead.

"Pull anything sneaky and I'll gut you." Kirsi turned back to watch the tree line. "Hurry Rave, I'm over this shit."

I continued to dig the candles into the ground. Breya fell to my side to help, keeping the white one to the north end of the circle. Lighting them in the proper order was the trick to the antidote, but the problem was, my head was pounding, causing me to question everything, and the blur on my vision was worsening.

I managed eventually and burned the slug's grass in the third candle, collecting the ashes into water. The antidote needed time we didn't have but we had to wait for the white candle to melt down far enough. Seconds turned into minutes as time passed.

"Time's up, Rave. We need to go," Kirsi said, raising her arms again as she continued to study the tree line, Scoop and Talon both full size and pacing along an invisible barrier.

Willow had cast on Scoop for one reason only. To make sure she could. And now that she knew it was possible, Kir wouldn't take any chances. She'd kill her long before Willow could take out her familiar.

"More," I answered, but it was nearly unintelligible.

"No more. Do it now," Nym cried, casting a spell that sent a snake slithering from her hands into the forest where a battle cry had rung free.

I glanced to see Onyx coming toward us, palms raised. Time was up. I lifted the candle, pouring white wax over the top of the horn, as I used my amplifying spell to hurry the process along.

"Stay back," Kirsi warned.

"It's just a game, Kirsi." Onyx's sing-song voice made my heart pound. "You're taking this too seriously."

I heard him fall to a knee as I took the mixture of wax and ash from the horn, pouring it into my hands and rubbing it into a smooth wax ball.

"Sky above us, earth below, healing waters, I invoke thee."

I spoke the words over and over again until I was sure it was ready. Breaking off a piece of the antidote, I shoved the doughy texture into my mouth, pushing past the horrible taste as I swallowed. My vision cleared almost immediately.

"Here." I broke off pieces for the others, putting the last of the ball into my satchel.

Breya sobbed as she swallowed the antidote, and I knew then that saving her had been a mercy, but she likely wouldn't last much longer in the Trials if she was left to her own. She'd need our help. And maybe someday we would need hers.

"Please," Onyx begged.

Nym's magical snake rose from the grass before Onyx, causing him to fall backward. We used that window to run. Every second, every step was a rejuvenation from the earth. The antidote healing each of us. As the clearing came into sight, I wondered about Ophelia and Zennik. If the old witch had destroyed the other candles, were they able to find others? I'd left all the ingredients behind at the river. A wise witch might have sat back, watching us, waiting to take the items for themselves. Perhaps I was foolish to leave them behind. Or merciful.

I thought it was Grey waiting in the clearing, until we got closer, until dark hair and hidden wings became clearer. I faltered my run, breath finally stinging my lungs as the adrenaline crashed. He was alone. We were the first ones back.

"Go first," Kirsi said, only loud enough for the group of us to hear. "Raven, this was your win, your antidote. Go first."

The others slowed their run, agreeing. I didn't want to. I would have argued. Had those silver eyes of his not pulled me forward, though my heart leapt into my throat as flashes of his hands on my face, my neck, came to mind. I stopped before him, curtseying, though it felt odd in pants.

"Eight points, Ms. Moonstone." His cold voice matched the glare in his eyes and the tick in his jaw at my presence. "And a five-minute head start for the next Trial."

I said nothing, moving away from him as I watched him bestow his award of points among the rest of my party.

Breya came to stand next to me and placed her hand into mine. "Thank you, Raven. Thank you," was all she said as she faced forward, staring into the line of trees.

Then we waited. And waited. And waited. Until I could feel the cool kiss of the moon on my neck. Willow was the fifth back, only minutes after us, looking no worse for wear. Onyx came strolling up in sixth place, the smug look on his face a deep contrast to the begging he'd been doing when we saw him last. The king remained steadfast in his cold stance. Saying nothing more than point totals as the witches arrived.

My feet ached and the looming autumn solstice kept a sharp chill in the air. Still, we remained silent, watching and waiting as if we hadn't each just battled each other. As if the core of who we were, Moon Coven witches, meant nothing when the Trial began.

I thought I knew. Thought this would be more about personal challenges than anything else. I was wrong. A lump grew in my throat and tears pooled in my eyes. I could not let them see me cry, could not let them see how weak I truly was. Because the Trials were not a game. They were dangerous. And if they continued the way they'd started, the real winner would only be the king that hated us all.

Swallowing, I felt a tear move down my cheek. Knowing I couldn't wipe it away without them knowing, I let it dry to my skin. Its trail a cool reminder that I was still good. I was still a compassionate person.

The leaves rustled; the tops of the trees swayed. All attention fell to

Yetu, the troll that stepped from the clearing carrying the limp body of the final Moon Coven witch. Old Ophelia with her cloak billowing beneath her as he moved.

I knew he lived in the mountains of the Forest Coven lands. I thought when I'd seen him it was purely coincidence. But as he lay the hardly breathing body of the final witch at the feet of the Dark King, I wondered whether it was, in fact, not a coincidence at all.

"One point," the king said, his voice as cold as before.

"Yes, Lord King," Yetu said, bowing, before he turned and disappeared back into the forest.

The king cast a spell and a door appeared before us. My jaw slackened. It was *his* magic that had created them. His magic that crafted such beautiful artwork.

"Dinner will be served to your rooms. Go back to the castle." He stepped back, his wings spreading like that of a soaring eagle, as each of the Chosen entered the doorway and disappeared, from last to arrive to first, apart from the woman still laying on the ground.

"And her?" I asked when all the others were gone. "Will you leave her there to die?"

His wings dropped as he placed his hands into his pockets, pushing back the hilt of dagger strapped to his belt, staring at me as if I'd offended him simply by speaking.

"That woman is your subject," I continued. "She's here to perform in the Trials for our coven and you would let her die?"

"She knew what she signed up for, as did the rest of you." He moved in, invading my space as he so loved to do. "Did you think this was a game, Ms. Moonstone?"

My nostrils flared and hatred so pure and raw moved over my body. "You are no king. You are no man. You are simply a crowned thief with far too much power." I kneeled beside the woman and pulled the remaining antidote from my satchel. "I would have saved them all."

My skin turned ice cold, tingling as the shock of my words registered. What right did I have to speak to him like that? Why hadn't I held my tongue?

Shoving the antidote into the old woman's mouth, I pinched her nose until she swallowed, then gasped for breath. Refusing to acknowledge the king again, afraid of what I might say, I lifted her from the ground. It wasn't graceful, but well enough to walk through the door and leave the king to his own construed misery.

Or so I thought. Until I nearly tripped over the dead body in the hallway of the Dark King's castle.

16

Six pairs of eyes stared back at me as I crossed the magical threshold and stepped into the castle with an unconscious old witch in my arms, avoiding the slain person lying in a pool of blood. Kirsi and Nym helped me with Ophelia as my stomach twisted at the dagger, black as night, protruding from the man's back.

"What happened?" I asked.

Willow shrugged and Breya shook her head as the Dark King stepped through the threshold.

He looked down to the body and then up to us with a half-smile on his face as he drew in the horror on ours. "Something wrong?"

No one dared speak.

The Dark King stepped over the man on the floor and placed his hand on Ophelia. To my utter shock and dismay, his shadows, cool on my arms, surrounded her until she vanished.

"Go back to your rooms," he barked. When no one moved, he spun on his heel, his wings skimming the walls of the hallway. "Now!"

Breaking the trance, the witches jumped and then ran to their respective rooms. I was no exception. Hustling down the dark corridor, I found my room at the very end of the hall, ripped the door open and hid within. But it didn't feel safe. Not from him. Not from the

Chosen. Not at all. He'd made it clear he did what he pleased regardless of morality and somehow, I hated him more now than when I hadn't known him at all.

I padded through my rooms, afraid to even remove the boots from my feet in case I needed to run. I thought of Nikos then. Testing my heart to see if I missed him at all. He was mostly kind and safe, but there was no passion with Nikos. No fire. 'Only a fool would be tempted by fire,' he'd said . . . Only a fool.

I wanted my home. But part of home was already here. Gripping the sconce of the secret door, I pulled it open and stepped into Kirsi's sitting room, but it was empty. Her bedroom door was closed. Placing my hand on the cool doorknob, I let myself in.

She was pacing the floor as her familiar often did, biting the tip of her thumb, and I could nearly see the wheels of her brilliant mind turning. But as her face darkened, her eyes moved over to me and she shook her head without a word.

"I know what you're thinking," I soothed. "But you have to stop."

"We're going to have to kill each other. You realize that, right? This isn't going to be a game of skill and ingenuity; this is going to come down to the last one standing."

"Today could have been different, Kir. Willow and Onyx *chose* to turn on us. If we would have worked together, everyone could have been saved. I hate to say this, given our return, but the Trial outcome was what *we* made it. Just like my grandmother and the other coven leaders said."

She threw her hands in the air. "So what? We endure this near-death shit until one of us gets brave enough to take out Onyx and Willow? Is that how it's going to go?"

"I don't know. Maybe. But if it has to happen, we do it together. We live, no matter what."

"Swear it," she said, turning to stand before me. "Swear that you will not sacrifice yourself to save anyone in these Trials."

"I swear I won't sacrifice myself to save our enemies. That's as much as you're going to get from me."

This was not Kirsi. She was strong and resilient. She could not be broken. But as I looked into her face, the turmoil in her eyes, her ragged breath, I knew if she could be broken, this would be how it happened.

"I'll take that for now. But I'll kick your ass if you do something reckless, Raven. Don't think I won't."

"Deal."

I stayed in her rooms that night for as long as I thought safe, but afraid to be caught by her maids and still unsure whether the door was actually allowed or meant to be a secret that could be taken away, I snuck out eventually. Changing out of the clothes that I never wanted to look at again, I stared at myself in the long mirror, wondering if the woman that stared back would ever be strong enough to murder. When a dark and dangerous presence appeared behind me, silver eyes locking with my blue, I didn't bother turning around.

"Get out," I said with more callousness than I'd ever spoken in my life.

He ran his fingers over his shallow beard before chuckling low and slow. "You forget yourself, witch."

"If you want to kill me, King, get it over with. I'm tired of these games already."

He vanished and appeared between me and the mirror in an instant, towering as he stared. I clenched my jaw so tight I thought my teeth might crack from the pressure alone. He leaned in close. I stepped backward. He followed. I stepped again until I collided with the bed and fell onto it. To my utter dismay, his eyes lit with delight.

"Don't even think about it."

He tilted his head, those eyes piercing my own as the shadow of a smile crossed his face. "Think about what?"

Heat rose from my neck onto my cheeks as I whispered words that felt like they'd been dragged from my lips. "Touching me."

His shadows reacted, scattering along the floor, though he remained the picture of calm and collected, his tongue moving across his bottom lip. "I wouldn't dare."

I stood, taking one firm step. "Oh, but you would. You have." I didn't mention I could still feel his lingering touch. Didn't mention the way it stirred something I preferred to be left dormant within me. What kind of woman sought the touch of a murderer?

"Only when you've disobeyed, Raven." He stepped away, crossing the room to sit in the only chair, relaxed with his arm draped casually down the armrests, wings gone.

"What do you want from me?"

"I think you know." Dipping his chin lower, he looked at me beneath his drawn brow.

Mouth falling open, I blinked slowly at him. "I am not available."

A corner of his mouth lifted, though he kept his chin tucked. "I can assure you, Ms. Moonstone, *that* is not what I meant."

"Then elaborate."

He shifted forward, elbows to knees as he held his hands together, looking up at me. "I want to know why your spells are hidden."

"Get in line." I crossed my arms. "I'm not here to amuse you or become some kind of obsession."

He moved so fast I hardly saw the action. One moment he was in the chair, the next he was behind me, lifting my curls away to whisper into my ear. "On the contrary my dear, you *are* here for my amusement. You are here for my pleasure. You are here for anything I request of you, because unless I say otherwise, there is no escape. Trials or not."

I shuddered at the way his words lifted something in my body. At the way my legs trembled with the vibrato of his deep voice. The way those shadows called to me, lured me, intrigued me as much as I did him. He reached his arm around me, gripping my throat and pulling until my back was against his chest, his pinky resting on my collarbone as his breath fell on my ear. I should have been terrified. Should have pushed away from him and run, but I was frozen, breath halted as I waited for him to say something, do something. The small bit of heat grew until every part of my sensitive body was swollen with a desire that had begun the moment I'd walked through his magical barrier that night on Gravana Lake. His hefty power drawing on mine.

"There is more to me than the monster you have imagined."

"I am quite sure you wish that to be true," I said, far more breathless than I wanted.

He chuckled again, his chest vibrating against my back. "You know nothing."

That thing within me roared to life at his audacity. I spun, placing my hands on his chest to push him away, but he grabbed my wrists and held me there. "You're angry with me. After I gave you a door to your friend, you're mad."

Eyes doubling in size, I shoved him as hard as I could, all desire and passion and fear of him gone. "Of course, I'm angry with you. I've spent the majority of my life angry with you. As most of the witches have. The Thrashings? Letting the witches starve? Stealing the Grimoires? Any of this sound familiar to you? One time my very own father narrowly missed one of your scattered massacres. You left a pile of bodies to rot in the Storm Coven territory when I was sixteen."

He'd barely moved when I pressed into him, his muscular build far greater than mine. I considered casting a spell on him, something to send him a message. But I knew, among all things, that would be crossing a line I couldn't come back from.

He put his hands in his pockets as he began to pace back and forth in front of me. "I am not in a position to explain myself to anyone," he said, his shadows growing from the ground, rolling under him. "But I feel intrigued by you, Ms. Moonstone. No markings on your body, though I can feel the magic within you. You are kind to others, yet you're brave enough to not only speak but openly disagree with me. You're a woman that will stand beside a friend, consequences be damned. You'll save a stranger, yet chastise a king you hate. You are a puzzle. Tell me about my greatest offense toward you."

"How does one rank the murder of loved ones?" I answered through gritted teeth. "How does one put a level of heartache on family lost and treasures stolen? How does one decide if nearly losing their own life is worse than watching their grandmother's taken?"

My voice broke on the last word I spoke as tears filled my vision. Angry tears that burned like venom. Sad tears, a myriad of emotions bubbled to the surface as I stared at a man so full of hatred, he likely could not see his own reflection through it.

His shadows pooled below him, cascading over the floor in waves of smoke as I spoke the words. The draw to step into them, to let them consume me took over as I stood there. And then it hit me. The familiarity of that pull. "It was you, wasn't it? In the woods that day after Tasa's funeral. The draw I felt. You were there. The witch's sickness they call it. It's not real. It's you. You tried to kill me."

He looked stricken as his face filled with rage. His calm, steady demeanor changed, grew into something roaring with callous and contempt. "I did not pull you into the woods. But I was there. Watching." He rubbed his thumb across his lips in an effort to calm himself. It didn't work. "Whatever conclusions you've drawn of me, know this. You. Are. Wrong. That final wave of magic you felt, the one that saved your God damn life? You're welcome." Wrapping his wings around himself, he vanished.

He'd lied, of course. What reason would he have to do anything more than that? Murderer. Thief. Liar was just another title for his long list of crimes against witches.

"IT'S TIME TO WAKE, LADY." TAVIA'S VOICE WAS SOFT, THOUGH WEARY.

I sat up, rubbing my eyes as I took in the dark circles under hers. As if she hadn't slept. The red an indication that she'd been crying, though she hid everything behind a forced smile. I wanted to ask. Wanted to care. But she worked for him. Chose to be here. I would not pry into her burdens.

"Where am I to go today?" I asked, my voice neutral.

She turned her back to me, but I didn't miss the tissue she dabbed at her eyes. "Simply breakfast for now, my lady. A bath and breakfast."

"Am I able to take it in my rooms?"

She shook her head. "I'm sorry. The king has demanded everyone's presence."

"Of course, he has."

The dress she put me in was simple enough, with billowing sleeves and lace embellishments. The pampering had been kept to a minimum, leaving my hair down in organized curls with a few small braids and twists at the top. I appreciated the simple. Needed it more today than I'd known.

As much as I wanted to skip breakfast, I realized I hadn't eaten anything yesterday and, while poison and a dead body would probably do that to a person, it didn't help the way my stomach groaned.

Kirsi sat between Nym and I toward the end of the table. You'd never know she'd nearly broken last night as she sat with a happy smile, whispering back and forth with Nym, smitten as ever.

Grey stood casually in a corner, that familiar light in his eyes gone as he stared straight ahead, very much the solemn soldier and not the bantering smartass we'd seen of him on previous days.

I traced the intricate pattern on the silverware as we waited for the king to join us so that we might eat. I didn't want to see him at all, but then I didn't think anyone did. Especially not the witch that sat across from me. Old Ophelia. Slightly more gaunt than usual, but otherwise, unscathed. She was alive and, after the king's display yesterday, that was a blessing for her.

The king's kitchen staff filled the room with dozens of covered golden trays. Lining the tables with all the dishes felt too much like a celebration after yesterday. My eyes flashed to Onyx who whispered into Willow's ear. She looked uninterested, but listened.

I nudged Kir with my knee and jutted my chin toward them. "The more those two scheme, the more dangerous the next Trial could be, and that's going to be a problem."

She nodded, but didn't say anything else. It was clear the other contestants were sizing each other up far more now than they had two days ago. The tone of the trials had been set. I watched the Chosen carefully, remembering everything I could about each of them. Spells I'd witnessed, stories I'd heard of them from our coven. Anything from our childhood was now relevant because, like it or not, my life depended on it.

My eyes flicked to the banner I'd been avoiding. The one on the wall with each of our names and current point totals. My name graced the top of the list with eight points, followed by my companions. If I hadn't had a target on my back the day I'd challenged him to acknowledge me, I certainly did now. Why had I stared down the face of a lion and had no fear?

The king swept into the room, taking his seat at the head of the table. He waved his hand through the air and all the lids on the dishes vanished. I wondered if he'd invite Grey to come sit at one of the empty seats at the long table, but he didn't.

"Eat," he said by way of greeting as he sat back in his chair, glaring at the lot of us.

Some filled their plates to brimming, some picked warily. As I sat on my hands and stared at a painting on the wall, I could feel his glare on me as thoroughly as if it were his hands.

"Something wrong with your breakfast, Mr. Moonfall?"

Zennik, the witch with one green eye and one blue, shook his head. "No, Your Grace."

I thought of everything I knew of him, ignoring the conversation as he began to fill his plate with sausage and fruit. Zennik's sense of humor had been keen when we were children, but he had always been mischievous. He'd carried a spider around with him for a whole year, pretending he was spirit blessed, so Kirsi would talk to him. It was only when the spider bit him, putting him in a bed for a week, did he confess it'd been a ploy to try to be with her.

"Ms. Moonstone?"

I took a deep, steadying breath as I realized I'd shut out the room, and whatever the king had said to me, I hadn't heard.

"He asked if you're avoiding his cook's food," Kirsi whispered, so quietly I could barely hear.

I'd decided that I would back off from engaging with the Dark King. Whatever game he meant to play with us, I would not stand out of line. I wouldn't point out that the last time we'd eaten in the room he'd poisoned us all. The rest of the witches were right to fear him and I needed to fall in line.

"No, Your Grace." I reached to the nearest tray and selected a piece of chilled fruit.

He didn't answer and I didn't look his way the rest of the silent meal. I took two slices of buttered toast and three strawberries. I'd eaten. If only just. And that was enough for now.

We were dismissed back to our rooms without any insight on the man we'd found dead in the castle the night before. It was clearly none of our business even though his markings identified him as a witch. The guards seemed to double in number, several of them brawny enough to be full blooded shifters, marching up and down the hallways until the ambiance of the castle was drowning in shifted metal and heavy boots on marble floor.

Kirsi was already waiting for me when I entered my rooms. I considered telling her about the king's visits, but it was possible he was visiting all the contestants. And surely whatever interest he'd had in me vanished after last night. Instead, I went straight to battle mode.

"We need to go down the list of Chosen and share everything we know of all of them."

"We can start with Onyx," she said, nodding. "He's going to be ruthless. We can't underestimate him, nor expect him to do anything with honor."

"He had a knife in the last trial, even though we were only supposed to have our satchels. It's spelled to him with some kind of magic, so we'll have to be careful. It's a permanent loophole. He can also draw things to him with a spell because he was trying to take my satchel, and he blasted down a cottage door."

"And how did your arm get cut?"

I sat down on the chaise across from her, pouring us both a lavender tea. "Well, he's got a spell that can slice you, so watch him." I pulled my long lace sleeve up, showing her the cut from yesterday. "It wasn't deep nor terribly painful, but I imagine if he got any more powerful, he'd be able to use it like my grandmother could. And it caused enough blood loss with the poison to knock me out."

"It was hard to tell as we were running yesterday, but Willow might be working with Ophelia. Willow can't control the wind and Nym and I both fell, trying to fight against it. It was so strong yesterday it was hard to run through."

"That leaves us with Breya, Zennik and Nym."

"I'm fairly certain Breya is the weakest link. She's not above begging for help, and she's nice enough. But we could have turned on her in an instant yesterday."

"I don't think anyone here is weak, Kir. We're all foolish. And fools will be reckless when they have to be."

"Speaking of fools." Kirsi set her tea down and leaned back against the couch, clasping her hands. "I need to know what's going on, Rave. Why did we get a secret door between our rooms? And don't tell me it's always been there because I saw the outline appear. Scoop stared at it for nearly an hour."

I shook my head. "I don't know."

"Bullshit." She stood. "Nym says everyone thinks you and the king know each other. That he's helping you. What am I supposed to say to that? I know you knew the antidote spell and I had your back on that, but why are they saying that?"

"I ... I don't know. Witches talk? But it's not like that."

"What's it like, then? Because something's going on."

I wasn't ready to tell her anything when I didn't feel like there was anything to say. But Kirsi was like a sister to me. There was no competition here. Not when it came to her.

"He's been here."

She narrowed her eyes. "Here, where?"

"Here." I swept my arm forward. "In my rooms. It happened the first night. And again last night."

She stumbled backward. "You're sleeping with the Dark King?"

"No, Kirsi. I swear it on the moon. I'm not. He keeps showing up. But I'm sure last night was the final time." I stood, walking to the fireplace to light it, though the room wasn't cold. I needed to keep my hands busy. "I know how it looks. I know how it sounds. But he just appears. And last night I made him angry enough to leave."

"He's dangerous," she warned, her voice deep and quiet.

"I know that as well as anyone else." I wanted to keep going. To tell her that he didn't scare me anymore. But when I turned, searching for the words to say, she was already gone.

17

Lunch was served on a golden tray, and there it sat by the door, untouched. I was learning I could deal with a lot of things. I could run a shop and balance my overprotective parents. I could go toe to toe with the Dark King when pushed hard enough, but I couldn't fight with Kirsi. I couldn't live a life where she wasn't by my side.

I went to the door and knocked three times, but only silence answered. Eventually, I pushed my way in and found her sitting on her unmade bed, stroking Scoop as she stared off into space.

"I didn't ask for his attention. I've never invited him into my room. I have no control over what he's doing."

She nodded, but didn't look my way.

"What do you want me to say? He's probably pestering everyone. He's doing it to get a reaction. It's not like his visits are pleasant."

"He doesn't visit me," she whispered.

"Well, he's probably afraid of Scoop," I said, lifting the feline from her and settling him into my arms. "I would be."

She sighed. "He is a fearsome beast."

I waited, letting the soothing sound of feline purrs fill the room until I couldn't handle it anymore. "Please don't be mad at me, Kir. We

144

need each other. I'm sorry I didn't tell you about the king. I couldn't process it for myself the first night and I would have told you about it last night, but you were so upset. He was in my rooms after I left yours."

"What if he is visiting everyone else? What if it's only me that he's avoiding?" she asked, picking at the seam of her thick blanket.

"Then I'd say to count your blessings."

She shifted, facing toward me. "What does he do? When he comes to you?"

"Fluffs his feathers and starts arguments with me."

She laughed. "I can't imagine you arguing with ... him. Don't get me wrong, I've always known there was fire in your soul, Rave. But ... he's the Dark King."

I bumped her shoulder with mine. "Underneath that black heart of his, I'm pretty sure he's just an insecure man with small dick syndrome."

"Raven Moonstone! Who *are* you? Can you imagine if he's listening right now?"

My heart skipped a beat in fear for only a moment. "Honestly, I hope he is."

"But thanks for the door," Kirsi said, "Just in case," she whispered.

TAVIA AND CLARISS DIDN'T COME TO DRESS ME FOR DINNER, WHICH I considered a blessing. Dinner arrived the same as lunch, only this time, the boy from the kitchens handed me a note.

"I'm to watch you read it, miss."

I rolled my eyes as slowly as possible, realizing the king must have known I could never deny a child.

Ms. Moonstone,

You will eat, or I will feed you myself. And while that's something I would greatly enjoy, I have a feeling you would not.

Impatiently waiting,

~Bastian

Stamped with his royal seal, there was no doubt it was from the Dark King, but only now did I consider he was a real person who bore an actual name.

"Stalker." I huffed, crumpling the paper and throwing it into the fireplace. I reached for the tea tray and another black note fluttered down from the ceiling, landing atop the handle.

Ms. Moonstone,
  Would stalking be another symptom of small dick syndrome?
  Keeping notes for future reference,
  ~Bastian

I spoke to the fireplace as I tossed the second note inside. "Let's go with yes. And don't you have king stuff to do? Go badger the other Chosen."

A third note dropped from seemingly nowhere. I snagged it from the air and threw it into the fireplace without reading it. Another appeared. I did the same.

"Are you not even a little bit curious about what I have to say to you?"

I felt him behind me, that darkness he commanded, but when I turned, he wasn't there. Instead, another black note was suspended in midair with the words '*Look up*' scrawled in beautiful handwriting.

Unable to resist my curiosity, I tilted my head back in time for a black rose petal to land on my nose. I brushed it away as thousands more rained down from the obsidian ceiling like raindrops.

Guilt hit me as the petals felt like poison on my skin. A direct and pure form of betrayal to all the witches who'd fallen at the hands of this bloodthirsty king. To my grandmother. Tasa. To the man in the hall. To Kirsi, who'd been exactly right when she'd warned me of the danger.

"What happened to that man in the hall?" I asked. "You killed him, didn't you?"

"Yes."

With a swish of my arms the petals flew into the fire. All of them. "I hate you. Don't you get it? I don't want this ... this gesture of kindness with a side of chaos and murder. Leave me alone." Gripping my hands into fists until my nails broke the skin, I screamed. "Send me home. I'm done. I don't want to be here."

He flashed in front of me, angry eyes meeting mine. "You cannot leave. You're here until I decide otherwise."

"You do enjoy the control, don't you?"

"You signed up for this just like everyone else."

"No!" Magic crackled beneath my skin. It sat waiting to be called. A seduction at my fingertips, should I have use of it. "I did *not* sign up to be stalked by you. I did *not* sign up to watch bodies fall. I wanted to make a change. I wanted to try to help the Moon Coven witches from a place with real power. I wanted to prove to them all that I was worth more than what they all thought of me. I did *not* want this." I gestured between us. "I did not, nor will I ever want you. You are not likable, certainly not lovable. If I survive this maniacal torture you find so much pleasure in, I'll go home and be ten times the person you are. Now get the fuck out of here. Or kill me where I stand and be done with it."

He took a step toward me, but I thrust my hand out to stop him.

Shadows pooled at his feet, coalescing as his cold anger grew. "If you so much as think of drawing the power that sits under your skin forward, twenty guards will be in this room before you can finish the hand movement."

I dropped my hand. "Leave."

He dipped his head and vanished.

I was confident that would be the end of the king's visits to my chambers.

"WHAT ARE WE DOING HERE?" BREYA ASKED, STANDING BESIDE KIRSI and I the next morning.

After bathing and putting on another elaborate gown, we'd each been escorted by a guard through a wing of the castle to an ostentatious hall. The cavernous room had a fireplace so grand a man could stand inside with plenty of room. Couches and lounge chairs filled half the space, with paints, musical instruments and shelves of books and plants along the other half.

"We're about to try to kill each other for a title again," Kir answered, walking across the room to plop on a couch. "Might as well get comfortable."

"Actually," Grey said, stepping into the room, "the king has made some changes to the rules."

The Chosen inched close enough to hear the messenger, but all were on guard. Willow stood away from everyone, but Onyx stayed close to old Ophelia. An interesting choice. Kirsi caught my eye, and I knew she was thinking the same thing.

"What happens during the Trials is a result of your competition, but you're not to harm one another or cause problems in the interim. The king has decided to expand your boundaries to this hall. You're to call for a guard to escort you down, but this space is now yours."

"Pretty birds in gilded cages," Nym said, sitting casually beside Kirsi. She shared a wink with Kir, the bangles on her arms rattling as she adjusted them, wholly unamused. "It's the autumn solstice soon. Will the prisoners be set free to go home to their families, errand boy?"

I felt a genuine pang of pity for Grey at that moment. The king was our enemy in more ways than one, but Grey had to bear the weight of the king's actions on his shoulders when he acted in his place.

"I can put in a request," he said simply, tucking his hands behind his back as he turned to the fireplace, lit it, and stood there, watching the flames.

As the Chosen scattered throughout the room, I walked to the plants, checking the soil first and then the smooth texture of the leaves.

"Pretty, isn't it?"

"Fitting is more like it," I said, turning to find Grey a few steps from me.

"How so?" he asked, still holding his hands clasped behind his back as he stepped forward to examine the plant.

"It's devil's ivy," I answered. "It grows well in low light and indoors. But if you let it out into your gardens, it will choke and kill the rest of your foliage."

"Fitting, indeed." He reached for the leaf, rubbing it between his fingers.

I smiled, tilting my head to him. "You may find that especially true when you consider the environment. Unlike many things around here, I expect that plant is only present because it's hard to kill."

A full belly laugh filled the room, and possibly the castle, with more happiness than it had probably seen in a long time. But then Grey was always smiling, it seemed. The eyes of the other witches in the room each landed on us, one by one. Some glared, some stared, but they all looked, even Kirsi. I stepped away, lifting my skirts to quickly bob before I turned and walked away.

It didn't take long before Grey had mingled through the other women, landing solidly on Willow, who he'd spent the most amount of time with as she laughed at whatever he'd whispered in her ear, taking every opportunity she could to touch him.

"Encroaching on your territory, Raven? What would Nikos have to say about your new lover?"

I hadn't seen Onyx approach because I'd been watching Willow with Grey too closely, but his final words struck me hard. Did it matter what Nikos had to say?

Side stepping, I tried to cut around him. "Don't be ridiculous."

"Ridiculous?" he repeated far too loud as he stepped away from me. "Are you denying the king shows you favor?"

"No. I ... yes." Flustered, I tried again to get away, tripping over a small side table and falling to the floor. Caught in the ridiculous layers of skirts, I couldn't get myself up until Kirsi came to help me.

"I'd be careful if I were you," Onyx warned. "The bed of the king may be comfortable, but I've heard that's where witches go missing. Or so old Endora says."

I couldn't argue. I had nothing I could retort as every pair of eyes settled on me once again. Kirsi turned toward Onyx, but I gripped her arm, pulling her away.

"Don't break the king's rules over him. He's not worth it."

Once she conceded, I hurried out of the room, hustling toward mine as the guard that had taken me to the hall chased after me. Fortunately, he took the lead, directing me through the maze and to my door. Sealing myself inside, I ripped at the bodice of the dress. Flustered and furiously trapped within the fabric, I managed to get the dress off, but I couldn't reach the ties on the corset.

"Do you see?" I didn't know if he was there, listening or spying. "You are going to be the reason I am killed."

A soft knock came to my door, and for a moment I thought it would be him. But then, he didn't knock, nor was he the consoling type. Expecting Tavia, as Clariss hadn't been back, I swung the door open, hoping she could help me.

Instead, Grey leaned against the door frame in his casual way, though his smile was gone. "You okay?"

"As if you actually care," I answered, trying to cover myself.

He stepped into the room and closed the door behind him. "Let me help."

Taken aback, I turned away. "I will not."

"I have some experience. And you can't reach the laces yourself. Stop being your stubborn self for one minute and let me help you."

Dropping my hands, I refused to turn, but stepped closer to him. "If you could loosen them for me, I can handle the rest of it. I don't know why these things have to be so tight."

He laughed. "Tiny waists and curvy hips, I don't think there's a mystery here to be solved."

I rolled my eyes.

"I saw that."

He was gentle, pulling on the laces one by one without touching me at all. "I should have stopped him," he said as he tugged. "It's not my place to interfere. I have to stay out of it. But I should have done it anyway."

I shook my head. "No, Grey. The king would have you punished, and

Onyx is not worth that." The last of the corset came loose and I stepped away, holding it in place. "Thank you for your kindness." I looked at him then. Really looked at him. His eyes were a soft green, kind and full of light. He and the king were not cut from the same cloth. Grey was definitely the rougher of the two, though they carried the same build.

"I should go," he said, breaking the silence.

"I could make us tea? If you give me a moment to change."

"I shouldn't." He shoved his hands into his pockets leaning back on his heels. "They'll wonder where I am ... But also, I don't care, so yeah. I'll stay for tea."

"I'll be right back."

Hustling into the bedroom, I pulled the rest of the ties loose, let the layers of dress fall, and untied the strings around my waist until I was finally free. I threw on a pair of trousers similar to the ones we'd worn in the first trial and a loose shirt. When I walked back into the room, there was already a tray sitting on the table between the chair and chaise. Grey stood watching the flames dance in the fire that hadn't been there when I'd left.

"Hope you don't mind. That took you six full years."

Of course, he'd used a spell to summon the tea service.

"I don't mind." I poured two cups and breathed in the steam infused with peppermint as it steeped.

He sat across from me, hanging his arms along the back of the couch, broad enough to nearly cover the entire thing.

"Would you tell me about the castle?" I asked, lifting a cookie from the tray.

He tilted his head. "What do you want to know?"

"Has it always been this dark and mysterious?"

He looked away, letting a memory play in his mind for a while before he answered. "It's strange the things we remember from our childhood. It never felt like a dark and dreary place back when I used to run through the halls as a boy."

"Is it as massive as it seems from the outside? I asked, sipping the hot tea.

"Oh, it's probably bigger. It is a shame the witches cannot be trusted. I'd take you on a tour if I didn't think you'd wander off in search of your Grimoires."

I bristled at the casual tone he'd taken in reference to the book my grandmother had died for. Setting my tea down, I chose not to engage, but rather educate.

"Those Grimoires belong to the covens' caretakers, Grey. The first and last drop of each witch's blood is supposed to be ritualized into our families' books. It's a direct line of our power and our magic. A chronological story of our power's origins. The king has no right to keep them."

"I didn't mean to offend you. I only meant to say it's happened before. Witches have broken into the castle and tried to take the Grimoires. Bastian keeps them veiled for the good of everyone."

"Does *Bastian?*" I mocked. "They say Endora's daughter gave the Moss coven's Grimoire freely twenty years ago and *Bastian's* father, the old king, had her killed before he hid it away."

Grey lifted his teacup, far too small for his hands and blew the steam toward me. "That's a lie."

I stared into his eyes, daring him to say more. To reveal some grand secret about the missing woman and Grimoire.

He moved a hand through his straight blond hair. "The Moss Coven Grimoire has been missing for as long as Eden Mossbrook. You'll not find it here, nor find a single soul that knows where it is, and if you know what's good for you, you'll let this go and never mention it again."

I nodded, sinking back into my seat. "I'm sorry. I don't want to argue. It's hard being here. Knowing my family's Grimoire is so close I can nearly feel the power of it, yet I may never lay my eyes on it again."

"The king will grant an audience with a Grimoire for first blood, Raven. Someday, if you have a child, you'll be allowed the honor."

"How generous."

"I should go." He put his palms to his knees and hoisted his giant body up, strutting toward the door before he stopped, hand gripping the handle. "I'm sorry again. About Onyx, but please let this pass. It'll only bring you danger."

"Don't worry, Grey. I'm not interested in hunting down the Grimoires. I really am only here to win the Trials."

He nodded, his shoulders releasing the tension they'd built from our conversation. "Be ready for tomorrow, Raven. The second Trial is going to be harder than the first." He stared at me then, as if he was trying to say more with a look than he was allowed. "Trust your instincts and try not to die."

With the click of the door, I leaned my head onto the high back of the satin covered chair. Those last words would keep me up the rest of the night.

18

This was the first time I'd seen the king since his last unpleasant visit to my rooms. He hadn't come to breakfast, and I was grateful for it. But now we stood in the catacombs of the Dark King's castle and, though I'd convinced myself I could handle whatever was thrown at me, everything changed the deeper below we'd gone. The castle above was black and dark as shadow, the warm candle lights along the corridor's alcoves giving a foreign sense of familiarity. We couldn't see the details of the castle, but in a strange way, it was what we'd come to know of it. Below the fortress, the obsidian floors turned to dirt, the candles became torches, the walls … red stone. We passed tombs with statues of shifters, wolves and bears alike, that had ruled this world long before the war with the witches.

I wanted to wander the castle, to discover what the king might hide behind the walls, maybe even search for the Grimoires, but this wasn't what I'd had in mind. As each day passed, that feeling grew stronger, though I knew I'd likely die if I followed through. Still, my intuition nagged at me all the same.

I decided the shifters were definitely gifted with better sight than witches. Which would probably be a benefit for the spirit blessed witches who could use their familiar's sight via their magical link.

That did nothing for me though, now shrouded in darkness, deep below the castle, surrounded by ancient tombs of shifters that had owned this castle far longer than the half witch bloodline that ruled it now.

The king hadn't so much as glanced in my direction the entire trip through the mysteriously dark castle, and he stood before us now with two guards on each side, his hands in his pockets, wings tucked tight as the fire from a nearby wall sconce lit his hard face.

"You will each be timed as you enter the labyrinth. You're to work your way through each elemental roadblock as quickly as possible. Your timer will stop the moment you've conquered the end task. Make no mistake, you'll know the end when you get there. Ms. Moonstone will have a five-minute head start during her turn for winning the last Trial. The winner for this Trial will be given the gift of the other's deficit; the loser will only gain one point from this round but will also find themselves deaf for the next Trial. Willow Moonhollow, step forward."

Willow walked to the king, curtsying low. He locked eyes with her for a brief second, saying nothing as he stepped aside, indicating she was to begin. She was handed a lit torch and, needing no more provocation as one of the guards flipped an hourglass, she ran. We waited. Her scream the moment she was out of sight rattled us all.

I found myself looking up at the king several times, but he ignored me entirely. He did, however, cut several deadly glances toward Onyx, and I couldn't help but wonder if Grey had told him what happened. Or if he was doing his creepy stalker thing. Probably both. But then I thought of Grey helping me undress in my rooms and I wondered if the king would have been jealous to learn that. But why should he? And why had my mind wandered to such a dangerous place? He'd looked at Willow. Really looked at her, and that was worth more than words. Perhaps I was saved from his attention.

Though it seemed like it had taken forever, and she was white as a ghost when she stepped through one of the king's magical doorways, Willow made it back relatively unscathed, save for a few scratches and an arm she held tight to her body. She was immediately escorted back to her rooms.

"Forty-seven minutes," the king announced. "A decent time."

I ignored the intrigue in his tone. I couldn't let someone else's success distract me. There was no way to know how much time had passed once you went in, so it was irrelevant.

"Onyx Moonshade."

He moved, bowing before the king. Though he kept his tone steady, there was no questioning the threat behind his single word. "Run."

When Onyx returned, silent and with a gash on his head, he didn't look a single person in the eyes as he was escorted away. He did fairly well but didn't beat Willow's time. Eventually, the rest of us tired, waiting in shadowed silence, listening for whatever commotion we could hear beyond that first curve that seemed to startle everyone. Breya's time went beyond two full hours and the moment she stepped through the doorway, she fainted and had to be carried back to her rooms.

Only then did the king look at me. Only then did his eyes say a thousand words before his lips muttered two. "Raven Moonstone."

I stood, following the pattern of the Chosen before me, curtsying as my ears began to ring. The fear that had slowly been building came raining down as I waited for him to step aside. We shared one final glance before the hourglass was turned, and I was running. I'd get five minutes knocked off my time, but who knew if that would be enough?

Feeling completely unprepared, I carried the lit torch in front of me while flying forward, but as something reached out and grabbed my ankle, the light went soaring from my hands. I crashed to the ground, but held my scream, knowing the other contestants were waiting for it, just as I had.

I cast the spell to yank the torch back into my hands as I was dragged through the maze of dirt covered halls beneath the castle. Vines, I realized, wrapped around my feet, holding them together, pulling me. Small pebbles scraped against my back as the hallway began to narrow. I wiggled and pushed, but the more I squirmed, the more vines came, wrapping further up my body. The devil's ivy from upstairs. I should have known.

I had no doubt they were dragging me opposite of the direction I needed to go, and if I wanted to get a decent time, I needed to get free, quickly. I cast the spell to heal my back as a face drifted past me. Startled, I twisted, looking behind me to see several wraiths reaching their translucent arms for me as if they'd help free me.

With one hand on the torch, I held the other toward them, but the vines reacted, binding my body more, all the way to my hips. I reached still for the closest wraith, her expression blank. Until a cruel smile spread across her face as realization dawned on me. I would not be able to grab a being that was not corporal. The wraiths had only wasted my time. And the devil's ivy was now tightening across my stomach.

Unlike Onyx with his magical knife, I had no spells with blades to cut the plants. The tunnel had grown so narrow, my arms scraped the sides of the walls as I was dragged on. I lifted my head and terror erupted within me. If I didn't think of a way out, within minutes, I'd be smashed between the walls. Panic set in as I realized I'd let this go on too long. Adrenaline surged through my body, pumping my heart faster and faster.

Fire. Of course. I didn't think, casting the magic forward, hoping it would sever the end of the vines from the roots. The flame spider-webbed over the deadly vines beyond my feet, working beautifully as it recoiled in response, slowing.

Kicking myself free of the plants, I tossed the torch into the remaining mess of magical foliage and, as it caught fire, I sidestepped in the opposite direction, bringing my shirt up to help breathe through the smoke.

As soon as the tunnel was wide enough, I ran, following the markings on the ground where I'd been dragged through the thin layer of dirt. The wraiths from before created a barrier at one point in the hallway, but rather than turning, as they were likely meant to make me do, I passed through them. Their figures chilled me to the bone, but that was all, until they began to follow.

The labyrinth of halls and twists and turns was light enough I hadn't needed that torch. It was only a distraction. I'd be behind now for sure, even with the five-minute bonus awarded at the end.

Having no clue when I lost the original trail, I moved cautiously, though the wraiths followed close behind.

"You're going the wrong direction, Raven Moonstone," one's haunted voice called.

I ignored her, still pushing forward as I listened for sounds or clues through the passageways. There was nothing to lead me.

"Listen."

It was his voice. The deep and smoky tone of the king echoing off the walls.

I whipped around, staring at the ghostly beings. "Which one of you said that?"

The one in the center drifted forward, the edges of her floating gown billowing in a breeze that did not exist. "It was your king, was it not?"

"It couldn't have been. He's standing with the other contestants."

"But he favors you." She shifted forward, her form changing until she became his twin. Her voice changed, dropping in tone to mimic his. "You are the Chosen I prefer, Ms. Moonstone."

"I don't have time to play your games, wraith. What is your purpose here?"

"I've asked them to aid you," the king that was not the king said.

"Yes, you were so helpful before," I snapped, moving away from them.

"Raven, listen."

I couldn't help the way his voice halted me. Even when I was so angry with him, he still commanded me in a way I could not deny.

I turned, staring at him. Really staring. I never could have done this if it were truly him. Stepping forward, I peered at him through heavy lashes, slowing my breathing as I reached for his face, letting my fingers hover above the dark shadows along his strong jawline. "Tell me, my king. Which way should I go?"

Eyes that were not the king's lit with delight as he stepped to the side. "That way."

I tsked, shaking my head as I turned and ran in the opposite direction. 'Trust yourself,' Grey had warned. And it was time to listen. I'd evaluate my reaction to the king's voice another time.

The wraiths shrieked and shrilled behind me, but they did not follow. What started as a maze of halls, turned into cavernous rooms full of cobwebs, rocks and high ceilings as if I'd gone so far, I was no longer beneath the castle, but instead, I'd crossed one of the king's magical barriers and was now deep within the belly of a mountain somewhere else in the world.

I could hear the grains of sand falling in that hourglass as I moved, attempting to keep my breathing in control as my legs grew tired. Passing a room full of giant boulders, I couldn't help but wonder if Willow had made the stones upon the floor grow in size for what lay ahead. I left the room behind, taking a narrowed path, until I came upon another sizable room with a wall of water held by an invisible barrier. Pressing my hand through the barrier to test the liquid before I jumped in, the current yanked my arm so hard I thought I'd dislocated my shoulder. If I stepped in, I'd be whisked away and never come back.

Fortunately, it took me no time to come up with a plan. Calling my magic forward, I cast a spell on one of the boulders from the other room. Heavy enough to combat the flow of water, I moved the rocks beyond the barrier, building two walls with only enough room to pass through the middle. The mist of water passing through the gaps of the stones was cold, but the smell on the other side told me things were about to heat up.

The burning scent of sulfur grew more and more potent. Lungs burning, I left behind the second phase of the Trial and entered the third.

Skidding to a halt, I nearly went over the edge of a cliff leading down into molten lava, swelling in waves of orange and red below me. A threadbare rope bridge crossed the open space, but as the heat smothered the air in the room, I was sure it wouldn't hold me.

I thought of the seconds ticking by as I tried to make a plan. There was none. I'd have to keep my back against the wall and slide all the way around the small ledge that led to the other side or reach down for the ladder and take my chances on the bridge. I called forward a spell rarely used. Frost. It helped to protect the plants in the gardens from an early freeze, but I'd used it on the occasional hot summer's day as well. It would not save the bridge, but it would keep me from overheating above the pit, I hoped.

The ledge around the room wouldn't work because it was too time consuming. I gripped the edges of the rope, the frost coating my skin sizzling at the contact. I moved as quickly as I could. The bridge swayed and boards fell into the fire below me as I ran, but I did not stop and did not look down. Until the roar.

I slipped, falling onto the bridge, my feet dangling as I scrambled to find the source of the sound.

"Oh fuck."

A giant fire serpent leaped from the lava, a cascade of flaming orange and red scales concealing the scattered spots of blue deep within the beast's body. Frost wasn't going to do shit to save me now.

I ran. Committing to falling to a fiery death or escaping by the skin of my teeth as I studied the ramshackle boards flying below my feet, trying to avoid the ones that were barely there, while thinking quickly enough to remember where to step.

The serpent leaped from the lava straight for the bridge I was nearing the middle of. The beast's blazing jaw opened wide as it surged up and up, straight for me. There was no escape. If I ran forward, I'd be lost to the fiery pits of its bite. Having no other choice, I spun, running back to the ledge I'd come from as the bridge snapped behind me. I fell backward, desperately gripping the old coarse ropes as I plummeted, the rope burning into the palm of my hand.

The shoulder I'd injured in the water burned like a thousand suns, but I managed to catch myself. I climbed up the broken bridge, thanking the moon I hadn't gotten any further ahead before a hiss sounded below me. I glanced down, ignoring the tendrils of the rope bridge on fire racing for me. A wave of heat scorched my legs. Two beady eyes stared directly into mine as the fire serpent coiled below, ready to strike once more. And this time, it would not miss.

Every instinct I had came rushing forward as I closed my eyes, drew every ounce of power I could and hoped like hell I could move the water from the previous hall into this one. I had the power to make it rain, but that would do no good this far below ground. It was this or nothing.

Like a raging storm, the river of water rained down upon the fiery pit, consuming the serpent with a thundering hiss as it turned to steaming black rock. I scaled the ladder, using a healing spell on my shoulder, though I knew it would not be enough. And unfortunately, I was back on the wrong side of the wall.

There was not enough water to cool the lava and even if there was, I wouldn't survive the thick steam that would fill the room, nor the likely explosion from combining the hot and cold. I studied the wall, really hating the only other alternative.

The ledge, barely thin enough to stand on, circled the pit of fire. With no other choice, I began.

It took ages. I used muscles I never knew I had. I nearly fell four times, but by grit and stubborn will alone, I made it to the other side of that pit. Alive. Weary, beaten down, and completely exhausted, I stepped from the room that would have been my gravesite and found myself standing atop a cliff. I turned, but the door behind me was gone. As were any ledges for escape.

There was nowhere to go, only down. The pit below was so far, I could not see what lay beneath the bed of low-lying clouds. I went through my spells one by one. Uncomfortable using anything that shook the ground or affected the weather, I resigned. There was only one way out of this. To have courage. To trust that small voice inside of me that knew this was the final task and the only way forward.

And so, I jumped.

19

The world passed me by in a blur as I fell, thrusting my arms out and wondering if this was what it felt like to fly. I thought perhaps I would see the faces of my parents, of Nikos, even as I said goodbye to my life, but I didn't. Instead, I found myself wondering if the Dark King's wings were for vanity or functionality. If I had wings, would I spread them during this fall and soar across the world?

The ground came rushing toward me far too quickly. The euphoria of letting go ended more abruptly than I'd planned as I began to scream. But then I slowed. More and more, until I floated to a gentle stop before a door lit by moonlight. Exhaling, I rushed forward and threw the door open.

I couldn't look at my own time. I knew I hadn't been fast enough. Not to beat Willow, probably not even Onyx. The others watched as I walked forward, but Kirsi's glance was the only one I returned as her shoulders slumped with relief. I'd lived. Survived two trials. Not gracefully. Not with poise. But I'd made it. And that was enough for me.

Clariss was the one to join me in my rooms after the Trial. Her healing spell was far superior to mine as she mended my shoulder and helped me into the bath. She left me to soak and that's exactly what I did, tracing my fingers through the water as the suds remained in place, the warmth never cooling. I could have fallen asleep had it not been for leaving Kir behind. No matter how much I tried to convince myself she could handle it, probably even better than me, I worried too much to truly relax.

A banging at the door yanked me out of the bath as I thought of my friend, imagining all the ways they would tell me she'd died. Wrapping only a robe around myself, I rushed to the door and flung it open.

The same little boy from before quickly covered his eyes and spun around as he held up a note. "I'm to watch you read it."

Sighing, I pulled the note from his hands. "I guess you'll have to take my word for it."

I pushed the door closed as I listened to him giggle on the other side. He couldn't have been more than eight years old, and I wondered what a child was doing living in a place like this.

I unfolded the note, unable to control a small smile as I thought of the boy's laugh.

Ms. Raven Moonstone,
  Thanks for not dying.
  Ever the Stalker,
  ~Bastian

"It would have been your fault if I had." I threw the black paper into the fire and waited.

A fresh note fell from the ceiling.

Ms. R. Moonstone,
  Untrue. The trials are set by ritual and magic.
  Not at fault,
  ~Bastian

I sat on the sofa, picking at the tray of food Clariss had left, demanding I eat 'at once'. "What sort of spell lets you stand in the catacombs, yet listen into my rooms?"

I didn't want to ask, didn't want to let him know I was worried. But I wasn't strong enough to resist. "How's Kirsi doing?"

I'd barely finished my sentence when the next note came from the ceiling.

Ms. R. M.
> *Are we on speaking terms now?*
> *Intrigued,*
> *~B*

"Well," I said, swallowing a bite of cheese. "I'm the only one speaking. And you're avoiding the question."

R
> *Kirsi has not yet started her Trial. The letters are magic, of course.*
> *B*

"Oh, magic? Haven't heard of it. Are you standing down in the catacombs right now with that angry face casually sending me notes? Do you not have to flourish your hands to cast?"

R,
> *Just a finger wiggle if you must know. Which is hardly discernible with my hands in my pockets.*
> *B*

I smiled foolishly. "I'm pretty sure with everyone afraid to breathe in your presence, they've all noticed your little finger movements. They've already drawn their conclusions."

And what conclusion might that be, Miss Moonstone?

My cheeks flushed as I dared myself to answer him, but could not. "What do you do in this castle for fun?"

Work. Being the Dark King requires an exuberant amount of attention to other people.

"Hence the spying. But there has to be something else? Do you do nothing for entertainment? Aside from casual murder and master-minding?"

I like to sculpt. What do you do for entertainment, Ms. Moonstone?

I jerked upright, noting the statues in my assigned room. "What? You sculpt? As in …with your hands?"

Is there another type of sculpting? One of my pieces is in your sitting room. In the alcove by the door. The Goddess Elite, I call her. Also, you didn't answer my question.

"Wait, you carved this naked lady and stuck her in my rooms under the guise of being a goddess? Kind of twisted. Not surprised."

The female form is quite … Alluring.

"Quite." I smiled, studying the statue with long tresses falling over one shoulder, gathering in careful curls between her legs, her face, serene and lovely. I hadn't taken the time to study the sculptures before. He was exceedingly talented and I couldn't help but wonder what Kirsi would think.

Another note fell from the ceiling and I found the smile hadn't faded as I opened the carefully written black paper.

Ms. Studying My Handywork,
 What does Raven Moonstone do in her free time?
 Bored,
 B

I moved away from the art, sitting on the edge of the couch, trying to keep the thoughts of Kirsi running through the catacombs from my mind. "I don't know, really. It seems like I'm always at work. Even when I'm not physically there, I'm working with plants at home, studying the crystals. Whatever I can do."

Another note.

I guess we have more in common than we thought.

"Let's not get ahead of ourselves, Mr. Dark And Moody." I picked another fruit from the tray and popped it into my mouth. "May I ask you a question?"

I could almost see his dark eyebrow raise as the next note appeared before me.

Yes, but I may refuse to answer.

"Do you really think there's a place in this world for the shifters and witches to live in peace? Or do you think one day we will stand on separate lines of a battlefield?"

Several moments passed. I traced my hand over the smooth fabric of the dark couch, drawing a pattern into the velvet material, convinced I'd gone too far. A large paper landed in my lap, rolled, and tied with a black, shiny ribbon. I tugged on it, letting the paper unroll.

Ms. Raven Moonstone,

Should there ever be a war on these lands, I hope that you and I would not stand on opposite sides of the field. I hope the line is drawn between right and wrong and not species and power. Because I would not stand blindly with the shifters. There are the stories the witches tell, the stories the shifters tell, and somewhere in between lies the truth. In many ways, though it may not seem like it, I straddle that line.

Don't think that I haven't seen you suffer. Don't think that I am unaware of the state of the world. It is perhaps my greatest failure. Maybe you should find solace in the man you left at home instead. Good night, Raven.

His Royal Highness,
Bastian Firepool

The mention of Nikos stole the air from the room. How did he know of him? Clearly, he hadn't heard of the breakup. Still, guilt took over as I considered my casual tone. Friendly even. My heart changed, no longer interested in conversing with the enemy that simply confused me. I just wanted to go home.

I didn't say another word. I left Kirsi a note to wake me when she got back and crawled into bed. Closing my eyes, I thought of my parents. Of the regulars at the store. Of anything and everything but darkness. I needed to remember I was here to win the Trials and nothing more. Everything else was a well-placed distraction from my potential future as coven leader.

At some point during the night, Kirsi must have crawled into bed with me. She was there when I woke the next morning, her hair still damp from her bath and the scented oils still fresh on her skin. I tried to slip away quietly, but she was a light sleeper.

"We lived." She groaned, wiping her eyes.

"Barely."

Sitting up, she patted the side of the bed. "I'm tired and sore. This day sucks already."

I leaned against her as we rested our heads together. "That trial was a disaster."

She huffed. "Understatement of the century. How did you get past the fire asshole?"

"Moved the water. You?"

She tapped her spirit blessed marking. "Controlled him. Those fucking wraiths were creepy, right? The mouthy one took the shape of your father."

"My father?" I shrieked. "That's ridiculous."

"Well, he scares me. I almost listened to him. Who did you see?"

"The king, of course. He's terrifying." As soon as the words left my mouth, I glanced up to the ceiling, as if he'd answer immediately with a note of discontent.

Kirsi leaned into me, looking up as well. "What?"

"Oh ... nothing." I moved my hands through the tangles of curls fallen over my shoulders. "Thought I saw a spider."

She shuddered. "Better that than a wraith."

I COULDN'T HELP BUT JOIN THE OTHERS CROWDED AROUND THE TAPESTRY with the updated scores before breakfast. The king hadn't joined us yet. Most of us were worn down, especially old Ophelia with her crazy hair a bit wilder today, her stance more hunched. But we'd all made it out alive. Willow had come in first, Onyx second and me third, solely because of my time advantage. With fourteen overall points, I still held first place, but barely. Kirsi and Willow were tied for second with twelve points each, and Nym and Onyx were tied for third. Willow receiving an advantage in the next Trial was going to hurt a lot. She was a fierce competitor.

"I'm never going to catch up now that I have to be deaf in the next trial," Breya said, gesturing to her single point gain. "I might as well give up."

I took her hand. "It's only the second Trial. There's still time."

"False hope for the hopeless," Willow said, smirking from her end of the eight as she took Onyx's arm.

"What was your name again?" Nym asked Willow, though she knew very well who she was. "Onyx has made so many rounds, I can't keep up with you all anymore."

"Jealous?" Willow asked, adjusting the salacious cut of her dress.

"Why would anyone be jealous of a witch with hardly any markings?" Breya snorted.

My cheeks burned red as one by one everyone turned to me.

"Oh Raven. I'm sorry. I didn't mean you, of course. You're ... different."

Onyx stepped forward, his perfect window to pounce. "You are different. King's whore, aren't you? Even your friends know you can't win this."

"That's not what I meant." Breya crossed her arms over her chest.

"What was it you'd said about Raven the night before we came here? Right before you got out of my bed? Something about how she'd have to cheat her way through, being a silent witch and all. Guess you were right, doll."

"Raven, I didn't. I swear." The red-haired witch reached for me, but I stepped away.

"Oh, but she did."

Breya rushed forward, shoving Onyx as a marking on her neck flared orange. Before she could be stopped, she'd taken him to his knees with a spell I'd heard of but never seen. Pain.

Instantly, Breya dropped her hands, stepping backward, shaking her head as she realized what she'd done. "I'm sorry. I didn't mean it. I never use that spell."

"You stupid, little bitch." Onyx pulled his trusty knife from his boot and tossed it through the air in a blur.

Without thinking, I rushed for Breya, swiping the knife away with magic. I'd been fast enough to save her life, but not fast enough to avoid the blade all together. It was only a graze across my ribs, but it tore my bodice and blood trickled down my stomach.

Kirsi raised her arms, ready to retaliate, and Nym took her side as I hissed, clutching the wound.

"Enough. Stop this," Ophelia cried, stepping into the newly formed circle. "You're all foolish children. We are not each other's enemies. Remember who the real enemy is here. Remember why you put your blood in that cauldron."

Pushing away from the Chosen, I carefully took my usual seat at the end of the table. I could heal the wound well enough, but I didn't. I sat in my own fury, the sting of pain a reminder that this was not a game and few of these witches were my friends.

The king swept into the room, Grey behind him and three guards on each side as he took his seat. No one said a word as they sat and waited for him to allow us to eat. His eyes bore into the side of my head. I kept mine trained on the other side of the table, content to look anywhere but there. To him.

A small note appeared beside my plate. I slid my palm over the paper and pulled it into my lap. There was such a large part of me that didn't want to open it. That wanted to let the amiable terms of that final note last night be it. I didn't want to be a woman having secret conversations with a dangerous and deadly king. But I was weak, it seemed.

Why the fuck are you bleeding?

I crumpled the note and it vanished. I couldn't speak the words aloud. Could hardly handle it as I finally peered down the table and saw eyes full of rage as he held a bent fork in his hands.

My body's immediate response was pure fear as I cast a healing spell to the wound and shifted my gaze, lifting my fork to my mouth in a slow and steady motion, taking another bite of sausage as my hand trembled. I realized then that I was not afraid for myself. I was afraid to be the reason someone died. And that simple glance had said more than enough. The king had warned us we were not to harm one another outside of the Trial, and Onyx and Breya had both broken that rule.

Bastian abruptly stood from the table and stormed out. It was as if the room itself breathed a sigh of relief when he was gone. That's when it clicked. The fear the king had so callously brewed among his people filled the witches with the animosity they now turned on each other and the other species of the world.

It was not Eden and her coven Grimoire's disappearance, nor the single act of stealing the remaining Grimoires, nor a mysterious death of a coven leader. Rather, it was a culmination of all those things with no mercy, no apologies, no regret. It was starving the witches day after day until they became desperate for change. It was the shadow that a powerful king cast across his black lands until fear was the only emotional response left. And the only response to that fear was hatred. And that's what sat so heavily in my soul. The angry words of Onyx, the desperate response from Breya, were a direct consequence of an environment the king had created. So, who was he to blame but himself?

I waited until the others began to leave before I followed suit. Sandwiched between the guards that always waited in the hall to escort us to our rooms, I let the cadence of their march surge through my blood, empowering me for the man I knew waited in my rooms.

Only I didn't make it that far. The king's men had strategically separated us as more and more joined the hall. While the others were sent to their rooms, likely unaware, Grey pushed in beside me, taking my arm and leading me in the opposite direction. He said nothing, but the silence was louder than anything he could have. He was on the king's orders now. Whatever friendship that might have blossomed between us sizzled out as soon as he'd taken the murderer's side.

We stopped at a peculiar set of light wood doors that stretched all the way to the ceiling. The intricate carved branches that snaked all the way up the panels felt so out of place in the rest of the cold, stone castle. Grey gestured for me to enter. I wanted to ask why he wasn't following, but I couldn't find the words as I took in the room. A room that wasn't a room at all, but a glass covered greenhouse larger than the hall we used for meals.

Inching my way inside, I expected the king to be there, seething as he demanded answers for an event he hadn't spied on. Instead, water trickled from a mossy fountain in the center of the room and the sun, the glorious sun, shone down on me and the only thing I could wish for was for it to be night. To finally have the beam of the moon upon my skin, even filtered through the high arches of dirty windows. I missed windows, and the sound of nature, and the feel of grass below my feet.

The room looked as if it hadn't been tended to in ages, the plants far too overgrown and likely root bound. The shrubbery had grown so much you couldn't tell where one plant ended and the other began. The air. Heavens, the air. As fresh as spring soil and winter's first frost.

Slipping out of my shoes, propriety be damned, I had only one single desire. I lifted my skirts and buried my feet in the dirt. Grounding myself until my heart was calm, until my breathing was so steady, I could curl into a ball and lie there forever. Until the doors slammed open, and the king marched in, his raven wings straight out as he closed the space between us, grabbing my arms as he leaned down into my face.

"Who hurt you?"

Jerking my hands free, I stepped away from him. "It was an accident, and I'm fine."

"There's power in your blood."

"Yes," I said calmly, as his shoulders heaved with rage. "I'm a witch. It is my nature."

"Tell me who it was, or so help me, I will kill them all."

My heart stopped beating. Those would have been empty words from any other man. "I cannot."

He tucked his wings in, eyes wide as he stared me down. "I can hand you the role of coven leader right now. I'll slit all their throats and be done with this fucking nonsense that has my castle turned upside down. It's as if the witches think they are the only people I rule over." Rubbing his face, he groaned. "King of the magical beings. Ruler of the divine." The anger in his voice rode the edge of control. "You see the shifters in my guard, my father's heritage. There was to be peace with my parent's union. Only the witches cause issues. Did you know the coven leaders are demanding the right to watch the Trials? To see for themselves what's happening? How can I trust them within my walls when I cannot even trust the few that were Chosen?"

I curtsied, refusing to remove the barrier of formality between us. "Reaping what you sow is such an unfortunate part of life."

"Indeed." He moved in close, his fingers trailing the rip in the bodice of my dress as he so clearly tried to control his anger. "It was Onyx and his boot knife, wasn't it?"

Keeping my face forward as his fingers practically burned into me, I swallowed, my flesh rippling with unwanted desire at his touch. "It was not."

"Willow with her magic?"

"No."

I hadn't realized I'd been shuffling away from him until my back collided with the cool glass of a window. I was brave in my soul, but on the outside, clearly, I was still a coward. And now there was nowhere to go. He rested his rough hand upon my throat, but I would not meet his gaze. Though his grip was loose enough, his thumb resting on my racing pulse, the implication was there. "Tell me who broke the rules in my castle, Raven. My patience is growing thin."

I swallowed again, refusing still to look up at him, instead concentrating on the strong line of his jaw. The way his chest rose and fell with each measured breath. As if his control was wavering, the beast within him barely caged. The Dark King's tongue moved slowly across his full bottom lip as he moved one hand into my hair, gripping tight, then tugging down, forcing me to finally look him in the eye with a small wave of glorious pain.

Nose to nose with the greatest villain I'd ever known, the burning sensation of his hand still gripping my throat, I couldn't bear the way my core reacted to him. As if every nerve in my whole body longed to be touched in that way by him.

"Who hurt you? I will not ask again."

Through gritted teeth, I answered. "Allow the witches to come into the castle. Allow the Chosen to go home for All Hallows Eve. Grant me those two favors and I will tell you anything you want to know ... Your Grace."

"Denied," he answered, moving so close his lips were nearly to mine, his breath warm on my skin. "I will not bargain."

My entire body could have been on fire, and I'd have never known it from the heat that had taken over. Whatever was between the king and I ignited in that moment. All the myriad of emotions aside, he woke my senses like no other man. He was fire. And I was the fool.

I lifted my hand to the hollow of his cheek, letting the coarse hairs of his short beard burrow into my palm as I stared at him. Not the Dark King. But Bastian, the man with a terrible temper and enough passion to light the world on fire.

The rage melted from his face as his shoulders dropped, his wings vanishing as he took a step backward, blinking as if trying to clear his vision. "The gardens are yours, Raven. Come here as often as you like." He stumbled backward again. "I'll allow you to return home for one night. But I won't let those bitches into my castle."

I wanted to thank him for conceding when I'd given nothing away. But my lips couldn't find the words as he disappeared.

20

A week had passed since I last saw the king. He had announced our granted departure that night at dinner and had been gone since. Beyond the secret trips to the gardens, I still hadn't found the courage to leave my rooms, though every day I grew more and more determined to find a way to search the castle. There were no trials and no lush dinner feasts. Hardly any visits from Clariss or Tavia and, when they did come, it was a short visit with few words. We were to leave for home in two days and each hour that passed made me more and more anxious. There should have been a Trial. We were there to compete. I didn't know what the king was doing, but if he was lurking in shadows and sulking, it was putting everyone on edge.

The day he'd given me the gardens, I'd stayed until the nearly full moon had risen above the castle walls and shone its light upon my skin, rejuvenating me from the inside out as I sat on the window ledge dreaming of home. Of a simple life with tricky gardens and over-bearing parents. Life with a doorknob that stuck and blankets that were not quite warm enough on chilly nights.

When I finally had the courage to leave the gardens, one of the king's personal guards took me back to my rooms. His stocky build, round face, and hairy arms led me to believe he was likely a bear in beast form. I considered the hardship of balancing and ruling all the magical creatures, as the king did. The witches caused him trouble he deserved. But what of the others? The time of peace after centuries of war was still tumultuous.

But that was because of Eden. Endora, the Moss coven leader, had sent her daughter to marry Bastian's father, unaware that Eden had taken their Grimoire. When King Dristan denied her and she went missing, along with that magical book, he'd damned himself and his future son. Because although he married a witch, a Fire Coven leader from the most powerful bloodline, the Moss Coven had lost their link to their heritage. And no witch could ever let that go.

"You should come," Kirsi said, sitting on the edge of my bed as I brushed through my hair. "It's entertaining if nothing else."

"I have no desire to be in a room with them when they'd all rather see me dead. Mealtimes are more than enough."

"They don't want only you dead, to be fair. They want me dead just as much. And Onyx has set his sights on Ophelia now. He decided that since she's the oldest, she's the weakest."

Setting my brush down, I let my shoulders sag. "Fine. But if the knife comes out, I'm not responsible for what happens."

Kirsi picked at the loose seam in her red sleeve as she smiled. "That's the best part. Grey has made it his personal mission to torture Onyx. There's no way he's got the balls to pull that knife out again. The king would kill him, but I'm pretty sure Grey would do some hefty damage first."

"FANCY SEEING YOU HERE," THE KING'S MESSENGER SAID AS WE ENTERED the hall we'd been given. His blond hair fell across his brow as he dipped his chin to me.

"Messenger." I shared a stiff smile and small curtsy before walking directly to the couch, sitting beside Nym.

"Hey, stranger," she said by way of greeting, handing me a cup of steaming coffee as her stacks of gold bracelets slid down her arm. "It's black, like Onyx's soul."

Onyx sat near the bookcases, but as if Nym had shouted his name, he strode across the room straight for us. I gripped the hem of my dress, fighting the desire to strip him of the knife that was surely in his boot.

"Should you talk so openly of souls on the cusp of All Hallows Eve?" He sat directly across from us, slumping back as if he had no cares in the world.

"Scared of a little wraith?" Grey asked, leaning his arms across the back of Onyx's chair as he stared down at him.

"Not at all. In fact, when I become coven leader, I hope to make use of the wraiths."

"Oh, do tell," Willow said, coming to sit in his lap. She adjusted her red dress, but there was no helping the low cut in the chest, or the high rise slit exposing her thigh. She was gorgeous.

Onyx ran his fingers up and down the satin fabric at her waist as he answered. "I find the wraiths to be quite ... useless as of late. They have no need for tangible things, so they do not contribute. They need someone to lead them properly."

"You do realize we're competing for Moon Coven leader, not king of the world, right?" Kirsi asked, sitting on the arm of the couch beside me.

"Oh. Nearly forgot that title was already taken. Seems the king isn't pulling his weight either."

Grey shoved the high back of the chair forward, dumping the two witches on the floor. "Oops. Sorry. Don't know my own strength sometimes."

"It comes with being the castle fool, no doubt," Onyx snapped, standing and dusting himself off while Willow still lay on the floor, her arm extended as if Onyx was chivalrous enough to attend to her.

The second it was clear that he would not, Willow helped herself up, dusting off her gown before storming off to a corner to sulk.

I bit the inside of my cheek to keep from laughing as Onyx jerked upright, ambling away, and Grey took his seat, bringing one leg up so his ankle rested on his knee.

He lifted a discarded book with a worn title from the small table beside him and thumbed through the pages idly. "We know why Onnie wants to win the trials. But why do you?" He looked up at Kirsi, still seated on the arm of the couch, Scoop poised like a statue at her feet.

"It's no secret the witches are suffering. I want to win to bring fresh ideas to the other coven leaders."

I reached for her hand and squeezed. "You'd be amazing."

"What about you?" Nym asked, adjusting the small tiger sleeping in her lap before looking at me.

The room got quieter.

I took a sip of the bitter coffee, wondering how much I should say. But what would it matter? What would it change if they knew the truth in my heart?

"I almost didn't enter my name into the cauldron. As much as I wanted the chance to be here, to do something I admired my grand-mother for, I was terrified. But I decided I could spend my life afraid, or I could inspire change. If I had to be at the front line of that battle, standing toe-to-toe with an evil man to be heard, I'd find the courage to do it. If it meant the killings would stop. I'd do it."

Ophelia joined us then, looking down on me with old eyes, some of her markings hidden beneath the cavernous wrinkles in her skin. "If there was a change to be made, girl, our coven leaders would have done that long ago. You cannot barter with a tyrant. You can only hope to go unnoticed."

"And yet you're here," Willow said, leaving her corner to lean against Grey's chair as if her attraction to Onyx had expired. "Right under the king's nose, not at all invisible."

She raised a silver eyebrow to Willow. "I've lived a long life unno-ticed, Ms. Moonhollow. I don't not want the world to change. I simply want to slow the implosion."

"I don't really see anything wrong with the world as it sits," Zennik said. "I'm just here for the glory. And the food. The food's the best."

I didn't believe that for one second. But to each their own.

TWO MORE DAYS PASSED WITHOUT THE KING'S PRESENCE. I DIDN'T bother going back to the hall because there was no comfort for me there. Not like the greenhouse that I poured all my extra time into. I'd barely scratched the surface on the work that needed done, but the windows were clearer, and a fraction of the weeding was finished. If nothing else, it kept me busy. I hadn't told Kirsi. Not because she didn't deserve to come to the gardens, but mostly because I couldn't explain them away. I couldn't tell her how the king had gripped my neck and I still felt those coarse fingers on me. I couldn't tell her he'd threatened to kill everyone for me. I couldn't tell her I hadn't thrown myself at his feet and begged him not to. She was distracted by Nym and hadn't seemed to notice my absence more than the occasional invite to the Chosen's hall.

"It's different."

I whirled around, nearly falling over at the voice I hadn't heard in so long. He stood silent at the door, his wings gone as he held his back straight, his hands behind him. I opened my mouth to speak, but what could I say? Thank you for leaving me alone? Thank you for giving me a reason to lie to my best friend? Thank you for taking everything I thought I'd known about myself and turning it upside down?

He stared at the night sky. The pause, the silence, was awkward between us. Whatever boundary we'd crossed for a moment the last time we were in this room, we'd both run in the opposite direction, back to a place we both felt safe. Controlled.

"Grey will go with you tomorrow. He'll take you as far as the square and then he will return. The carriages will retrieve you all again the following morning in the same spot."

"Okay." The word was nearly whispered as I watched him. Focused on the space between us.

He took in the room one final time, gave a curt nod and turned, walking out the door. I stared at the space he'd been standing until a letter fluttered above me and fell into my waiting hands.

Raven,

> *Please come back.*
> *~Bastian*

"I think we both know I have no choice," I said, tossing the note into the air, watching the glow from the burning edges until it disintegrated to ash.

A CHILL HAD SETTLED INTO THE AIR AS WE STEPPED FROM THE DARK castle for the first time since arriving weeks ago. All Hallows Eve was a time for rebirth, as much as it was a time to say goodbye to the past. It was a day to manifest and a day to celebrate. To eat, drink, dance around a bonfire and laugh with family and friends. But it started with Grey taking most of the space in my carriage once again as we headed over the king's bridge and back to the Moon Coven territory.

"You look nothing like him."

I shifted in my seat, bringing my feet up onto the bench as I rotated to face him.

He smirked, showing that infamous dimple. "We're cousins. And of course, we don't look alike. I'm prettier."

I laughed. "Are you? Cousins? Which side?"

Grey rolled his eyes. "I'm a witch, aren't I?"

"Yes, but ..."

"It's not uncommon for the Fire Coven witches to fall in love with the shifters. Years ago, our territory was full of lush grass and towering trees. Things have changed since then, but we've always been a peaceful coven."

I shook my head. "I don't understand. I've always thought most of the Fire Coven was unfriendly. They don't attend gatherings. I only know one that visits the shop and isn't too good to be seen in our territory. The king hardly even sits on the council."

"It's different for him," he said, twisting in his seat to get more comfortable as the carriage bumped along the road. "He's the king and the Fire Coven leader. He has a lot to juggle. And the other covens haven't been very welcoming since ..."

My breath caught as I realized what he was trying to say, but stopped himself because of last time. "The Grimoires?"

"Yes. But even before that. Since Eden Mossbrook went missing and Endora convinced the rest of the leaders that it was Bastian's father that orchestrated it. Murdering her and stealing the book."

"Can we not?" I reached for his hand. "We're never going to agree on this topic, and I want to keep the peace between us. Can we let this go for today?"

He shook his head. "Of all the Chosen, I thought for sure you'd be the exception. If not to believe, at least not to blindly follow."

I opened my mouth to retort, but he held up a hand. "In the spirit of the holiday, I'll stop. I want you to have a great time today and tell me all about it when you come back."

Something occurred to me then. Grey was a cousin to the Dark King. He'd spent every day I'd been there within the walls. He'd only left when ordered. I narrowed my eyes. "Have you ever been to an All Hallows Eve festival?"

"No."

"Not even with the Fire Coven?"

"No. I've grown up in the castle and when you are in the presence of the king, the kingdom comes before the coven, always."

"What a miserable life. Cooped up in the castle, at the beck and call of a king that doesn't understand joy and happiness. You should come. Forget him for the night."

The corners of his mouth lifted, but he still shook his head. "I respect him. I don't mind answering to him."

"You should stay. Feel the power of the veil, manifest with us. Eat. It's fun."

"Fun, huh ..." He peeked out of the small window in the dark carriage. The sun lit the hollows of his cheeks, the blond in his hair practically white.

"What's the worst that could happen?"

He glanced at me with a lifted eyebrow and I couldn't help my giggle. His eyes doubled in size to match the wide grin that spread on his face at the sound.

"Ms. Moonstone, if you promise to smile like that all day, I'll be at *your* beck and call, king be damned."

All happiness left my face. "Be careful what you say aloud, Grey. The king is always listening."

He wiggled his eyebrows. "I meant every word. Also," he said, talking to the roof of the carriage. "You still look like a troll, Cousin."

I snorted and he laughed that full belly laugh of his that reminded me no matter how dark the king's castle was, there was still something light to be found there, even if you had to seek out a cousin with a penchant for mischief.

"I NEED TO STOP AT THE SHOP. KIRSI AND I ARE MEETING THERE FIRST to make our masks and the giving wreath for my parents." I took his hand, stepping out of the carriage.

"Are you sure you don't want me to hide in here and sneak over so the others don't give you a hard time?"

I turned, putting my hands on my hips. "There's nothing they can say that hasn't been said already. I'm not afraid of them and you shouldn't be either."

"There's not an ounce of fear within me, Ms. Moonstone." He bent at the waist, sweeping his hand before himself. "Lead the way."

The doorknob stuck as it always did, and I apologized profusely while throwing my hip into the door.

"It adds character," Kirsi said, walking up behind us. "Hey, handsome."

"Ms. Moondance," he said, wiggling his eyebrows.

"If I weren't madly in love with women, I'd marry you, sir."

He gripped his chest. "I can't bear the pain."

The door finally gave, and if not for Grey's instant reaction, grabbing my waist, I would have landed in a heap on the floor.

"Raven?"

My head jerked sideways, still tangled in Grey's arms, to see Nikos standing in the shop with a fresh bouquet of flowers wrapped in brown paper.

21

"Nikos? What are you doing here?" I asked, scrambling to move out of Grey's arms.

He cleared his throat awkwardly, gaze shifting between me and the king's cousin. "Your mom gave me her key. She thought it would be fun to surprise you. We both knew you'd stop here." He held out the flowers. "Who's your friend?"

"Oh, that's just Grey," Kirsi said. "He's my husband should I ever find the need for one." She lifted the golden skirts of the dress she wore from the castle and swept into the shop, quite possibly the nicest dressed person to have ever entered Crescent Cottage.

Scoop darted in after her, heading directly for his favorite spot by the window, and settled in. Nikos nodded slowly, struggling to take his eyes from Grey. He knew exactly who he was. The question remained: how would he react?

"These are beautiful," I said, taking the flowers, letting the brown paper crumble in my hands as I crossed the room to find a vase near the sink. In an attempt to fill the silence, I asked, "Did my mother help choose the flowers? I think I recognize the cornflower from her garden."

"She did," he answered, quickly following me. "Let me help you."

It hurt. Seeing him there, very much the man I knew him to be before everything had gone so awry. Everything about Nikos was familiar. From the way he wore his shirts tucked in, to the easy smile he carried most days.

But he'd pushed too hard. Had taken everything too damn far and while I'd let the Trials distract me from life outside the king's castle, I should have been more prepared to come back here and face the man who'd hurt me with his vicious words.

Grey, oblivious to the tension, clapped his hands together. "All right team. What are we making again?"

"Masks," Kirsi answered, clearing off the counter. "You have free rein to use anything in the shop. I'll be sure to bill the king. You'll want to make one that represents something you'd like to let go of on one half, like evil kings, and the other half is a manifestation. Something you want to conjure or bring into reality while the veil between the living and dead is the thinnest. If your ancestors think you're worthy, they will help grant your wishes."

"What's he doing here?" Nikos murmured, joining my side while Kirsi and Grey moved about the shop looking for items for their festival masks.

"He's my guest. What are *you* doing here?" I whispered back.

"I wanted to see you. To —"

"I know where this is going, and I can't —"

"No. I'm sorry," he said, taking my hands so that I would face him. He kept his voice low and slow. "I was such an asshole to you. Every day I woke up and worried you'd been a victim of the Thrashings, or the Harrowing. The stress of life just got to be so much. Too much. You didn't deserve how I treated you. But I've got no one else, Raven. You, me and Kirsi have been friends for a long, long time and I can't let that go. I messed up. I got so used to the idea of the two of us, and forgot we need independent lives and goals and dreams as well. I thought I had this all figured out. There's right and there's wrong and there is no in between. I want to do the right things, be the compass that always points north. But the pressure to be that person for myself and for you was just too much."

"Nik —"

"Please let me finish. I know it bothers you, me showing up here. But I need you in my life. As a friend. That's all I'm asking. Come on, Rave. I don't want to be alone. I can't lose you." He moved his hand up and down my arm. "I'll do better. We can go back to the way things were before ... us."

Being friends with Nikos was easy. Before *us*, he was kind and chivalrous and everything a man should be. He'd gotten lost along the way, but as I stared at the plea in his eyes, listening to the tone of his sincere voice, I knew I could never cast him aside. No one was perfect. Especially me. How could I fault him for that? He'd been ridiculed by the witches in this coven his whole life, simply because of a decision his parents had made. What was he to do as a child? Refuse to come with them? My heart ached as my mind swept through the years of taunting I'd witnessed. No wonder he was broken. No wonder he was so desperate to hold on to us. Kirsi and I were the only true friends he had.

I peeked over his shoulder, locking eyes with Kir. We had a single conversation in the span of a stare down. First the judging glare, but then the surrender. The understanding that we couldn't turn our backs on him. Because, while I could be friends with Nik, she'd never let things be comfortable if she didn't agree with it. That's what sealed the deal in my own heart. Kirsi held a grudge like a bad habit. If she was willing to let it go, I could, too.

She grabbed onto Grey's arm and moved him further away, distracting him with various crystals while I leaned against the sink. "We were pretty amazing as friends."

He lifted an eyebrow, leaning in. "Right?"

"Okay, Nikos. Friends, then."

"Great!"

We stood there for a moment, the awkwardness of trying to take a step back from each other nearly tangible.

"Can I ask about the Trials?" he blurted, trying to fill the silence.

"Depends on what you want to know."

"I know you're bound to secrecy, but can we know the standings?"

"I'm doing well, I guess." I bit the inside of my cheek, debating my response. Nik knowing the truth of the dangerous Trials would cause tension with him, no matter what we'd agreed upon. We weren't allowed to say much anyway. "First place for now, but only two done so far."

"First place? You're sure?"

I narrowed my eyes. "Does it surprise you I'd be in first?"

He flashed a smile. "Not at all."

"You know what the silver lining here is?" Kirsi asked, coming to stand next to Nikos as she threw a dried flower at him. "I don't have to be a third wheel for you two anymore," she said, answering her own question. "Speaking of ... Raven, backroom. Now."

I glanced at Grey across the room who was scanning the shelves and then back to Nik. "Play nice."

"Pinkie promise," he said, holding up his smallest finger.

I hid my eye roll at his overly friendly manner and followed Kirsi behind the vines of ivy to our backroom, which gave only a small bit of privacy from the others. "What?" I asked, peeking out to make sure the men were being cordial.

"Remember that time when we were seven and you asked me to punch Davey Moongrass in the nose because he said your mother was ugly?"

I dropped the ivy and flashed her a curious look. "Yes. Why?"

"And that time when we were sixteen and we snuck into Crescent Cottage with that old bottle of wine and when your father found us, I took all the blame and told him you were just regular old sick and not alcohol poisoning sick?"

"Yes, Kirsi. Get to the point before they kill each other out there."

She stuck her bottom lip out. "But that's half the fun."

I pinned her with a glare.

"Fine. Fine. I promised Nym we could go on our first real date tonight. I'm taking her to the festival."

I threw my arms around her in the most dramatic and annoying way. "That's fantastic."

"Mmhmm. You're choking me."

"I know." I squeezed harder.

She laughed and shoved me. "I've loved that witch from the second I laid eyes on her. I've been distracted, going down to the hall every day to be around her. And now it's really happening. She and I."

"Of course it is. You're a catch."

"Right. So back to Davey's broken nose ... Can I have the house tonight?"

"What for?" I wiggled my eyebrows.

She slapped my arm. Hard. "You know what for. I don't want it to be weird for her. Knowing you're on the other side of the wall."

I sighed. "Yes, but we're fighting now. It's my only night to sleep in my own bed."

She shoved her long blonde hair over her shoulder in a huff. "As if that thing holds a candle to the bed at the castle."

"Good point. I'll stay at my parents' house tonight." I stepped back into the store, away from the ivy wall, reaching down to grab a terra-cotta pot from the floor, and wiping it clean of dust.

"You're the best. I promise to never bring up that time you burnt Ophelia's garden to a crisp ever again."

I whipped around, eyes wide. "You just did." I turned to Grey, whose smile covered his whole face. I pointed at him. "Don't you dare."

"Tell old Ophelia you're an arsonist? I wouldn't dream of it."

My lips twisted into a half smile. "I don't believe you for a second."

He winked and went back to pulling dry petals from a collection of flowers in front of him.

Nikos cleared his throat, still standing at the sink where I'd left him. "Rave insisted we walk the long way home for two weeks after that."

"Listen, Ophelia is cordial and all, but she's scary, okay?"

"I'm telling her," Grey answered.

I narrowed my eyes. "Traitor."

The word left my mouth before I thought about what I'd said. But Grey ignored the word he'd probably been called a thousand times as if I'd never said it at all.

Nikos crossed the room. "Shall we get started?"

Kirsi rubbed her hands together. "Let's do it, *friend*."

I had only enough material to make the bare bones of four masks from birch bark and twine. Nikos and I strolled through the shop, collecting the things we each thought appropriate for our projects. There was a hint of familiarity there. The husk of a friendship reemerging as I tried to be the bigger person and leave the hurt behind me. Nikos had few friends. I'd have never wanted him to feel like he had no one in the world on his side.

I decided on a magical webbing for half my mask, hoping to represent that which I wanted to leave behind. I needed to let go of who I thought I was, and embrace the woman I was becoming, and potentially would become if I won the Trials. The other half was a myriad of flowers, fresh and dried. A representation of manifesting growth and change.

Laying all the materials down at the table, I asked Grey what he'd chosen for his mask. He pulled one of his flowers from the table and showed it to me. "This is to represent our dark past and the hope of letting it go. I'm going to cover one whole side in them and a few black tourmaline crystals to banish the negative energy."

Nikos coughed. "Sounds like you're trying to get rid of the Dark King."

"No, it's great," I reassured him. "The black bacarra roses are some of my favorites. And I think that's an excellent idea. What about your manifestation side?"

He pointed toward a handful of snow owl feathers and clear quartz. "I'm manifesting healing and purity."

"So black and white but both equal in intention. I like it," Kirsi said, setting down more things than she'd likely have space for on her mask. "What about you, Nik?"

"Same as every year, Kir," he answered. "I picked things at random, trusting the universe knows what I need."

"You'd think after all these years, you'd learn." Kirsi set the adhesive on the table beside the scissors. "Self-reflection and exploring what you desire is half the fun."

"Not for me," he answered simply, reaching for the adhesive.

He'd barely gotten his grip on it when it slipped and poured all over the floor. I rushed around to help clean the mess but didn't miss the smirk on Kirsi's face, as if she'd caused him to drop the glue. I gave her a look but said no more.

He knew, though. Kirsi and Nik had always picked on each other. Her more than him, but he never begrudged her for it. I wondered how he'd feel in front of Grey, knowing he was already wary around him. A brief pause swelled, filling the room with tension. But rather than lash out, as I'd expected, a marking on his neck lit up.

"Nik ... don't you dare," Kirsi said, turning to run around the table, hoping he'd miss her.

He didn't. Water from nowhere came pouring down, drenching her as she screamed.

"I take it back. We can't be friends with him, Rave."

She shook her arms, water dripping onto the floor as I shared a smile with Grey, who seemed to take it all in. He flourished a hand and Kirsi was dry as a bone.

"I'm replacing you," she said, pretending to scowl at Nik as she linked arms with Grey.

"At least I'll deserve it," Nikos answered, going back to his mask.

Emotionally, I swayed between okay and completely comfortable as the time passed. Nikos made small comments about the king here and there, testing Grey, who never once took the bait. But he also spoke of old memories and times we'd had together.

An hour into mask making, Nikos had dropped nearly everything he picked up, couldn't get his items to stick and had somehow glued his thumb to the table. Twice. Kirsi had come at him with a vengeance, but then he'd attacked back, and he'd been ruthless. Even making her fall asleep once. I thought he would have kept that spell secret.

"Shit. Is that the time?" Nikos said, setting his mask on the table, as he peeked out the window, noting the warm hues of the early evening sunlight. "I've got to go. I'm supposed to stop at the record hall before I go to the festival."

"But you've hardly got the stick on your mask, and it's only half covered."

I reached to pick it up for inspection, but he pulled it away. "It'll be enough for the ritual and that's all that matters." He circled the table, patting me awkwardly on the back. "I'll see you there tonight?"

I followed him toward the door, out of earshot of the other two. "Thanks for today. I'm glad we have peace between us."

He nodded, his shoulders sinking. "I couldn't let things end the way they did. We've been friends for far too long."

Watching the door close, I stood there for a moment, trying to evaluate how that felt. The healing, the friendship, the peace. Wondering why he couldn't have been that man when we were together.

I snagged a sage stick before walking back to the others and lit it, grabbing a black feather to push the smoke around the room. I hoped it would enhance the power of the mask I'd made. But after putting the stick away, smudging done, I lifted the mask and the birch wood had cracked down the middle, splitting the mask in two.

"Oh no." Kirsi snatched the pieces from my fingers, examining the damage.

"Please tell me that's not some kind of bad omen," Grey said as I took the pieces and dropped them in the trash.

22

"**S**wear you're still coming?" Kirsi asked of me, wrapping a heavy golden cloak around her shoulders.

Nym had arrived, still wearing her long mauve gown made of velvet. Aside from the meals, letting go of our castle wardrobe, with layers of warmth and beauty, would quite possibly be the hardest thing once the Trials were over. Though I doubted many of the Chosen would wear their castle garb to the festival, unwilling to show off the king's riches, I would have bet Willow would.

"I swear I'm still coming. Go have fun."

Kirsi studied my eyes for a hint of a lie before dipping her chin to Grey and walking out with Nym, Scoop and Talon, their beastly familiars, leading the way.

Grey leaned his forearms down on the tall work table, staring at me with a smile soft enough to conceal the single dimple in his cheek.

"What?" I asked, drawing back.

"Let's remake your mask. I could even fix that one with magic."

I shook my head. "You can't use magic on the mask because it's an offering. It's genuinely sad you don't know these things."

"I've never been to a festival, but I do know how the rituals work and you're wrong. I could use magic to hold the mask together all night. Then before the offering, I withdraw my magic. Simple."

"The last thing I want to do is offer something broken to the ancestors." I shrugged. "It's really fine. I'll go without."

"Not an option, Moonstone. Grab those flowers over there, I have an idea."

I lifted the basket of flowers and set them on the workbench. "I have to make an offering for my parents' hearth. There won't be time for both if we don't want to be late."

He pushed his blond hair away from his face, studying the mess on the table. "I'll make your mask, and you make the offering. Deal?"

"I don't have enough birch to make another mask."

"I'm resourceful. You just have to let a tiny bit of that control go."

I pressed my lips together. "I'm not hoarding control, I ... okay, fine. Make the mask."

"Perfect," he said, swiping a piece of mesh fabric I used to make spell satchels from the wall behind him. "I hate to see a quitter. I need attitude and sheer stubborn will from you, or I'll have to go hang out with Ophelia."

"You wouldn't." I laughed.

"I hear she might need some help in her gardens." He winked before waving a hand through the air, building a small wall of magic between us. "No peeking."

I pressed my lips together, fighting back the laugh. "You could have asked. You didn't have to make a literal wall."

"I trust no one," he answered, glancing over the barrier. "Get to work, Moonstone."

The next half hour passed with no shortage of his curses and my laughs as he settled into whatever he was crafting behind his barrier. He scrunched his face, concentrating so hard he ignored several of my judgmental glances as he stood lost in concentration.

"Done," he announced proudly, rubbing his hands together before removing the small, magical wall. "It's not exactly the same. I had to improvise. You'll wear the floral wreath on top of your head and then the veil will act as a mask. It'll work. I tried to use the same materials you had before."

I lifted the floral crown from his hands, surprised at the detail. All of the vines and stems hidden beneath plush flowers, the veil pinned with tiny black tourmaline crystals was easy enough to see through.

"Who knew you'd have such a hidden talent for arts and crafts," I teased, placing the floral crown on my head.

He stepped forward, adjusting the angle. It was hard not to think of the king while standing this close to his kin. Similar in stature, though not in temperament, he towered over me. Every inch of him, invading my space as he surveyed his work.

"If I ever lose my job with the king, I know which direction to take now," he said, plucking a loose petal from the crown.

I moved away, reaching for my cloak. "You could have a small corner in Crescent Cottage until you got on your feet. I'm very generous."

"Indeed." He laughed, lifting the wreath I'd made before walking toward the door.

I paused mid-step, remembering I'd have to take him to my parents' house. My father was already unhappy about the Trials. He'd seen Grey before. He would know exactly who he was and not be kind.

"You could wait for me here if you want. I can take this to them and then come back and get you, or we could meet in the clearing."

He held his back to me, unmoving. "Do you not want me to go?"

"No. I mean, of course, I do, but I can't promise my parents will be welcoming."

He shrugged. "The outside witches never are."

We hustled through the cobblestone streets of the Moon Coven territory, working our way to the old road that would take us to my childhood home as the sun set with a billion hues of fiery orange, melting into softened purples. As if the goddess had gifted the witches a glorious backdrop for this day of gathering and fellowship.

We stood shoulder to shoulder on my mother's doorstep, and I knocked, moving back to Grey's side. A show of solidarity. My mother opened the door the next second and nearly passed out the moment her eyes landed on my guest.

"Mother, this is Grey. He's been sent as a guard." I held the wreath up. "We won't keep you, but we've brought the giving wreath for the offering."

She pulled the wreath from my hands. She would later lay it on the hearth of her fireplace, light seven candles placed over a white salt circle and ask our ancestors to bless our harvest. The candles would be melted three quarters of the way down, blown out and then buried in the garden.

Her words were a forced whisper, as if that's all she could manage. "I hope you're doing well in the Trials, dear. Perhaps I'll let your father rest a bit more as you go on ahead to the festival." She half closed the door, sinking inside as she glanced again at Grey.

"Please, Mrs. Moonstone. Forgive my presence," he said. "I don't mean to be a hindrance to your festivities."

"Actually," I said, linking my arm with him, "he's my guest. Grey's never been to an All Hallows Eve festival."

"Oh," my mother answered, without trying to understand. "That's wonderful, dear. We'll see you later, then."

She closed the door in our faces and something in that single latch click brought back several memories of the aftermath of the Thrashings. People screaming. Blood pooled on the ground. Funeral after funeral. I swallowed, remembering my arm was linked with the king's man. The representative of the villain. And I'd asked him to come. I'd asked him to subject himself to all of the hateful glances he would endure this night. I didn't regret that decision, but I felt the weight of it all the same.

As we walked, mothers pulled their masked children away from us, glaring as if I'd personally murdered a loved one. As if I'd been the hand that delivered blow after blow to the condemned witches. I might have been used to the stares and whispers, but not that hatred. In so many ways, Nikos and Grey were similar. Both broken by association, but equally endearing and redeemable.

"Put your mask on. And you have to take off your boots," I told Grey as I sat, unlacing my own within the clearing. "It's important to be grounded before the festival. The veil between the afterlife and this one is at its thinnest tonight. If you are not anchored to our world, you could be snatched into theirs."

"We wouldn't want that," he said, pulling at the long laces of his leather boots. "I've got a lot of problems to create before I leave this world."

"Do you, now?" Nikos asked, sneaking up behind us.

"Something like that," Grey answered, his smile wavering.

Music filled the night air, rolling over the soft hills. Though most people avoided us—the misfits—barefoot children danced, their unbridled laughter like a faint memory amongst the witches. With masks upon their faces and ribbons trailing them as they moved, even I didn't miss Grey's dimpled smile. Voices filled the air with fellowship, and as always with a large gathering, the magic, the power of the witches, sat heavily among us.

"I'm glad you came, Nik." I stood, letting my toes sink into the soft grass.

"I said I would, didn't I? What happened to your beautiful mask?" He picked a petal from the crown on my head and tossed it away.

"I accidentally broke it, but Grey made me a new one."

"It's not bad. Suits you, I think."

I reached up, pinching the veil between my fingers. "Thank you."

The ground of the large clearing nestled in the middle of the forest was chilly but bearable, covered in leaves of all colors, some dried and some freshly fallen. The cold made me grateful we hadn't stopped at home. I'd intended on changing into the traditional plain white dress so many others wore, but the layers of the scarlet gown I'd worn from the castle provided enough warmth to feel comfortable. Though I was now that person, representing the king's wealth, with his representative close by. Fortunately, most of the other Chosen I'd glimpsed had decided to wear their castle wardrobe as well. There was honor in being chosen for the Trials. I just needed to remind myself that it didn't make me the enemy.

Grey walked behind Nikos and me, his hands in his pockets as he smiled at the witches that passed by. No smiles were returned, but it didn't seem to bother him. Likely, he'd expected as much. They'd spent the last decade terrified of him and the man he represented. Of the Thrashings and the king's guard.

The gathered witches moved into circles around the scattered bonfires that had been prepped in advance. Holding hands, we surrounded them, chanting, letting our feet bind us to the earth. The Chosen seemed to be enclosed by other witches asking about the Trials, but no one stopped us. No one came close to Grey.

Some of the witches' masks covered so much of their faces, I couldn't decipher who they were. Others wore ties across only their eyes. I was the only one with a black veil that went to my chin, rather than a traditional mask.

"Are you hungry?" I asked the two men when the seance to open the line of communication to our ancestors was over.

"Starved," Grey said, rubbing his stomach.

"Perhaps not a wise choice of words amongst the people your kin refuses to feed, though he is clearly capable of doing," Nikos said.

"A servant is not responsible for the will of his master," I retorted, giving him a stern look.

"Agreed, but I don't believe Grey is a servant to the king. He chooses to serve by his side, I'm sure," Nikos retorted, opening a window for Grey to disagree.

But he didn't, instead staring at Nikos as if he'd not completed his accusation.

My cheeks heated. I knew the truth of it, but I didn't want them to fight.

"Please don't—"

The entire world went still as stone. I tried to move, but my spirit had lifted from my body. A receiving. The timing was awful, but I was grateful for new magic, nevertheless. Pure, unrelenting peace settled in my soul as I listened quietly for my ancestors to bestow upon me a power of their choosing. Though I remained in the clearing, the witches around me slowly faded away, as did the sounds of murmuring, crackling fire and even my own heartbeat.

A door appeared before me, and then another to the left, then one to the right, and only inches behind me, and then more and more. Some appeared with carvings, some of glass and others of wood. Some framed in vines, some floating midair, some more portal-like than actual doors. I waited, watching. Wondering what I was supposed to do to unlock the spell I was to be gifted. As with every time before, it was up to me to decipher the code of this spell.

I inched forward, studying the doors, wondering if I needed to choose. But my intuition told me that wasn't the task. Placing my hand on the golden door directly in front of me, I tried to open it, but the door was locked. I turned to the one beside me, pearl in color and cool to the touch. No luck.

Each one of them was locked. I weaved between them, not at all understanding, until I turned back to face the spot I was standing. On the other side of the doors were bolts and chains and latches. Walking back to the golden door, I stayed on the backside of it, unlocking the handle. Content, I went around to the front side of the gilded door and turned the knob, it swung open, and the vision faded. I'd received the power to unlock doors.

The night had gotten slightly darker. Grey and Nikos both waiting beside me, the tension between them heightened, it seemed.

"That was a long one," Nikos said, realizing I'd come back to earthly consciousness.

He eyed me carefully, likely waiting for me to tell him which spell I'd acquired, but as several other eyes watched from the crowd of witches, I simply shrugged, pushing away the wariness of receiving a new spell and began walking toward the tables in the distance.

"Did you guys eat without me?"

"Of course not," Nikos said. "Your guest wandered off for a bit, but I stayed here."

"Thanks for waiting for me."

"Working on that friend thing," he said with a wink.

The tables were not as full of food as the palace feasts we'd been privy to, but there was more than usual, with plenty of witches donating from their own harvest so there would be enough. The Moon Coven witches traded crops for wine with the Whisper Coven witches. They lived on floating isles, barely able to grow anything more than fruits and simple herbs. For that reason, the drinks were easier to come by.

After eating, and several drinks, Grey wandered off again, avoiding most of the witches who spat and scowled in his direction as he watched the festivities, though he did seek out Ophelia and I'd seen him talking to Willow several times. He was a grown man with his own agenda. As long as he was enjoying himself outside the castle, that was enough for me.

"When will you come home?" Nikos asked.

We sat in front of one of the fires, watching the flames lick up the side of the towering wooden stack. It was the perfect blend of cool and warm as the fire hypnotized us, the silence that usually lingered friendly and comfortable.

"I'm not sure, to be honest. There doesn't seem to be a schedule, but the king makes it seem like it's more ritual and less in his control than we thought."

"Raven. Of course the king would not take responsibility for his actions." He huffed, shifting sideways, no longer interested in the fire as he reached for the lace detailing on the sleeve of my gown. "I worry for you. I don't want you to be so blinded by these comforts you forget what life is like at home."

"Have more faith in me than that. I haven't forgotten a thing."

"I hope most of all you haven't forgotten the way you fit into my arms."

It could have been the warmth of the night, the ease of conversation, or the fact that we'd spent most of the evening together, but somewhere along the way, he'd forgotten our new boundary.

"Rave. You can't tell me you can easily reset our history. I tried today; I really did. But, it's so hard to be only your friend. To have you within arm's reach and not hold you. You don't have to answer now. Think about it. When you come back, we can start over."

The guilt I felt threatened to smother me whole as the king flashed into my thoughts. His hands on me, the way he melted into my touch. The way he'd lit my soul on fire that day in the gardens. That passion was not there with Nikos. No matter how much he wished it was. And he was so hot and cold I couldn't keep track of him anymore. I'd never known him to be so erratic before Tasa died. I opened my mouth to shut him down, but a nearby cough caught my attention. I whipped my head to find Grey staring down at us. How much of that had he heard?

"I think I'm going to head back now. You know where to be in the morning?"

I stood, adjusting my dress. "You're leaving? You should stay."

He closed the space between us, taking my hands. "Thank you for inviting me. It was a wonderful day, truly."

I nodded, letting go of his hands as Nikos rose from the ground, rubbing his hands together to warm them as he looked at me expectantly. I'd have to let him down gently, right in front of Grey.

"Nik—"

"Nikos?" a familiar voice called from behind us.

"Mother?" He jerked upright, his casual step away from me not unnoticed.

His mother had never liked me. She and her husband had left the Moss Coven without giving an explanation. Performing a bloodletting to join another coven was nearly unheard of, but they'd done it with approval of Tasa and Endora the year after the last of the Mooncrest family died. The Moon Coven witches were content to be a coven of twelve families instead of thirteen, but it seemed Nikos' parents had other plans.

I didn't hate them for it, knowing they'd brought Nikos with them, but I couldn't help but blame them for the hardship and hatred he'd battled his whole life. It wasn't fair, but it also wasn't his choice. Even still, she held her own prejudices against me.

"You're needed," she said, hands clasped in front of her, the waves of golden blonde hair a perfect match to his. Her eyes flicked to me, and she scowled. "Now."

He turned and left without a goodbye. The most telling thing of all was my lack of emotion about it. I didn't need anything from him anymore.

"I can walk you home?" Grey offered.

"I'm not going home. Kirsi has Nym over so I'm going to my parents' house. You could walk me there if you're sure you don't mind."

"Not in the least," he said, holding his arm out for me.

"Oh wait, my mask." I lifted the crown of flowers from my head and stood before the fire. "By the moon's brightest light and the sun's deepest shadow, ancestors, I invoke thee. Two halves of a whole, hear my intentions and bless me." Tossing my mask into the fire, I watched as it was incinerated. A wish sent to the heavens.

The walk back to my parents' house was fairly quiet. Grey seemed to be deep in thought, or content to listen to the sounds of night, and I couldn't stop thinking about the steps we took. Wondering if I'd die in the Trials and never walk this path again.

My thoughts were morbid. But they carried me home, nonetheless. Grey walked me as far as the door before he vanished. I let myself in, noting my parents hadn't come home from the festival and likely wouldn't be back until morning.

Crawling into my childhood bed, I was haunted by the memory of what had put me there the last time. The Harrowing they called it, a sickness. But the more I thought about that day, the illness that fell over me, the power it took to save me, the more I knew it wasn't true. It was an attack from a witch with powerful magic, or something completely unheard of. It was not a sickness. I thought of the words the Dark King had said to me ... He'd claimed to save my life. If that were true, then why? He hadn't known me. Even now, he didn't.

As I fell asleep with thoughts of Bastian Firepool circulating my mind, it was no surprise to find him standing in my dreams.

23

The shadows of the king's royal magic rolled around him like dense autumn fog on a lake as he strolled across his empty throne room, greeting me within my dream. The edges of my vision blurred, as dreams often do, and I wondered if my mind had gotten his likeness exact or only close. So far, he was flawless. His dark hair swept up and tied behind him, his black coat fitting tight, perfectly tailored. Even the massive wings he held close to his body didn't seem to have a feather out of place.

In a dress made of shimmering black with a train that seemed to disappear into the dark marble floor, I curtsied, greeting him in my dreams as formally as I would in front of an audience. "Has it ever occurred to you how elaborate this castle is in contrast to the rest of the world?"

He dipped his chin. "A family heirloom, nothing more."

As a million floating candles bathed the room in warm light, I found myself curious about the king's wings. Each feather as black as night and perfectly laid behind him. "Do you only have wings, or can you shift into a bird and fly?" I approached him, reaching out to stroke them.

A shudder rippled through the silky feathers as he stared down at me, piercing me with those silver eyes. He ran his tongue over his lips. "I could show you?"

"Perhaps another time," I whispered, walking up the aisle, the sound of my steps sharper than the boots that followed me. I sat lazily on his throne, the obsidian stone chilling my legs. "Surprising."

He squinted, an unspoken question on his face.

"Your seat is not very comfortable, Your Grace."

He sat on the arm of the throne, lifting my arm and dragging his fingers languidly over the soft flesh. "You have no idea how right you are." Raising my fingers to his mouth, he kissed my knuckles.

My skin heated beneath his touch. "You make the rules, you break the rules. If you're suffering, it's self-inflicted."

"Agreed. Tell me, will you rekindle your relationship with Nikos?"

Even in my dreams I could not escape the conflict of him, it seemed. But though I'd made up my mind, something within me still wanted to protect him from the king. Even a fictional one, far too amiable to be real.

"What was it like? Growing up in this castle?" I asked, ignoring his question.

He held my hand in his lap, circling his thumb over my palm, staring at our fingers. "I thought my parents would live forever," he answered, seemingly lost in his thoughts. "I hated it most days. Training with the shifters in physical combat, sword fighting with the Old Barren. World studies and long boring meetings. The best part was training with the Fire Coven witches. I gained markings so quickly I think I surprised everyone."

I glanced at the dark marks that snaked up his neck and couldn't help but wonder how far down they went. As if he could read my mind, he lifted his brow. My eyes fell to the floor, and he gently tucked a finger under my chin. "You will look at me when I speak to you."

I couldn't help my laugh. Nor the way my body responded when his eyes lit with desire at the sound that echoed through the room. "You would command me, even in my own dreams."

He leaped to his feet, holding a hand out to me as he bowed. "I'm not fond of this room. Let's find another."

Leaving the throne room behind, my gasp echoed as the midnight castle changed entirely to crisp white. The walls were beaming, the light filling every nook and cranny. My dress melted into the simple nightgown I'd crawled into bed in. I spun in a circle, looking up to see the ceiling for the first time. Before, it felt as if we'd wandered through a dark cave, but this? This was certainly dream worthy, with paintings of gold stretching all the way down the hall.

"What is this?" I gasped.

The king followed my gaze. "A memory," he breathed.

"Come on." I yanked his arm, speeding up our pace as I explored the castle, white as snow.

His deep voice was full of wonder and void of all traceable danger. "We should check the gardens."

"Lead the way, Your Grace."

He tugged me along now, looking back to watch my smile as he navigated the bright halls of his home as if he thought I'd somehow vanish. When he pushed open the doors, a thousand familiar smells filled the air. The foliage had grown so beautiful, the gardens so well taken care of, the smell of rich soil didn't overpower the vines of ivy or the hyacinth. Lily pads filled the pond as water trickled from the flowing fountain.

"I hope one day to see this greenhouse truly look like this."

"I'll see it done immediately," the king said, his eyes glued to me as I ran my fingers over the soft petals of a nearby hydrangea.

"I wish the real king was as kind as the dream king," I said, moving to stand before him.

He reached for my arms, tugging me close to his chest. "Who says he's not?"

"It is just a dream." I tucked a dark strand of his hair behind his ear. "So, if I wanted to kiss you, I could."

"You could," he said, the air becoming stifling. He pulled me so close my chest pressed into his. "Put me out of this misery, Raven Moonstone."

I didn't hesitate, closing the space between us as everything that had drawn us toward each other, every pent-up emotion, all the passion and hatred collided into the single moment my lips brushed his. All the times I'd been pulled to him and his darkness built up to that one fictional moment of answered curiosity. The world fell away as we were enveloped in the midnight shadows he commanded. He held me tight to him as the room around us changed. No longer in the pristine greenhouse, but instead standing in my rooms at the castle.

He buried his fingers into my unruly curls as he pulled my face to his for another kiss, sending a pulse of desire straight to my core. A second became infinite as he devoured me, but as if someone had shouted at him, he jerked upright, stepping away with his eyes closed as he seemed to be battling himself. But this was my dream, and I was in charge. I pressed myself into him, lifting his chin with my finger.

"Again, Your Grace," I demanded.

He fisted my hair into his hands again as he smashed himself against me, pressing me into the post of my bed, kissing me with no restraint, his soft lips massaging mine while his tongue did the same. A very small part of me remembered that I despised this man, but this was the answer to every one of my forbidden daydreams. This was what I needed. Wanted. To purge my system of the frenzied desire that wracked my body every time I was in his presence.

His grip was not gentle, the groans more beast than anything, but damn if he didn't bring my body to life in ways I'd never known possible. His fiery lips moved as he kissed a trail down my collarbone, then back up to my earlobe. Every inch of flesh sensitive to his touch. He lifted me off the ground, kneading my thighs as he kissed me again. I couldn't help the moan against his mouth as his breaths became ragged and mine nearly nonexistent.

"Tell me you want this." His dark eyes held mine as if they would be his release.

"I want this," I whispered.

His wings opened wide, then closed us in total darkness until we were falling backward, moving again. We landed on a bed wider than his wingspan, covered in black silk sheets. Holding himself up by his arms on both sides of my head he stared down at me. He felt so real, the details of his face so perfect, I had to look away.

"No," he commanded. "You do not take your eyes from mine, understand?"

I swallowed and nodded as he laid his forehead against mine.

"I want you so badly I can hardly restrain myself."

"I am yours, Bastian. For tonight. Take me."

He moved his lips to the pulse in my throat, brushing softly against my skin, the sensation rippling down my body in waves. Gentle kisses moved up to my jaw, as his fingers traced the flimsy gown I wore. Reaching down, I grabbed the hem, trying to lift it, but he clutched my wrist, holding it in place.

"There are things even I cannot resist, and your naked body is top of that list. Do not tempt me."

"Then don't resist."

His laugh was dark and far too controlled. "We both know you do not mean that, but I'm happy to make you beg for it."

I raised myself up on my elbows. "You wouldn't."

"Oh, I would."

The challenge lit his silvery eyes as he pressed his hips into mine, showing me exactly what I was missing. I moved my hips, rubbing against his hardened length until the feral moan that left his mouth threatened to undo me. The need for him, for release, surged between my legs, every part of me swollen and molten with desire. I needed him.

He traced a finger down my neck, as he pulled his body away from mine. Tracking between my breasts to my navel, I lifted my hips again, urging him to continue downward. To keep going until he hit that spot that throbbed with longing. He consented, moving slowly downward as our eyes held each other. He was close, so damn close before he circled away, moving those heated fingers to my thigh, so close yet so far away as a smile, dark and delicious spread across his face.

"I hate you," I whispered, wishing my voice held more conviction.

"You want to hate me." He chuckled, bending down to drag his tongue up my thigh. When he was close again, he pulled away, eyes still locked with mine. "But you do not."

A brush, a single touch between my legs would have given me the release I needed, but he refused. Moving again to hover above me, he kissed me slowly. And I let him, because that was all he would give me and though I needed more, when he pulled away, expecting me to beg him, I would not.

He crashed to the bed beside me, grabbing my hand and moving his fingers into the spaces between mine. "In another reality, it would have been perfect."

"Believe me, it would have been perfect in this one."

"I wish we could stay like this," he said as he pressed his soft lips to my fingers.

"If only you were real," I answered.

He rolled to the side, pulling me to his chest as he kissed my forehead. "If only."

THE KING WHO HAD OCCUPIED MY DREAMS ALSO CAUSED ME TO oversleep. And the real king would likely kill me for being late.

Racing out of my parents' home, stopping only to make sure they'd made it back, I hustled to the square, mortified to see that all were waiting on me. Grey stood outside the carriage with hard eyes and lips pressed into a fine line.

"Glad you could join us," he said as he swung the door open.

"I'm sorry. I overslept."

He shut the door without getting in. I wanted to call after him, to ask if he was really that cross with me, but as he crawled into a different carriage, I let it go. I had enough troubles with men these days. I didn't need another.

Arriving at the black castle felt very much like putting myself back into prison. The faces of the staff were somber, more so than usual, and all the life and spirit I'd witnessed at home had been left behind. We were escorted through the halls and sent directly to our rooms.

"You're not to leave. The Chosen's Hall is off limits as is the old greenhouse until further notice," Clariss said, pulling a key from her pocket.

"Did something happen?" I pressed my nails into my palms, preparing for the worst.

"A witch from the Storm Coven tried to break into the castle last night. She caused some damage with her magic and the king had to ..."

"Kill her?"

Clariss dropped her head. "Yes, my lady."

"But why? Surely there's a different way to punish someone than death?"

Clariss looked at me as if I'd struck her face. "You'd defend this witch?"

"Yes. No. I'm not defending her. I'm appalled at the level of punishment."

"Stay in your rooms, girl." She walked out without another word, locking the door behind her.

In an act of pure defiance, perhaps a bit of annoyance and anger, I swiped my hand through the air and unlocked it with my newly acquired spell. If I was to be a prisoner, at least it would be on my own terms.

I walked through my rooms to the secret door, but because Kirsi's maids were still with her, I wasn't able to enter. She'd done everything right. She'd mingled with the contestants, found us allies, and taken note of everyone's spells. I might have been in first place, but she was the clear winner here. Especially because I'd still been lying to her about the greenhouse and depth of my issues with the king.

He was haunting my dreams now too, it seemed. And I wasn't entirely mad about it.

24

Nothing happened for several days. The king kept us isolated, and meals were delivered to our rooms. Kir and I were the lucky ones with the door between our rooms opened, consequences be damned, but none of the staff seemed to care. We slept in our own beds, but spent most of our time playing cards and talking about all of the things we'd like to do in the shop in the future. We'd heard a Moon Coven witch had received an intuition spell and she'd been giving palm readings out of her home. If we could bring her into Crescent Cottage, it could help our revenue.

"What if one of us wins this? Does the other run the shop alone?" Kirsi asked.

I knew what she'd really been asking. The shop was my grand-mother's and we'd taken it over by inheritance alone. If I won, would she still have a job?

"If you win, I'll find a way to keep the shop running even if it means moving into the back room and restocking some of my grand-mother's elixirs. I could probably handle luck, youth and happiness potions without killing myself."

"And if you win?" She sat cross legged on a pillow resting on the floor, a hand full of cards.

"If I win, would you consider running the shop? And before you answer, I'd understand if you didn't want to."

She tapped her lips with her index finger, scrunching her nose. "I'd consider it."

Laying my cards flat on the table to indicate she'd won the hand, I smiled. "We'd still live together though, right?"

"Of course. I need you to feed me."

"And I need you to acquire wine and do all the social things."

She rolled her eyes. "You like people way more than I do."

"True." I giggled.

A knock sounded at the door to Kirsi's sitting room. Scoop rose from his position on the rug beside her, arching his back as he hissed.

"Who is it?" Kirsi asked.

"Your next trial is to begin in ten minutes. You're to meet in the hall with the other Chosen," a guard called from behind the closed door.

"Perfect. I'm tired of sitting around." I stood from the table and gathered the cards, pausing as I stared down at her. "Good luck."

"I hope we're together again," she said, standing.

"Me too."

I didn't bother changing. I simply walked through my rooms and out my door so the other Chosen wouldn't know Kirsi and I had been allowed to speak to each other in private. But, as I saw Willow at the end of the hall talking to Ophelia, I realized we may not be the only ones. It was likely the king had granted everyone secret doors. I caught a glimpse of Grey down the back end of the hallway talking to Breya. She twirled her hair in her fingers as she batted her eyelashes and smiled. His single dimple was showing on his cheek as he leaned in and whispered something before walking away.

Four of the king's men were in beast form surrounding him as he rounded the corner nearest Kirsi and I at the front of the long, dark hallway. Still wrapped in black armor, metal scraped against metal as the animals moved in perfect formation. Aside from that very quick goodbye in the gardens before All Hallows Eve, I hadn't seen him in over ten days, apart from the version of him that my mind created in my dreams. He'd been there every night. His arms around me, his breath on my neck as we talked and lived in an imaginary world of peace. I had no control over what my mind was doing when I was sleeping, but as my cheeks blushed, I couldn't bring myself to look him in the eye. The collective group of witches in the halls all bowed before him.

"Follow me," he said simply, leading us through the castle as more of his guards moved in, flanking us as we walked.

The dim light and darkness of the king's castle remained steady throughout the halls we were ushered down. From my position, I was first to see the arena we were escorted into. Rows of empty seats filled the space above us as we entered the outdoor space. Only a handful were occupied. It seemed the coven leaders had forced his hand after all. My shoulders stiffened, happiness settling into my soul as I felt confident they'd make sure we were all safe during this Trial. A hedge taller than the king himself, taller than the bear beside him, filled the arena floor.

"A maze?" Kirsi whispered.

"Shh," one of the guards hissed.

Four intricately woven tapestries hung from the north, south, east and west. Each of our names were listed, similar to the one in the dining hall with our ranks, only there was no tally of points. My name graced the top of the list, marking me in first place. Kirsi and Willow were on the next line, tied for second, then Nym and Onyx tied for third.

"As you can see," the king said to the group of Chosen, "I've allowed the leaders from the other six covens to join us today. They will be able to see what you will not. You'll be blinded and released into the hedge maze based on current rankings with a thirty second gap between. You're not to use a single spell for this Trial. If you do, you'll be eliminated and take last place. Find your way to the exit on the other side. Trust your intuition. It will be your only guide.

"Ms. Willow Moonhollow will be given the gift of sight for winning the last competition. Ms. Breya Moonbranch will lose her hearing for coming in last place. Win this race and you will be given a valuable hint for the next Trial. Lose, and you will be given half the information needed for next time."

For the briefest of moments, I caught his eye, a tick in his jaw as he said my name. "Ms. Moonstone, step forward."

Exhaling, I lifted my chin and moved. I'd struggled in the last trial. But this was completely different because the coven leaders could see me. Could all judge and evaluate my weaknesses. Should I do poorly, they'd never trust me to take Tasa's place and I couldn't bear that. I needed to win this.

Standing in front of the gaping hole in the hedge, I steadied myself. I could do this blind, but Willow had a major advantage. And beating her would be a miracle. There was no magic, which meant I probably wouldn't have to fight beasts or tangle with wraiths. It was simply a maze. All I had to do was run.

A mallet crashed into a hanging metal orb somewhere in the distance, causing me to dash forward where darkness swallowed me whole. The problem was, it was his darkness, his magic that surrounded me. The same beautiful power that had seduced me in the barrier the first time I'd ever felt the press of his shadows. Trapped inside my own body, I couldn't force myself to run. I knew I needed to, knew that Willow would come plowing into me within seconds, but I stood frozen. It was only a second, but it could have been a lifetime as I panicked, overwhelmed by that seductive magic.

But I could not be weak. I could not let those women I admired watch me break. So, I ran, relying on my other senses to help carry me through. The sound from outside the hedge melted away until the only thing I could hear was the rustling of branches through a phantom wind, my feet pounding the grass below me, and my steady breaths.

Blind and holding my arms before me, it was only a moment, the span of a thought, before I crashed into a hedge, scraping my arms and essentially eating the damn bush. Every part of my body wanted to run, but I couldn't. I'd have to take my time, dragging my hand along the wall of branches as I leaned on my intuition. As a witch, instinctively, I wanted to pull on my power, but that was the challenge. No magic. So, I kept that desire at bay, moving along the hedge.

The gong rang clear again. I jolted, whipping around. Thirty seconds passed by in a flash. And so did Willow as only seconds later she collided with me.

"Move it, Raven."

With no magic and no weapons, her only form of attack was to grab me and shove me into the prickly bush. I swung, connecting with flesh, but she still managed to dart away. The hedge consumed me, scratching my back and shoulders, ripping at my dress as it seemed to hold me down. I cursed her to the moon as I fought my way out, doused in annoyance with a renewed sense of competitiveness, I started after her. Willow could see and if I followed her, even coming in second, I'd keep first place overall with my two-point lead.

Kirsi had entered with her because they were tied, but I couldn't hear her behind me as I moved, following what I hoped were Willow's footfalls. Unfortunately, she was faster than I could be, and before the next gong, I'd lost her entirely. A rustling sound came from behind me. I turned, arms out, braced for attack. Try as I might, I could not see a single thing, not a shadow, nor a flick of light. Only pure darkness. I backed into the wall of bush, holding my breath as I listened for someone new to pass me. One second. Two.

Nothing was there.

Stepping out, I started again, letting the thorns of the bushes shred my arms as I used the walls for guidance, scurrying down the path. Colliding with a dead end, I cursed out loud, my voice echoing through the perceived emptiness. But then it wasn't only my voice, it was a thousand voices, so faint I couldn't make out the words, so haunted I couldn't help the shiver that ran down my back. And then there was a hand on my ankle. I kicked my foot, pulling away with ease. I ran again, convinced I was losing my mind trapped in the darkness. A set of claws ripped into my shoulder, half turning me.

Sweat formed on my brow as I pulled away and ran forward, blind. I collided with another branch and the echo of voices grew in volume, turning to laughter carried on that phantom wind. My muscles ached with the tension I carried as I hit another dead end. I turned and kept going, my pace quick but erratic. Dead end. I turned right, another wall. The hedges were moving in on me, the voices that didn't speak words were drowning me, the branches that grew talons were cutting me to pieces. Left was right and up was down and no matter which direction I went, which step I took, I was turning and spiraling into an oblivion of sheer panic and claustrophobia.

I tripped, falling to the ground. A hundred hands, all sinew and sharp nails punched from the ground, grabbing me, threatening to drag me down into the Earth. To hold me there for eternity. I kicked, adrenaline shooting through me until I was back on my feet, pushing away the feeling of dread.

Disoriented, sore, and full of panic, I stopped. I willed the entire world to stop. To silence. Until I felt the Dark King's shadows press into my skin. Until I could feel his calm and powerful presence commanding me to breathe. To collect myself.

"Turn around." The king's quiet voice sent shivers down my spine. "Turn around, Raven."

It could have been a trick. The maze was crawling with magic meant to distract us, send us in the wrong direction.

"No," the king said firmly. "Listen to me. Go right." A brush of shadow crossed the hollow of my neck. I paused, my body instantly reacting. Without a doubt, it was him.

I gulped. "Unless you're helping the others as well, go away."

His voice was less than an inch from my ear. "Are you commanding me?"

"Yes," I whispered.

The breeze picked up, and as I willed myself to be as calm as the king's low voice, the hedges rustled loud enough to drown out all other sounds.

"Go forward, don't turn."

"Go away." I could practically see the half smile on his face as I snapped at him. "I haven't seen or spoken to you for days and *this* is when you decide to have a chat?" I turned instead of following his direction to move forward. "And don't think I didn't hear about the witch you killed while I was gone."

"It was necessary. You're going the wrong way."

"Murder is not necessary on any day, and maybe if you weren't distracting me, I'd be doing a better job."

It was an absolute lie and he knew it. But he remained silent as I walked, as I turned this way and that, taking some form of control while navigating. Shrouded in darkness, his heavy presence was my only companion, I couldn't help but feel alone with him, even though I knew I wasn't. Space and distance didn't exist with his voice directly in my ear. His shadows lingering nearby. I stopped. All signs of panic from before, gone.

"Better?" he asked, cool fingers brushing my arms.

"They'll see you," I breathed, still halted.

"I control what they can see through my magic." His shadowed hands gripped my throat as he tilted my head back and whispered, "I asked you a question, Ms. Moonstone."

His magic moved directly up my body, swirling around me as it lifted my heavy curls and caressed my neck before lingering over my lips. The cool vibration of the king's power halted me as my body immediately responded. Betraying me. I stopped, closing my eyes, though I didn't need to. But then I felt the breeze on my face again, the power within it. I didn't need the king's direction. I needed to use my instincts.

He practically purred into my ear. "Go left."

"I can't focus," I said, the quiver in my voice giving me away.

"What's the matter?" he asked in a playful tone. "Cat got your tongue?"

The shadowed hands moved inch by inch down my breasts, over my stomach and stopped to hold my thighs firm. Power pulsing against me, I gasped as I backed into the hedge.

"I'll never finish like this. Please stop."

The shadows vanished, leaving a chill where they'd been.

The king's dark laugh vibrated around me as he growled, "Go left."

I ran. Knowing he'd chase me. Knowing I'd deserve each and every time I collided with a dead end or an edge of the maze. Still I ran, following the direction of the wind, not giving him time to direct me, not listening to the words he whispered into my ear, not giving in to my baser instincts that begged me to forget everything and let the king have his way.

A phantom hand reached for me time and time again, moving smoothly through my hair. I ignored it all, knowing I'd probably not be the first one done thanks to the king's distraction and my own panicking, but hoping I wouldn't be last as I followed the direction of the breeze and eventually found my way through. I had no idea I'd reached the end. One moment the world was black and silent and the next it was bright as the day.

All the coven leaders stared down at me before returning their attention to the maze. They hardly regarded me at all, which could only mean I hadn't impressed them. But then perhaps they hadn't seen me whispering to the king either. Unless he really was distracting everyone.

Searching for the closest tapestry, my shoulders sank. Willow, Nym, Onyx and Kirsi had all beaten me out. I refused to meet the king's gaze, even when I heard his whispering voice in my ear demanding I do so. He'd distracted me. I'd taken fifth place in this Trial. Willow, grinning ear to ear had gotten first, taking the overall top spot from me as well.

We stood together, staring at the names shuffling magically on the tapestries as we waited for the others to finish. Fortunately, I wasn't last, but poor Breya was. Following Willow's twenty points, I held second place with eighteen. Nym and Kir were tied with seventeen and Onyx was right on their tails with sixteen points.

The longer we stood there, the more I began to worry for the witches that had demanded entry to watch this Trial. The king ... he could strike again. And with no remorse or explanation. And he'd justify it with something unforgivable and the dangerous cycle we were all on would continue.

Something needed to change. But apart from his interference, he'd been avoiding me, so it wasn't like I could sit him down and ask what was happening. What kind of explanation could he truly give me? Or would he give me any at all? Perhaps it was time that I start looking for my own answers.

Steel filled my veins as I resolved to discover the truth behind the king who killed witches for sport. I turned finally, looking him directly in the eyes as I smiled, lifting an eyebrow. I wouldn't dare him to kill me, that would be foolish. But I would dare him to underestimate me.

25

The mechanism within the lock on my door clicked as I stepped inside. They could bolt me in, but it was only temporary. Leery of someone hearing me unlock the door with magic, I waited. Buying time, I dressed in all black, braiding my hair back and contemplating gloves, as if they'd somehow keep me from being tracked.

The coven leaders had requested an audience with the king, and I knew he'd be distracted there, not worrying about what the Chosen were doing in their rooms. Or perhaps he'd be more distracted by Willow, who had given him so much attention after she'd won, and I'd given him none. She'd stayed behind to speak with him as we were escorted away, and I knew it was the perfect opportunity to start digging into the Dark King's castle. I decided against the gloves. If I was caught by anyone at all, I'd likely just be another one of the king's 'necessary' tragedies anyway.

I told Kirsi I wasn't feeling well and was going to bed early. Lying to her was becoming an awful habit. One I'd need to break sooner rather than later. But as I pressed my ear against the door, listening to footsteps fade down the hall, I knew I had to do this. She would never have let me go alone. My life was one thing, but being responsible for the loss of my best friend was entirely different.

Gritting my teeth, I used the lock spell and inched the door open far enough to peek up and down the hall. The flames of scattered wall sconces were my only company as I tiptoed out of my room, shut the door, and leaped into the first shadowed alcove I could find.

The king's castle was a maze of darkness, like the Trial we'd just completed. Though there were small alcoves carved into the halls, only a few of them were lit. The rest was near darkness and deep shadows. My heart raced as my conscience warred with my heart to turn around and go back to my rooms. I couldn't do it, though. I needed to take advantage of this opportunity. The nagging sensation in my mind told me I needed to do this and, of all the things I'd learned in my life, ignoring a witch's intuition was always a terrible idea.

It was as if something in the castle called me. But in that moment, it wasn't bravery that pushed me on, not the intuition of a witch; it was sheer panic as I realized I'd actually walked out of my rooms and was now wandering the castle as if people hadn't died for less.

Waving my fingers, I cast the spell to make me silent. If a soldier passed by, he could see me if I wasn't careful, but he would hear neither my breaths nor my footfalls. Turning corners, and peeking around corridors, I hustled forward until I was well and truly lost within the king's castle. It became so cold and dark, I felt as if the halls were closing in on me, as if gnarled beasts would crawl from around the dangerous passageways and rip me to shreds. The lights faded. Even those I didn't touch with magic seemed to produce less light than when I'd left my room. As if even the fire feared the wrath of a ruthless king.

Three guards shuffled by as I dashed into a darkened recess in the wall. My heart dipped into my stomach and I held my breath unnecessarily. Pressed firmly against cool obsidian stone as they passed, I wondered if the castle had always been this dark and dreary. I recalled the white palace from my dream. It couldn't have been real.

When had the soldiers stopped searching the shadows? Had these walls heard the laughter of the Dark King as a boy? Had they witnessed his mother, the witch, fall in love with his father, the shifter, bringing our two clashing worlds to a measure of peace?

Silence fell once more and with it, my resolve. I shouldn't be here, shouldn't risk my life for mere curiosity. Surely, I'd eventually find something worth hunting. Perhaps the Grimoires themselves, but at what cost? My own life? I turned, intending to walk back to my rooms, to save the adventure for another day. But the moment before I stepped from the shadows, my eye caught the movement of red hair, the shuffling of a figure walking pointedly forward. Breya.

She lifted the blue edges of her hood as I sank backward, holding my hand to my throat as if it would mask the surprise on my shadowed face. With wide steps and clear direction, there was no doubt she knew exactly where she was going. But how could she? Breya was the weak link in the competition. She'd come in last in every Trial but the first. She'd cowered away from the king, sinking away from all confrontation. She'd allowed Onyx to target her and only once defended herself. How did a woman like that walk through this dark castle as if she'd done it a hundred times?

I followed, curiosity prevailing once more. The hem of her navy cloak dragged behind her on the floor, billowing as she quickened her pace. The cadence of metal grew in the distance, soldiers drawing near. She hid. But there was nowhere for me to do the same. I'd kept a safe distance, only staying close enough to see her through the darkness.

Spinning on a heel, I hustled backward, the only option turning into a hall we'd passed. If the guards came this way, they would not miss me and there was nowhere else to go. This hall, for some reason, was not like the others. There were no alcoves where Bastian's statues might have once stood, or paintings once displayed. The wall was flat.

I took out all the lights in the hall as far down as I could, smothering myself in darkness. With the scattered light throughout the castle, I doubted the soldiers would notice which halls were lit and which were not. But the king's men were shifters. They were beasts, even in human form. They would see far better in the dark than I could and that is why this castle was an advantage to him and his men. Why, even within the walls of the fortress, where men would otherwise be equals, he would have the advantage.

"Dark down here, innit, Soliad?"

Boots halted on the hall floor around the corner. There were two options from here, they'd continue forward, or they would turn toward me, and the odds were, even though it was dark, they'd see me if they turned.

"Probably the king's magic close by. Best hurry. I hate it down here."

I didn't move a muscle, squeezing my eyes shut as I waited for them to round that corner. I'd have to throw them back and run, hoping they wouldn't have enough time to see my face. Magic crackled under my skin, ready, should I need to attack. I held an arm to my chest, just in case.

But as fate would have it, they continued straight, passing me by with no clue of my presence. I waited longer than I wanted to, assuring my heart they'd well and truly gone and no one else was coming. Peeking around the corner, only small orange orbs of light were to be seen from the alcoves down the opposite hall. I inched forward until I reached the last spot I'd seen Breya. But she was gone.

Rushing forward down the corridor, I hoped to catch sight of her again. Though my footsteps remained silent, my breaths were nothing more than a whisper even as I panted. The window of opportunity for me was closing. Eyes seemed to fall on me around every corner as paranoia swept in. I was sure I'd run directly into the king any second. I'd be caught and Breya would get away.

There was nowhere to go at the end of the passageway but to the right, into an enormous sitting room lit thoroughly. I stopped at the door, studying the room carefully to make sure no one was inside. Paintings of horses and landscapes covered the walls. Textured rugs lay on the floor, framed in golds and reds, and a fireplace, twin to the one in the Chosen's hall, roared with heat and flames. If it were the same, it never needed tending. Never burned away the log in its belly, never choked the chimney with years of built-up ash.

I flew across the room, darting into the opposite hallway and continuing forward, though I wasn't altogether convinced at this point I was moving forward. The king's magic created doorways. Without a doubt, he'd purposely made his own labyrinth of this castle, making navigating near impossible.

Magic pulsed in the hall now, dense enough that if I dragged my hand through the stiff air, I might have felt it in physical form. It didn't take an astute witch to know something powerful, something that nearly called me by name, was close by. I walked on the tips of my toes, cautious as I approached the source of such heady magic. Rounding the final corner, I was nearly blinded by a room so bright it might have held captive the sun.

Every hair on my body stood on end as I neared, squinting beyond the power. A warning of danger rippled over me. I chose to ignore it, completely enthralled by what I knew would be in that room. As I crossed the threshold, my heart stopped. My breaths stopped. Ears ringing, I fell to my knees and crawled across the golden floor toward the seventh pillar. Pulling myself to standing, I placed my hand onto a book so ancient, if not for the magic that preserved it, the leather would have withered away. The moon shaped stone pulsed below my fingers. The first and last drop of blood from every Moon Coven witch lending to the power vibrating within our Grimoire. I could nearly hear it whisper to me, as if it were sentient.

I'd seen this book a thousand times. The record of my ancestors' markings, the family trees that extended far beyond any extent of time I could grasp. All there. But it was different here. Only a piece of an unfinished puzzle. Not a relic sitting in Crescent Cottage. I turned then, finally taking in the rest of the gilded room.

Seven pillars, six books, one dead body.

Breya.

I swallowed the scream in my throat as I flew across the room to her. So consumed by the power of six combined Grimoires, I hadn't noticed her. I rotated her to the side, hoping I was wrong. That she had only tripped and fallen, but as I brushed her beautiful red hair from her face, vacant eyes stared back at me. She was dead. My stomach rolled, bile rising in my throat.

"Raven?"

I gasped, turning to see Grey standing right outside the door, white as a wraith. His eyes flicked to Breya in my arms, both of us on the floor.

Mouth falling open, he uttered the word, "How?"

I moved away from her, struggling to stand. "It wasn't me. I swear it."

"Get out of the room, Raven." His voice was low, laced with warning as he stared at the door frame and then back to me. "You have to leave now."

"But Breya ... and the Grimoires. If I could—"

"Now," he barked, stepping away from the door as if it were poisoned.

I lifted my hands in surrender as I walked carefully toward him. "I saw her running in the halls and I followed her here. I was too far behind and, when I finally found where she'd gone, it was too late. I didn't do this, Grey. You have to believe me." Stepping out of the room, I grabbed his hand. "Please, Grey. The king will kill me."

He shook his head, backing away slowly. "How did you get into the room?"

"I don't ... I don't understand. I simply walked in."

"That's not possible, Raven."

I looked away from him, shriveling back from the tone he'd taken. There was no escape for me now. Not without attacking Grey and making a run for it, but even then, the king would find me before I could leave his castle. "Grey, please," I begged. "You know me. You know I wouldn't do this."

"I know you didn't kill Breya."

"You do? I mean, of course you do. I would never ..." My voice faded as he stepped away from me.

"Who are you?"

I shook my head in confusion, scrunching my nose. "What do you mean?"

He pointed toward the room, his voice growing in volume. "How did you walk out of that room? It's protected by the king's magic. Breya died because she crossed the threshold without his permission.

There's not an ounce of Fire Coven blood within you, but you ... How are you alive?"

I shook my head. "I don't know."

26

"You can't tell him. He'll kill me."

Grey walked with me through the shadowed halls, our voices in hushed tones as we hurried back to my rooms. I couldn't get the image of Breya out of my mind. Her ashen face, the emptiness in her eyes. Another witch's blood on the king's hands. If indirectly.

I glanced at the king's cousin, his mind clearly racing with thoughts as his mouth formed a line. But so was mine as I started to doubt whether I could actually trust Grey at all. He'd found me with a dead body. Perhaps he was making his own conclusions as we went. He could have been walking me to death's door and I would have been none the wiser.

"I won't tell the king. I'm not sure what saved you tonight, but do me a favor and don't try to go back. The power in that room is not meant for one witch alone. The only man in this land we can trust to protect and not wield that power is Bastian. If the witches know what happens when the books are together, they will find a way to bring this castle down."

He turned toward me, grabbing my arms as he lowered his voice until I could barely hear him. "I'm trusting you with the greatest secret. I need to know that it is not misplaced. You cannot tell a soul. Not even Kirsi."

"If you promise not to tell him a single thing, I will keep his secret. You have my word."

Unease washed over me, growing like a boulder in the pit of my stomach as I realized, like it or not, I was going to have to trust Grey with my life for my whole life. Because even when I left these Trials behind, as long as I knew this secret, I'd never be safe.

We carried on until we were just outside my door.

"What will happen to her? To Breya?"

He shrugged, his large shoulders seeming heavier than normal. "There's no way she would have found that room in one night. She had to be searching like the oth—" He stopped instantly, realizing what he was saying.

"So that's what the others were looking for?"

"Go to bed, Raven. Let this go. It won't do you any good to investigate further."

I nodded. I wasn't sure I wanted to know anything else. Ignorance was bliss and curiosity was misery. Leaving Grey in the hall, I let myself in, going straight through to my bedchamber.

"You snuck out?" Kirsi didn't even try to hide her anger. "I've been doing everything I can to help us succeed in these Trials and you're hiding stuff from me."

"I'm not ..." I paused, a lie sitting on the tip of my tongue waiting. But I couldn't do it. She deserved better than that, and I needed her. "I'm sorry."

She circled the bed, crossing her arms as she stood in front of me. Her messy hair haloed in candlelight as if she'd just crawled out of bed. "Tell me the truth. What's going on?"

I couldn't tell her about Breya. Not yet. Maybe not ever. But she needed more than the careful lies I'd been weaving. "I think the king likes me."

"Yeah. No shit." She lifted an eyebrow. "You've been sneaking out to sleep with him?"

"Uhm, no. But he gifted me access to the greenhouse and I've been working there at night sometimes. And he ... Well, he's been avoiding me. But before we went home for All Hallows Eve, we had a moment."

She walked backwards, sitting heavily on my bed. "A moment?"

"I thought he would kiss me, but he was so mad and then I ... and then he wasn't. And he just vanished. He loves to do that."

"You've completely lost me."

The anger melted off her face and, though I felt guilty for distracting her from one truth with another, at least this she could know.

"I haven't been back to the greenhouse since we returned from All Hallows Eve. I don't know a lot, but I do know there are witches trying to infiltrate the castle without the king's permission."

"Without his permission? He infiltrated our homes and stole our Grimoires without permission. I'd say it's his own fault."

"What if he has a reason for taking the Grimoires?"

Her eyes doubled in size as she gasped. "Do you know something?"

I lifted my hands. "No. I'm not making excuses for him either if that's what you're thinking. It's just ... I can't help but wonder if there's more to the story than what we know."

"You know your father would say that's exactly what he wants you to think."

"I know," I said, sitting beside her. "And besides all that, you've been doing so much for us. Keeping tabs on all the Chosen and being social while I've hidden away. I'm sorry I'm not pulling my weight. I never expected it to be like this."

She laid her head on my shoulder. "I'm always going to be here for you, Rave. Even if you fall in love with a murderous bastard. I'll still cut him if he hurts you. And if he has you under some spell, if he's been slipping you elixirs, I'll put that fucker in a grave."

"Shh." I giggled.

"What? It's not like he can hear me."

All the color drained from my face as I realized, even if Grey hadn't betrayed me, the king could have overheard everything. He could know. But surely, he would have been in my rooms waiting for me, or maybe he'd be here soon. I couldn't let Kirsi get caught up in any of it.

"I think I need some sleep."

"I woke to check on you and when you weren't here, I was worried sick." She took my hands. "Seriously, Raven, you're not in this alone. I'm here if you need me."

I pulled her into my arms. "I don't deserve you."

"Not even a little bit." She kissed the top of my head and went back to her rooms.

The king never came. I stayed up for hours, pacing the floors of my rooms, too scared to call him by name, but also too anxious to fall asleep. The second my eyes finally closed, a banging sounded through the rooms as someone knocked on the door. I crawled out of bed, so tired I could hardly keep my eyes open. The door opened with magic before I managed to get all the way to it. The Dark King stood, beard freshly trimmed, eyes as sharp as ever, wings tucked behind his broad shoulders, flanked by two giant men, all clad in black, smooth leather, as they stared me down.

I curtsied low, my nose parallel with the obsidian floor.

"Stand," the king demanded.

I rose, gripping my fingers to hide the tremble.

"You will dress for the day and meet my advisers and I in the hall in exactly ten minutes."

I nodded, afraid of the way my voice would break if I spoke a word. The king and his men stepped aside and Tavia and Clariss rushed into the room, shutting the door.

"Undress, quickly now," Clariss demanded. "The king is in no mood to be delayed."

"Has something happened?" I asked as innocently as I could while pulling the long nightgown over my head.

"There's been another," Tavia said, her voice little more than a whisper.

"Snap out of it, girl," Clariss barked. "Go get the black gown with the silver buttons."

They dressed me quickly as I stood there like a fool, the terror on my face every bit as prominent as theirs. Tavia used her beauty magic on my face as Clariss plaited two braids in a crown on my head, the rest of my curls getting nothing more than a brush through as we flew from the room and into the hall. And not a second too soon. I wondered if the Chosen had noticed Breya wasn't there. Her rooms were at the very end of the hall, so there would be no reason for me to know she was dead. Not yet.

I locked eyes with the king. Though his face was hard and his stature as fearsome as ever, the look he gave me was neither one of anger, nor intimidation, nor the myriad of other emotions I'd received from him. It was pity. I wished he hadn't looked at me at all. I wished I didn't know what it felt like to have his hands on me. I wished I hadn't dreamed of him exploring my body. I wished I could take back every stolen moment with him. Because as he looked at me with those soft eyes I'd never seen him take with another, I mirrored them. I pitied him as well.

"You'll follow," one of the king's men advised. "Should anyone step out of line, you'll be taken at once by the soldiers. There's been another casualty, and I'm sorry to say, it's one of the Chosen."

I feigned shock, aligning myself with the others. I couldn't meet eyes with Kirsi as I looked back. I could fool the king's advisors, maybe even the king himself, but she'd see right through my face, especially after our talk last night. So, I turned my head down and faced forward, grateful for the staff between us.

We were taken back to the hall outside the throne room, similar to our first day at the castle. The king and his men left us with all the soldiers and staff as they went inside. I watched Grey approach Kirsi. They talked for a few minutes, though their voices were quiet. He stepped away to console old Ophelia and I wondered how much the other Chosen actually cared that one of us had died. Breya had always been kind and helpful where she could be. But I'd never seen any of them too close to her.

"You're to be questioned," Tavia said, leaning toward me. "The king will sit with his advisors as they discuss the plans and then each of us will go in and answer whatever questions they have. It happens frequently. Don't let the Old Barren rattle you."

"The Old Barren?"

She nodded. "That's the one who takes a bear shape in animal form. He used to work with Bas—uh—the king's father."

"Thanks for the tip."

"She'll be fine," Grey said as he approached. "Only guilty parties have anything to fear from our young king."

I swallowed, casting my eyes to the floor.

Grey's massive hand landed on my shoulder. "Chin up, Raven."

I nodded as the doors behind me opened.

"Grey Firewing, the king will see you now."

Grey winked at me before marching through the doors that closed behind him. My ears began to burn as I wondered why I'd put my faith in the king's cousin. He could be telling them everything right now and I'd be none the wiser until the soldiers closed in on me. And try as I might, I couldn't hear what happened beyond the barrier of the door.

Seconds turned into minutes as time crawled slower than a passing slug. I played the whole thing in my mind. The shouting from behind the door, the way they would fly open as the soldiers surrounded me. The look on Kir's face when she watched them drag me away, knowing I still hadn't managed to tell her the full truth last night. Because in this castle, the king could murder for sport, but walking in the halls was cause for instant death.

The second the doors flew open, I squeezed my eyes shut, ears ringing as I waited for my fate.

"Kirsi Moondance, step forward."

Every ounce of blood drained from my face as my best friend's name was called. What had Grey said? There was a full line of witches in the hall along with a massive number of servants, and she'd been called first. The entire corridor fell silent as she walked forward. She looked at me then. A blanket of fear upon her face as she dipped her chin and carried on into the king's throne room. When the doors shut between us, I stepped forward, as if I had no control of the movement. The desire to protect her, no matter the cost, overwhelmed me. Even if it meant a full confession.

Again, time slowed. Each second felt as if an hour had passed. No one in the hall spoke a word as we all stared at the backside of that door, waiting for something, anything to tell us that Kirsi was fine. She'd made her mark with the Chosen as she had with all the people around her. Full of sass and humor, Kirsi was fiercely loyal and doubly lovable.

Again, the doors opened. Her demeanor had changed entirely. My shoulders slumped and my exhale was easier as she slipped right back into her typical self.

"Someone get that bear a snack. He's in a mood." With that, she smirked at me and was escorted down the hall, and likely back to her rooms.

"Raven Moonstone, step forward."

I nodded, primarily to convince myself entering was my choice. The throne room seemed bigger than the last time. With only three occupants, I supposed it should. I carried my chin high, strolling down the center aisle of the room and kneeling before the king and his two advisors. My dress pooled around me in black waves as silence filled the room like smoke in a spell jar. Uncomfortable, yet necessary. The coarse feel of crinkled paper landed in my palm. I couldn't look at the note as they stared me down, but as I rose, the king waved his advisers closer to speak in hushed tones. Holding my breath, I chanced a glance.

CALM!

I nearly snorted at the secret demand. As if he had no idea that he was the one I feared the most. I looked at him then. Truly looked at the man who had lived in my mind as an enemy for far longer than he'd been an actual living being. As if the monster that lived under the child's bed had crawled from the shadows and was revealed to be just a person. Bastian was just a man. With heavy burdens and questionable morals, but the way he rubbed his bottom lip with his thumb as he spoke to his advisers, the way his broad shoulders carried the weight of the world, the way he created a sense of peace within me by a simple piece of paper, he was just a man. A man that, despite his faults and serious lack of judgment, had somehow inspired loyalty from all the shifters of the world and a sliver of the witches.

His dark eyes flicked to me as he nodded, listening to whatever they'd been saying and I couldn't help the small step forward, the lift of my hand as I wanted to reach for him. To simply tell him the truth.

"As you've heard, Breya Moonbranch is dead," the shorter of the two men said as their secret meeting came to an end.

"Make no mistake," the king interjected. "She chose to leave her rooms, breaking the rules." He stared at me, and I couldn't help but feel bare before him. "She is dead because of her own actions. You are not called here today to prove yourself innocent of murder."

I opened my mouth to speak, thought better of it, and snapped it shut. It was quick, but not quick enough.

The bear, or the Old Barren they'd called him, moved down the steps until he towered over me, inches away as he nearly blocked my view of the king. "Have something to say?"

I shook my head.

"You will speak during this meeting, or you will not like the outcome, I can promise you that, witch."

Something in the way he'd said 'witch' ignited that rebellion inside of me. The one that sent fear right out the window, wholly replacing it with stupid.

"Do you even hear yourself speaking?" I balled my hands into fists.

"Come again?" He bared his teeth to me in warning, but I was a fool.

"We are all lambs for slaughter, waiting our turn in line for you animals." I stepped to the side, so I could look directly into Bastian's hardened face. "I'm done playing your games."

"You're done when the king says you're done and not a moment before." The Old Barren's face grew redder with each word he spat. "How many times have you left your rooms?"

"I will not answer to you."

"Oh, you will answer to me, or you will die as swiftly as your friend. How many times have you left your rooms?"

I said nothing, chin high as I stood toe to toe with the man that would see me dead.

He raised his fist faster than I could have seen coming and the blow would have sent me to the floor had the king not appeared between us, catching the shifter's fist mid-strike.

"You're excused, Barren."

"I beg your pardon?" He seethed, staring down the king as if he was the one in charge.

Bastian's voice was teetering on the edge of danger as his shadows began to roll below him, a threat, if nothing more. "Leave. Now."

They stared each other down, a pissing match if ever I'd seen one, but in the end, the bear stormed out.

"How many times, Raven?" Bastian asked, turning toward me.

The other man stood watching the door the Old Barren had walked out of, his face void of color. The king's eyes were hollow; the silver dulled to a simple gray with nothing kind in the way he looked at me now.

"How many times have I gone to the gardens? The single room we're allowed to visit? The dining hall? Call me crazy, but I hadn't thought to count."

Steady hands slipped into his pockets, his casual demeanor like a shield of armor between us. "Let me rephrase the question, Ms. Moonstone. Was last night the first time you left your rooms unaccompanied by a member of my staff?"

My eyes flashed to the shadows curling around his feet like smoke and I wondered if they'd betrayed me. Cheeks burning red, I clutched the paper in my fist. "Yes."

"Why?"

"No. You don't get to ask questions when you refuse to answer any of mine."

He turned away, his jaw set as he pinched the bridge of his nose. "Yes, I do." His voice started so quietly, but as he spoke it grew in volume. "I am not your fucking enemy. There are rules in place for your safety."

"What are you saving us from, if not the real villain in this world?"

"Better a villain by truth than a hero by lies. I'll be the devil in your story if that's what you need, but I will not apologize for what I choose to protect." He looked at me then. His eyes lit with passion and anger and a thousand other things I couldn't define. "That includes you."

27

Ms. Moonstone,
   Meet in the hall for your next Trial.
   Be careful.
   ~Bastian

T crumpled the paper in my hand and lit the fireplace just to throw it inside before it could burn away. He'd dismissed me from that interrogation not three hours ago and already we were back to this. I didn't bother responding as I stepped out into the hall once more, joining the other Chosen. I wasn't sure my mind was in it, but at this point, the sooner we got through these Trials, the sooner we could go home.

The separation in the hall was not lost on me. Alliances formed were breaking apart as we neared the middle of the competition. With three Trials behind us, though Willow was still ahead of me by two points, I was more determined than ever to win the role as coven leader. Something needed to change.

We were led to a large room in the castle. I couldn't pull my eyes from the line of black pillows on the floor dividing the room in half. Floor to ceiling paintings of haunted shadowed figures filled the walls and the guards marching beside us carried in six high-backed chairs, setting them in a line directly across from the pillows. Grey marched to the corner of the room and stood, silent, mirroring the other guards. I imagined in these moments it was a challenge for him to pretend he had a semblance of free will in this castle. The Chosen studied each other, but it was clear only Willow, knowing a clue was coming to her, felt confident with her chin held high, a smug grin on her face. Were we going to turn this room into a bloodbath? Would we be fighting each other or working together?

The rest of our collective steps were heavier, smaller than they had been, as we were ushered to the center of the room and instructed to each find a pillow and sit. We waited in silence until the king joined us, taking the tallest chair in the line across from us. He nodded toward the two guards at the door, and they let in the other witches that would fill the opposing seats. The coven leaders, surrounded by more guards than I'd yet seen at the castle. I marveled at the collection of markings upon the old women's bodies. All of their lives were in danger if they did not abide by the king's exact rule. But perhaps their magic, their combined power would keep them safe, should anything happen.

Endora rested her wrinkled hands in her lap, her jaw clenched tight as she stared straight ahead. The Moss Coven leader had always been known and respected for her no-nonsense way of leading. Nikos' parents had left her territory and joined the Moon Coven years ago, but he still always respected her. And so did I. As did the rest of the witches. Maybe they weren't perfect, but they'd helped lead the witches through these hard times and, even though the covens were drifting apart, these women led our kind with the strength and courage of our ancestors. I longed to be revered alongside such powerful and influential women. My grandmother had wanted this for herself, and for me, and now that reality was within my grasp.

I sat straighter on my pillow, determined to impress the women I hoped to work with. The Trials were only temporary, the role of coven leader was until death. I glanced at the king. He watched me closely, trying to read my mind it seemed, as I looked at the older women. A tiny piece of paper appeared in my hand, but I could not read it. I could not let temporary distractions deter me from lifetime goals. So, I crumpled the paper and pushed it under my cushion.

The doors opened once more, and an ancient woman entered the room, leaning heavily on a carved wooden staff. She wore gold bands up her brown arms just like Nym, and her gown seemed so thin it hardly covered the hundreds of markings on her body. She was magnificent, inching across the room, each clang of her staff upon the obsidian floor louder than the last. I looked to the king then, wondering if he would offer her his chair, but he hadn't taken his eyes off the old woman as he pointed to Willow.

"This is our prior winner."

The woman moved to stand before Willow, taking her hand and tracing patterns up and down her arm until Willow nodded in understanding. She'd just been given the clue she'd won, and I envied every second of it.

The old witch walked in the gap between the coven leaders and Chosen, keeping her back to the leaders as she struggled to get herself down to a kneeling position, laying her nose and palms flat on the floor as if she bowed to us rather than the king that was directly behind her. He didn't seem to notice, more enthralled by the old woman and the chant she began singing than the propriety of it all. Her haunting tune carried throughout the room until the air was thick with magic I had never felt before. It rested upon my skin. I could feel it in my lungs. My head grew light as I swayed, bathing in the power she conjured.

"The mind is a puzzle, a deep vat of memories, of fears, of loss, of love, and regret. An intricate map of your own moral compass and a dictionary of words that drive you. For your next Trial, you will all be put under a spell that will take you into your own mind. You will face those fears, relive those memories, discover all the hard truths there is to know about yourself. You must find your way out of your own mind, but I warn you, not all who venture so deep into themselves return."

I locked eyes with Bastian. He'd known, of course. I couldn't mistake the look of worry on his face, even as our gaze broke, and he looked upon the others. First at Kirsi beside me and then Nym beside her. Even down to Onyx. Was he actually worried? More so than he'd been when we faced the fire serpent.

A throat cleared and my head snapped to Endora, who stared only at me, her hard eyes surrounded in wrinkles as she finally moved her gaze to Zennik, who sat on the other side of me. I watched him out of the corner of my eye. He may not have feared the king, but the sweat that dripped down his forehead was a clear indication of how he felt about the other coven leaders.

I cast my eyes to the floor, listening once more to the old woman's chanting as I pushed away that accusatory look from Endora. She'd seen me staring at the king and I couldn't begin to wonder what conclusions she'd conjure in her own mind.

Again, the woman's sound enraptured me so heavily it was as if I'd unwillingly become intoxicated by her tune, carrying me along her foreign lyrics like a pirate to a siren's song. Several markings on her body began to glow a bright green color. She looked each of us in the eyes, nodding as one by one, we fell into our own minds, leaving the castle, and our bodies behind.

Traveling into my subconscious was painless, yet terrifying. For a brief moment, I'd forgotten who I was, or where I was. I was simply a little girl tracing the dark markings down her grandmother's arms with tiny fingers as she was cuddled to sleep. Light blue eyes, a match to my own, stared down at me, so soft and familiar, even as a babe I knew it was the safest place I'd ever be.

My grandmother held me in an old rocking chair that squeaked in protest if she went too far back. She smiled down at me as she spoke with a voice I thought I'd never hear again. "You listen here to your grandmother, Raven."

"Mother, she is four. Let her be little." My mother swept into the room, and for a moment I hardly recognized her. A smile lit her whole face as she looked down upon us both, far younger than I ever remembered her being. Perhaps the years since my grandmother died had not been as kind to her as I'd thought.

"Nonsense. This is a Moonstone witch. She will hear our teach-ings." She swiped a wild black curl from my forehead. "Never make an important decision when the moon is gone from the sky."

My mother tossed her hands into the air. "Oh, here we go."

My grandmother continued as if she hadn't said a word. "Do one thing each day that is just for you. Whisper your wishes to the full moon. Sing to the peonies to help them grow. A little sugar in your soil will sweeten your tomatoes." She ran a finger down the bridge of my nose and my eyes grew heavy. "At least once in your lifetime there will be Trials held. Win them."

"Mother!"

Yanked from my grandmother's arms, my heart instantly yearned for her warmth. The four-year-old version of me began to cry, reaching for her, but my mom held me away, lifting a brow as she stared down at her own mother.

"Fine, fine. We will speak of farm animals and familiar colors. Give her back."

My mother's hesitation was short lived as she placed me back into those waiting arms, though I'm sure my wailing had a good deal to do with it. "Our dear friend Tasa lives on a farm. She has an ugly goat. What does the goat say?" she asked, rocking once more as she watched my mother out of the corner of her eye. When I answered, twirling her wiry, silver hair in my fingers she nodded, humming a tune as a marking near her throat illuminated.

You can never be too careful with who you trust, dear girl. Trust our coven leaders. Tasa will never steer you wrong. Protect the book at all costs. She tilted her head toward the pedestal in her shop.

My conscious mind jerked as I remembered this was not reality, but a memory I'd long since forgotten. As the edges of the memory began to fade, I heard the old matriarch one final time.

One day, it may be yours to protect. There is more power in that than you know.

Falling away from the memory, I wondered why I'd been taken there for this Trial. What significance that memory had when really all it brought was pain. In that moment, I was content. But then the loss of her slammed into me all over again. I tried to remember the touch of her skin beneath my fingers. The lilt of her soft voice, the deep wrinkles around her eyes. But the harder I tried, the faster the details were swept away from me.

Falling deeper into my mind with no control, the second time more erratic than the first, I felt a jerk and sway in my subconscious, a tiny bit of chaos in the transition from one stage to another. Until I realized the next part would not be a memory, but a feeling. One that oozed over my skin, causing my heart to race, though I was separated from my body. Mouth dry, I tried to swallow but couldn't as fear gripped my throat.

Landing in a pool of shadows, my form was corporeal as I lay on the floor panting. The inexplicable dread caused my fingers to tremble and cool sweat to bead on the back of my neck. A dark form loomed over me, its features hidden. The embodiment of fear, it seemed. Crawling backward on the icy floor, I held a palm out, magic sitting, waiting.

"Don't come any closer."

The shadowed figure tilted its head in an odd angle as it looked at me. "I do not fear you, witch." The rasp in Fear's voice was chilling.

I released a spell, intent to send it soaring backward, but it did not move. Instead, it cackled, growing larger as it inched forward, looming over me. Until Fear changed, melting into the embodiment of the Dark King, pure evil in his eyes as he looked at me with such hatred my heart nearly stopped.

His gaze lifted to a spot behind me. I stood, turning to see the soldiers whose faces I would never forget. Those that murdered my grandmother for doing her job. Eyes hard as stone, staring forward as they took commands from a young king.

"Take them all. Take them by force. If anyone stands in your way, you kill them on the spot. Do not hesitate."

"Sir!" they shouted, turning and fading away.

"You're a monster." Though my heart was in my throat, I couldn't help but say the words. "You just ordered her death. I loved her and you took her away."

The king's head tilted in an odd way as a wicked smile spread across his face. "Did I?"

Again, his gaze flicked to someone behind me. I turned to see another group of shifters. The Old Barren directly in front of them, a smile that matched the king's slathered on his face as he held his hands in fists to his side.

"They must not thrive. Spoil the gardens, destroy the farms. Leave only enough for them to chance survival through the winter months. No animals are to be left alive. No crop unturned."

I gasped, my mouth hanging open as I watched the shifters surge forward, a garden nestled behind a witch's home taking shape as they destroyed it all. When a young witch came running from the cottage, begging them to have mercy, a scythe shot through the air, rounded blade slaughtering her. More and more witches came, the outcry of injustice rattling the vision, but they too were murdered with no remorse. Until the only thing left in the monstrous act was a pile of dead witches, pouring their final drops of blood into a witch's desecrated garden. I'd just witnessed my first Thrashing and though it was only a vision, my stomach rolled at the reality of our kingdom.

Everything faded to darkness as I glowered at the king in the maze of my mind.

"Not only are you refusing to help the witches, but you're also murdering us. Starving us every year. Everything I thought I knew about you was true," I said, storming forward. "You're the devil."

The king whipped out a sword and held it to my throat, his eyebrows peaked and a terrible smile on his lips as he held my life at the point of his weapon. I stood frozen, my fear waning until Breya appeared, her eyes void of life, fixed straight ahead, her skin lacking any color. She skimmed the top of the floor, floating by like a wraith until her head snapped sideways, pinning me with a hideous glare. I jumped away from her, nicking my throat on the tip of the king's blade.

I couldn't feel the blood as pure terror washed over me. Bodies. So many dead bodies filled the floor. Some I'd known, some I hadn't. Tasa lay dead below my feet. I scrambled away, tripping and landed face to face with my decaying grandmother. The scream that left my throat was all but silent as her face changed into mine. Staring down at my desiccated form, heart pounding, the sharp edge of a blade rested on the back of my neck. I closed my eyes, refusing to look at my lifeless face, refusing to accept this twisted form of reality my mind had created.

But was it twisted? Weren't the king's demands real?

"How could they be?" my voice asked.

I opened my eyes, expecting my dead body to have spoken. Instead, I lay on the floor, all the bodies, all the death, the blade at my neck, gone. I scrambled to my feet, turning to see myself standing in the void of darkness with the king's infamous blade in my hand.

"What is happening?" I asked, stepping away from whatever had taken my form.

The smug look on the mirage's face rattled me. I tried to move away again. To step backward, but my feet would not comply. Stuck to the floor by shadowed hands, I panicked. Magic I'd suppressed for a long time grew within me, the loss of control of that magic would be devastating. Even in the boundaries of my own mind.

Nikos appeared beside my other form. I watched her turn to him, burying her hands in his short blond hair as she kissed him. He moved his hands up her back, staring down at her with so much love, my own heart ached. And then she stepped away, smiling sweetly to Nikos before pivoting on her heel. The Dark King appeared before her. Opposite in all ways to Nikos. He lifted her from the ground, wrapping her thighs around him as their clothing vanished. My stomach churned as I watched her slide down him, taking as much of him into her as she could. She leaned back, moaning in pleasure as he lifted her hips, slamming her down onto him again. I could hardly pull my eyes away, could hardly help the envy that crept over me until I saw Nikos' horror-stricken face.

"No," I said, trying to move to him. "It's not real."

Together or not together, this would hurt him and I didn't want that. But I also didn't want his judgment.

The sounds of their pleasure, their bodies moving together grew so loud, her feelings became mine, his hands gripped my hips. I was naked, being taken by the king in front of the man I once thought I'd marry. I couldn't help the gasp that escaped, the moan on my lips as he leaned forward, pressing his burning lips to mine as he filled me, commanding my body as he also ruined me. Rich desire pooled low in my belly with each thrust. Each blink of the king's beautiful eyes while I stared down at him. This man, this king, for all his evil, was raw power and lust.

"Raven," he rasped.

"Raven," Nikos demanded.

"Raaaveeeenn," my own voice called from behind me.

Just as I thought I'd explode from pleasure, the world stopped. The king vanished from below me. Though I ached with need, the two men were gone, and I was left more confused, more erratic than ever.

"I don't understand."

"Of course you don't," the mirage said, coming to stand before me as she twisted my hair in her fingers. "This is your mind. These are the truths that you've created. The confusion you've construed. The king was your villain before you met him. You didn't try to save your grandmother. But she didn't try to save herself either. She could have stepped to the side, you know. The king's men were taking the Grimoire no matter what. The outcome could have been so much different, had she only listened."

The mirage paced in front of me, tapping her finger to her lips as she gave words to the darkest parts of my mind. I'd thought that of course, but never spoken the words aloud, never let my grandmother be responsible for anything that happened to her. She could have lived, and the book would still be in the same place it was now.

"And don't get me started on Breya. You followed her through the castle, could have shared her fate. Yet you didn't once call out to her. Didn't try to warn her, though you know of the king's evils. What if she was merely sleep walking? Or under someone's spell? You didn't save her, you let her die."

"I didn't. She wasn't asleep. She knew—"

"You don't know anything. You assume a lot and know very little."

I opened my mouth to protest, but she—I—was right. I didn't know her motive, just as I didn't really know the king or his motives. I'd cast him as a villain and that was that.

"Oh, but Nikos ..."

"Yes, I know. Please stop."

She shook her head, staring at me. "Are you afraid of your own truths?"

I nodded, admitting the shame that came when I thought of Nikos. "We would have never been a good match. He deserves better."

She shook her head again, the eerie head tilt jarring. "Perhaps it's you that deserves better. Perhaps that's why your mind strays so easily to the Dark King."

"Nikos is ... in the past. Maybe I left him wondering on All Hallows Eve, but my heart knows, my mind knows we are done." I paused considering her words. Every day I battled these things in my mind. Was the Dark King truly bad, with all his flirty notes and giving me access to Kirsi and the greenhouse? Could he be both?

"He could."

I locked eyes with myself one final time as the acknowledgment seemed to be the answer to this Trial. The evil vanished as quickly as the weight on my shoulders. And then I was falling again, only this time, I was truly tumbling, spiraling deeper into my mind than I thought I should go. I couldn't stop the freefall. Too deep. This was dangerous. I could no longer feel my corporal body, no longer remember where I was. Shadows of myself zipped past me. I couldn't reach out, couldn't control my mind, my thoughts, my racing heart.

"Raven!"

That voice. I knew that voice, all sass and loyalty. Kirsi.

Even now, in my desperate moments, she was there. Embedded so far into my mind, she was the only anchor. Mentally, I reached for that voice. And real or not, she reached back. I could feel her. As real as the full moon on my skin in summertime, as strong as the power that grew within me. I thought of the earth, of planting my feet deep into the rich soil and grounding myself. Another anchor. I felt the magic within me swirling, crackling, pulsating until I could feel my skin. Until I felt the surface of my mind as I dragged myself away from that dangerous oblivion that would have swallowed me whole. The world around me rocked as I opened my eyes.

Thunder shook the castle. Bastian's eyes were glued to me, no pretenses, no concern for the coven leaders, pure panic on his face. I pulled my eyes from him, tasting raw magic on my tongue, feeling the magic sitting in the air surrounding us. I'd never wanted anyone to know the extent of my magic, the power that I held dormant. But now there was no hiding it as each and every coven leader stared, mouths open at me sitting on the floor.

My cheeks burned red hot. Thankful they could not see into my mind, I looked around in confusion. Perhaps if I pretended it wasn't me, they would believe it also. I wanted to be one of them. To sit among them and help make decisions to bring peace and prosperity to the witches. I didn't want their judgment, even now as I felt their greed.

The thump of a body hitting the floor finally took everyone's eyes from me. The old witch that manipulated the minds moved forward, standing before Zennik. Ophelia and Willow both gasped at the same time, waking from their Trial just in time to witness tragedy. I slowly slid my hand to grasp Kirsi's, even though she was still in a catatonic state, Scoop sleeping in her lap. She seemed to come back at that instant with a deep inhale, but no one noticed as we watched the old witch turn to the king, pointing at Zennik.

"Strong of will, but not of mind. This one is lost."

My heart broke into a thousand pieces at those words. I could not move, could not protest, for fear of the coven leaders' unwanted attention. This was wrong. Lost did not mean dead. Lost things could be found.

Clenching my teeth together, I forced back the tears as Bastian dipped his chin. The old woman had marked Zennik for dead and my stomach swayed at the sheer misuse of power. This woman was unlike any witch I'd ever seen. And while every single inch of me wanted to leap from my seat and demand them to see reason, I did not. I remained still, tears streaking down my face because I was too much of a coward.

I thought I'd find comfort in a kind glance to Kir, but she hadn't looked away from Nym, who, like many of the others, was still navigating her own mind, fighting her own fears. Scoop crept from Kirsi's lap, crawling into Nym's as a spell on the back of Kirsi's arm glowed. Likely, I was the only one to see it. Scoop nudged Nym's familiar. The small tiger opened one drowsy eye, yawed and fell back to sleep.

Nym woke with a start, whipping her head around to orient herself. Finding the two felines in her lap, she dipped her chin, a tear rolling down her cheek. She'd fought her own battles in this Trial.

The king cast a spell and Zennik vanished. Another Chosen gone within the span of hours.

We waited in collective mourning as finally, Onyx crawled out of his mind and back to this equally dark reality. Mentally exhausted, we sat in silence as the coven leaders were excused. They simply stood and strode out of the room, though I didn't miss old Endora's final glance at me before she exited.

Bastian rose from his seat then, looking down upon us all. He rubbed the back of his neck as he looked back to Grey, who hadn't so much as glanced at us. Purposefully avoiding my gaze and the spot where Zennik's life was forfeit, the king's wings spread behind him as his jaw ticked. "Raven won the Trial, followed by Willow, and Ophelia took third. Ms. Moonstone, an item of your choosing will be gifted to you before the start of the next event. The full moon is in three days. As tradition and the other coven leaders demand, there will be a feast and a ball. Your attire will be selected by your attendants."

I wanted to stand, to protest such an announcement seconds after a man had died. But I didn't need to. I could see that even though the king had locked himself away for so long, he still knew this was wrong. There was regret within his eyes and that was enough. For now.

28

It took me hours to fall asleep that night. Tossing and turning, Zennik's face was always there when I closed my eyes. One green eye, one blue, staring directly at me as if I'd had a hand in his death. I wondered if the king felt the same level of guilt. But if the Trials were ancestral based and not his choosing, was he to blame, even if he'd been the one to nod his head?

When my eyes finally felt heavy enough to sleep, it was no surprise to see the object of my last thoughts within my dreams.

"Did he have to die?" I asked the king, who sat on a bench, staring over a pond on what looked to be a warm summer's night.

He wrapped his arm around my shoulder, and I leaned in, taking in all of his warmth and strength. Dream king was safe for me. No one ever had to know the images I'd conjured in my mind every night. There was no guilt here, no shame.

He nodded with a deep sigh. "Once you are lost in your own mind, there's no coming back. The deeper and deeper you go, the more tortured you become until you're in a constant state of purgatory. Eventually, your body will weaken, and you'll die anyway, but it's a cruel way to go. No one should suffer that."

The moon glistened over the top of the water as the smell of tart apples growing on the trees filled the air. A chorus of calling insects and the croaks of pond frogs serenaded us as the occasional fish leaped from the water and came down with a splash. There was more peace in this spot than I'd felt in a long time. It was exactly what my soul needed.

"I think sometimes I miss you when I'm awake," I told him, listening to his heart beat in his chest.

"I think sometimes I miss you when you're awake, too," he answered.

"Why ask me to come to the gardens if you're not even going to be here?" I grumbled as I yanked on a patch of weeds beneath the moon's gaze.

Two days had passed since the mind Trial. Though I'd won, Willow remained in first place with twenty-five points. I was in second with twenty-four and Kir held third with twenty. I'd hardly looked at the tally marks at dinner that night, and couldn't bring myself to look down the list to two vacant spots.

Zennik's family had come to retrieve his body after giving his final drop to the Moon Coven Grimoire. The king had offered to let the Chosen go to the funerals for him and Breya, but no one did. I couldn't get past the guilt I felt. I should have stood for Zennik. I should have protested, even if the explanation I'd conjured was real. I was a coward. Because I'd lived, and he hadn't.

A paper drifted down from the glass ceiling above me. I didn't bother reaching for it. Instead, I watched it flutter into the fountain and disappear.

"No. You will come and speak to me like a normal person, or I'll go back to my rooms."

"Demanding today, aren't we?" he asked, his voice stealing all the air from the room as he appeared before me, a cloak hanging over one arm.

There were times when I'd forget the man I summoned into my

dreams was not the same as the one that stood before me now, his boots nearly touching my knees. I pushed myself off the ground, though I still had to look up to see his face. "I could say the same, you know."

"Fair enough." Scratching his dark beard, he looked down to me, weighing his words before he spoke. "I'd like to take you somewhere. To show you something."

I noticed the hint of dark circles around his eyes, the flush of his skin. "Have you been sleeping?"

He smiled down at me. "I'm sleeping when I can. Are you avoiding my invitation, Ms. Moonstone?"

I folded my arms across my chest. "Is it dangerous?"

"Do you truly believe I would ever let anything happen to you?" he asked, handing me the cloak.

Taking it from him, I swung it over my shoulders. I opened my mouth, ready to deliver a snarky comment, but I paused. He was right. All the times I'd doubted him and feared him and swore he'd kill me, he'd never even come close. He may not have been the king that filled my dreams, but if the Trial into my mind taught me anything, the prejudices I'd held against him might have been unfair. I needed to witness his discretions with my own eyes.

"Where are we going?"

He lifted the hood of my cloak to hide my face, reaching his hand out for me. "You'll see."

We walked through the door of the greenhouse, but rather than moving into the castle and meeting with the guard that always waited there, we stepped into a place I didn't recognize. A valley between two enormous peaks covered in grass. The few scattered trees varied in color from greens to reds, and birds of all kinds flew overhead, squawking as they swooped low, hunting the lush grass.

"Where are we?" I asked Bastian, who stared straight ahead, all visible kindness gone from his features.

He didn't break his stare as he answered. "The outskirts of the Moss Coven territory."

I followed his gaze, surprised to see several of his soldiers carrying wooden crates. He pulled me along, my hand still secure in his as we followed them, staying far enough behind that we would not be seen. Without thinking, I cast the silencing spell on our feet, and he paused for a moment to wink at me before we continued on. I realized then that he probably could have done that with some form of his shadow magic.

"I brought you here because I wanted to address one of the offenses you have against me. The crates you see are full of fruit and vegetables I purchase from the other territories in small increments. I typically send Grey or another of my men to the markets and we buy what we can, putting money into the witch's pockets. I've even sent people into your shop."

I stopped short, jerking him to a stop. "You have?"

"There's a woman that visits you on the third of every month, she buys all the dried flowers you'll sell her."

"Agatha Rivercast?"

"Her true name is Agatha Firecast," he said with a smirk.

Admittedly, Agatha's purchases had kept us fed on many slow months, but I still couldn't believe it. "But why didn't you mention it? Why don't you do this under the name of the king so the witches know?"

"Watch," he said, pointing toward the men stacking the crates in front of a line of Moss Coven witches I didn't recognize.

There were no words exchanged as no less than fifteen crates of food, wider and taller than my arms could reach, were lined up. The king's men retreated, though clearly uncomfortable with turning their backs to the witches. The very last soldier walked backwards, watching the Moss coven witches as they fled back down the path.

"They wouldn't act like that if they hadn't been attacked before," I said more to myself than the king.

He nodded, bringing his finger to his lips as he jutted his chin forward, motioning for me to keep watching. The moment the witches thought the king's men were gone, the one in the middle with bright red hair and a crooked nose stepped forward and cast a spell, igniting all the food and letting it burn to ash.

My heart dropped into my stomach. I couldn't watch, couldn't believe they would waste such valuable nourishment when everyone knew there were witches in every territory starving.

"Why?" I whispered.

He didn't answer, instead pulling me away into the shadows where he conjured another door. Stepping through, we landed on a floating isle in the Whisper Coven territory. Hiding once more, we watched as winged shifters deposited similar looking crates before flying away.

I'd always imagined each of the floating isles to look as if we were standing on the edge, no matter which way we turned, the tumultuous ocean below angry and raging. Just as they seemed during our tour, but that was not the case.

I'd thought living on the isle bred fearless witches that traveled on the rope bridges or were marked with the ability to fly. But standing here, I realized a lot of their territory looked similar to the Moon coven, with more trees and grass and great patches of land mass. I could see the edge of the isle but did not fear it.

Once all the king's soldiers had flown away, while he and I remained hidden, we watched as the witches of the Whisper coven lifted his offerings with magic similar to one of my spells and dropped it over the edge of the floating island directly into the ocean.

"I don't understand. There's no way Tasa would have agreed to destroying food. There has to be more to this."

"Shh," he said, pulling me out of the line of sight. Once we were far enough away, a thick line of trees between us and the other witches, he sat on the ground, gesturing for me to join him. "The reality of the world is far more complicated than the coven leaders would have you believe. I've been sending food since I took the throne, just as my father did. I'm not sure when this started, but it's been the same ever since. They either accept it and destroy it, or they let it sit to rot. The coven leaders are all individual pieces of a whole. They act together, likely believing that I'm poisoning them."

"It's no secret that you've been openly murdering the witches," I snapped at him. "You can hardly blame them for not trusting you."

He sucked in a short breath, the anger he would have unleashed under control as he stood. "I take a life when it's warranted based on the laws I've put in place. Like it or not, when impoverished people get desperate, they also get dangerous. These Thrashings that I'm accused of?" He shook his head. "The Fire Coven is under attack, my castle is under attack, constantly."

"Maybe you should let the coven leaders assign punishment instead of taking it upon yourself to murder. You can write off the food, sure. But the Thrashings have been witnessed. You're so disconnected you don't even see the guilt when you look in the mirror."

"I am the king," he roared, his control gone as he fisted his hands to his side. He turned his back to me, his broad shoulders rising and falling with each measured breath. "My parents married, joining the shifters and the witches. And though they may not like the witch my father married, my mother was a good person. They loved each other and they were happy. There was peace. Until the witches ruined it all."

"The witches?" I asked, leaping to my feet as I yelled at his back. "The witches are trying to protect themselves. You can't tell me Tasa Moonbreak was a threat to you. She was wise and gentle. Nor was she overly dangerous, and you killed her."

He broke then, the anger in his voice shifting into sadness "I did not murder Tasa Moonbreak."

Before I could speak, a barrier as clear and thick as glass shot up between us. I spun, screaming as three cloaked witches, arms raised and markings glowing, inched toward me. I turned back to see the king still facing away, unable to hear my panic within the veiled dome of magic.

I didn't hesitate, striking one of the witches in the chest with a spell that sent her flying backward. I turned on the second, igniting the ground below her feet, but I wasn't fast enough to avoid the spell she'd thrown. Vines as strong as muscled arms grew from the ground, winding themselves around my wrists and feet. I fell. A witch with chestnut hair leaped on top of me with a knife.

Out of the corner of my eye, I could see the king just as he turned to see the barrier. His face shifted into pure rage as he smothered the barrier with his shadow magic, plummeting us all into darkness. The weight of the woman on my stomach was nothing compared to the strain of my wrists and ankles. I writhed, trying to buck her off, but hardly able to see anything.

"The wall is thinning, Cavian," one of the other witches said.

"Let him come. Let him watch." The brown haired one on top of me answered as she took her knife and pressed the sharp tip into my forearm.

Another second later and the barrier they'd created shattered, shadows pouring over us as Bastian moved into the circle, roaring. Unable to see what was happening beyond the pain, I heard the squelch of a blade strike true and a body fall.

The witch on top of me yanked the knife out with a laugh that would haunt me forever. Another vine came from the ground, winding itself around my neck. I tried to cast a spell at her but without control of my hands, I could not aim. So, I burrowed deep into the pool of magic within me, knowing what I was about to do could bring down the whole isle.

The ground below began to rumble, shaking violently as I cast blindly. The witch on top of me shoved her blade into my stomach— the cool knife edge a contrast to the warm blood that seeped from the wound immediately.

Bastian was above us in an instant. Gripping the witch by her hair, he threw her off me, moving like a dancer as he twisted, shoving his knife into her chest. One moment she was alive, the next, she was dead. His shadows smothered the ground, slicing away the vines, allowing me to roll into the fetal position as I pressed my hand to my belly, the blood pouring free. And then it was silent. I peeled my eyes open to see him boiling with anger, looming over the three dead witches.

"Bas—" I couldn't even manage his whole name. Without a doubt, something had been severed in my abdomen.

He ran for me, lifting me gently from the ground as he conjured a door and stepped into my rooms at the castle.

"This is why we kill first and ask questions later," he said, face serious as he looked down at me in his arms. "I shouldn't have turned my back. Shouldn't have hesitated."

The door to my room flew open as several healers poured in. He'd notified them with his magic, of course. The largest looking up at Bastian with pity before I turned and vomited all over her, the pain ripping through me. Kirsi must have heard the commotion because she rushed in, Scoop massive at her heels, his blue eyes identical to hers as she heaved with fury, pinning the Dark King with a look that would have sent a lesser man running.

"Scoop," she said with quiet fury. "Kill."

29

"Kir, no." I could hardly get the words out as I was taken from Bastian's arms and laid on the floor. "Not his ..."

She didn't move a muscle. Not even to breathe. The mark on her forehead glowing blue, an indication that Scoop was more than prepared to pounce. He'd die. Bastian would kill him with less than a thought.

"You tell me what you did to her right now, King, or I'll put you in a grave by whatever means necessary. Consequences be damned."

Scoop stepped forward on her final word. One paw in front of the others as he lowered his hind end toward the ground, nearly disappearing in the shadows pooling beneath Bastian.

He raised his palms to her. "Calm, witch. This was not my doing."

Her vivid gray eyes flashed to me, though her chin remained lowered. I could not respond as powerful magic slammed into my stomach, stealing my breath and all my attention as I cried out, squeezing my eyes shut. I was terrified. For me, for Kirsi, for Bastian, even for Scoop. The tension in the room was as thick as churned butter. As much as I needed to intervene, to tell my best friend, the sister I always needed, the one that would kill a king for me, to stop, there were no words.

There was shouting, hers or mine, I wasn't sure as the world sank around me, the fire within my belly surging through my veins, into the small wound in my arm, into every crevice of my soul. As if something within me had stolen that healer's magic and taken it to places it had never been. White, piercing light filled my vision. The goddess herself must have reached her divine hands into my deadly wounds and wrenched me back to life.

I jerked upright, gasping for air as the world righted itself. Time had passed. I was no longer lying on the carpeted floor surrounded by healers. Bastian lunged for me, saving me from falling off the sable couch in the sitting room as he pressed a hot cup of tea into my hands. I sipped slowly, letting the warmth of rich honey coat my dry mouth and throat before trickling into my healed stomach.

"You're all still alive, I see," I said, gripping the teacup with trembling fingers.

"For now," Kirsi sneered, from where she stood in the doorway to my bedroom, Scoop laying at her feet though his eyes watched the king. "A mutual agreement until we made sure you were healed. But now that you're back," she whipped her head toward Bastian, who was still kneeling beside me on the ground, "explain yourself, Dark King."

Scoop rose to his feet in one graceful motion as Kir crossed her arms over her chest.

"It truly wasn't his fault. He's been giving the witches food. We went to the Whisper Coven so he could show me, and we were attacked."

"I'm not seeing how that's not his fault." She stepped into the room, coming close enough to grip the back of the chair across from us. "Had he not been trying to pursue you, you wouldn't have been there. As far as I'm concerned, that's enough." She turned her cold eyes to me, a plea within them. "I told you he was dangerous."

"Kir ..."

"No. Raven. Look at you. You're covered in blood. I've witnessed you almost die twice now. This needs to stop."

"A Whisper Coven witch buried a knife in my belly because I was there with him. I will not condemn him for the choices of others."

"And you, King." She jutted her chin in his direction. "What do you have to say for yourself?"

I could probably have counted on one hand how many times Bastian had been talked to like that in his whole life. But rather than drawing up his power, rather than attacking or becoming overly defensive, he simply sat back on his feet, taking my hand into his as he looked into my eyes so deeply I could hear the apology before it left his beautiful lips.

"I haven't been as careful with you as I should have been, and I'm sorry. I never meant for any of this to happen." He turned to Kirsi. "I have no excuses to make. For one weak moment, I was tired of being the enemy and your friend paid the price for that. It won't happen again."

Her eyes shifted between us as the tension in her shoulders melted. She would have fought him. Would have tried to kill him, but as her eyes landed on our hands, she knew me well enough to know it was a battle lost. So, she circled the chairs, lifted her skirts, and plopped down. "I like you better when you're the asshole."

"I can assure you nothing has changed on that front," he answered, a gleam in his eye.

"Great." Kirsi rubbed her hands together. "So, when do we go kill the Whisper Coven bitches?"

I set my tea down on the tray with a half-smile. "While I do appreciate that you are such a vengeful little thing, they are already dead."

She lifted an eyebrow, and I tilted my head toward Bastian.

"Could've at least saved one for me." She pouted.

Bastian dipped his chin. "Noted."

"He said it was your choice," Clariss announced, gesturing to the two elaborate gowns draped over my giant bed.

A room full of witches preparing for an ostentatious ball within the castle of the Dark King was never something I thought I'd be a part of. But as I stood, overthinking every little detail, I accepted that life was happening around me, and I could either embrace it or fall victim to it.

"I'm sure my opinion doesn't matter, but I'd say the black and gold," Kirsi said, sipping tea as she leaned against the door that connected our rooms.

I lifted an eyebrow. "You know that's what he'll be wearing."

"I know." She shrugged.

"The scarlet is very beautiful, my lady," Tavia said, clutching the edges of her apron to contain her excitement. "But the black is divine."

My hair had been pinned up to expose my neck, but some wild curls were left loose around my face. Clariss had insisted on a small golden diadem, and I knew Onyx would give me so much hell about it, even though the jewel hanging down was crescent moon shaped. It sat nicely in my hair and was the finest piece of jewelry I'd ever worn, with drips of black diamonds from the peak at the front.

I moved to the bed, feeling the luxurious fabric of both dresses. It was not about what the dresses looked like, or what they felt like. It was about him. It seemed it was always about him. The king that graced my dreams and shattered my reality.

I lifted the black gown, holding it to my shoulders as I turned to the three witches in the room. "You know what they will say."

Kirsi moved to me, taking the heavy dress from my arms and laying it back on the bed. She took my hands into hers. "Let them say whatever they will, Raven. You know the truth. You know the king. You know your heart. It's just a dress, not a marriage proposal."

"Is it?" I asked, the hysteria in my voice too strong to conceal. "Shouldn't I consider the fallen witches? How choosing to match the king, tiara and all, will make me look?"

"Do one thing every day for yourself," Kirsi said, knowing she was quoting my grandmother. "Tomorrow you can decide what you want. Tonight, go to the ball. Match the king. Be happy."

I nodded, a tear slipping down my cheek as I gathered the dark gown, beaded with black diamonds that resembled the diadem I wore. "Black it is."

Even stoic Clariss clapped her hands with joy standing behind me as I stared at myself in the mirror. Tavia had used a heavy hand with the makeup, keeping my eyes so dark the blue in them popped. She'd given me a soft lip color, though, and could hardly contain her sigh when she stepped away.

"You're beautiful," Kirsi said when she rejoined us sometime later. Her blonde hair, now curled, had been left down to cascade over her bare shoulders, showing off the markings along her collarbone.

"Nym's not going to know what to do with herself," I answered.

"Wait until you see Scoop." She snorted, the spirit blessed marking on her temple lighting as she called her familiar.

Scoop waddled into the room, his head a bit higher than usual. The four of us burst into laughter at the small cat, content to wear a perfect little blue bowtie to match his witch.

"Well, isn't he adorable?" Tavia said, kneeling to scratch his ears. "My mother was spirit blessed. Her familiar was the most beautiful stallion."

"Was?" Kirsi asked, color draining from her face.

Losing Scoop was her greatest fear and, since she only knew a handful of other witches with familiars, she didn't know what would happen to her if he died. She likened Scoop to being her soul and, in many ways, I believed that to be true.

Tavia's brown eyes fell to the rug on the floor. "She passed away recently. She was doing something for the king and was attacked."

I thought back to the day that she'd seemed so sad, yet still came to do her duties. I hadn't even been kind enough to ask what was wrong.

"I'm so sorry to hear that," Kirsi said with no hesitation as she opened her arms to hug her.

After several seconds, Tavia pulled away, kneeling to lift Scoop off the ground.

It was Clariss that answered the questions on Kirsi's mind, though. "If you go first," she said, "he will remain, though they say he'll spend his life wandering the world searching for you. And if he goes first, your heart will never be the same. Your magic will change, as you can no longer channel through him as you do now."

Kirsi's eyes were wide as she listened to the maid speak. She'd wondered for so long, ever since she was little and Scoop appeared just as much a kitten then as he was now, though Kirsi's magic could turn him into something far more fearsome.

"Thank you," she whispered, sharing a brief smile.

"You're quite welcome." Clariss gathered the sleeping gown I'd been wearing and tossed it over her arm, moving to the door as she addressed Kir. "Back to your rooms now, my lady. It's time to go."

The feast was held in a far more elegant room than the one we usually used. The ceiling had been charmed to appear invisible, showing a glimpse into the night sky, the full blood moon staring down at us, though it didn't comfort me the way the real moon did. The fresh flowers, placed perfectly in tall vases lining the long table, gave a sense of warmth and peace through the castle I'd only ever found sitting by the fire with Kirsi or working in the covered gardens. There were more servers tonight than I'd ever realized the castle held and while the walls were lined with the king's soldiers, the table seats were filled with witches and shifters alike.

"The Fire coven?" I asked Nym as we moved toward the far end of the table.

"It must be," she answered, straining her neck to search the crowd for Kirsi, who hadn't joined us yet.

"She'll be here." I laughed. "And she's jaw-dropping."

Lifting her golden, sequined gown, Nym grabbed a chair, meaning to sit, but used it to steady herself as Kirsi finally entered the room. She appeared to glide across the floor, eyes locked on Nym, who seemed to have been dipped in gold, from the bangles up her arms, to the dress and rings of jewelry tied into her hair. No one else in the world existed to the two women as they collided, kissing each other more passionately than anyone I'd ever seen.

After several moments, I cleared my throat and they pulled away reluctantly.

"Sorry," Kirsi said, pressing her fingers to her lips as if wishing she could hold that feeling in.

I snorted. "No, you're not."

"Not really," Nym answered.

"Nor should they be." Grey stepped beside me, adjusting the cuffs of his jacket. "Maybe kiss my wife one more time for good measure."

Kirsi leaned forward, punching him playfully in the arm until his dimple showed.

Nym lifted an eyebrow. "Your wife?"

Grey shrugged. "You can use me, too, if you want. Two wives are fine."

We laughed together until Grey turned toward me, only now paying any attention to me at all. His eyes raked up and down my body. The corset that pushed my breasts to brimming, the delicate black lace that snaked up my arms and down my back.

"Perhaps three wives, then," Nym said, breaking his stare.

"Won't you sit with us, Grey?" Kir asked, her eyes shifting between us, searching for something more than surface level attraction.

"Ah," he tucked his hands behind his back. "Can't. I'm on duty." He bowed low, flashing his easy, dimpled smile as he turned and walked away.

"You know, if things don't work out with Nikos, you could always come back for Grey. He's alright, for a Fire Coven witch," Nym said a bit too loud, drawing a few wandering eyes.

"Shh." Kirsi grabbed her by the arm. "Rave hasn't told anyone, but she and Nikos aren't together. Also, don't forget where we are. I refuse to get kicked out of this thing before we get to dance."

Nym lifted a bare shoulder, a flirty look on her face as she winked a Kir. "I'd dance with you in the hall all the way back to our rooms."

"Okay then, carry on," Kirsi said, taking her by the waist and pulling her close.

Feeling very much like a third wheel, I slowly crept away, giving them space to fawn over each other. Bastian and I had made an agreement that we would not sit near or engage with each other during the meal so as not to draw unwanted attention to me. And he'd reluctantly agreed to pay me no more attention than the other witches. After the attack, he was certain I would become a target and that was the only reason for his concession.

I still felt him when he entered the room, still knew exactly when his eyes landed on me, on the black dress I'd chosen to wear over the scarlet. The dress with gold embroidery that matched the filigree on his jacket. It could have been a coincidence, I suppose, something that others wouldn't even notice in a room full of witches dressed for a ball, but he noticed. Our eyes met across the room and in that single second, the rest of the world paused. The king, for all his faults, carried himself like a god with a level of calm and certainty that said he knew he could bring this entire room to their knees if he wished it.

And so, he did as one by one, the witches, the shifters, Grey, and his guards along with the Chosen all stopped what they were doing to bow to the man that did not take his eyes from me. Dropping my gaze, I lifted the sides of my dress and did the same.

He cleared his throat, dipping his chin. "Thank you for coming. Please enjoy your dinner." He turned on a heel and marched directly back out of the room.

Feeling alone in a room full of people, I inched my way through the crowd, pulling out a chair next to Kirsi and Nym. I'd meant to give them their space, but if not me, then someone else would be sitting there anyway. As dinner proceeded, I couldn't help my glances toward the door, even the ceiling as I thrummed my fingers on the table, picking at the food.

"For goodness sake," Kirsi hissed, leaning toward me. "Just go to the door and ask a guard where he went."

I shook my head. "I don't care where he went. I'm just enjoying my dinner." I lifted the chicken from my plate and took a massive bite, stuffing my entire mouth.

Kirsi rested her head in her hands, watching me with a condescending smile as she waited for me to choke. "Tasty?"

I couldn't answer over the mouthful so I simply nodded, reaching for my wine. When I finally managed to swallow, I scowled. "I hate you."

"I know," she sang, wiggling her eyebrows. "Also, you dropped this."

I snatched the small piece of paper from her fingers.

"You were too busy staring at the door," she added with that all-knowing smile of hers.

I unfolded the paper, turning my back to her so she couldn't read it.

Ms. Moonstone,

On no planet could I sit in a room with a woman as beautiful as you and not make a fool of myself. Forgive me for leaving so abruptly. The first dance is mine.

In awe,

Bastian Firepool

"That's our murderous king?" Kirsi asked, breathing on my shoulder as she read the note.

The edges of the paper lit in embers as the king's secret note turned to ash. My cheeks flushed as I tried to force away the smile. "Go make out with Nym."

"I tried," she grumbled. "She won't let me." Her volume rose as she continued. "She said it's not polite at the dinner table."

"That's not what I said," Nym huffed. "I said you could have me for dessert, but let me eat first."

"That does sound more like you," I answered.

"Don't take her side." Kirsi pouted.

I leaned forward, talking around her to Nym. "She's dramatic when she's hungry. It'll pass."

After dinner, a massive set of glass doors appeared on the southernmost wall of the room. The king's men ushered everyone through the magical doors and into the ballroom. Off center, upon a stage, instruments played themselves as a nearby witch cast a spell over them, her markings glowing deep red in color. Next to them, the king sat upon a throne made of fire. He'd unbuttoned his jacket and sat casually, holding a conversation with the Old Barren as the opened room filled with guests. In a crowd this large I would have thought he'd be on edge, but I hadn't seen the coven leaders that were supposed to attend, and the other Chosen were huddled in a corner, looking down their noses at the rest of the guests.

Glasses passed by on trays, guests murmuring their appreciation for the event, and Nym and Kirsi stayed by my side as a gap was left in the middle of the floor. My heart raced as Bastian stood from his throne and descended the steps, eyes locked on me. The entire room fell deathly silent as he strode across the floor, stopping directly in front of me. Heat rose through my entire body.

He dipped his chin to me, holding his hand out. "It would be my greatest honor to have this dance."

I glanced up at the crowd, confident I'd have a myriad of hateful glares as I slipped my hand into his and let him lead me onto the dance floor. But the Fire Coven witches smiled, hugging onto each other as they swooned, watching their king as if they'd been granted the first dance.

"You are quite possibly the most stunning little witch I've ever laid eyes on, Ms. Moonstone."

I blinked rapidly, swearing Dream King had come to life as Bastian spun me around the dance floor. "Th-Thank you," I muttered. Unable to think of words, to process thoughts in my brain, I blurted, "I wore the black."

He laughed. "I can see that."

Embarrassed, I dropped my face, watching our feet as the music grew louder, the crowd closer. He tucked a finger under my chin and lifted until I was looking him in the eyes. "You will look at me when I speak to you, Ms. Moonstone."

I smiled then, remembering the words he'd spoken to me the first time we met. "Everyone's staring at us."

He shook his head, pushing me away to twirl, the skirts of my dress fluttering out to show the lace beneath. "No. No one is looking at me".

"So much for keeping the target off me."

"I will dance with the others, as we discussed."

"Something tells me that won't matter."

He spun me once more as the song grew in crescendo. Pulling me against his chest, his eyes burned into mine, sending a wave of heat and desire straight through me. "Then let them come."

The crowd burst into applause as we moved apart, still holding each other's eyes until his head snapped up, staring at the door. I turned, horrified to see Nikos standing there, watching the exchange between Bastian and me.

The king held my wrist, pulling me to the edge of the dance floor as it was filled by all the other attendees, content to dance the night away. "What's he doing here?"

"How do you know who that is?" I asked, narrowing my eyes as I remembered the last interrupted conversation I'd had with Nikos. In my head, I'd denied him immediately. Outwardly, I hadn't the chance to say a word before he left with his mother.

"Don't change the subject."

"He's here with a message from the other coven leaders," one of the king's guards said, approaching with an envelope in his hands.

Bastian peeled open the letter, releasing my arm to do so. I turned, staring at Nikos who was dressed in the nicest clothes I'd ever seen him in. He didn't look hurt. Nor confused. He stared at me with such anger, such disgust, I had to look away.

"Raven?"

"Huh?" Glancing back at Bastian, I hadn't realized he'd been speaking to me.

"The coven leaders have sent their regrets, announcing they're unable to attend tonight. They've asked for a favor. I'm to let you speak to your *betrothed* outside."

The world began to spin as I took in that word. *My betrothed.* Were the coven leaders trying to tell me something? Was Nikos here to warn me?

"Are you promised to him?" he asked, more hurt than Nikos had appeared to be.

I weighed my reaction carefully, knowing I needed to play safe on both sides until I knew what Nikos wanted.

I took Bastian's hand. "I don't know why they've chosen to use that word because I am not. Things are changing, and I don't know how I feel." I lowered my voice, hoping only he could hear me. "Every time I'm with you, I'm more confused than the last. I just can't make decisions about my future right now. I have to focus on the Trials."

I think the words hurt me as much as they hurt him. But rather than fighting it, rather than demanding I stay in the castle or go to my rooms, he simply nodded, all emotion falling from his face as he raised his chin.

"Please see Ms. Moonstone and her *friend* out of the castle. Do not leave her side."

The castle walls seemed to close in on us as I followed Nikos outside without a word. The guard remained just as the king had asked, but the moment we were alone, Nikos cast a sleeping spell on him, and he crumpled to the ground.

I wanted to reach for the guard, to make sure he was okay, but held myself in place, confident it would only anger Nikos more.

"Explain," he demanded.

"I ... I know what it looked like, but if you went back in, you'd see, the king will dance with all the Chosen women at the ball."

He shook his head. "You're wearing the same thing as him. You even have a crown to match. And you think I'm too stupid to see the way he looked at you, Rave?"

"It's not a crown and I—"

"I told you to be careful. I told you the king would manipulate you. I'm saying this as your friend. He's brainwashed you."

I rubbed my arms with my hands, the autumn air brisk under the full blood moon. "He hasn't."

Nikos stepped so close I nearly backed away from the plea on his face. "Then prove it."

30

"How am I supposed to prove to you that I'm not brainwashed by the king?" I asked, feeling the power of the blood moon on my skin, coaxing the magic within me. I couldn't decide if I owed him a true explanation, but the way he looked down at me, the conclusions he'd made on his own were hard to want to combat. What could I say to make him understand when I, myself, didn't understand?

"The coven leaders wish to see you. They've sent me here to sneak you out of the castle."

"Me? Why?"

He lifted his shoulders in a shrug. "I'm not privy to that information. Endora asked me to come. I'm here. Loyal to witches. As I thought you were."

"No," I said, lifting my hand. "You can be mad at me for what you saw. You can choose to never speak to me again, but you will not tell me you're my friend and then use that as a weapon against me. You haven't given me a chance to explain, but now I won't bother." I stood ramrod straight staring him down. I'd gone toe to toe with the king. Nikos was not nearly as intimidating as he thought.

He ran his fingers through his cropped hair, turning to watch the pair of guards at the gate. Fortunately for him, they could not see the sleeping guard within the shadows of the night, but who knew how long that would last.

"Fine. I'm sorry. I'm not trying to be your enemy, but you just make it so hard to be your friend. We need to go now if we stand any chance of getting out of here."

Going with him would be a direct betrayal to the king's orders. He'd lose his mind if he knew I'd left. But I'd be safe with Nikos and with the coven leaders and, if something were important enough to sneak me out of the castle, I needed to know what it was. I wanted to work beside these women as matriarch of the Moon Coven and if I could prove myself to them tonight, that would make my life easier in the long run. There had to be another side to the king's story about the food they'd been destroying. And maybe tonight would give me the opportunity to ask.

"How are—"

I didn't have a chance to finish my sentence as Nikos approached the two guards and cast the same sleep spell on them that he had on the first guard.

"We only have a few minutes to open this side gate and get out of here without the next set of guards passing by."

I cast a spell to move the guards away from the gate, their slumbering figures hovering just above the ground before laying them gently beside the other tucked in the shadows. Casting the spell to unlock the gate, I stood with my arms crossed, watching it swing open. "Let's go."

I knew the simple gesture wouldn't change Nikos' mind about what he saw, but if it gave him hope that I still had the witches' best interest in mind, that was enough for me. The king would be livid, but I was no longer afraid of him.

Chasing after Nikos, my mind ran nearly as fast as my feet until he skidded to a stop and I slammed into him, my gown nearly tripping me. The barren ground, a signature of the Fire Coven territory, offering no real place to hide but within its own darkness. Perhaps it was a blessing I'd chosen the black gown.

"I'm not supposed to go with you. They told me to send you down that path," he said, pointing ahead of us to a faint trail.

I turned back to the castle not far behind us. "The Dark King will be here within minutes. You can't stay out here in the open."

He shifted from one foot to the other, staring down the path. "I'll do what the coven leaders have asked. I have faith in them, and you should, too."

"Just be careful," I said, lifting my skirts and running ahead.

I slammed into a wall of magic not twenty paces beyond where I was standing. It coated my skin, my eyes, my mouth until I fell to the ground, the world around me vanishing.

"Finally, she comes," Endora's voice croaked from above me as I peeled my eyes open. "There's not much time, Raven Moonstone. You must stand."

I twisted, still able to see the silhouette of the Dark King's castle lit by the full blood moon behind it. Five coven leaders surrounded me, each standing on the point of a star made from black candles, every other one half melted. And me, directly in the center of the spell.

"What's happening?" I asked, my mouth going dry as dread gripped me, fully aware of a powerful spell created by five mighty witches beneath the blood moon.

"There's no need to be afraid. We are not your enemies," Xena Foresthale said, her kind eyes and rosy cheeks prominent in the chilly night.

I shook my head, trying to clear the fog. "Of course you aren't." With heaving limbs, I struggled to my feet.

"Good girl," Endora said, lifting her cloak in unison with the others. "You have the ability to wield immense power."

I swallowed, shaking my head slowly. "No."

"There's no point in denying what we've seen with our own eyes. Apart from that, you and the Dark King seem to …" she paused considering her words. "You have a connection with him."

I said nothing, biting the inside of my cheek to keep from revealing anything that might land me in trouble.

"You know you can trust us, don't you? We've always done what's best for the witches." Circe Rivervale said from behind me, her golden hair near orange under the red moon.

"My whole life I've been taught to trust the coven leaders above all else."

"Good," Isolde said. "We've reason to believe the king is grooming the future Moon Coven leader. He believes that you or your friend Kirsi will win the Trials and as such, has spent a lot of time weaving a web of lies."

I turned to face her, noting the candlelight from below elongated her face, making the markings on her neck more vivid. "I don't know what you mean." Surely, they meant Willow, but who was I to educate them?

"A witch with power to move the earth was with the king's men when they delivered poisoned food to the Whisper Coven," Dasha Whispercove said as she leaned on her cane. "We know you were there, Raven. We know the lies he has spun."

"And poor Breya and Zennik? Dead at the hands of the king. You saw him give the order," Isolde added.

Spinning to face each of them as they spoke, along with the heavy power of the invisibility barrier, made me feel as if I'd had several glasses of wine instead of only one.

"I believe the best way forward for the witches is one of peace and forgiveness," I said quietly, holding back the accusation of the Whisper coven attack against me.

"Forgiveness?" Endora croaked. "He knows where my daughter is. He's hidden the Moss Coven Grimoire and stolen the others. There is no way forward except one."

Circe Rivervale, the youngest of them, held out a hand. "Please Endora, let her speak."

"There's no time," Dasha said from behind me.

I spun again, to see her staring up at the moon. The blood moon. The star of varied candles. Five witches of influential power. My breaths fell short as my heart began to race. This was a seance and I was standing directly in the middle of it.

"Who are we calling from the dead?" I asked, swallowing my fear.

"Don't be frightened, dear," Circe said, her voice nowhere near soothing enough to calm me. "You must acknowledge the dangerous path the Dark King is leading you down. Use your mind, Raven. He doesn't let you out of your rooms. You are all prisoners in his castle."

True, but only half. I had the greenhouse and access to Kirsi and the Chosen's hall. But, how had she known that?

"You're beholden to his orders, not allowed outside even on this day, when your heart aches for the full moon. You've witnessed him order a witch from your own coven dead, without even attempting to help him navigate his mind. He is using you, child, and if you truly want to be a coven leader, if you want to stand among us and lead the Moon Coven, you must see the truth that is in front of your face."

I nodded, numb from the piles of truths I'd avoided in order to fill my fantasy of a king with a kind heart.

"There," Circe said, smiling. "I knew you were smart enough to see reason. Now, we must ask you for something, Raven Moonstone. But you must bind your words to each of us. What happens here must not be spoken of until the deed is done."

I could trust the coven leaders. It was a truth my grandmother had embedded into my mind whenever we were alone. It was important to her that I knew that. Maybe on some level her intuition had known a moment like this would come.

"Moon above, earth below, I bind my will to thee," I said, holding out my trembling hand.

Without moving from her spot, Endora held out a knife and I took it, poking the tip of my finger and smearing the blood across my lips, officially binding my promise of secrecy.

As one, the witches raised their hands, casting a foreign magic upon me. It started as a tingling on my lips where the blood sat, the source of my power, but as the world around us vanished, I realized the spell was far more sinister than promising to keep a secret.

Searing pain burned my forehead, taking me instantly to my knees. As the witches began to chant in a language I'd never heard, I felt my soul leave my body, spiraling into a vacant oblivion. One I'd been to many times when I'd received a new spell.

A red substance oozed down the walls of the room I found myself in, pouring into a deep crimson puddle. A girl appeared before me.

Bone straight black hair, and skin as pale as the moon, she stared up at me with the innocent look of a child untainted by the filth and lies of the world.

"This is wrong," she said, looking around the space. "You're not supposed to be here."

Gripping my trembling hands, I agreed with her. "No. I don't think I am."

The little girl titled her head to the left and then to the right, studying me. "Where are your markings?"

"I don't know." I covered my arms, feeling bare before the girl.

"Oh!" She giggled, the sound distant and haunted. "There they are."

I jerked, lifting my hands to see what she had, but there was nothing there.

"Who are you?" I asked, backing away.

"Indeed." She smiled, her lips a bit too wide for her face, her eyes a bit too innocent. "You shall have what you've come to take, witch. But there is a price for taking that which is not given."

My back slammed against the red wall. The suction as I stepped away confirmed my fears. Blood. The child laughed again, stepping closer as she watched the panic take over with eerie delight.

"Please, I did not choose to come here."

"Moon above, earth below, I bind my word to thee." My voice spilled from the child's mouth as she repeated my bonded vow to the coven leaders.

I could only hope those witches knew what they were doing. Especially as the little girl stepped closer. Like a snake, she struck, snatching my wrist, the immediate pain taking me to my knees as my eyes rolled back. Fire surged through my veins. The eerie little girl laughed.

"The price you pay, Raven Moonstone, is greater than the spell you've come to steal. You could have been good, great even, but the spells will no longer come. This will be your last receiving."

I couldn't process her words as I writhed in pain, so debilitating I thought my head would explode from the pressure, my bones would shatter, my life would be taken. Every muscle stretched beyond its natural ability. In any other instance, I'd have already passed out from the agony.

But then I realized what she'd said. This would be my last receiving. Shaking my head, I begged. "Please. Don't punish me."

I could feel the world crashing down around me, the limitless possibilities swept away. Everything was wrong. Everything was broken. And I was just a pawn in everyone's game. Still on my knees, drenched in blood, throbbing with pain from the girl's toxic touch, I gripped my stomach, sobbing. They could have it all. The shop, the coven leader's spot, my home even, but no. They'd taken away the future of my magic.

The child's unnatural smile became a blur beyond my tears. "He comes."

My trembling body went still as the blood drained from my face. If the child was only the receptionist, who the hell was *he*?

"You are right to be afraid," she whispered, shrinking away from the spot where she stood like a shriveling spider, ankle deep in crimson blood. "You've cheated him twice now."

As I rose to my feet, she twisted her head to the side, listening. Her eyes grew wider still, her face ashen until she flourished a hand and vanished, less than a second before a cloaked figure appeared before me, the face hidden in shadow.

The hair rose on the nape of my neck as shivers ran down my spine. My natural instinct was to run and hide, as if this was Death himself. The moment the thought crossed my mind, the figure nodded, reaching a long bony finger from the folds of his robes, pointing above us.

Reluctantly, I followed that haunted finger with my eyes, gasping at the sight above me. Bodies. Hundreds of bodies hung from the ceiling, lifeless and in various shades of gray. All dressed in long gowns, their yellow toenails like talons on their feet. So many bodies filled the space, I could hardly see their faces, but those that I could see were plagued with opened eyes, clouded over from death.

The figure pointed down to the floor. More death rose from the pool of blood. Faces missing half their skulls, some missing both eyes, all with gashing, deadly wounds. The gore was enough to bring a strong man down.

"You truly are Death, aren't you?" I managed, barely above a sound. I couldn't help but remember the death card I'd drawn. The accuracy.

"You dare speak my name, witch," he snarled, his voice penetrating the very core of my soul.

Holding his long finger toward me, he flicked it upward and my feet left the floor, a coiled cord wrapping around my throat as I was hanged from the ceiling like the others, packed so tight the stiff limbs of bodies around me pressed into my own.

I knew now what the coven leaders had sent me for. And though I could hardly believe it, hardly fathom how I would manage it, they wished me to acquire a spell I'd never known to be. Death. But how? The cord tightened around my throat, the coarse hairs digging into my flesh. I couldn't cast here, couldn't save myself. Instead, I did the only thing I could think of and stilled, taking a final deep breath as I accepted my own death.

31

"Is it done?" Endora's voice scraped against the walls of my mind.

"Give her a minute," another said.

I pushed my aching body from the ground, the blur of candlelight coming into focus before the faces of the five women surrounding me. My dress was ruffled but ultimately unscathed, the diadem on my head still intact, though I half expected the world to have broken somehow.

"Did it work, girl?" Endora demanded again. "Tell me you've acquired the spell."

"It is true?" another coven leader asked. "You cannot see the marking."

"What did you do to me?" I demanded, pressing a hand to my throbbing temple.

"Come dear," Xena coaxed. She wrapped an arm around my shoulders, leading me back to the path that led to the castle. "You understand, don't you?"

"I ... why?" I pulled away from the woman whose voice was as smooth as honey.

She stared back at me with kind eyes and a hesitant smile on her spell-marked face. So old, so many spells, they'd begun to form on her temple.

"You are the unmarked witch. A spell such as death ..." she worked her wrinkled hands together. "Well, it requires decent power, but all of our studies have told us that the two other witches that were blessed with such a spell had not an inch of their body left unmarked."

I shook my head, a lump forming in my throat as my tears threatened to escape. "You have no idea what you did to me. The price I had to pay for taking a spell."

"True," Isolde said, walking up from behind us. "We did not know if it would work, the legends have only whispered of such possibilities. But now that we know it can be done ... beneath a full blood moon ..."

"No. You mustn't. You cannot do that again. They took ... she... it ... took ..." I couldn't form the words. Couldn't prepare my devastated heart to hear the declaration allowed.

"What, dear?" Circe asked, stopping me to take my hands.

"I'll never be blessed with another spell again. That which I have is all that I will ever know. And for a choice that was not my own."

"Consider the spell of death a different kind of blessing, then," old Endora said, marching forward as she brushed by us. "It's time for you to kill the Dark King and change this era."

I'd known, of course. I'd put the pieces together. But it didn't make the truth any easier to swallow. The coven leaders had forced a death spell onto me because I was the only one that could get close enough to Bastian and he'd never know I carried it. I was, as they'd said ... unmarked.

"Ready?" Nikos asked, standing with his hands in his pockets, waiting casually where I'd left him.

"Did you know?" I snapped. "Did you know what they would force upon me?"

He couldn't speak a word before Endora cut him off. "He simply did as he was told, and you will do the same if there's to be any peace in this world. You must get back to the castle before the king grows suspicious.

I couldn't hide my incredulous snort. "I think it's fair to say Ba—

the king remains in a constant state of suspicion. I'm sure Nikos proclaiming we are betrothed did *not* help that."

His eyes jerked open, mirroring my surprise, the words tumbling from my mouth before I could filter them. But who could I trust here? A band of witches that just forced their will upon me? A man that had once sworn to love me, but treated me like a child? A king that hid more than he shared? Everywhere I turned, I was faced with people I could not trust. Nothing made sense anymore, and as my head pounded with a migraine, I nearly cast a healing spell and thought better of it. If one of them could detect the magic ... I didn't need any of these witches knowing anything more about me than they already did. And maybe I deserved the pain for being so incredibly naive with every person in my life.

I pushed past Nikos, carrying the weight of the beautiful ball gown as I stormed back to the castle. Gravel crunched behind me as he kept up, taking obnoxious, wide steps so he could lead as we left the coven leaders down the path.

"And what will you do when they wake, Nikos? Have you considered that you've cast magic upon the king's men? He'll hunt you down and kill you just for that."

"And yet I found you in his arms tonight," he answered, no sign of anger on his handsome face.

"Yes. You did. And had you shown up ten minutes later, it might have been Kirsi, or Willow or Nym. He's to dance with each of the Chosen." Clenching my teeth, I pushed back the tears again. He did not deserve them. Maybe he hadn't known what he'd been a part of, but the betrayal at stealing so much of my future stung worse than the blade I'd taken to the gut. "Wake the guards. I'll take it from here."

Having had enough of this evening, after staring death in the face, after having my power stunted, I wanted nothing more than a quiet place to sit and think about what my next move would be.

Nikos made a simple gesture and woke the guards. I cast a memory spell the second they oriented themselves enough to stand. I hated using that spell, twisting the mind in a way it shouldn't be, manipulating people for my own gain, but it was this, or thrust the man I'd known for many, many years into the hands of a man I didn't think I could ever truly trust.

I did very little with the magic, keeping their minds as clear as I could as I planted the memory of them watching Nikos and I just arrive, having no time pass at all. For a moment, staring at the king's closest guard, I wondered if it had worked, or if that creepy little girl had done something else to my magic when I broke the rules. But his dazed face, evened over as I turned back to Nikos.

"I can't believe you would tell the king we were betrothed just to get a moment alone with me."

For all his ignorance tonight, Nikos was not a gullible man. He understood immediately what his role was to be if he wanted to leave this castle safely.

"I know. I'm sorry. But I needed to see you. I've missed you."

"Do you not appreciate the tradition of the Trials?"

He stepped toward me slightly, reaching to grasp the back of my arm. The king's soldier moved in, forcing him to maintain distance. Any other night and there would have been droves of guards patrolling the outside of the castle rather than in the halls. I suspected the witches deducted that much, knew of the blood moon's influence and that's why they forced the ball on the king. A distraction if nothing else, on a night of strong spiritual power, to burden me with their plans.

"I do. But I worry for you. You never answered my question that night on All Hallows Eve. Can we start over?"

I pinched the bridge of my nose, tilting my head back as I released a long, heavy sigh. This was not an act. He meant those words, and now I would have to mean mine.

"We cannot be together, Nikos. I'm not sure I'll ever forgive you for tonight. I'm bound to the Trials until they end, and you know that." I inched backward, closer to the king's guard. "I know you mean well. I know you care and that's why you came tonight. I might have done the same if our roles were reversed. But you should go now. Let me see this through."

The frown on his face, the way his brows turned as he looked down on me, at the dress I wore, the implication it held, I could see nothing but his mother's face. The way she'd always peered at me, at the lack of markings on my skin and held it against me. Nikos was not upset with me, he was disgusted.

I dipped in a small curtsy. "Good night. I wish you safe travels home."

The guard led me back inside, casting glances at me as if I'd combust at any moment.

"What?" I asked finally, halting before we entered the ballroom.

Eyes wide, he simply shook his head, a tuft of brown hair falling forward over his brow. "You're not going to cry, are you?" he asked. "Because of the fight?" He tilted his head toward the door we'd come from. "It's just tears make me uncomfortable."

I slowly shook my head, but something familiar about the guard raced through my mind. A face I'd seen over and over. Cleaned up, with a pressed leather vest and clean boots. I stepped away, realizing finally who he was. "You're alive."

"Uh, come again?"

"You. I knew you looked familiar. You're the thief! But the Dark King killed you for stealing a goblet weeks ago."

He shook his head again, raising his palms between us. "You're mistaken, lady."

"No. I don't think I am." I ran my hands down my skirts, letting the memory of our first day replay in my mind. The other guards had dragged him through the throne room, kicking and protesting, until the king cast a spell and his body went limp. But the coven leaders had said only two other witches had ever received the spell to kill, and they were covered in markings. The king didn't have the power to kill with a spell. That's why he kept a knife on his side. "Why put on the act?"

He kept his feet planted as he looked up and down the hall before leaning in to whisper. "King's got a reputation to uphold."

I bit my bottom lip, considering what he'd admitted. Though better than the alternative, it was still proof the king was lying. I'd keep this secret for now, though. "I see. Shall we?"

The guard pushed into the room, the heavy doors swinging open in unison as we entered. I'm not sure what I expected. Kirsi standing there worried to death, the king pacing the floor, all music at a stand-still, everyone turning to stare. But I was thankfully met with none of those things. The room was full of Fire Coven witches dancing below the illusion of the blood moon. Kirsi was nowhere in sight, but I was sure she was occupied with her lover, and I watched as the king grace-fully swung Willow around, her red dress skimming the floor like a flickering flame.

Her smile was as genuine as the king's. They whispered back and forth, more casual than I'd known them to be. Maybe I was blind to what was really happening around me. I reached for a passing tray, grabbing a glass of whatever was closest and gulping. The liquid was sweet and syrupy, gliding down my throat with ease, leaving the heavy burn of strong liqueur behind.

Bastian took Willow by the waist, his hands massive on her small frame, and lifted her, spinning as a small crowd opened in the middle of the floor for them. His wings made him so large compared to her, so much stronger and controlled. Her tanned skin glowed beneath the illusion of the blood moon peering down on the crowd. Onlookers clapped at the display, Willow's dark curls cascading along her shoul-ders as she tossed her head back and laughed. When the song ended, he bowed to her, kissing her hand before walking her to the edge of the dance floor.

His not-so-dead guard approached him, tapping him on the shoulder and whispering a few words. As if on cue, his eyes shot across the room, locking on me for only a brief second before he turned away, pulling Willow back onto the floor, his hand comfort-able on her waist.

He knew I'd returned safely and that was enough for me, and clearly him. I wanted out of the dress, out of this stifling room, and away from everyone. Grey refused to make eye contact when I passed him and that only added fuel to the fire raging within me. When the guards stopped me at the door, reminding me that I truly was in a lavish prison, I simply asked to be escorted back to my rooms. And for once, they didn't try to stop me.

I twisted, turned, bent sideways and exerted every ounce of left-over energy trying and failing to get out of the Dark King's black gown. After over an hour, Clariss entered my rooms, startled to find me sitting on the couch, smothered in black satin and lace.

"Help?" I asked around a mouthful of the cookies that had been left on a tray in my room. Perhaps the ladies thought the king would be joining me after the ball. Guess they were wrong.

"What in the world are you doing here so early?"

I rolled my eyes, ignoring the look she'd given me for my lack of propriety. "I don't want to talk about it."

She gestured for me to stand and turn. Pulling on the corset ties, she worked her magic, releasing me from the organ-smashing contraption. Finally able to take in a full breath, I reached for another cookie.

"Many more of those and we'll have to roll you to the bedroom," she scolded.

"Or I could just sleep on the couch," I answered, picking a chunk of chocolate from the soft dessert.

After half an hour of removing the pins from my hair and helping me into my nightgown, I thanked Clariss for saving me and crawled into bed. I couldn't look her in the face, couldn't unwrap that feeling of hurt that settled into my stomach. Could I be the one to kill him?

32

The ballroom was empty. No discarded drinks, no orchestra, not a single sign that only hours ago, it had been full of witches dancing beneath a full moon. But then, this was my dream and maybe I didn't want to remember those parts. I stood in the same place he'd spun me a final time just before everything changed. Before I was charged to kill him, before my future spells were stolen from me. The silence in the air grew so loud my ears rang. I spun, a scarlet dress fanning out below me as I moved.

"May I have this dance?"

His voice filled a void in me I hadn't known was there. I hardly wanted to open my eyes and look at him. Full of shame and fear of what was to come. Knowing the end of his life lay dormant within me, all I needed to do was cast and he'd fall. I'd win the favor of the other coven leaders, save the witches the torment of his dangerous rule, and ... and then what? Go home? Back to Crescent Cottage as if this experience had meant nothing? Prepare for a guaranteed war with the shifters?

"Something on your mind?" he asked, his chin brushing my shoulder as he stepped behind me.

I nodded, holding my eyes closed as I held back the tears that would surely give my feelings away.

"I need to know if you're good, Bastian. Truly good. But I can't seem to decipher who is the villain and who is the hero in this realm."

He spun me around, tugging me to his chest. I could hear the heart I was to stop as if it called to me.

"Even the villain is the hero of his own story."

I nodded, pulling away from him. Dream King was a figment of my imagination. He'd never really be able to help me.

He tucked his finger under my chin, lifting my face. "Raven, look at me."

Opening my eyes, a single tear slipped down my cheek.

He brushed it away with his thumb, resting his hands on my collarbone before sliding them up around my neck. "I was a fool to think you'd stay with me."

"You weren't. But I can't make life decisions right now. Not during the Trials, when I have to focus. When my biggest problem is supposed to be gaining points to win, not hearts to break. And how did you know about Nikos anyway? Do you stalk everyone?" I looked up, another tear falling as I stared into his silver eyes.

"Grey told me about him after All Hallows Eve. I thought maybe your heart had changed."

I released a hesitant laugh. "I'm not sure what my heart is doing anymore. This isn't really you and that's hard to discern in my mind. I'm safe here with you. In my dreams. This version of you would never hurt me. But you're a conjuring of my own desire. You aren't real." I turned away from him, moving out of his arms to find space. "I know what you did."

An awkward pause hung in the air as he waited for me to elaborate.

"Your guard? The man you *killed* when we first arrived. It was a show. An illusion from the king of shadows."

"I've paid for that deception a thousand times over. Every time you look at me, you remember that moment. You remember Tasa, the rumors, you remember your grandmother. Your mind ticks off all of my offenses before you speak a word."

I shrugged, willing my sadness to become something he could truly feel. "Some wounds never heal."

"As far as I can tell, you have a choice. A moment. Right now. You can choose to keep circling these same things over and over in your mind, or you can take a step back and look at the bigger picture." He stepped away, standing before me with his hands locked behind his back. "I charge you to find a single person in this world that isn't full of regret, rash decisions, and misguided judgment."

"You're not being very 'Dream King' tonight, sir." It was a deflection mostly, but I meant it.

Letting out an exasperated sigh, he grabbed my hands. "It's time to end this."

My ears rang, my heart transforming into a fist in my chest. I wasn't ready to let him go, and that very truth seemed to finalize my decision. If I couldn't let my heart stop the way it felt for him, there was no way I could kill him.

I nodded slowly, backing away from him as everything in the ballroom faded away and we stood in an empty space, no walls, no ceiling, just an expanse of empty.

"Please try to understand," he said, reaching for me.

"Understand?"

He waved his hand and again the space changed, transforming into my rooms at the castle. I was there, lying in my bed, dreaming. It was exact. The scuff mark on the wall where I'd bumped the bedside table, my handprint on the mirror from trying to get the dress off after the dance.

I turned to him, eyes as wide as I studied his features. The depth of his gray eyes, the scar on his left hand, the texture of the leather that tied his hair back. "You're real," I breathed. "You've been manipulating me this entire time?"

"No. We were just spending time together."

I shook my head, the shock more overwhelming than I could handle. "We've kissed. Not even my dreams are safe from you?"

"Raven ..."

"Prove it to me. Come into my room and wake me up."

He hesitated for a moment before vanishing, leaving only a tendril of black shadow where he'd stood. The room faded away as he called my name, an echo at first, something far away and foreign. But then I sat up in my bed, staring at him. His black shirt semi unbuttoned, his hair a bit more disheveled.

I pushed myself out of the bed, away from him. "Why?"

Running his fingers through his hair, he'd never looked so nervous. "Is there anything I can say that would justify it in your mind?"

I folded my arms over my chest. "Scars fade. They don't vanish. This was an absolute violation, and while we're at it, since this has all been a pile of lies, what else are you hiding?"

His wings fluttered behind him and somehow, I knew he wished he could wrap them around himself now and escape the scrutiny of my glare. But he'd made his bed and it was time to lie in it.

"Sit down," he ordered.

"I think I'll stand."

"Fine." He sat by himself on the edge of the bed. "I didn't want to hold the Trials. I knew you'd all come here and the only thing you'd want is what every witch before you has wanted when they come to my castle. The Grimoires."

"Bastian, we have ancestral magic. We need those Grimoires to keep our power. Handing them over to a man that would see us all dead is a threat to the very core of who we are. If you don't want the witches hunting you, or the books, just give them back. Why do you need them?"

"You saw what happens when the books are put together. If the coven leaders have those books and learn of that power, it would turn the very small amount of peace we have on its head."

"Okay, let's table the fact that you get to decide that for the world. Why host the Trials if you didn't want to?" I gestured for him to continue.

"There was no way out of it. I consulted my coven, the elders insisted I hold them. I thought I'd oversee and keep my distance, holding the Chosen in their rooms to avoid conflict and wandering witches." He looked up to me then, his eyes a vat of vulnerability as he audibly swallowed. "But then you walked into the throne room, and nothing made sense anymore. There was something about you, so familiar and yet so foreign, I couldn't explain it. I still can't."

I nodded. "I'm not justifying your decision to manipulate me, but I felt that too. As much as I was absolutely terrified, something in me recognized something in you."

"I thought you'd figure it out. I thought you'd know it was really me and not a dream. But I couldn't stay away. The way you looked at me, the way you reached for me. There was nothing negative between us there."

"How convenient for you." I jammed my hands onto my hips. "Do you visit the other Chosen as well? In their dreams or otherwise? Do you have several greenhouses hidden in this castle, or do you gift them with markets and libraries? How many of your magical notes have you passed to the other witches here?"

"Life would be so much easier if I wasn't totally enthralled by you alone."

"I can't even begin to believe you. I can't trust you. Whatever was between us was fragile at best, and you've shattered it."

He stood from the bed, towering over me with his broad frame. "I was a fool to use Willow tonight to make you jealous. I wanted you to know what it felt like when you turned and looked me in the eye, asking me to give you permission to go with Nikos. I wanted you to feel that pain."

His forward steps pushed me backward until he had me pressed against the wall, his large hand on my waist. "I wanted to ruin you as thoroughly as you've ruined me."

"Mission accomplished," I breathed, that pull to him just as strong as the first day we'd met, no matter how much I wanted to hate him.

"You make me crazy," he whispered, inching closer. "You consume me."

The way the deep resonance of his smoky voice curled around my body made my breasts ache with need. His fingers gripped me tighter as he brought his lips to my jawline, brushing them over my skin, leaving a trail of warm breath.

"Bastian ..."

"I'm sorry for deceiving you. But it was worth every moment you'll spend mad at me." His shadows moved, surging up my body. "You'll think of me, of the darkness that calls to you. The second you lie in that bed and your heart stops racing. Because you've always known that I don't play by the rules." He pushed his fingers into my hair, grabbing a little too hard as he tilted my head back to look into his face as his wings enclosed around us. "Be mad, Raven. Be furious. Let me know when you're done pretending that isn't exactly what you find so irresistible about me."

33

W e'd lost two of the Chosen thus far and the vacancy of those spots as we sat for breakfast felt enormous. The king had left without another word last night and, just as he'd predicted, I didn't get another ounce of sleep, thinking only of him until my thoughts moved on to the witches that died, the witches that lived, of the death spell and the task I was to complete.

Working myself into such a frenzy of anxious nerves and loneliness, I wound up in Kirsi's rooms, laying on her couch so I wouldn't wake her. Scoop had known I was there, coming to curl into a ball on my stomach, allowing me to trace patterns of vines and markings into his soft fur. When the maids announced a mandatory breakfast, I honestly wasn't sure what to expect.

As we sat, half the group yawning, exhausted from the ball, the other clearly on edge, we waited, casually whispering to each other as if any loud sound would shatter the small bit of peace we'd found amongst ourselves. Even Onyx had calmed these past days, his glares and quiet threats only half as frequent as they had been.

Bastian strode into the dining room at last, gesturing for us to begin eating as he took his seat. I couldn't help but notice Willow had taken his right side, leaning toward him as she tried for small talk. I remained at the opposite end of the long table, unwavering in my conviction to keep the distance between us, but also because I just couldn't trust myself around that man.

Piling her plate and then mine with sausage and fruit, Kirsi looked half awake. She claimed she'd drank too much last night before finding a dark corner to hide away with Nym. She was glowing. Blissfully happy. And as I looked over her shoulder to Nym, whose smile hadn't left her face either, I couldn't help the pang of jealousy. Letting myself love the king would be an uphill battle and I was not a warrior.

The screech of Bastian's chair sliding across the floor yanked me from my thoughts, and he stood, steepling his hands and pressing them against his lips, as he looked down the table. "The fifth Trial begins immediately following this meal. Find a way to communicate with an ancestor that has competed in the Trials. Get a list of the thirteen contenders in their event. You're to say them out loud and that will be your official entry. We will check the history books to confirm. The person with the greatest number of accurate names wins. We will not be announcing the standings until the beginning of the final Trial."

He waved and the pennant banners with our names and scores vanished. Before Bastian could leave the room, my mind was already running with ideas for this Trial. But glancing around, listening to the murmurs, I knew I wasn't alone.

Kirsi leaned toward me, whispering, "Can you get into those gardens?"

I nodded. "I won the last Trial, remember? I get to choose an item. Salvia tea?"

"Exactly," she whispered. "Meet you in your room in ten?"

"Nym?"

Kir shook her head. "She has her own plan."

As if on cue, the majority of the room stood. Ophelia and Nym remained. Ophelia seemed to be lost in thought, but Nym picked through a handful of meats, shoving them in a satchel nestled onto her hip. Feeding her familiar was top priority for a spirit blessed witch.

"THERE WAS ONLY A SMALL BATCH," I SAID, DROPPING THE LEAVES OF THE diviner's sage onto the coffee table.

Kirsi lifted a shoulder, scrunching her nose at the scent. "It's basically useless if you don't know how to use it."

The corner of my mouth rose at her nonchalant comment. "Unless you want to hallucinate your life away."

"Now that you mention it ... We should plant more of this. Sell it in bulk."

"Let's circle back to that suggestion." I laughed, placing a pot of water into the fireplace.

With a wave of my hand, I lit a small fire below the kettle, heating the water. Kirsi gestured, a marking on her arm glowing as she removed all moisture from the plant, drying it instantly. Scoop was as curious as ever, burying his maw into her hand, then yowling and scurrying away.

She laughed, coaxing him out of his hiding spot to reassure him he'd be fine. For all the fire in her soul and sass she carried, I loved watching the vulnerability she shared with him. He knew her heart better than anyone and had deemed her worthy years ago. She may not have had much in the way of real family, but she'd grown her own and I was so proud to be a part of that.

"Do you think it's fair we're working together?" she asked.

I sighed. "If there were rules, he would have said. And besides, we're brewing tea together, the hard part comes after this."

"When we're high." She giggled.

"Basically."

Once the teapot whistled, I used magic to pull it from the fire and pour into our glasses. A small purple hue leached from the dried leaves as we dropped them into the steaming water.

Looping my finger through the handle on the teacup, I blew on the plumes of steam as Kirsi and I locked eyes.

"We should lay on the floor. That way, if this works, we won't fall and hurt ourselves."

"Are you worried it won't work?" I asked, moving to sit beside her.

"Raven, this is dangerous. If it wasn't, you and I both know you'd have already visited your grandmother. You're going to have to force your soul from your body and then seek out her spirit. It won't be easy. Just don't linger," she warned. "You will want to stay, but the clock is ticking and you'll be forced back whether you've succeeded or not. Get the names, say them aloud if you need to, and let the magic send you back."

"What if it's like the mind Trial?" I asked, still scared from watching Zennik's untimely death.

She shook her head. "It's not. You'll have to fight to stay there. That's why you have to hurry. If visiting our dead family were easy, it wouldn't hurt so much when they die."

"Good point. Bottoms up."

She clinked her glass with mine and in three searing hot gulps, I swallowed the tea. Nothing happened. I'm not sure what I was expecting, but the only thing I felt was the warm liquid trail down my throat and into my belly. Still, I laid back, reached for Kirsi's hand and closed my eyes.

I'd forgotten how tired I was. How long the day of the ball had been and the night even longer. My heartbeat slowed. My breathing slowed. I thought maybe I was drifting off to sleep instead of separating my soul. It was only then that I realized Kirsi knew exactly how to do this, and I hadn't questioned it. But that was a fleeting thought as inch by inch, my limbs grew heavier and heavier.

The weight of Kir leaning against my arm faded away along with the room. The heat of the fire licking down the right side of my body also vanished. I was supposed to be doing something important, but I couldn't remember what it was. So sleepy, the world seemed to pass by me, pulsing as my soul drifted through a forest.

Hallucinating. I was absolutely hallucinating as I spun to my back and stared up at the treetops, the sun peeking through the branches in dappled beams of warmth. I had a passing thought that it should have been autumn outside, the leaves a countless variable of colors and stages in their lives. But I was met with greens of all shades instead. As I wondered about the season, my brain ticked away with reasons I'd be casually floating through a forest. I was certain this wasn't a typical day for me, confident I hadn't joined the ranks of the wraiths. Certainly, I hadn't died.

Died. I covered my mouth with my fingertips, trying to suppress the giggle. I hadn't died. But I'd met Death and he was creepy. I gasped.

"Kir, I forgot to tell you what happened." Turning to my side, I remembered she wasn't there. And neither was I. I was dead. But not dead.

"Oh!" I laughed. "Never mind, Kir, I can't tell you anyway."

Again, I giggled, realizing she couldn't hear me. Because we were doing a Trial. Right! A Trial. About death. Dead people.

Drawing in a deep breath, I bolted upright, leaving the forest behind. "Focus, Raven."

I sat in the rocking chair that had once been a staple in Crescent Cottage. My grandmother's. My thoughts turned linear, remembering that I had a goal. A reason for taking a tea that warped the mind. Standing from my grandmother's chair, I glanced over my shoulder, surprised to see that wooden pillar at the back of the shop, an old leather book lying there as if it had never been stolen.

Crossing the room, stepping on each of the boards that squeaked when you walked on them, I reached for my grandmother's knitted, white shawl, hanging on a hook near the back room. I knew I was where I was supposed to be when my hand didn't surge through it, but rather caressed the soft, aged yarn. I lifted it to my nose, smelling the fresh dirt and peppermint that always reminded me of her.

"Grandmother, can you hear me?"

Placing the shawl back on its hook, I moved to my workbench, which was still hers at this time. Deep grooves from her knives embedded into the wood took me right back to the time I'd sliced my finger when I was eight. She'd asked me to trim the stems on several bunches of dried herbs. She'd meant for me to use the sheers, but I'd gone right for her favorite knife with the ivory handle. Now though, the workbench was full of glass jars, drying upside down, water still gathered around the rims.

I walked out into the gardens half expecting to find her drawing clean water from the well, that old wooden bucket leaking as it always did and her cursing the sun. Not there either.

"I need to speak to you."

But of course, she wouldn't be here, in this place full of memories. This wasn't real. I closed my eyes, focusing on intentionally projecting my soul beyond. Beyond the memories, beyond the place she'd been murdered, landing in the clearing where we'd had her funeral pyre. Her final resting place.

I sat on the ground, dipping my chin to my chest as I rested my hands on my knees, visualizing her face, her voice, the markings I'd memorized. With a jerk on the magic, the strength of the tea wavering, I was running out of precious time. A wave of incredible sadness washed over me. My body turned cold. I tried to clear the lump that had grown in my throat but couldn't push it away. An overwhelming urge to break down in tears weighed heavy on my soul as my beautiful grandmother appeared before me.

Believing I'd never see her face again, I sat, stunned, taking in every single feature the edges of my memory had forgotten. The scar on her temple, the perfect arch of her brow. The age marks and wrinkles that came with a century of life and wisdom. The spattering of markings that seemed so much darker than I could remember.

"My baby," she whispered, tears falling as purely as my own. "What mess have you gotten yourself into?"

"Are you real?" I asked, leaning forward, a gasp escaping as I placed my hands on the sides of her face, bringing her nose to mine. "You are real."

Someone could have reached inside of my chest, gripped my heart and squeezed until it stopped beating and I wouldn't have noticed. Possibly wouldn't have cared as I stared into the old face of the woman who had left such a deep void in my life.

"I've missed you so," she said, her silvery hair tangling with my own as I pulled away.

The world tilted as, again, the magic infused in the tea wavered.

"Quickly now, child. We don't have a lot of time."

I nodded, swiping away my tears. "I need—"

"I know. You've joined the Trials." She reached for my hands. "I'm so proud. I always knew you'd be Chosen. The names—"

"You watch?" I nodded, smiling through my tears.

Her grip on my hand loosened as she looked behind me, panic on her face.

"Agatha, Elaine, Widrow, Venket. Say them back."

"Agatha, Elaine, Widrow, Venket."

"Good. Agatha, Elaine, Widrow, Venket, Trusella, Viana, Tasa, Maebh, Faythe, Lillith. Say them back.

"Agatha, Elaine, Widrow, Venket, Trusella, Viana, Tasa, Maebh, Faythe, Lillith."

The world tilted again.

"Quickly now. No granddaughter of mine is going to lose on my watch. "Agatha, Elaine, Widrow, Venket, Trusella, Viana, Tasa, Maebh, Faythe, Lillith, Archer, Ivy, Ingrid. Go."

I nodded, repeating the names like a chant. Over and over. She smiled at me, her form fading, and I hated myself for spending so much time dazed in the woods. I could have been with her longer. Could have felt her hands in mine for several more minutes.

"I think you've got it." Though she sat before me, her voice echoed as if she were at the far end of a long hallway. "You must let my death go, Raven. Your mother ..."

I couldn't make out her final words as the world I'd conjured vanished around me, the fire heating my legs, Kirsi's arm pressed against mine. I held my eyes closed, chanting the names.

"Agatha, Elaine, Widrow, Venket, Trusella, Viana, Tasa, Maebh, Faythe, Lillith, Archer, Ivy, Ingrid."

Content I'd completed the Trial, I opened my eyes, staring at the ceiling. My heart was so full, my face ached from the pain of smiling. At that moment, I didn't care if I'd come in first or last or somewhere in the middle. She wanted me and my mother to let go of her death. We'd suffered for so long. But as I'd said to the king, some wounds don't heal.

Standing, I stretched, walking a few paces away to soothe my aching body before turning to check on Kirsi. She could have still been under the tea's spell, she could have even fallen asleep. But neither of those were real options ... because of the dagger hilt-deep in her chest.

I wanted to scream, to cry out, to do anything but fall helplessly to my knees, the scream trapped within my throat as I forced myself to crawl through a pool of blood to get to her.

"Open your eyes, Kir. Open your eyes."

This could not be happening. Not to her. Not to Kirsi Moondance, the best friend and only sister I'd ever known. The witch that always smiled through her pain, always, always had my back, no matter what. I never knew a person could hear their heart crack until mine shattered.

"Kirsi?"

Reaching an unsteady hand forward, I brushed a stray hair from her face, ignoring the sticky blood on my fingers. Her eyes fluttered. A hint, a trace of hope bloomed in that single gesture. I clung to it for dear life as I placed my palm on her cheek, daring to say her name. "Kirsi."

"Rave—"

"Shh. It's okay. You're okay. I promise you're okay." I could hardly speak the lie over the rigid lump in my throat, the sickness that swelled in my stomach. I begged time to stop. To go back. I pleaded with the goddess to change her mind about this cruel, cruel fate.

I couldn't bear the fear in her eyes as she looked at me. That single stare speaking all the words our hearts could not. She knew. Scoop lay at her side, his fur drenched in her blood as he nudged her over and over again, yowling.

She tried to move the dagger, but was too weak to pull it.

Placing my hand over hers, I squeezed gently. "No, Kir, you have to leave it, you'll make it worse."

"Doesn't hurt," she managed, a tear falling from her eyes.

"Good. See?" I gulped, unable to hide the fear in my eyes. "Every-thing is going to be okay. And we're going to go home, Kir. You and me and Scoop. We'll go home. Tomorrow if that's what you want. We'll lay in front of the fireplace and drink all the wine and laugh until we cry."

My voice broke on that final word. I'd filled the room with empty promises, watching the blood leave her. Watching her breaths slow. Throat burning, I tried to heal her, but the spell was not strong enough. I needed to do something. Anything, but I could not leave her like this. I could not bear the thought of her dying alone.

"Help." The word was only a whisper in a luxurious room of despair. I tried again. "Please. Help." Unable to force the volume into my broken words, I closed my eyes, lifting my chin to the ceiling as I burrowed deep and screamed from the very pit of my soul. "Help me!"

Kirsi's eyes rolled back as a ragged breath rattled through the wound in her chest. Short sobs came from me as I brought my face to hers, whispering, "You cannot leave me, do you hear me? We have plans. We're going to grow old working in the shop. You're going to marry Nym and get a million markings and be more fearsome and less wrinkled than Tasa. Scoop needs you. But I need you, too. You cannot die, sister."

Her shoulders did not move, another breath did not come.

"You cannot die."

There were no words. My hands rested on the dead body of my best friend, covered in her blood as I sat there, stunned, sobbing. This wasn't sadness. Nor devastation. Not heartache or misery. This was something far deeper.

I peered at the cat, who'd stood, moved to the space between her neck and shoulder and crawled into a tiny black ball, resting his face over her throat. "Who was it? Who did this?"

He couldn't answer me. Not the way he did for Kirsi. He'd never be able to answer anyone again. But the dagger was undeniable.

The Dark King.

34

I hugged my knees to my chest, rocking back and forth in a chair as the healers swarmed the room. He had come. The moment I'd screamed, he'd known. I had stared up at him, the look of horror on my face undeniable. He didn't stay. Instead, his eyes fell on Kirsi, and he left, sending healers in droves.

Magic filled the air in such a stagnant way, I wasn't sure if it was my lungs refusing a full breath, my heart, or the power. I couldn't think beyond the blood beneath her. I knew. Without the looks of pity they each gave to me, she was gone. Murdered as I lay beside her, pining for a few more minutes with my grandmother.

Her hand lay still on the floor, and I wondered if she'd been holding mine when she'd been stabbed. If she'd felt the pain, the cool pierce of that knife. How many times had I held that hand in my own? I gulped, the lump of sadness not budging as I remembered every step of my life that she'd been there. The day we'd unlocked the door to Crescent Cottage as owners and she'd sworn I added extra layers of dust just to piss her off. When we were twelve and she kissed Nafe Moonstaff and then swore off boys forever because he'd stuck his tongue in her mouth. The first night we'd stayed in our home, and she'd insisted Scoop sleep with me so I wouldn't feel homesick.

She'd never known she was my home. My safe place. I clenched my teeth together so hard my jaw ached, willing the tears that welled in my swollen eyes to stay put. They couldn't see me as weak. None of them. My throat thickened, threatening to expose me as I held my tears in when that final healer looked over her shoulder to me and shook her head.

That was it. She was gone. Unsavable.

The healer slipped out the door, closing it silently behind her. Black shadows grew from the ground, smothering Kirsi. I leaped from the seat, screaming at him. Begging him not to take her. But it was in vain. Her body vanished, the blood disappeared, and I was left on my knees, sobbing as I crawled to the door, screaming for him to bring her back.

He didn't answer.

Of course he didn't.

I reached up, gripping the cold handle. Locked.

Anger soared through me, the death spell crackling within my soul as I used my power to unlock the door, surging out of the room. Two guards flanked the door. With less than a thought, I sent them flying into the others down the hall. If he was going to hide from me, I was going to hunt him down. Consequences be damned.

My hands shook with rage as I stormed through the black castle, ears pounding. Another set of guards approached, this time on high alert as I moved. They shifted. It didn't matter. The wolf and the lion were merely heaps of tangled limbs as I continued.

"Bastian!" I screamed. "Do not hide behind your soldiers, you coward. You liar!"

Fresh tears formed, fueled by the anger that consumed me. He'd be a fool to show his face. I wouldn't hesitate. I'd kill him. I'd rip him to shreds with my bare hands. I had been wrong to show him kindness. So wrong. And the person I loved most in the world had paid the price for my misplaced trust.

A door appeared in front of me. I gripped the handle and threw it open, storming in, hoping the king would save his men and show his face. He didn't. The door vanished behind me, and I was trapped in a small room full of his shadows. Power surged from me, shaking the room violently. I screamed and screamed and screamed until my throat was raw. Until blood dripped from my palms from my nails digging in. Until I could no longer see straight.

Defeated, my heart a dull thud in my chest from the loss of adrenaline, my limbs heavy, I curled into a ball on the floor and sobbed until I was sure I'd drown in my own tears. The king's shadows inched closer, testing me. I didn't even have the strength to wish them away.

I woke, numb. Closing my eyes, I saw her face. The tears began again. A shriveled piece of paper crinkled in my palm. Dragging my heavy arm across the cool floor of my prison, I peered at the blurry letters through my tears, noting the blanket over me that hadn't been there hours ago.

Raven,

I thought if I gave it the night, I'd have something worthy to say. But after hours of pacing, of hunting, of coming up empty handed, the only thing I can tell you is that I swear on my life I will avenge the murder of your friend. I know you think it was me, but I can assure you, it was not. My blade has been missing since the ball.

Ever yours and truly sorry,
Bastian

I crumpled the note and it disintegrated into embers and ash. "I don't want to play these games anymore, Bastian. I'm tired. And sad. And I give up. I just want to go home."

"I watched the coven leaders kill my parents when I was fourteen." He stood in the corner, half smothered in dark shadow. His voice, careful and quiet. "Four of them attacked their carriage. My father sacrificed himself for my mother, but in the end they both died. The witches had no idea I'd been following them on horseback. When the attack came, I ran away like a child. I let them die."

I stared into his gray eyes, full of sadness, still laying on the hard floor. I was supposed to kill him. Needed to kill him. But I didn't want to be a pawn in their battle. I couldn't tell him, though. I couldn't tell anyone; the coven leaders had seen to that.

Bastian fell to his knees and crawled until he lay beside me in that empty room, his nose so close to mine, I could feel his breath on my face.

"Did you really kill that man in the hall after the poison trial?" I asked, flashes of the dagger in the man's back filling my mind.

His lips formed a thin line as he audibly swallowed. "Yes."

"Why?"

"He attacked one of my maids in the hall. He tried to force her to take him to the Grimoires and when she refused, he pinned her to the floor with magic and cast illusions over her that made her believe he was peeling the skin from her body."

"Tavia?" I asked, remembering her reaction the next day. Her surprise that I would defend the man. Be appalled by his death. So much death.

"Clariss, actually. But Tavia found them. And called for the guards."

"Are you responsible for the Thrashings?"

A slow inhale of breath held my attention as I put the king on trial.

"Have you ever witnessed a Thrashing? Have you, or anyone you know, aside from a coven leader's story, ever seen anything other than the aftermath?"

I was sure they had, confident in the pictures painted across my memory. But no. I could not think of one time when someone other than the coven leaders had personally witnessed the massacres. "No," I whispered.

"The reality of the world is far more complicated than the bleak images they conjure to invoke fear." His voice remained soft and calm as he spoke to me. "They may not have announced it, but the coven leaders have waged a war on the people. They are kidnapping the staff in my castle, the guards I send to the territories, and various Fire Coven witches. They torture them in the most cruel and vile ways. One of the coven leaders is able to manipulate the mind. I'm not sure which one, but they are controlling the witches and forcing them to their will. They want to get to the Grimoires. And they will stop at nothing to wield that power. I believed for a long time they didn't know about the heady magic of the books when they are combined. But now I think they might."

I hesitated, waiting for my clouded mind to take in what he was saying. I just wanted facts and truth and no pretenses. "What are the Thrashings, if not a massacre dealt by you?"

"Death delivered at the coven leaders' hands when my men go in to rescue the innocent. I will not say that I have not taken lives. But I've never murdered masses of people. The coven leaders lie and kill to make me their villain."

"I hear the words that you are saying, but I cannot see right from wrong right now."

He brushed a curl from my face. "I know this is incredibly hard for you and I'm so sorry. If I could take this pain, I would."

"I don't know who to trust anymore, Bastian. There are lies and deception around every corner."

He slid his body even closer to me, grabbing my hands and pulling them to his chest. "I don't know why the coven leaders don't want us to be together, but it's the only thing that makes sense. They want to frame me for Kirsi's murder so you will deny me the only thing in the world I want."

"I know why." And of course, I did. If I'd gotten a chance last night, I would have killed him and that's what they wanted. The lump in my throat formed all over again as I realized Kirsi's murder had been a direct result of my own actions.

"Why?" His eyes shifted between mine, his head lying on the floor.

"I cannot say."

He nodded, no pushing, though I knew he wanted to.

"I want to go home. I want to find Kirsi's familiar and go home. Just a carriage. No magic."

"Okay," he whispered, pushing off the floor. "The cat is with Nym. He was howling in your rooms, and I wasn't sure what else to do with him."

He helped me to my feet and before I could protest or move away, he enveloped me in a hug. The kind with no pretenses, no expectations, just his heart willing mine to find a sliver of peace in the suffocating heartache. I needed it so badly. The comfort. The security of those wings wrapped around us. I hadn't even realized I was crying again until my shoulders shook with sobs. I didn't want this, any of it. But as I replayed my grandmother's words, to let her death go, I couldn't help but wonder if she was pushing me into these arms. Wishing I'd stop holding it against him.

I thought he probably held me longer than either of us had expected. But I needed to be reminded that someone cared. Even if his way of showing it was messed up, even if my mind and my heart would always be at war with each other, that seed of doubt had been planted, the soil turned, and I couldn't deny something was growing there. Be it regret or otherwise, at least it was fueled by passion.

Bastian rested his head on mine, moving his hands in circles on my back until my skin warmed beneath the friction of his palms. I wasn't sure if the king knew how to treat something so fragile he'd shatter it with a breath, but he was trying.

Stepping away, I wiped giant tears from my splotchy face. "It's time."

His eyes studied mine. "Will you come back?"

It was all I had to simply lift a shoulder and commit to nothing. There was heartache to come as I faced the next few days and I couldn't, wouldn't, be selfish with these moments that belonged to Kirsi. As the first to see her death, I'd have to light the initial candle at her funeral. That thought alone consumed me as the king waved a hand and a door appeared on a wall in the vacant room.

Opening the door, we stepped just outside the castle gates, rain of my own making falling steadily from darkened skies, matching my mood entirely. I walked numbly through the puddles, swallowing as the guards kept sharp eyes on me, likely scared from the show last night. I still didn't feel shame. Utterly shattered, but unashamed.

The king took my hand, helping me into the carriage, though he held the door open. letting the rain drip down his face, weighing down his wings, he stared up at me, something akin to torture on his face.

"Your Grace?" A guard ran up behind him, his coat bulging as he approached.

Bastian lifted Scoop from the inside of the man's coat, and turned, setting him onto my knees. The feline rubbed his head into my hand, spun in three circles and settled into my lap. Bastian stroked behind his ears and Scoop did not howl or hiss or swipe at him. I'd seen that cat attack a man in our shop when he would not back away from Kir. If Bastian had something to do with Kir's death, Scoop would have alerted me. I was sure of it.

"Raven?"

"I'm sorry, what?"

The Dark King's eyes turned down, rain droplets gathering on his lashes as he studied the iron step of the carriage.

"I asked if you were going to see Nikos."

Taking a deep breath, tension knotted in my shoulder blades as I stared upon the king I'd once feared and saw him as nothing more than a man with a title.

"I ... I don't know." I hadn't thought about Nik one time since last night. But Bastian didn't know that. Didn't know that I'd denied him. His insecurity could have been endearing, if not for the circumstances.

The sky ripped open, sheets of rain pouring on him, soaking the dark wings that hung heavy at his side. I reached for the door, but he grabbed my arm, coaxing me toward him until we were a breath apart. Angry shadows covered the ground below him, mirroring those silver, beautiful eyes. "Go to him, watch him fight with himself over morality and love. See if he would deny a coven leader. Because that's the difference between him and I, Raven. I would break every fucking rule, I would burn the world down for you. I know you're worth it without needing the time to figure it out."

"Maybe that's the problem, isn't it?" I whispered, brushing a rain-drop from his cheek.

"Maybe it's the solution."

His eyes bored into mine as the rain continued to pour. So much passion, and hurt, and anger lingered between us, there was hardly anything I could say to break away from the command he held over me.

Tucking a curl behind my ear, his stunning face twisted with anguish. "He'll do what the coven leaders expect of him. He'll fall in line and be the man to keep you there." He shook his head. "If you want to go, if you want to leave the Trials, I'll find a way to get you out of the blood oath you made when you put your name in the cauldron. I won't force you to do anything you don't want to do, even if it means I pay the price for that. Or the world does. Because you're worth whatever the cost." His eyes burned into me, and I could not look away. "The benefit to being the villain is there's nothing they can do to me that I won't repay tenfold."

The horse in front of the carriage nickered, breaking the spell between us. The Dark King pulled away, never taking his eyes from mine, even when the door was shut, with only a small window between us.

When I could no longer see him, Scoop nestled into my lap, I sank into the bench, lowering my chin to my chest as I rubbed my eyes, feeling utterly defeated. There had never been a future for me that wasn't wrapped around Kirsi's. I couldn't make myself care about the Trials, or whatever lay ahead. Bastian wanted me to go back to him, but to what end? In my heart, I knew the coven leaders had a hand in Kirsi's death. They meant to force me to kill the king. And I almost had. What good would winning the Trials do for me if I was stuck side by side with them? The minute I opposed them, I'd be dead by winter solstice. They'd see to that, regardless of the death spell I carried.

Watching the Fire Coven's territory pass by the window, nothing notable beyond the blackened, dead ground smothered in the pouring rain, I wondered what it would be like to be one of them. Cut off from the rest of the covens. Or did they separate themselves? Did they see the poison in the water when the rest of us had been so blind?

It wasn't long before we'd crossed the stone bridge into the Moon Coven territory. Knocking on the wall between the driver and I, he pulled the carriage to a near stop.

I yelled out the window, "Please take me to Crescent Cottage."

I couldn't go home. Couldn't bear to see Kirsi's things. Walking into my grandmother's shop wouldn't be much better, but there was nowhere in my life I could go that didn't have memories of her all over it. At least I was used to the pain at the shop.

I didn't have a key with me, but I didn't need it. Waving a hand, I hustled through the rain, and fought with the sticky handle before letting myself into our store. A bit more dust had gathered than I preferred, but the smell was the same, like standing in a wildflower field on a warm summer day. I lit the candles through the shop and made it to the cot in the back room before I collapsed, the grief overtaking me again as I remembered every laugh, saw every smile.

Scoop wandered the shop as if he'd find her. If there was anything that made me sadder than my own memories, it was that poor cat who would suffer more than anyone. Eventually he came to me, walking up and down the cot, yowling until I lifted him from the ground and buried my face into his soft, black fur. The tufts on his ears twitched when I breathed on them, and he twisted away, seeking comfort on my belly.

I felt as if his sadness seeped into me, or maybe mine to him, but either way, we were a pair of shared misery, laying there, tears flowing from my eyes all over again. A letter fell from the ceiling, landing on my face. My tears had smeared the ink before I could read it, but the message was clear enough to decipher.

Raven,
> *I'll have dinner delivered by sundown. Please eat something.*
> *Bastian*

I watched the paper disintegrate and closed my eyes, letting Scoop's gentle breaths soothe me into a dreamless slumber. My body needed rest, but my mind needed it more. I could have stayed in that escape forever. Where my mind forgot the hole in my heart. But a banging on the door before I heard it open yanked me from that reprieve.

"Raven?" Nikos' voice was the last I wanted to hear, hauling me back to two nights ago when everything had changed. Still, he didn't deserve my anger when he was only a pawn in their wicked game.

"I'm in the back," I croaked, lifting myself from the cot, carrying Scoop with me, who let out a low growl. He wanted to be left to mourn. So did I.

The ivy over the door rustled and he stepped inside, looking down on me with pity. "I've just heard about Kirsi. I wondered if you'd be able to escape the king. Are you okay?"

I shrugged. "I don't really know what I am."

"Come sit with me," he said, gesturing toward the cot.

Keeping Kirsi's familiar in my arms, we settled, a heavy silence between us as I stared at the floor, flashes of what Bastian had said rippling through my mind. He didn't know Nik. Not like I did.

"What happened?"

"I can't ... I can't bring myself to retell the story. I'm sorry. Maybe one day, but not this one."

Placing a palm on my back, he rubbed in circles until I could feel the heat of magic trying to bring me solace.

"Please don't. I need to feel. I need to think. I need to process."

He pulled away, turning to pick at a plant that had gone dry until all the dead leaves were gone. Using his magic, he watered the soil to kill time before turning back to me. "What are you going to do now?"

"That seems to be the great question, doesn't it? My whole life was wrapped around Kir. She was everything." I gulped, the tears threatening to return. "This place is full of memories, my home is the same. She's everywhere. I don't want to live without her memory around me, but I also don't want to drown in it."

He sighed. "Maybe it's time for a clean break. You can let this place go. You can let it all go. Start over."

I stopped. Processing his words. They hurt to hear, but there was truth there. I could start over. Maybe even go to the human lands. Run away from all the magical beings and power struggles, living in a place that had none at all. But even as the thought crossed my mind, I knew I couldn't actively sever myself from my power.

"I can never leave this shop. There's a piece of me here, too. And all the women that came before me."

"You know you have to go back to the castle, right? I hate to say it. I hate to even think it because who knows what that monster will do to you. But there's no choice."

"He said I could leave forever," I whispered. "He gave me a choice."

Nikos shifted on the cot, eyes widening. "But you need to go back to the castle and complete the assignment the coven leaders have given you."

"You know what they asked me to do?"

"I know they've given you an important task. And nothing has changed, so I assume it's incomplete."

I lifted Scoop, placing him gently on the ground while I stood, needing distance. "You know, I don't understand you, Nikos. Why are you so devoted to the coven leaders? Why are you *so* sure we should blindly follow them?"

He looked at me like I'd grown another head. "You're not ... you're not thinking clearly. Those women are the only way forward. They will vindicate the witches; they will see us set free of the Dark King's reign." He stood, crossing the room so he could grip my arms. "Tell me again that he hasn't brainwashed you. Tell me that you haven't been so manipulated that your best friend's death means nothing."

The numbness within my soul melted away as I jerked my arms from his grasp. Was this a battle I was willing to fight right now? Could I make him understand?

"Kirsi's death will always be the turning point of my life. I don't know what that means or what the future will be now, but I can tell you there's no going backwards. Do not draw a line in the sand and ask me to pick sides right now, Nikos. You will not like the direction I take."

He shook his head, backing away. "You don't mean that. You have the death spell. You can kill the king. You can end this today."

My heart stopped. The entire world stopped as I took in those damning words. They echoed through my mind as though screamed through a cavern. He knew. He knew they'd force that spell upon me, shutting me out from ever receiving another spell. He knew, and he'd lied.

"Five seconds ago, you were clueless. And now you're just a liar." I pulled the devil's ivy hanging from the ceiling to the side. Fire burned through my veins, the world rattling below me as that tumultuous magic threatened everything. "You need to leave."

All pretenses of friendship melted from his face as he turned back into the scorned lover he'd been the day I'd told him about joining the

Trials. "Stop this. You're just upset about Kir. You'll feel better soon, after the funeral tomorrow we can talk."

"This is over, Nikos. All of it. I don't want to be with you. I don't want to be your friend. I don't even want to look at you. Leave."

He stepped out into the shop, making his way to the door as anger rolled within me. Hands fisted at my side, I waited for him to go, to walk out that door and never come back, but instead he turned, hand on the doorknob.

"Endora is our only salvation. She's doing everything she can to make this world a better place. You're going to end up on the wrong side of this battle if you're not careful. Go back to the castle. Do as they've commanded and end it. This can be forgiven."

"I don't want your forgiveness. Get the fuck out."

He swung the door open only to find the king's guard standing there with a basket full of food. He snatched it from the guard's arms and launched it into the street, slamming the door behind him.

35

The rain never settled. I listened to it patter against the rooftop until it became so damp, the only sound left to be heard was a low rumble of scattered thunder. I leaned against the soggy door frame of the shop, watching the morning pass by as if the world were as sad as I were. I knew I'd cast the rain when my magic had gotten out of control. No one else did. Puddles gathered on the cobblestone streets were avoided by passing carts. No one stopped to talk to anyone. No cheer. No peace in familiarity.

When the king's carriage pulled up in front of the shop, I took a final deep breath, adjusted the heavy canvas bag on my shoulder and stepped out into the rain toward the waiting cabin.

"Thank you for coming," I told Grey as he held out a hand, helping me inside.

"I wish it were for something different," he said, staring out the window as the cart carried us on to mine and Kirsi's house.

The bag in my lap shifted. I reached inside and pulled out the black cat, setting him on the bench beside me. He didn't hesitate, crossing the carriage to settle onto Grey's lap. Those giant hands came down, stroking the feline as if he found comfort there while still staring absentmindedly at the trees.

"He sent you? The king?"

Grey looked at me then. His eyes ringed and sad. As if he hadn't slept. "I wanted to come."

"Right, of course. I just meant ... will he, the king, be coming as well, or ...?"

He lifted a shoulder, looking back out the window. "If he came, it would only cause a scene and I don't think anyone would want that."

"I guess not." I worked through my hair with my fingers, realizing I hadn't actually brushed it in days. I'd have to light the first candle and I was such a mess.

"Do you want him there?"

Saying yes would mean admitting things I wasn't ready to face or admit. So, instead, I pressed my lips together and picked at the seam of the shirt I'd been wearing for two days.

Approaching the cottage, I didn't know how I was going to feel, but as I stood where Kirsi had hundreds of times, it was like someone had punched me in the gut. I gulped, taking short steadying breaths, trying to hide my emotions as a fresh lump grew in my throat, threatening to reveal everything. Thankfully, the rain hid my silent tears as I took one careful step after another toward the door still marked with faded blood.

I unlocked and pushed the door open with magic. Grey stayed behind, but Scoop raced inside, searching for her. Everything was just as before. Threadbare, but ours. Homey and warm. Our wood stove in the corner, properly neglected, old pans with varying stages of tarnish hanging from the ceiling, cockeyed shelves we'd hung ourselves holding small jars of herbs, books, and the like. I clenched my teeth, trying not to double over as every memory swarmed me again. The only solace, a gentle knock on the open door behind me.

I spun to see Tavia and Clariss staring at me, pity all over their faces. Tavia marched forward, enveloping me in a hug and Clariss was only a second behind.

"There, there," Clariss said, her voice softer than usual. "We'll get through this. Poor dear."

Tavia sniffled, pulling away to wipe the tears from my cheeks.

"The king sent us. We're to do as you wish." She cleared her scratchy throat. "If you don't need us, we can wait outside."

With a shaking voice, I answered. "I think I need you more now than ever."

I had no one else. Not really.

Clariss broke away from us, going back to the door. "Come in, everyone."

"Everyone?"

"A cook and several guards," Tavia said, clearing her throat.

Grey appeared in the doorway next, lifting an eyebrow to me as if he could read my mind. "You sure?"

I wasn't. But the other option, being here alone with my thoughts, attempting to make myself presentable was far more daunting. So, I forced a smile and nodded, knowing today was only going to get worse anyway.

I ate by practical force as Grey stared me down, holding the plate in front of me while Clariss finished my hair. They'd brought a beautiful, intricate lace gown with them, but I chose to wear something of my own, content with a simple black funeral dress and black veil to cover my face. Within a few hours, we were smashed into the carriage together, Scoop in Grey's arms as we headed toward the clearing in Whorlwood Forest where the funeral would be.

The rain had stopped, but the ground was soggy. Knowing I'd have to face Kirsi's aunt and my parents made my stomach turn. Everyone would stare because she was like a sister to me. And I'd have to get through all of it, being gracious for the pity and condolences when my mind would be a million miles away, anywhere but here, living any life but this.

I let the king's guards flank me as I took my place at the front of the small gathering, avoiding the sight before me. Sometime during the day, a pile of branches had been gathered, a funeral pyre assembled, my best friend's body laid atop. Magic would have protected the branches from the moisture, but had they protected her as well?

A hand slipped into mine on one side and then the other. In my state of numbness, I hadn't even heard my parents move past the guards, but they stood like statues beside me, silent and staring straight ahead. My mother squeezed my hand as I forced back the tears that threatened to come. My eyes met Nym's across the circle from me, already holding her candle. She dipped her chin slightly, a tear streaking down her face. I swallowed.

Slowly, a small crowd gathered, intimate and meaningful as I looked over the faces of all the Moon Coven witches closest to her. Kirsi's aunt and father stood together holding candles, and I wondered how they'd learned. If the king had sent a messenger or whether Endora had passed on the news. It was hard not to look at her father and see her. They shared so many similar features, even his long blond hair was a mimic of hers.

The crowd cleared as old Endora, hunched over, made her way into the center of the clearing nestled within Whorlwood Forest. Only one coven leader was required to attend a funeral and Endora was the matriarch, having held the title the longest, so there we were. The numbness that had settled into me vanished. I didn't know how, but I knew she'd had a hand in Kirsi's murder. And now she was to preside over her funeral, pretending she gave a fuck. I squeezed both of my parents' hands, rocking back on my heels as I looked up to the sky and let my stubborn will drown out the sound of everything else. Until my father held out a candle and nudged me forward.

I still couldn't look at her, couldn't even see the shape of her covered face as I moved. Stepping forward, I swallowed the thickness in my throat as I lit my candle with magic, blinked away the final tears I would shed, and ignited my friend's pyre, consecrating her and her magic to the earth, to be born again.

"As steady as the moon that reigns over the dark, sister, we consecrate thee."

One by one, the others stepped forward repeating the phrase until all were done and the fire grew in size, way too hot to handle standing close to. Still, I remained, my parents anchored beside me as I let those flames carry me away, through a vat of memories and what ifs and moments that would never be. Until I was punishing myself with those thoughts, just to feel the pain of them.

Eventually, after my mother tried and failed to pull me away, they retreated into the background, letting me stand with only the king's guards as the fire was more ash than flame.

"Raven?"

I turned, staring at Nikos who stood a few paces away, his chin down, hands in his pockets as he kicked at the ground.

"I know I was a full ass yesterday and I just wanted to tell you how sorry I am."

Tone flat, I responded. "Thank you for your apology."

He stepped forward, placing his hand on the back of my arm. "I know you didn't mean what you said, but I need you to say the words, Rave." He pinned me with a look before glancing around us to make sure we wouldn't be overheard. "You're going back to the castle, you're going to use that spell, become the Moon Coven leader and we'll figure the rest out from there."

I shook my head, trying and failing to pull away from his grip.

"Let go of me."

His fingers dug in. "Not until you promise to do what you said you'd do."

"Why do you even care so much? You're hurting my arm. Let go." I yanked myself away, but he grabbed the other, pulling me to his face.

Through clenched teeth, his face red, he seethed. "You will do it."

A throat cleared behind me. "If you don't get your hands off her, I will end you here and now."

The honeyed tone of that deep voice melted over my spine as Bastian stepped into view, his hands clasped behind his back, his wings gone. Nikos released his grip, backing away slowly.

"This is just a misunderstanding," Nikos said, a forced smile on his face as he bowed to the Dark King. "Tell him, Raven. We're fine."

Bastian didn't bother looking at me as he took my side with casual confidence. "I'll be sure to ask her later."

Nikos' jaw set tighter, his hands turned to fists, but he did not engage the king, which was the smart choice.

"If you could just give us a moment alone?" Nikos asked, his eyes glued to the ground. "I would like to say goodbye to my love before she's taken back to the castle."

Bastian rubbed his thumb over his full bottom lip as he seemingly considered Nikos' request. He looked toward me, lifting a dark eyebrow. I managed a small shake of my head, which was returned with a wink.

"Request denied."

Nikos opened his mouth to protest, but as dark shadows rose from the ground, coiling around his legs, his mouth snapped shut, fear holding him in place.

"You're excused."

Needing no further provocation, Nikos turned and hurried away. We watched him in silence until he disappeared within the tree line.

"You came," I managed, turning toward the king. "I didn't think you would."

"I planned to pay my respects after everyone had gone, but then I saw him put his hands on you and I couldn't stay away."

"Thank you," I whispered, holding his gaze. "I'm not sure I could have managed these last days without you."

He tucked a wild curl behind my ear, and I knew the other witches would be watching. I couldn't care, though. Not today. Not after every step he'd taken to make sure I was cared for.

"I've sent Scoop back with Grey. Would you come with me? Away from here?"

I turned over my shoulder to stare at the burning embers of the pyre. "I'd rather be anywhere but here."

Shadows enveloped us both, a simple door appearing within their depths. He took my hand, pulling me through the door and away from all the prying eyes.

36

"This is where I come to get away," Bastian said, gripping my hand as we stood on the porch of a tiny cabin, nestled high into snow-capped mountains.

I hadn't pulled away from him and he hadn't let go. Instead, we stood, shoulder to shoulder, staring over what seemed like the entire world, filled with variations of landscapes and floating isles far in the distance. The mountain was completely silent and still, the crisp air a welcomed change from the soggy forest and funeral pyre.

"Kirsi would have loved it here."

He nodded. "Come inside where it's warm. I'll find us something to eat."

I lifted an eyebrow as I followed him. "You're going to cook?"

He smirked, rolling up his sleeves, baring some of his markings. "Contrary to popular belief, I have many skills. But no. I'm not a chef."

The inside of the small cabin was not at all what I expected. There was nothing grandiose, no black marble, nothing regal about it. It reminded me more of my home than his, with quilted blankets, stacks of books, and mismatched furniture, Bastian walked behind a counter on the far side of the room, and I lit the fireplace before moving to the floor-to-ceiling window beside the door.

One by one, stars appeared in the sky, the waning moon joining them as the sun began to fade in the distance. Flurries fell from the clouds that had settled just above the cabin's rooftop. I sank down onto the high-backed chair between the fireplace and window, wrapping a blanket around me as I pulled my knees to my chest and stared out into the abyss, letting myself get lost in the beauty of the world. For all its cruelty, there was still something to be grateful for.

Bastian vanished and returned within minutes, a savory smell filling the intimate space, making my stomach twist in hunger. I truly hadn't eaten enough the past two days. Lifting items from a basket he'd procured, he was in his own world, several strands of hair falling from where he kept it tied back. The veins in his forearms were visible, his muscles taut, as he lifted a bottle of amber liquid from the basket. The firelight caught his gray eyes, lighting them in a way that made them warmer. Kinder. His shirt was casually open at the collar, revealing several markings with symbols surrounding a circle. I wondered if those were the ones that commanded his shadows or controlled his doors.

"You're staring, Ms. Moonstone," he said without looking up.

"I'm aware," I answered, boldly.

His eyes cut to mine, his fingers stumbling with the glasses in his hands. "Nice to see you're still in there somewhere."

"Somewhere," I echoed, rising from the chair, the wool blanket still wrapped around my shoulders. "What did you bring?"

He opened a cabinet, shifting things around as he searched. "Just a vegetable soup for tonight."

"Smells divine." I turned to stare at the flames of the fire, listening to the crackle of the dried wood. "How'd you find this place?"

"I built it with my father, actually," he said. "I was twelve. I wished I'd known then that I'd only have two more years with him. Might not have been such an ass."

"Sad that you were only fourteen when your parents were killed."

A dark shadow crossed his face as he pulled the tie from his hair, swept the loose strands back, and retied it. "Seems like a lifetime ago really."

"A year later you ordered the confiscation of the Grimoires. Why?"

313

He filled the glasses with liquor. I could tell by the look on his face, he was not only reliving those moments, but weighing his words, debating if he should tell me. Scooping two healthy bowls of soup, he placed them on the counter.

"Eat and I will tell you."

I crossed the room and lifted the spoon, dipping it into the steaming broth and bringing it to my lips to blow. My eyes locked with his until the warm liquid coated my tongue in the most glorious mix of peppered and savory. I couldn't help the moan that escaped as I closed my eyes and took another bite. He cleared his throat, staring at me with that deathly gaze as I moaned again.

"You're doing that on purpose," he said.

"Maybe, but I believe you owe me a story now, Your Grace."

He growled low. "Do not forget I am half animal."

"Are we sure it's only half?" I couldn't help my smile. It seemed like a lifetime ago when I'd last done it.

He must have noticed too because he tossed his head back and laughed. "My mother used to say the same thing." He brought the spoon to his lips, blowing before he tasted it. Satisfied, he tossed the spoon, lifted the bowl and drank the rest as if it were a cup.

Setting his empty bowl down on the counter, he grinned ear to ear until I rolled my eyes and giggled.

"Everything I'm about to tell you has to stay here. With us. It's incredibly important that this information doesn't leave the cabin."

I swiped a finger over my chest in an 'x'. "Cross my heart."

"Endora Mossbrook sent her daughter Eden to marry my father, but she had no idea her daughter was already trying to escape her clutches. Nor did she know my father had already planned to marry a Fire Coven witch they said had great power and visions about the future. The morning Eden was to leave, she convinced the Moss Coven's bookkeeper that Endora had asked for the Grimoire.

"They had no reason to believe she'd lie, so they gave her the book and when she was escorted to the castle the next day, she kept it hidden. As my father tells it, Eden didn't want to marry him. She wanted to go somewhere she could never be found by her mother. She asked my mother to protect the Grimoire, but when the books were put together, they began to glow, compounding the power.

"My mother had a vision that night very clearly. Testing what she'd seen, she placed her hand on her family's book and performed a simple spell to light a candle. Everything in the castle turned black. The Fire Coven lands turned to ash below their feet. None were harmed, but the power was a warning, my mother had said, condemning us to live in shadow.

"So, my father sent Eden and her coven's Grimoire away, and my mother used a spell to conceal her, so she could never be found by any but our bloodline. Not even scrying would work."

I set my spoon down, immersed in his story. "I don't understand. Why wouldn't your father just bring judgment against Endora? Have her daughter speak against her? Why haven't you?"

"My father wasn't willing to put Eden at risk, nor let the knowledge of what happened when the Grimoires were put together come out. He didn't think Endora was a real threat to him."

"That's why you have the spell over the Grimoire room? Once someone enters, they know the secret and have access to the power?"

He nodded, leaning over the counter. "That room is sealed so the power cannot escape. There are whispers of what happens when you put the books together, but no one knows for sure except a select few. It's the only safe place for them. I'd hate to think what would happen if I cast within that room. The power is even greater now that there are six books."

"But after all this time, you could have condemned Endora. You watched her kill your parents."

He waved a hand and the dishes disappeared in a gathering of shadows. "Endora is cunning and dangerous. Killing her would make her a martyr and it would break the very fragile bond between the shifters and the witches. They think I'm their enemy because of her poison, but they haven't outright begun a war. The only way to keep the shifters from attacking when my father was killed was by promising I'd make several of them advisers and give their opinions fair weight on important decisions."

"The Old Barren," I said, nodding.

He smiled. "Yes, and a few others. The witches remain afraid of my rule. It's the best I can hope for until a new leader takes over the Moon Coven and convinces her people that I'm far more handsome and charming than murderous and moody."

"Oh." I tapped my finger to my lips. "So, you admit you're using me for personal gain?"

"I admit nothing."

I stood from the chair and moved to the window, staring out as I processed everything. "There's a flaw in your plan."

"What's the flaw?" he asked, wrapping the blanket I'd left behind around my shoulders.

"I still have to win the Trials."

"You're tied with Willow."

I felt no reaction to his admission. "You weren't supposed to tell me that. Now, with ... Kirsi gone, Onyx is close as well and he's ruthless. But even still, they will never truly accept me." I turned to face him, tracing a finger over the circle marking on his chest. "I'm unmarked and the coven leaders aren't exactly pleased with me at the moment."

He shuddered beneath my touch, lifting his gaze from my fingers to my eyes. "And why is that?"

"I cannot say."

"Cannot or will not?" he asked, the fire within him rising as he grabbed my wrist.

"Cannot," I whispered.

"They've bound your words?"

I nodded.

He buried his hands into my hair, gripping tight as he pulled me to my tiptoes. "Can I trust you?" His words were no more than a plea on his lips. Those full, beautiful lips.

"I think so," I answered, inching closer to him.

He broke away from me, far too soon, moving toward the door and grabbing the handle before I could stop him.

"Where are you going?"

He swung the door open. "I'm not sure *I* can be trusted." Stepping out of the cabin, his wings appeared behind him. He spread them wide, the blackness within them nearly stealing the light from the stars.

"Wait!" I yelled, chasing him out of the cabin. "Take me with you."

He turned, darkness filling his eyes as they roved over me. "Do you have a penchant for danger?"

"Please," I begged. "I need a distraction. I need to feel something other than grief."

He stalked toward me, lifting me from the ground with ease, before walking straight off the cliff of the mountain. I screamed the majority of the way down, until his massive wings opened wide, catching a current of cold air. Laying my head against his chest, we rose, his wings flapping in the night. We soared amongst the stars, diving and lifting back up, a complete symphony of adrenaline, fear, and ecstasy as he carried me closer to the moon than I'd ever been.

There was something intimate in those moments with Bastian. His strength and will alone, the only thing keeping me alive as the Earth passed below us, the cold mountain air tangling my hair. Soft snowflakes landed on my lashes, tickling my cheeks as I blinked them away. I was happy. So unfairly happy on a day that should have been filled with so much sorrow.

As guilt settled into my stomach, the smile faded from my face. The joy from my heart. Within a minute, he landed, setting me down gently as he gripped my face and pressed his forehead to mine.

"I know this isn't what you want to hear, but she'd want you to be happy."

"I know," I answered, swallowing back the pain. "It's just not fair that I get to be, and she doesn't."

He pulled me to his chest, his arms so firm around me that any other time I'd have struggled to breathe. But his warmth seeped into me, his heartbeat in my ear, and I refused to move. I needed him in that moment. Desperately. And somewhere in my soul, I thought maybe he needed me, too.

"Can we stay? In the cabin?"

He pulled away, staring down at me. "Are you sure?"

The snow fell harder now, covering his dark hair in flakes. I'd only then realized, though chilly, I wasn't nearly as cold as I should have been, standing on the top of a mountain at night while it snowed. He'd been warming us, of course.

Deciding I wasn't certain of anything anymore, whether spending a night with the king was a good idea or not, I nodded, wrapping my hands around his neck. "I'm sure."

37

The silence grew between us as Bastian looked down at me, brushing a thumb over my cheek. "I'm not a chivalrous man. I know you're hurting, and I should do the right thing, but I won't. If you need to use me to feel something, then use me because whatever I feel for you, it's agony. Every day. Every second. Every breath. Give me agony. If that's what it means to be with you, I choose it."

With his shadows firmly gripped around my beating heart, I reached for him, the dark stubble on his face grazing the palm of my hand. He turned into my touch, closing his eyes as he shuddered, his wings rustling behind him as if his grasp on the beast within was weakening. He lifted my hand, brushing my knuckles against his smooth lips, his breath warm.

Bastian's eyes met mine, every bit the villain I'd always known him to be, as darkness filled his features. His sun-kissed skin, the deeper hollows of his cheeks, the pointed set of his brow as he stared down at me, holding me in place with a glance, as only a king could do.

In a single motion, from one breath to another, he swooped, lifting me from the frozen ground and carrying me inside the cabin. The moment we were in, the door slammed behind us, and he set me down, leaning over me. Sliding my fingers up his chest, inside the open collar of the shirt he never buttoned, I clasped them behind his neck. His firm hands moved to my waist. So strong and steady as he pushed me up against the ice-cold window, the freezing sensation a complete contrast to the warmth pooling between my legs.

The gasp that left my mouth was swallowed by him as he closed all space between us, kissing me for the first time with more passion, more fierceness than I'd ever known. His tongue swept across my lips, tasting me, and I moaned, feeling utterly his to command. As he bit at my lip, I was convinced he could swallow me whole, and I would absolutely let him.

The heat within me grew. Moving his hands up my body, Bastian spun me to face the window, his lips finding the back of my neck as he gripped my hands above me.

"I hope you aren't in a rush, Ms. Moonstone, because I plan to devour you slowly."

My knees buckled at the weight of his promise, the way his words rippled down my spine. Bastian held me steady, one hand still holding my arms above me, his other circling my waist as he gripped me tight against his body, trailing kisses up my neck, around to my ear and across my throat as I leaned my head back on him.

"No rush," I managed, though the words came out far too breathy.

His deep chuckle rumbled against my back. Releasing my hands, his apt fingers began unlacing the black dress I was wearing. In a single motion, he pulled the gown over my head revealing only my undergarments. I closed my eyes, refusing to look at my reflection in the window. As punishment, the king bit my earlobe, sending a single sharp wave of blissful pain directly between my thighs.

"You will watch, or I will stop."

I nodded, forcing my eyes open, if only to prolong the pleasure of his warm fingertips. Within moments, I was naked before him, still staring straight ahead, his eyes burning into mine in the reflection as he took my arms and placed them around his neck once more.

"So beautiful," he said, stroking a finger down my stomach and pulling me several steps from the window.

I moved to my tiptoes without realizing it, trying to force his hand lower, to stroke that aching need growing like a storm within me. The fire of his touch moved only low enough to make the need worse before he changed course, moving to my breasts, pinching a nipple between his fingers as he watched for my reaction. I nearly dropped my hands, breathless and burning for him. But I could not look away, would not. I needed him. Needed to feel every inch of him.

Bastian's hands moved like a feather down my sides, making me squirm. The delight in his eyes when I gasped only stroked the fire within me. I pressed myself backward, purposefully pushing my ass into him, feeling him grow behind me with a growl.

He moved his leg between mine, pushing them further apart as he watched me, leaning all my weight against him. His shadows bound my hands above my head, and he stepped away, leaving me there, naked. He circled me like prey, as he so loved to do, sending those magical fingers up and down my body. After several rotations of the Dark King admiring me, he stopped before me, kissing me slowly as his hands took the place of his magical shadows.

"Do you want me to stop?" he asked, the strain on his voice raw and real.

"No, Your Grace," I whispered.

He held out his hand. The door flew open and an icicle from the cabin roof snapped free, surging forward into his waiting palm as the door shut once more and he looked at me with that devious smile. "Are you sure?"

I couldn't manage a word as I trembled, my body aching for him to touch me again. He brought the thick icicle to his mouth and bit off a chunk before tossing it to the floor.

My eyes remained glued to his as he fell to his knees before me, teeth clamped around the ice and dragged it up my navel. I squirmed, tossing my head back, though I remained held by shadows. He pulled away and I knew exactly what I had done. Snapping my head back to him, he sat on his feet, lifting an eyebrow.

"Sorry," I panted.

Waiting until he was confident I wouldn't look away from those brutal eyes again, he reached for the melting icicle and bit off another chunk from the narrow end. Smiling deviously, he stood, bringing the bitter cold to my neck before sliding it down my body, circling my nipples until my flesh raised to bumps, sending every nerve into overdrive.

He released his shadows around my wrists, and I slumped forward. He caught me, the cube still in his mouth as he laid me down on the bed which had appeared where the couch had been. I gripped the pillow tight in my grasp as he began anew with that icy torture, sliding it up my thighs. The chill from the ice, the burn from his gaze, all forms of glorious agony as he moved over my core, leaving the cube to melt in my navel.

"Cold, love?" He stood from the bed, walking to the table and lifted the candle from the holder. Moving across the room, he lifted the half-melted icicle from the floor, a smirk on his face as he came back to me. "Do you trust me?"

I nodded, ache growing. His eyes roved over my body again, full of hunger as he ran his tongue over his bottom lip. Holding the candle out, he poured the hot wax down the valley between my breasts. The stinging pain vanished within seconds, making the slit between my legs swell and throb with need.

As the wax cooled, he ran the tip of the icicle over my lips, the melted water dripping down my chin and pooling in the hollow of my neck. He leaned over and drank from me, sliding his tongue up, following the trail of cool water until his mouth was on mine, his lips pressed fervently over mine.

He pulled away far too soon, just as I began to squirm below him, the desire cascading over my body in lush waves of passion. Bringing the icicle to my lips again, freezing water dripping from his fists onto my body, I took it into my mouth, sucking down the cool water.

It was his turn to gasp, watching me with hooded eyes as I played a willing part in his fantasy. He pulled the ice from my mouth, this time trailing it down my body, the cold bite ravishing me, followed by slow drips of burning wax until my nerves were nearly undone with the varying temperatures. Sliding that icicle down my core, I wasn't nearly prepared enough when he pressed it into me, the cold forcing my body taut.

He was unrelenting though, pouring the steaming hot wax over my navel. The fiery heat, mixed with the icy cold as our eyes held each other. He moved the ice in and out as he continued to drip wax over my nipples. I couldn't handle the crash of nerves, the way he looked at me, the way my body responded. Squeezing my eyes shut, I knew he'd pull away, but I barely had control as I tilted my head back and screamed his name.

I faintly heard the sizzle of the candle's flame, the crash of the icicle shattering on the floor as he lifted my legs and closed his mouth over me, sucking on the sensitive bud. Everything that was once ice cold heated over. Every nerve ending in my entire body he'd commanded with his game came alive as his tongue, his mouth, his lips pushed me further and further toward the edge of that cliff I'd been begging for.

He pulled away. "Look at me, Raven."

I somehow managed, though I felt like I had no control over anything else as he closed his mouth over me once more, pushed two fingers inside, and watched as the orgasm shattered through me. I shook, unable to hold back the euphoria this man had delivered.

Sometime between that glorious bliss and the next moment, the king undressed, crawling up the bed and planting his arms on either side of my head. He brought his nose to mine, smiling as he watched me struggle to catch my breath. I slid my arms around him, rubbing my nails up and down his wingless back as he kissed me soft and slow. Bastian pressed himself into my opening and thrust forward without warning. I bucked, digging my nails in as I realized the size of him in reality had been just as big as I'd imagined. Perhaps the ice had helped numb the pain, because I felt nothing but pleasure as he pushed, staring down at me with more adoration than I'd ever deserved.

He took his time. Moving softly and slowly as he brushed hair from my face and traced my cheeks with his fingers. Brushing away the wax, he closed his mouth over a nipple, then bit down, inciting a wave of pain he soothed with his tongue as he lifted one of my legs to his shoulder, pressing himself further into me, though I was sure I could take no more.

He went fast, slamming his hard body into mine, his corded muscles never straining. Every groove of him, each inch, every sound he made, each breath, called to me, lured me closer and closer until I dug my nails into his back. He thrust forward with a groan, and we came together, holding each other for dear life as our bodies worshiped each other.

He fell to the bed, breathless and worn. Then wrapped himself around me, breathing on my neck until those short pants turned into the slow sounds of slumber. The king had utterly wrecked me in the best way possible and now, I never wanted to leave the mountain top.

WARMTH, UNLIKE ANY I'D EVER KNOWN, SMOTHERED ME AS THE SUN peeked through the large cabin windows. Clearing my mind, I realized the heat was a man, a king, with his arm and leg flung over me, his hot breath coiling down my back. I couldn't bring myself to wake him, though my body ached to shift. Instead, I watched the vibrant colors of the sunrise dance across the sky, so close to us here in the heavens, I thought if I walked out that cabin door, I could bathe in them.

"Can we stay?" he rumbled against my back, reaching his arms around to pull me closer.

"This is your world, Your Grace. The rest of us are just living in it."

He released a soft chuckle, kissing my shoulder blades before resting his mouth closer to my ear. "If only that were true."

I shrugged, tilting my head to prevent the tickles as he spoke again. "Do you see that clock on the wall?"

"If I say no, can we pretend it's not really there?"

"No," he laughed, a throaty sound this early in the morning. "My father built that clock specifically for this reason. When we'd come to hunt the mountain, I would always want to stay in bed a little longer. He'd say, 'midday waits for no man', and force me out of bed."

I rolled in Bastian's arms, our noses nearly touching as I traced a finger down his cheek.

He growled. "You can't just move around naked and magnificent in the morning. You're far too tempting."

Pressing my lips to his, I slid my hands down his stomach, far more interested in distracting the king than anything else. He protested for less than half a second before spinning me around, lifting my leg and pressing himself inside of me.

The morning was filled with soft pants, purposeful touches and more kisses than I'd shared in a lifetime. By actual midday, though my body was sore, he forced me out of bed, threatening to toss my naked ass in the snow if I didn't get up. He rewarded me with brunch when I eventually complied, but by the time the meal was done, I pinned him to the chair, lifting my skirts to take him into me again and again.

"You can only use me as a distraction for so long until we have to go back, you know?" he asked, pressing his lips to my bare shoulder.

"I don't think I can go back, Bastian."

He turned my face with his fingers, staring into my eyes. "What do you mean?"

Shaking my head, I stood, adjusting the dress. "I can hardly function without thinking of her. There's you and I, here, getting lost in each other or there's her, lying dead on that floor, knife in her chest, a pool of blood beneath her. I can't step into those rooms. I can't see the door between them and wish she'd come walking through. I'm not strong enough."

He took my hands, lifting them to his lips as he stared into my eyes. "I'd never force that on you, Raven. But please come home with me. I will get you new rooms."

"Can't I stay here? You could put one of your magic doors in that lead to the castle."

He shook his head. "If something happened to me, you'd be stuck up here with no food and no way down the mountain. Please come back."

I didn't really have a choice, it seemed. And I couldn't run from Kirsi's death forever. Eventually, I'd have to stop and face that heartache head on. For now, I'd just have to take it minute by minute. But at least I wasn't alone.

"Shall we, then, Ms. Moonstone?" he asked, holding out a hand to me as he bowed at the hip.

I rolled my eyes. "If you insist."

He yanked me to him, smothering me with a long and languid kiss. "I do, indeed."

True to his word, the minute we were back in the castle, he took me down a different hall than I'd seen before. Still very black and full of shadows, though it felt less ominous now, knowing it was an unintentional result of his mother's magic. Pressing open a tall set of double doors scrawled with golden filigree, I stepped inside, his hand firmly on the small of my back as I took in the scarlet room with carefully woven rugs, golden accents on every surface and deep red bedding. Golden frames lined the walls, holding pictures of landscapes and sunsets beyond my wildest dreams.

Scoop was already there, curled into a ball on the foot of the bed, watching us as I walked through to the bathing room and then the sitting room that could have housed half the kingdom, with a wall full of old books bound in leather and another of shelves with trinkets. I lifted one, a swan, studying its delicate features. Such a gem felt out of place in this castle.

"These were my mother's rooms," he said quietly.

I gasped, turning to him. "I can't take them, Bastian. Not when they mean so much to you."

He tilted his head. "Don't you see? You mean everything to me now. These rooms are just floors and walls and fancy things." He pulled me close. "You're the only thing that truly matters."

"Until the coven leaders come."

"Let them come." His eyes burned with fury. "I'll shred them to pieces."

38

Several days passed by with visits from Bastian when he could, food delivered to the room, and one trip to the greenhouse so I could lay in the dirt and let the moon bring peace over me. On the third day, I woke to Bastian already gone and Tavia and Clariss staring down at me. Lifting the blankets to cover my chest, I stretched, pulling Scoop closer and wishing I didn't have to get out of bed. As each day passed, the feline became more and more distant. Wandering, just as we'd been told he would, trying to find his witch.

"There's a Trial today," Clariss said, lifting an eyebrow.

"Think I'll die?"

"If you don't get out of that bed, it's nearly guaranteed," she answered.

I sighed, sitting up. "Good point."

"It'll just be pants and a shirt today," Tavia said, sharing a weary glance with her counterpart.

Clariss cleared her throat, tilting her head toward the bathing room. "Let's get started. You're going to need your breakfast."

"What aren't you saying?" I asked, dragging myself from the bed completely naked and heading toward the bath. When they didn't answer I stopped short, spinning just in time to catch another shared glance. "Did something happen?"

"No. No, nothing like that," Clariss said, pushing past me. "You're to take physical weapons today and it's got Tavia in a tizzy."

My mouth went dry. "I'm what?"

"That's all we know, so worry about it later. For now, in." She pointed toward the tub, full of steaming hot water. "And since you've decided to sleep in, there's no time to relax. Tavia, the oils."

Rushing through the bath and dressing in pants and a shirt, Tavia met me at the door with a satchel.

"There's rope, a knife, and ..." she looked down into the satchel again. "An empty jar."

"Fun."

"I hardly think now's the time for sarcasm," Clariss scolded, holding out the cloak for me. "We will see this through to the end together, so be on your toes. Observant. Smart."

"Love you too, Clariss." I smiled, hanging the cloak over an arm as we walked out of the room.

Bastian waited in the hall, his face twisted with worry. "A word, Ms. Moonstone."

Clariss and Tavia joined arms, dipping low before hurrying down the hallway. He watched them until they were out of sight before grabbing my waist and pinning me against the wall, one arm above me as he leaned down and kissed me frantically. His tongue unrelenting as he pressed his body into mine like he needed me more than anything, more than life. I pressed my hands to his chest, pushing him away as I caught my breath.

"If I didn't know any better, I'd swear you were worried, Your Grace."

He pressed his forehead to mine, the agony on his face clear. "Be careful. Be smart. I can't help you."

I ran my fingers into his hair, pulling out the tie just to feel his silky, thick locks "I know. I'll be fine, though. I'm not scared of them."

He leaned down and kissed me again, before forcing himself to pull away. "Wait here for two minutes and then join us. There's no reason to anger them right before this Trial."

I nodded, biting my bottom lip just to watch him falter as he walked away.

Shuffling through the dining hall, staring at that empty chair nearly gutted me. And the only Chosen I'd seen since Kirsi's death was Nym. We hadn't spoken a word, but the nervous glance she shared with me said enough. Willow grew taller in her chair as I passed, bowing to Bastian before I wandered down the table to my normal place. Onyx sat picking his teeth with a knife, staring at the remaining contestants. Once thirteen, now five.

It wasn't until I slid my chair toward the table, that I really noticed the rings around Nym's red eyes, her usually glowing dark skin a bit duller, her arms bare without her thirteen bangles. The only constant was Talon, the tiger pacing the floor beside her chair, his tail wrapping around the legs of it as he padded back and forth.

We ate in silence, a shared reverent state. An empty chair sat between us. Kirsi's. I scooted closer, reaching into her lap to take her hand, squeezing it as the rest of the room stared at us. Though her fingers trembled, and a tear streaked down her face, she squeezed back, staring straight ahead. I hoped she knew my kindness wasn't about an alliance, but I didn't get a chance to speak with her before the king rose from his seat, clearing his throat.

My cheeks flushed at the sound. But I couldn't feel guilty for what was growing between us. Whether we were together or not, the Trials would go on, unchanged. He had no more control than I did and there was peace in that knowledge. Knowing that come what may, it wouldn't be in the hands of someone I cared for.

Bastian waved an arm through the air, conjuring a door on a far wall with a clear silhouette of mountains carved on the surface. The tension in the air shifted immediately as the Chosen realized we'd be going directly to the Trial, armed with weapons, which meant there was a real possibility this would be the last time we all sat at this table.

"Rules." Bastian's voice cut through the room like a blade.

One of the shifters came forward, moving his glasses up his nose as he read from a rolled parchment. "This will be your final Trial. Raven Moonstone and Willow Moonhollow are tied for first place."

A tapestry appeared beside him with giant letters. I couldn't help my sweep of the standings, searching for Kirsi's missing name. The only sliver of hope was that Nym had held her position ahead of Onyx. It was a tight race, though, with only a few points spread between us. This was anyone's game.

"You've each been given three items. When you step through that door, you'll find yourself at the base of the Charon Mountains. Seven days past the blood moon, a hoard of deja take physical form for seven hours. Capture one, make your wish, and bring back proof it was done."

Though I could feel the king's eyes on me, I looked instead to Onyx, still holding that knife in his hands as he flashed me a smile and winked. Once the Trial began, I was free game, and he had a score to settle with me from the poison trial. He knew the king showed me favor, everyone did, and that was reason enough to come for me.

A slip of paper landed in my lap. I crunched it in my fist as we all stood from the table, now very aware of the cramped room, the weapons we each carried, and the small size of the door. Unwilling to walk into something I wasn't prepared for, I grabbed Nym's hand again, and ran. I slammed the door open with magic and flew through the opening, unwilling to look back as I dragged her behind me into the Moss Coven territory, the cloak and the letter from the king still clutched in my grasp.

Lush shades of green moss and sharp rocks flew by me as we ran, side by side, a baby tiger on our heels. The spirit blessed marking on Nym's forehead glowed as Talon transformed, taking his full size as a giant predator. He skidded to a halt, turning to roar as someone chased us.

"He'll buffer, but he won't be able to keep them all away. What's the plan?" Nym asked, swinging her arms as swiftly as I did while we ran through a valley of jagged cliffs covered in slippery moss.

"We need to find a decent place to hide. Willow is ahead of you in points, and Onyx is right behind you. We'll be their first targets. Long before the deja."

"Any idea what a deja looks like? Or how we're supposed to catch one?"

"Deja are supposed to be tiny winged fairies that blend into the night sky. I thought they were gone from this planet, though, after losing their ability to stay here."

"How do you find one?"

Shaking my head I turned, surveying the landscape. "No idea on the deja. We'll have to just get to higher ground and look for clues."

"Take my hand and guide me. I'll use my familiar's sight to watch our backs. You have to find a place that Talon will fit also, that's all I ask." She stopped running, looking me right in the eyes. "I can't lose him too, Raven."

"You won't," I promised, having no right to.

Her eyes turned white as the whole of her left arm's markings began to glow that bright orange color. I pulled her forward and she followed without hesitation, but I had to be even more careful than I already was on the slippery surface, as the ground slowly became wet and the rocks, dangerous.

"Onyx and Willow are together and not that far behind us. They have no idea Ophelia is tracking them, though. None have weapons out."

"Okay, you're going to have to come back to regular vision because we have a problem."

She blinked several times, looking around as I pulled her to a stop. "Oh shit."

A flock of phoenixes hovered in the sky ahead, swooping low enough their fiery forms blocked the only way forward.

"When was the last time you had to deal with a phoenix?"

"Pretty sure, never. Is the plan to just walk beneath them? While they are flying in circles and swooping down like that?"

"There's no choice unless you want to go back and deal with the others. We'll just have to be careful. My grandmother always told me they were hot tempered."

She pursed her lips, an eyebrow peaking. "You trying to be funny right now, Moonstone?"

I forced a laugh. "I wish I was. Let's push forward and hope to find a hiding place to make a plan once we pass them. Follow my lead. Better call Talon, just in case," I said, swinging the cloak over my shoulders and glancing down at the letter.

R,

It kills me that I cannot assist you. Come back to me safe and I will reward you in my own way.

Probably pacing the floor,

B.

I smirked as the note burned away. A giant white tiger surged forward. Any other day, any other task, and I'd be terrified. But that beast had eyes for only his witch as he shredded the ground beneath his giant paws, racing for us.

Climbing up the stacked slippery rocks as we moved, I lifted my hood and hid my face within the shadows. Talon charged ahead of us, his nimble body far more trusting than ours as we inched toward the phoenixes. I couldn't tell how many of them there were as we approached the giant red and orange birds with magical flames along the tips of their flourished tailfeathers. I stopped, waiting for Nym to stand beside me, and bowed as low as I could. Out of the corner of my eye, I could see her and Talon doing the same.

A piercing scream filled the air and I quickly looked up to determine which of the great flock was in charge. The phoenixes, though wild, were full of honor and grace. Typically, if you did not offend them, and kept your head down, they would let you walk below them. But their beady eyes and the heat rolling off them as we cowered below their flight still carried a heavy threat. If they attacked, it would be as one, swift, fierce and without fault. We'd be shredded by talons and burned alive.

So, we walked steadily across the flat top of the rocks, still climbing up the low slope of the mossy mountain. Sweat drenched my forehead and dripped down my back as we moved. We got nearly to the end of the path before I slammed to a stop. "Oh fuck."

I slapped my hands to my mouth, realizing the word would be enough to offend the beasts.

"What?" Nym hissed.

"The jars."

"Yeah, I have one too, so?"

I leaned in, hoping only she could hear me. "I think we're going to need a phoenix feather to capture the deja."

Her eyes doubled as she slowly shook her head. "There aren't enough titles on this planet to convince me to do something so moronic."

I'd love to just reach up, grab a handful of feathers and run like hell, but that wouldn't work for so many reasons, the first being the fact that if I stole the feather, it would turn to ash. It had to be freely given and any sort of damage would also turn it to ash. Delicate bastards. That's why we had jars.

"Keep going," I whispered. "Let's get past them and to that far rock. Then make a plan."

"Let's not forget we're being chased by people with knives either," she hissed.

Talon let out a low growl as we passed under the last of the phoenixes, watching us with his sharp gaze. My legs burned from climbing the slick rocks, but we made it to the ledge beyond them without falling. I scanned the path we'd taken up the rigid side of the mountain, looking past the birds to where the jagged cliffs met the valley below. We hadn't climbed nearly as far up as it felt.

I lay on my belly on the rock and Nym huffed, doing the same, though she was clearly over it already.

"The only thing I know of the deja is their old ties to the phoenix. They'd once been connected to them, using the feathers to prolong their time on earth. But as the phoenix became aware of the deja's obsession, they pushed them away, refusing to feed them their magic. I'm not going to force you to go on if you don't want to, but I'm guessing this is the only way we're going to catch one. And we have the advantage right now. The others are only a short distance behind us."

"Fine. Be logical. But I'm still going to bitch about it. What's the plan?"

"Unless held there by magic, why else would they be circling that spot?"

She watched the phoenixes swoop and circle, calculating their moves. "Food?'

"Exactly."

"And who's probably going to be able to hunt whatever it is they want in those rocks better than them?"

She looked at her familiar and back to me. "What if they attack him?"

"Then we hit them with all the magic we have and run like hell."

"I'm not a huge fan of this plan, Moonstone."

I looked her dead in the eye. "I'm not either, but I'm also not interested in dragging this out or waiting for Onyx with his spell that can slice you to pieces. He doesn't even need that blade. I'm not sure where we go from here, my plan was to get away from them. But there's only one reason they are going the exact same direction as us."

"Okay. Okay." The mark on her forehead burst to light as she commanded Talon forward. Though hidden still, we watched over the ledge as he padded back down the rocks and below the swirling phoenixes.

"Remember, we need to trade with them. He can't eat the prey. Only capture it."

"Tell him that," she mumbled, eyes closed as she coaxed her familiar forward.

Talon stooped low, his hind quarters lifted, his legs coiled as he stared straight ahead. Eyes locked on something. Two swishes of his backside and he pounced, sending the magical birds backward as he captured their dinner. Or at least dinner for one. The leader of the flock tilted his head back and screamed such a high pitch, I thought my ear would burst from the pain. The tiger ran back to where we were perched, a white stoat hanging limp from his massive maw.

I stood, throwing my cloak back as I caught sight of Willow shuffling toward us.

"Please," I said, bowing again. "We would like to offer a bargain."

The biggest of the birds swooped low, a trail of fire in his wake.

"Speak," the bird hissed, his word barely legible.

"This single stoat for five of your tail feathers."

Nym gasped beside me, but I remained still, watching the bird, ever wary of his claws. A sound, something that could have been a laugh, had it not been for the tiny beak, came from the phoenix. "No. But I could roast your cat."

"You could. But then you'd have to deal with all of us." I jutted my chin forward, pointing toward Willow who was still not within earshot, but definitely close enough to be seen with Onyx right on her trail.

"Witches?" he hissed.

"Yes, and we are closing in. They're over there too, beyond that ridge," I said, pointing to the side.

"I see no one," he answered.

"They don't want to be seen. As far I can tell, you're in for a rough fight. Or you can give up four feathers and my partner and I will go away."

"And the others?"

"Well, I wouldn't stick around to find out."

The bird tilted his head, staring at the stoat in Talon's mouth. "Two feathers and your beast must catch two more for my family."

"Two feathers, two stoats," I countered, looking beyond the phoenix to where Willow had slipped on a rock.

"Deal," the bird said, swooping to snatch the prey from Talon.

"Hurry," I whispered to Nym.

"You're either incredibly smart, or incredibly stupid," she answered as her familiar captured another of the tiny vermin for the phoenix and dropped it on the path.

The phoenix tilted his head back and screamed again. I pulled out my jar as Nym scrambled for hers. One of the phoenix's kin took the additional offering as the leader plucked two steaming feathers from his tail with ease and dropped them into our jars. He hissed something like a warning before flying away with the rest of them. They'd land somewhere close by, still hunting in the morning hours, but Nym and I wouldn't be around to watch. We were already moving laterally around the mountainside, away from our opponents. Unfortunately, that meant abandoning the path and climbing up and down the ledges that protruded the dangerous mountainside, but there was no other choice.

"Smart thinking, running off the phoenixes. I wonder if the others will chase them or us."

"I'm not waiting to find out. Keep moving over these flat rocks around this side so we can work our way back down."

Talon took his smaller form and leaped toward her. She caught him mid-air and dropped him into her satchel. "Down? I'm good with down."

A memory of Kirsi doing the same with Scoop flashed across my mind and suddenly the small victory didn't feel like a win anymore. Just a means to an end.

An arrow sliced through the air, narrowly missing my arm. I jerked my head to the side, looking back. Only Willow and Onyx pursued, which left Ophelia either chasing us and falling behind or potentially taking an ally position. I couldn't be sure, and it was too important to gamble. *Assume everyone is an enemy*, Kirsi had told me.

Willow's hands were up in the air as she cast. I stood, letting power crackle below my skin as I flung magic toward her, sending her flying into Onyx as if they were dominoes. I could kill them. A single thought, a flick of my hands and that would be it as the power of the death spell lured me. This whole competition would be over. But just because I bore the weight of death did not mean I had an ethical right to that magic, just like my memory spell.

"Raven!" Nym shouted as a rumbling came from above us.

Rocks poured from the top of the mountain like rain, rolling toward us as the ground shook.

"Run!" I screamed, realizing that wasn't going to save us on a trek down the rocky ledges of the mountain side.

A huge boulder rolled down toward us, bouncing off the steep plateaus, causing more rocks to fall. I cast as quickly as I could, using that boulder to sweep away as many of the others as possible, making it soar somewhere into the valley below. My heart twisted, hoping there would be no casualties from that rushed decision.

"Over there." Nym pointed, ignoring a cut on her forehead from where she'd already been hit.

I lowered myself from the ledge I was standing on, hustling until my feet slipped out from under me. Nym grabbed my hand, but I only pulled her down beside me as we slid, skin shredding, tiny rocks raining down upon us. Somehow, we managed to stop sliding, though both of us were bleeding. She hadn't used her hands at all, holding her satchel up so Talon wouldn't be injured. Achingly slow, stooped as much as we could be, we hurried under the protruding ledge she'd pointed out and tried to catch our breath.

I healed the cut on her head, before the ones on my side and calf. "It's not much, but I hope it helps."

"Thank you," she said with a sigh of relief. "Can you get my ankle?"

I nodded, dragging the spell forward as I considered my next words. "You're only going to be targeted if you stay with me. They want me, not you."

"If you weren't sleeping with the king that wouldn't be an issue."

I rolled my eyes. "I'm going to assume that's a joke."

She snorted. "Of course it's a joke. You'd have to be insane to sleep with that maniac."

I forced a smile. "Right."

"So, we split up?" she asked, moving to her feet.

"I think we have to. It's the only way to make sure you're safe."

She shifted the satchel over her shoulder, reaching a hand inside. "But what about you?"

"Kirsi would want me to make sure you were okay. So, I will. Because I think she loved you."

She froze, moving only to force her chest to rise and fall. "We can't talk about her right now. I won't make it through this."

I nodded, lifting the cloak back over my head. "Someday, when we're both ready, we can talk about it. For now, I'm going out there to cause the biggest distraction I can muster. And you're going to sneak out and get away. Because if someone's going to win this thing, it's you or it's me. As far as I'm concerned, everyone else is an enemy."

"Don't get dead, Moonstone," she said as I crept out of the safe cavern.

39

Once the dust from the falling rocks had settled, I stood tall, holding my hands out to my side as I called forth the spell that rattled the world. The spell that had only been a small tremor until recently. Until that veil within me, holding back whatever it was I harbored, had begun to thin. The coven leaders had known I had power, I had known I'd been suppressing magic, but none of us knew the extent. And certainly not why.

With Willow less than twenty paces away, I made my way to the final ledge of rock, leaping down to stand face to face with her as she shot an arrow out of her hands with magic. She missed. Heart racing, I backed up a few paces, steadying myself as the Earth continued to rock back and forth. Deep, rumbling thunder rolled overhead as I pushed and pushed my magic, preventing her from getting a good foothold while I watched for the most dangerous of the pack. But I couldn't see Onyx at all.

Gulping down my fear, I lifted my hands. "You don't want to do this," I warned as she inched closer, hard determination on her cold face.

"Oh, trust me, we do."

I shook my head at her. "It doesn't have to be like this. You can go on ahead. Catch the deja."

She snorted, taking a step closer. "You're a roadblock. I don't give a shit about the coven leader position. The only title I'm here to win is queen."

Willow took another step toward me and I lifted a hand, prepared to cast fire at her, but an arm slipped around my throat. Hot breath hissed in my ear as Onyx hauled me backward. I reached my hand in the satchel, fist wrapped around the carved handle, but Onyx was fast and smart. The knife surged from my hand, rotated in the air and planted itself deep into my thigh.

Buckling from the pain, I screamed. Still standing behind me, his forearm around my throat, Onyx chuckled, leaning down to rip the knife from my flesh. I screamed again, as he assaulted me with his magical cuts, marking my forearms. Another of Willow's arrows surged forward and planted into my other leg.

They chipped away at my morals, that singular thing in my mind that told me I shouldn't use the death spell on them. But why should they live if I couldn't? Willow moved, the blade in her hand now held to my throat. I burrowed into the magic again, ready to cast another spell I'd never used for harm, when out of nowhere, Talon roared, that great tiger bursting into the fray as he pounced on Willow, his sharp claws tearing the skin on her face.

Nym. She'd come back for me.

Onyx dragged me backward, away from the beast. Willow pulled out her knife, planting it in the tiger's side, and the feline bellowed a cry that sent a cold chill down my spine. The world fell to darkness, the sun vanished behind a fury of obscured clouds as Nym stood upon a ridge high above us, her arms spread wide while lighting cracked across the sky. She tilted her head back, screaming a battle cry as she cast a spell powerful enough to make it seem like her entire body was glowing, even her dark eyes, as she looked down upon us like a goddess about to unleash hell on the world.

"What the fuck?" Onyx whispered, his grip loosening as he stared at the spirit blessed witch, invoking the power she'd been gifted with.

At once, every animal that could feel her call surged forward at her command, pouring from the line of trees nearby, racing for Talon and Willow. I jammed my elbow into Onyx's ribs, escaping his grasp before falling to the ground, unable to hold myself up from the pain. I crawled toward Talon. I'd never be able to heal a blade wound, but now that he was free from Willow, I could help with the pain. I cast over him and he jerked in response to the magic. Onyx grabbed my leg, dragging me backward, the gashes in my thighs searing.

Overcome with a fury of forest animals, everything from birds, to bears, Willow cast a spell that forced them all into slow motion before she turned and ran for the tree line, hoping to escape. I looked up to see Ophelia appear over the ridge behind Nym. She stared down at Onyx as if all the years of her life had led up to this one moment. She lifted her hands. Onyx paused, watching. I'd hoped and prayed she'd make the right decision and see the danger of Onyx and Willow. But then, in one fell swoop, she reached for Nym and shoved her off the ledge, snatching the satchel from her shoulder as she turned and ran.

I screamed for Nym. The fall was not far, likely not lethal, but she landed hard and wasn't moving. Something within me broke. Whatever boundaries I'd placed on my magic vanished as fury ripped from my throat. Belly down, I dug into the satchel, pressing my hand to the jar to make sure it wasn't broken. Satisfied, I yanked the rope free and jerked around, tossing it into the air as I cast, sending it in coils to wrap around Onyx's throat, jerking him from the ground. He kicked and bucked wildly, grasping at the cords. I surged forward, reaching for the knife that had been dropped sometime during the fight. Still sticky from my own blood, the blade weighed heavily in my hand. But there was no time to think as Onyx cut himself free, falling to the ground and leaping to his feet. I hauled back and threw that dagger as hard as I could straight into his chest.

He stumbled, the look of horror and shock on his graying face burning into my memory. He fell to one knee and then the other as he looked down at the hilt, wrapping his fingers around it, until he went still, falling forward as death took him.

I forced myself to look toward the ledge where Nym had fallen. She was moving, pulling herself upward. I had no idea what type of wounds she'd sustained, but I still tried to heal her, even from this distance. I watched as Talon, wounded himself, lowered to the ground. She moved, dragging herself onto her familiar's back. The witch that had saved my life looked back at me with sheer resolve in her eyes as she dipped her chin, her spirit mark glowing. And then they were gone, racing after the old witch that had betrayed us.

I turned to survey the carnage of an unnecessary fight. A pool of blood from where Willow had stabbed the tiger. Onyx. Still and dead. I hadn't used the death spell. I could have, but there was still something in me that hoped I'd miss him or maybe he'd be wounded but not gone. The reality was I'd killed him. By spell or by knife, my choices had ended his life and I'd have to live with that truth forever.

In shock, I stumbled away, warm blood still dripping down my legs. I did my best to heal what I could, but it wasn't much. Enough to stop the bleeding, maybe take the edge off. That spell, though more powerful than it used to be, would never save my life. Wandering into the forest, my hand gripped tightly around that jar in my satchel, I knew the deja was now my only exit from the Trial.

I hoped everything I knew about the deja wasn't legend, but truth, as I continued on. I was certain there was more than one way to catch one and now Willow was on the run, and Ophelia had stolen Nym's feather, so she had a chance. If she came in first, or anyone really, with four points to gain, they could steal the lead and the title.

The feeling of spiders walking down my spine paused me, as if someone was watching, waiting. I turned, studying the varying colors of the forest, watching for movement, listening. Nothing. Gripping the satchel closer, I kept walking even though the sense of someone watching me was now as strong as the feeling that I'd been in this exact place before.

I spun, again, looking at the fiery orange and deep red hues of the leaves that reminded me so much of the blood moon. I knew I'd never been here, but there was something inside me telling me I had. Perhaps it was the late autumn feel of a forest that felt so familiar. As if I stood inside the home of the phoenixes. A flurry of vibrant colors and symphony of crackling leaves beneath my feet.

Aware that I could be alerting the deja to my presence, I dampened the sound of my footfalls as I passed a tree I was sure I'd seen before.

Knotty and split in half right at my waistline. Squeezing my eyes shut, I looked away and back again, my mind becoming fuzzy. I'd lost too much blood. Taking a deep breath, I pushed forward, winding myself through the trees, looking for any more signs of the creature I was to hunt. Again, I stumbled upon that tree, split in the same spot, the same fiery colors filling its branches. But I was confident I'd gone straight, purposefully not turning.

A twig snapped behind me. I spun, hands ready to protect myself. But there was no one there. I stared, barely daring to breathe as I listened and watched, assuming someone had used invisibility magic. Nothing. I turned back to the tree, noting the two small stones that sat at the base. One no bigger than my palm. I walked past the tree without turning. One foot directly in front of the other, as I studied the forest around me. As if by cruel joke, I came upon the same split tree again. Irritated, I kicked the rock at the base of the tree, realizing this time, there was only one rock.

I twisted, studying the surroundings. Everything else was exactly the same. A sapling four paces to the left, pine needles gathered in some animal's nest to the right, a trail of brighter yellow leaves that had fallen from a great oak beside the split tree. All the same. Except that rock. I walked forward with purpose this time, turning left directly after the deja vu tree. This was a trick. A task. I was meant to take a very specific path through this magical maze. One wrong turn and I'd have to start from the beginning.

A few more steps and I was back, standing before the split tree. Three rocks. I turned right this time, and when I arrived again, I groaned, seeing only one rock. I'd taken the wrong path and started over. Again, I had that eerie feeling someone was following me.

"Who's there?" I asked, spinning. It couldn't have been Nym. That only left Ophelia or Willow. But Ophelia had been up the mountain. "Has there not been enough bloodshed for you?"

No answer. I turned back to my task, accepting that if she was really following me, she was going to try to trap my deja and I'd have to deal with that when it came.

Back at square one, I turned left after the split tree this time. Two rocks. Last time I'd gone forward, and that was wrong, so this time I turned right. Over and over, I stumbled through the deja's trap until I finally cracked the code. Five rocks sat at the base of the split tree along with a long smooth offering stone. Convinced the little creature was nearby, waiting for me to pull the feather out gently so it could snag the magic within and disappear, I carefully sat the jar, lid tight, onto the stone.

"No fair!" a tiny voice shouted.

I spun, seeing nothing and completely unsure what the deja truly looked like.

"And tricking me through your maze was fair?" I asked. "If you want me to open the jar, you'll have to come out."

"Close your eyes," the little voice demanded.

"No. I don't think so. I'll just take my freshly plucked feather and head on home."

A gasp followed by a whoosh of wind lifted the tendrils of my hair as the tiny creature, no bigger than the palm of my hand, flew forward. With wings that looked like Bastian's, and hair and skin nearly as dark, she landed on the jar, pulling as if her life depended on it. Crouching down, I lifted the jar, taking her with it. She pulled and tugged on the lid, trying desperately to open it. I twisted the top and she flew back, clapping her hands as her eager eyes stared down at the feather.

"Yes! Please, oh please open the jar so that I may stay a little bit longer on Earth."

I gave a half turn and she trembled with excitement. "Where do you live when you aren't here?" I asked, holding the lid firmly in place.

She looked up at me with large, sad eyes and back to the jar, clasping her hands to her chest. "Among the stars, of course. Please, oh, please hurry."

I twisted another quarter turn. "You're not just going to steal my feather and fly away, are you?"

"Mm. No. I will not. Cross my heart." She made a tiny 'x' over her heart.

I sat the jar back down on the offering stone, knowing full well my magic would be faster than my fingers, trembling with adrenaline.

"Hey," the deja called, flying into my face to throw her hands on her tiny hips. "No fair. You promised."

I made a gesture with my hand and the lid slid off the top of the jar, just a sliver. The deja gasped, soaring for it. I slammed the lid down just as she wrapped the feather around herself and collided into the closed lid.

She jumped up and down in the jar, clapping her tiny hands together as she beamed at me. "You have trapped a deja, you clever fool. A wish shall be granted, but there are rules. No titles or riches, no lands or more wishes. No resurrections. No wishing for love. No hexes or death, no stars from above. One single wish that's well and truly yours, but heed this warning and be careful what you wish for."

It dawned on me then that I'd never thought about what I might wish for. I'd need something tangible. Something to take back and prove I'd captured the deja. I could save the wish and just take the jar with me, but she only had seven hours and I had no idea how long she'd already been back. Sure, the feather prolonged her stay, but I wasn't sure how long that would last.

"You are thinking?" the tiny creature asked, looking up at the lid and back to me, eager to be set free.

"Well, a wish isn't something you can take lightly. It's probably the only one I'll ever get."

"Very true, witch. Very true." She began pacing in her jar as she tapped her finger to her lips. "I once had a person wish for rain. And one man, a workhorse. And then there was the lady that wished to be invisible. Never saw that coming."

She giggled at her joke as my mind whirled. Something simple. Practical. I couldn't help but think of Kir and what she'd wish for. A new house or gardens that weeded themselves. A hefty sale every day in the shop, but then that would break the riches rule.

"I wish I could ask Kirsi," I mumbled, knowing that resurrection was against the rules as well so it wouldn't matter.

But the deja stood, bowing in her jar.

"No, wait. You said no resurrection. That doesn't count."

"You didn't ask for resurrection. You wished to ask your friend for help. There is a way."

"No," I said, reaching out my hand to stop her. "I have to take proof back or it doesn't matter. I don't need an answer. I take it back."

She shook her head, the jar glowing with the light of a thousand stars. She wasn't bringing her back. She couldn't. A branch snapped behind me and I jerked around, heart racing as I regretted my wish. As much as I wanted to talk to Kir, I couldn't see her dead form.

But it wasn't Kirsi standing there. Blond hair and green eyes stared back at me. "Nikos?"

He stormed forward and snatched the jar, throwing it against the trunk of the split tree. As it shattered, tiny pieces of glass glistened in an arc of flame as the phoenix feather crumbled to ash, the deja burned to a crisp. The world stilled. My heart aching for the little creature.

"What the hell, Nikos?" I asked, backing away as he turned to me, eyes hard as stones.

"I tried," he fumed. "I've sat back, letting you make these awful decisions. I know there's something between you and the king and I let it happen. I thought you'd see reason." He stepped forward, seemingly growing before me as his shoulders heaved. "I thought once the coven leaders asked you, you'd break and do what had to be done. But no."

"First of all—"

"No." He surged forward, grabbing me by the throat. "My parents left their coven. We snaked our way into the Moon Coven with a solid plan. I was just a child, but these things take time. We removed Tasa. We planted a hoard of witches in the castle with two goals. Find the Grimoires. Kill the king."

I choked, trying to pry his fingers from the throat. "You killed Tasa?"

"Not entirely. She killed herself." The devil himself showed through the smile on Nikos' face. "You'll do what you're told now."

He struck hard and fast. A spell I'd never heard of fell over me with the whip of his fingers. "Go to the castle. Stand before the Dark King. Cast the spell you were gifted upon him. You do not speak. You do nothing else until the task is done."

He released me, but I could not feel my feet, my arms, nor the tongue in my mouth. A hollowed echo sounded behind us. He jerked and ran for the tree line. My feet rotated, moving one step after the other. I couldn't stop myself, trapped in my body as I moved. The well of a scream grew in my throat, but my lips did not budge.

And then she was there. Kirsi. Floating up from the Earth, her specter just as beautiful as I remembered her. I could not resurrect Kirsi, but she could come back in another form. Not a resurrected body, but a wraith.

"Raven?" Her voice was hallowed, haunted. As if she stood in a vast empty hallway.

But I could not respond, could not even look back at her as I passed, mute and without any outward emotion, though my heart was breaking. Without the deja to complete the wish, Kirsi was stuck on Earth as a wraith forever.

40

One foot in front of the other, Kirsi following me, screaming my name and every profanity under the moon, I marched back through the forest, past Onyx's dead body, beyond the cliffs, and back to the door carved with beautiful wooden mountains. I pushed and pulled, tried to draw magic forward, tried screaming and stretching my muscles. Nothing worked. A shell of a person, moving mindlessly forward.

"Raven, stop," Kirsi said, moving in front of me.

I stepped through her, an aching sorrow striking the pit of my chest upon contact.

"Something's wrong," she said. "Give me a sign. What is it? What happened? Why am I here?"

I couldn't answer, of course, couldn't do anything but feel my heart break as I imagined responding to those hard questions. I stepped through the frame of the door, Kir hot on my trail, floating behind me as the dining hall appeared around us. He was there, standing near the table, staring at the door as if he hadn't moved since I stepped through it. His beautiful face was stoic, a show he put on for the others in the room as he restrained from showing me favor. I could see it in his eyes, though. The desperate need to surge forward and wrap me in his arms.

A mass of dark hair caught the corner of my eye. Though I couldn't turn my head, I saw her standing there, just steps away from Grey. Willow had beaten me back. The new Moon Coven leader. I'd failed. And now I would kill Bastian.

His eyes fell to the stab wounds in my legs, and he took a step forward, hands in fists.

"Healer," he demanded, those dark shadows pouring from him as if he'd begun to lose control.

One step toward him. His gaze flashed behind me.

"Kirsi? You wished for ... I thought you couldn't."

"Something's wrong," Kirsi echoed her words from before.

Another step.

"It's like she can't hear me."

Another.

"Raven, stop," Bastian demanded, his voice strong but eyes pleading.

I couldn't. Not for all the wishes in the world, for all the pulling and tugging and slamming into my own body. Nothing budged. Nikos' spell was absolute.

Another step.

I looked into those beautiful silver eyes. Those of a villain and a hero. Of a young boy who watched his parents murdered. Of a man who would never be given the grace to help the witches. Of a lover who swore he'd end the world for me. And I cast.

Deep, dark, roaring magic ripped from my body like a tidal wave, so utterly violent and cruel, my heart cracked as Bastian cast at the same time. His creeping shadows smothered me as I fell backward, looking into his face before he went still as stone. As if in slow motion, I soared, tumbling through a new door, Kirsi screaming and Grey's voice joining the fray, as I fell and fell and fell, landing so hard on the earth, I thought my body had splintered along with my heart.

The world faded to black.

I JERKED AWAKE, SURGING FORWARD AS I SUCKED IN A RAGGED BREATH, my lungs burning, my body on fire, my head pounding. For a moment, it was all just a dream. I'd never killed Onyx, never brought Kirsi back ... Didn't murder Bastian. But as I wiped the sand from my eyes, staring around at foreign lands, it all came crashing down on me. Tucking my legs, I moved to my hands and knees, screaming in horror. I was no longer a prisoner to my body, but now a prisoner to my mind, to the memories. To the man that had tried to love me, had let his walls drop for me only days before I'd killed him.

I couldn't breathe, no matter how many times I tried, the air wouldn't come in as I sobbed, discarded on a beach with silky sands and crashing waves. My stomach turned so violently I heaved, losing the contents of my stomach as I cried, confident I'd die of a broken heart.

"Bit dramatic."

I whipped around, shocked to hear Kirsi's voice. She floated beside me, arms across her chest, as she looked down on me with every amount of judgment she could muster.

"I can't ..." I dragged in a breath. "I can't."

"That's what we call a panic attack," she said, eyes hard as she stared down at me. "It'll only suck for a minute or two."

I wheezed, still trying to drag in breaths as my heartbeat raced within my chest.

"Better get that under control. He's about to wake up," she said, tilting her head toward a heap, half buried in the sand. "I have a feeling he's going to be kind of pissed at you."

For a moment, a very brief second, I hoped beyond hope it was Bastian. But when Grey shifted to his side, coughing, I couldn't help the disappointment. Or fear, as he turned, face as cold as ice, and glared at me.

"How could you?"

"Hang on, tall, gray and broody. She's having a panic attack," Kir said, moving between us.

I squeezed my eyes shut, trying and failing to calm myself. It made no difference as Grey tackled me, any breath I thought I'd caught whisked away with the blow.

"You're a liar and a traitor," he said, hands around my throat, startling me, though I could see the hurt on his face.

I shook my head, coughing. "No."

"No? No?" He leaned down, his nose in my face. "Please tell me how my eyes deceived me when I stood there and watched you cast death intending to kill my family. Why else would Bastian counter-cast with a spell to send you to the human lands? He was trying to stop your magic. Did you not see his face turn ashen? Did you find joy in finally besting your *Dark King*, the witches' greatest enemy. Tell me how you can sit there and deny anything?"

"Nikos."

He jerked, pulling his hands away. "Nikos what?"

"Oh, for fuck's sake. Could you give her one goddamn minute to catch her breath so we can hear this in full sentences?" Kirsi swooped low, putting herself in Grey's face as she scolded him.

He scrambled off me, sitting on the ground scowling at the ocean while I caught my breath, slowed my heart and tried like hell to push away the devastation of Bastian's murder.

I told them everything. Because the deed had been done, the spell cast over the king, the binding to the coven leaders was gone. Starting with the night of the ball, all the way through the cabin, to the final Trial. I struggled through most of it, but they listened quietly until I was done.

We sat in silence for a long time on that beach, watching the waves of the ocean rise and fall in a hypnotic pattern. I replayed everything that happened over and over again, thinking back to what I'd manifested with that makeshift mask on All Hallows Eve. Had the crown of flowers been a representation of Bastian? Had I asked the universe for him without realizing it? And the veil ... burning the veil had revealed the true villains. All of them.

Kirsi was the first to speak, her voice still a haunted semblance of what it once was. "I don't think I'll ever forgive you for bringing me back here."

I nodded, hugging my knees to my chest, realizing the friendship we'd cultivated over the years was gone with a single wish. A tear slipped down my cheek. "I'm sorry, Kir. I didn't mean to."

"Sorry is not going to fix this," she whispered, floating away. I didn't know if wraiths could cry, but if so, I was sure that's what she'd left for.

"We have to go back." Grey was sullen, quiet even.

I nodded.

They'd taken everything from me. I'd trusted them, had faith in them and they'd taken that and shredded it into a million pieces. How many witches had died at their hands while they blamed a man they'd been responsible for murdering? And Nikos? At least my conscience would be clear when I got ahold of him. I'd flay him. Tear his skin piece by piece from his bones as he writhed beneath my vengeful hands. I'd watch the blood spill from his body with no remorse. The coven leaders were problem number one, but he was absolutely going to pay for every choice he'd ever made in his fucking life.

THE END OF BOOK ONE

CONTINUE READING AFTER THE ACKNOWLEDGMENTS FOR A SNEAK PEEK INTO BOOK TWO

The Unbound Witch

ACKNOWLEDGMENTS

You'd think after doing this so many times, I'd have a clear picture in my head as to what I want to say, but that's never the case. I sit back and think about the tiny moments that breathed life into this story and the people that built it to what it is and it's such a culmination, I don't even know where to start. So, I guess at the beginning works.

To the readers, thank you. Every second of thought, of plotting, of building, of edits, of rewrites ... it was all for you. Each time you review my books, each time you engage with my social media, and each time you recommend my books to friends, I feel it. I see it. And I am grateful. I hope you enjoyed the ride and will be back for the wild conclusion of Unmarked.

To my husband, my poker aficionado, I don't care how we get to where we're going, as long as we go together. My ride or die. My best friend. My king. I love you.

To my girls, my beautiful girls ... I hope one day you'll remember what kind of work goes into following your dreams and still decide to chase them anyway. You each have power of your own. Even when you don't believe in yourselves, even when life sweeps you away and you forget what you're capable of, have faith in knowing I will always be there to remind you. I love you endlessly.

To Darby and Claire ... there are no words. I think I say that every time, but I mean it. From Darby's gasping moments during plotting crazy things, to Claire's final semicolon, I simply would not have published this book without you. The universe brought us together in a flurry of divine timing and I'm so glad to have you both in my corner. *insert upside down smiley emoji*

To Nichole, my spicy queen, thank you for your critical eye. For taking time I know you didn't have to read this book and love it. You've always supported me in the most solid friendship, giving me the safest space for rambling and never once complained. You never let me waver, believing in me when even I didn't. Thank you.

To Chloe, I wrote the witch, bitch. And then I rewrote her. And rewrote her. And you were there every whining moment of that. We climbed the same hills and had similar writing struggles with new characters, and it was so nice to have that kindred spirit. Dramatic as you are, I think I'll keep you.

To Jess ... I don't know how many times you'll read this story, but probably more times than me and that's saying something. Once upon a time we were having 3 am delirious conversations about people reading my books and coming to fangirl with us and it's been amazing to bring that dream to life with you at my side. Thank you for being here.

To my Tristopher ... If ever I needed a sign to write this book, our writing retreat was just that. I hope our lives continue to fill with the best memories together. From creepy massages to lunches delivered on long wedding days, you were put into my life at exactly the right time and now you're stuck with me forever. I love you, friend. Thank you for every second of your friendship.

To the Smidt clan ... the whole of you ... I don't think I could find words for how proud I am of the people that we have all become. Of the accomplishments, the wins, the loses, the camaraderie, the memories, and the laughter. I love you all.

To the street team that rocked the world ... Can you believe we've made it? Eight full months of the wildest marketing strategy I could have concocted and somehow, we're done. Thank you all for ALL the dedication, all the laughs, all the confidence boosting. For all the moments that we share in our chat. I hope you'll all stick around for book 2. I promise it will be tamer. Like, probably.

To Taire, who created the most beautiful cover for me with hardly any guidance. Who reads all of my books because she loves them, even though she doesn't have to, thank you, my friend.

And an extra special thanks to Tony Viento who created all of the current character artwork for this story. You brought these characters to life in a way I'd only dreamed of and I'm so grateful.

ABOUT THE AUTHOR

Miranda Lyn is the author of the trending, high fantasy series, Fae Rising and the witchy duology, Unmarked. Miranda has spent the past two decades reading romantic fantasy novels, and the last handful of years crafting similar worlds steeped in heartache, adventure, love, and loss. Her latest work will take her readers into the heart of a witch. And she owes it all to that one science teacher that made her write a paper on dirt and loved it so much he read it to the class. And then lectured her for missing class that day. But if not for him, because he probably doesn't deserve the credit since she missed the next day of class as well, then to that little, old English teacher that swept her into a world of creative writing. The only class she never missed.

Check out our website for extras, character art, and exclusive content. www.authormirandalyn.com

Also, click here to sign up for the mailing list and get access to more exclusive content and giveaways! https://www.authormiranda-lyn.com/subscribe

THE UNBOUND WITCH

CHAPTER 1 - KIRSI

There was life and death, and then there was somewhere fucked up in-between, and that's where I was sitting. Or not sitting, but hovering, because my soul had been ripped from the afterlife and plopped back into this lukewarm existence.

Shored up on the mysterious border of the human lands, after one night, I'd kill to feel the white sand between my toes, to leap into the cold autumn water for it to chill me to the bone. But as a wraith, that would never happen. The only thing I could feel was the overwhelming presence of sorrow deep within my gut. Haunted. Which made sense, because that's exactly what I was. Haunted by the reality of my future. Missing my familiar, the tie to Scoop had been completely severed by an unknown hand.

Whoever killed me deserved a fate worse than death, and I'd be the one to deliver justice. For as much as Raven was responsible for disturbing my afterlife, so was that person for damning me to it.

Slipping away from Grey and Raven for solace, I hovered above the ground, my ghostly form being a far cry from graceful as I swooped low, curious to see if I could manipulate the sand. I couldn't. Not a trace was left behind as I wandered further away from my gloomy companions. Something was different about them, but I couldn't quite put my finger on it.

Again, I tried to touch the sand. Descending to the beach in a frantic dive. The world became dark as I crossed the barrier of earth with nothing but silt around me. Twisting back and forth, panicking, I shoved myself out of the ground and thought only of catching my breath, of clutching my chest as the fear subsided. But there was no breath. There was no heartbeat. Invisibility had been the only thing that came easily.

Frustrated, I plunged again, intending to claw at the sand I couldn't move, couldn't leave a single mark upon. But within my fury, I jostled the tiny hill, sending several grains tumbling sideways. It was nothing, really. The saddest victory of my existence, but the only one I had now. So, nestled close to the ground, making myself invisible so no one could watch my shame, I tried again and again and again. As if my body were entirely numb, the rough texture of the sand nonexistent, I shoved my arm toward an abandoned sand-castle, sheer will and cold determination driving me forward. Nothing.

I crept closer to Grey and Raven, both content to brood silently on the beach. She'd condemned me to this ethereal body. Letting anger swell within me until I managed to grasp a small rock, I paused, tumbling it through my fingers, pretending I could feel the bit of lichen on the side, the cool temperature of the stone.

My mouth twisted as an idea sparked in my mind. I was invisible. Long gone, as far as Grey and Raven were concerned. Pulling my arm back, the pebble floated in midair. I chucked it forward, pelting Grey right in the thigh.

"What the fuck?" He jumped to his feet, whipping around until it dawned on him.

"One day in and you've discovered how to be a dick in a different form. That has to be some kind of record," he said, rubbing the spot where the rock had hit him.

"It's a skill." I flicked his ear, but my finger passed through, not making any sort of contact.

Damnit. I'd have to practice.

"Are we going to sit here and stare at this water forever or are we actually going to do something?" I asked.

Grey lifted one massive shoulder, content to speak to me though he couldn't see me. "We have no magic. How do you propose we do that?"

Raven sat hunched, holding her knees to her chest, those black curls of hers blowing in the wind. She'd killed the Dark King and would have to live with it for the rest of her life. Maybe that was enough punishment for her.

I reappeared before them. "There are these things called ships that float on water and carry you from one place to another."

"Oh, hey. Glad to see the smart-ass came back from the afterlife as well as the asshole," he answered, finally looking at me.

"They only let me pick two attributes. I felt like those were key." If I had it in me, I might have smirked, but it wasn't there. Only the haunting sorrow and the rage burrowed deep down. I didn't want to be here. I'd accepted my death on that castle floor. I'd seen Raven begging for me to live before I was taken.

The ocean waves roared as they tumbled forward, stretching as far as they could toward Grey and Raven before retreating, as if they were afraid of the witches on the shoreline. I couldn't be sucked into the lull of the tide, couldn't just stay here.

A line of trees, painted in a thousand different shades of autumn, created a barrier between us and whatever lay beyond in a land with no magic.

"How am I here?" I asked quietly.

Raven stiffened, turning to glance at me with red ringed eyes. "Because I made a mistake. Because I thought I couldn't bring you back, so I was careless with my words. You were only supposed to answer the question and then return to the afterlife, but Nikos killed the deja before she could send you back."

"Careless? That's the lightest word I'd use. But that's not what I meant. Are wraiths not magical? If there's no magic here, how am I?"

Grey dusted the sand from his black pants as he answered. "They call them ...er ... you a ghost here, but they exist all the same. Being a wraith is the nature of who you are. Just as a shifter can shift in the human lands, you can exist. It's not magic. However, the rules work differently for you here. You have to conceal yourself like you were a minute ago. The humans question your existence, but most don't believe it."

"How do you know that?" Raven asked, pushing herself from the ground.

"There're these things called books that people open and read for knowledge," he said, imitating my earlier tone.

Her eyes lit with fury. She did what she had always done. Held her tongue and kept absolute composure. She was nothing if not predictable when it came to conflict. Bastian Firepool was the only one I'd ever seen her stand up to and well, that ended poorly, to say the least.

"Don't be a dick, Grey." The words left my mouth before I could filter them. I was infuriated with Raven, but deep down, I would always protect her. I loved her.

He pushed his hands into his pockets. "Are we all friends again now?"

Before I looked into her face, before I could witness myself shattering that hope she would have, I said, "No," and floated toward that line of trees.

"I guess we're moving," Grey said in answer.

Footsteps followed me deep into the forest until sand became dirt and dirt became rock and somewhere on the other side, a whole new world awaited. Raven had wounds on her legs. Something that must have happened in the final Trial before Nikos compelled her to kill the Dark King. She wasn't bleeding, but if the tears in her pants and the dried blood weren't enough to know she was suffering beyond her mental state, the limp was.

"What will we do?" Raven asked, her voice a whisper, though it could have been a shout from the aching silence we'd let settle among us.

"Well," Grey said as we pushed forward. "Bastian is dead. Willow is the Moon Coven leader. The Trials are over. We could stay here together or go our separate ways."

"We can't split up," Raven protested. "You can be pissed at me all you want, but we have to stay together until we have a plan. We cannot assume it's safe for us here and we have nothing to survive on."

"As it turns out," I fired back, "I need nothing. I simply exist now."

She didn't reply as Grey quickened the pace. "We'll find the first town and figure it out from there."

"Fine," I huffed, floating forward.

"Fine," she echoed.

Hours passed as we continued. I heard the rumble in Raven's stomach and wished it were mine. Wished with all my being that I could long for anything but that peace I'd felt before. My eyes shifted between Raven and Grey until I finally realized what had changed.

"You look different without your markings," I said to fill the silence.

"More handsome or less?" Grey asked, plucking a stone from the ground and throwing it into the barren land before us, full of nothing but billowing clouds above and long tendrils of grass over rolling hills.

"Less. I prefer the sign of a witch."

Peeking down to my own translucent arms, I scowled. My markings were gone as well. Another robbery.

"You're going to be such a joy on this journey," he said.

"I've been a joy my whole fucking life, I don't see a need to change now."

"Where are we going?" Raven asked, ignoring the banter.

Grey stopped, pivoting as he placed his hands in his pockets. "I've got a friend here that might be able to help us but, the problem is, I only know the name of the town where she lives. I've no idea how to find it."

"How do you know anyone in the human lands?" she asked, shifting from one foot to the other, as if trying to ease the pain without drawing too much attention to her wounds.

"We've never formally met, but we've been in contact. I'm hoping that's enough to find a way back."

"Sounds less than promising," I mumbled, floating back and forth between them.

He ran his fingers through his cropped blond hair. "Well, let's just say she owes my family a favor."

"I guess it's better than no plan at all," Raven answered, still very much a shadow of who I'd known her to be.

I was far nosier. "So, who is it?"

He lifted an eyebrow, testing the tension between us before answering. "Eden Mossbrook."

Lightning Source UK Ltd.
Milton Keynes UK
UKHW041442090223
416762UK00017B/94/J

9 781736 833926